Changelings

Into the Mist

Katie Sullivan

Trade Paperback, 1st Edition
Copyright © 2014, 2018, 2020 by Katie Sullivan
Easter Rising Map, pg 122, copyright © Scolair 2007
All rights reserved.
Published in the United States by Marmalade Press

Changelings: Into the Mist / Katie Sullivan
ISBN: 978-1502903884
Fiction: Action/Adventure
Fiction: Historical Fantasy

For my child

Never stop following your dreams

". . . And I say to my people's masters: Beware.
Beware of the thing that is coming.
Beware of the risen people."
Patrick Pearse, *The Rebel*

Contents

Pirate

One

I sat in the grove of my own creation and stared out at a world and a people descended of mine own. As I watched, trees gave way to stone and the Many lost their claim to the priests of the One.

Then the wheel turned. The sacred trees grew around my effigy of stone and the Many came out of hiding. I sat in my grove and watched a world outside my imagination, willing it to see.

She saw. She saw me with uncanny green eyes – the green eyes of my mother and her mother before her: witch's eyes.

Joy rose in me. It was time – time to join the world after years of solitude, time to act after centuries of stillness.

I closed my eyes and reached across the barrier, to touch my future and my past.

Maureen O'Malley's eyes snapped open. The grove of ancient trees with their twisted branches disappeared.

Daydreaming. She took a shaky breath. It had just been a daydream.

Slowly – too slowly – her senses acknowledged the church, the hard pew beneath her, and the drone of Father's voice as he said the Epistle.

She was not stranded on a hilltop mired by mist.

There was no stand of oaks, and their gnarled branches were not creaking and groaning in the breeze.

There was no breeze, and the curls that had escaped her veil were not brushing her cheek – no, they were plastered against it. The late August heat, trapped amid the dusty black skirts of the nuns surrounding her, pressed in on her and stole her breath.

She gave her head a slight shake, as if the movement would free her from the grip of that dream world.

Sr. Theresa, her dorm mother, must have caught the movement because the nun turned from the mass to stare directly at Maureen, and for the briefest moment, Maureen thought she saw something canny and knowing in the woman's steely gaze.

Did Sr. Theresa know? Had Maureen cried out against the empty grotto at the grove's centre, looking as it did, like a forlorn prison? Had she flailed against the encroaching mist, which seemed to have a mind of its own as it wended its way around her feet and legs? Daydreaming during mass was one thing – she did it all the time – but if Sr. Theresa knew—

Stop.

She ground her teeth into the soft flesh of her cheek and mustered a grin for the nun.

This was ridiculous. There was no shrine of any sort in Carrickahowley – no matter how familiar that cracked and mossy stone hut had seemed. And Sr. Theresa couldn't know anything, since nothing was wrong. Maureen's hands were still clasped around her open prayer book, and her knees and ankles were primly together as she sat, just as the nuns had instructed – over and over – for the last nine years.

Sr. Theresa cocked her head at Maureen's smile, stared at her for a few agonizing moments and then turned back to mass. Maureen followed the nun's gaze and caught the eye of one of the servers. Sean McAndrew – her best friend and fellow orphan – smiled at her so quickly she would have missed it if she had not known it was coming.

That must have been why Sr. Theresa was looking at her. She never could resist the urge to distract Sean from across the guardrail, and the nun was ever vigilant.

It was the obedience that did it. He mouthed the Latin without question, as if his 'mea culpa' meant something. What could two fifteen-year-old wards of the Catholic Church get up to in the backwater of Ireland's west coast? They were about as far away from anything that mattered as they could be.

She watched Sean as he studiously went about his duties. Part of her envied him his quiet devotion, but the other part – the louder, more insistent part – knew: this was not real life. Real life was out there, away from the nuns and their rules, and away from the tiny village below, where nothing ever changed.

What was worse was Sean never complained – not outwardly. Piety aside, he wanted to be away to University almost as badly as she did, but he said it was pointless to wish – it just made the waiting harder. He had a point, but she preferred to believe escaping into the wish made the waiting go by faster.

Beside her, Sr. Theresa shifted. The nun still watching her from the corner of her eye, still waiting for her to do . . . what? Giggle, cry out, or make some sort of scene? She was tempted.

A horrible restlessness crawled over her skin, and the memory of the daydream settled on her unbidden. She itched to pluck at her wool tights or the pulled thread in her skirt. She wanted to scratch her nose, tear at the lace veil covering her hair – anything to break the vision's grip on her mind. She could feel it there, lingering with the mists, as if it was waiting to claim her.

"Stop it," she whispered. She no longer cared if Sr. Theresa heard her, or not. The nun's punishment was nothing compared to the buzzing in her head.

Except, the buzzing was not in her head.

It was all around her.

It surrounded her.

She clenched her teeth and fists as the sound filled her ears until they popped.

The silence that followed was absolute and Maureen blinked to make sure she had not slipped back into dreaming.

The air was dry and heavy with ozone that scorched her nose. Tiny flashes of light burst at the edges of her sight, and threads of mist slithered across the marble floor.

The mist rose. It whispered secrets in an unknown tongue as it gathered force. It obliterated the altar, the nuns and the priest. The servers vanished – all but one. There was no one left – no one but her and Sean.

And the man.

He stood proud in a tattered cloak, his raven head unbowed. His arms were bare but etched with tattoos that reached down to his hands, and a sheathed sword hung at his waist. The mist – the all too familiar mist – snaked up his legs and body.

It was dark with menace, but he ignored it.

His eyes searched the church. He was looking for something.

Or someone.

Maureen's breath caught in her throat as his gaze found her. Her body was screaming for her to move – to run, to do something – but all she could do was stare back into his bright blue eyes until she feared the mist would reach out to swallow her whole.

She blinked.

The image vanished.

She was at the edge of the pew – nearly on her feet – but caught herself and slid back, even as she searched the church for signs that the man was still there.

There was nothing.

Father's voice continued to rise and fall in a familiar cadence; his sermon was almost over. Sr. Theresa was beside her, silent and still. No one seemed aware that anything had happened.

Except Sean.

He was aware.

His eyes darted from her to the altar and back again. Like her, his hands had turned to claws, the knuckles white as his fingers clenched the edge of his seat.

Her heart hammered in her ears. She had no idea what they had just seen, but it had been no daydream. That man had been looking for her, and she knew, without any hesitation, she would answer his unspoken call.

Two

Maureen clasped two identical boxes beneath her arms as she slipped into the boarding school common room. She shot a bright smile at Sr. Theresa, but the woman barely acknowledged it. She was sitting comfortably in the corner with a dog-eared James Stephens novel. It was a hard-won indulgence in the nun's otherwise austere life, and Maureen knew she would be a complacent chaperone for the abbey's only summer residents.

Sean was perched on a chair in the opposite corner, reading a comic book – another indulgence. As soon as he saw her, he leapt to his feet. Brightly coloured pages fluttered to the floor.

"There you are!"

She curtseyed. "Here I am."

They always met in the common room on Sunday evenings, after chores were completed and supper eaten. Sean always finished first, but tonight she had not been delayed by some creative punishment. She shifted her cargo and grabbed his comic. He would be annoyed later if he'd left it there.

He squinted at her and then eyed the prize in her arms. "Oi, those are—"

"Our boxes."

The squint turned into an arched eyebrow. "But mine was in my room."

"And I went to the liberty of getting it for you." She tried to sound nonchalant as she deposited said boxes on the low table in the middle of the room. It was not the first time she had collected them – she knew where to look.

"I wasn't aware I wanted it." He ran his hands through his short, jet-black hair and laced his fingers behind his neck. The arched eyebrow was firmly in place.

"You did. You want to help me find the man." She stopped and clenched her hands. She had no idea what he had actually seen during mass, and she found herself not wanting to say too much. If Sean had not seen—

She took a breath and forced her nails out of her palms. She rested them on the tops of the sturdy cardboard and lifted the lid on hers. These small troves of personal treasures set them apart from the other students at the school. She and Sean called them the orphan boxes, and their contents were all that remained of their parents, and their lives, before becoming the responsibility of distant relatives, and thus, the Benedictine nuns of Carrickahowley Abbey.

"The man with the blue eyes?"

Maureen froze. Slowly, she lifted her gaze from the jumble of trinkets and photos. Sean was staring at her, his cornflower blue eyes guarded.

"They're like your eyes," she final managed, "only different. They're more—"

"Deep, intense? I only saw him for a few seconds. I – it happened so quickly, I don't—"

"Did you hear him?"

Sean's mouth fell open and she cringed. The man had been looking for her – for them. He had to have been. There had been a promise in that outstretched hand, but the more she tried to figure out what it was, the more tangled in the memory of *him* it became. His presence had filled the church – the powerful warrior with the wild, blazing eyes.

Sean did not answer her question directly. Instead, he settled on his knees in front of the table and riffled through his box.

He did not need to answer her – with that one movement, she knew what he could not say: he had heard.

Raised together by their widowed mothers, she and Sean were close enough to be brother and sister. Sr. Theresa always complained that the way they read each other's mind was uncanny. Changelings, she called them.

As if being foundlings was not bad enough.

Sean plucked a photo – its edges worn from handling – from his pile. It captured a group portrait taken when they were barely six months old. Well, he had been six months; she had probably been four months old.

Mary, Sean's mother, jostled him on her knee while Katherine held Maureen in her arms. Their fathers – Royal Air Force uniforms starched and faces merry – stood behind.

James McAndrew and Patrick O'Malley died six months later, shot down during an attack run on Nuremberg on March 30, 1944.

Maureen leaned over Sean's arm and smiled. She had a similar picture, one in which everyone managed to compose themselves for a proper pose, but she preferred the one in his hand.

Practically disowned for joining England's war, their mothers had been assigned to Pat and Jamie's unit in 8 Group as part of the Women's Auxiliary. According to the surviving letters, romance bloomed early. The foursome was inseparable, even to the point of marrying in a joint wedding ceremony.

She flipped through her own photos. This ritual, once done weekly, and now monthly at best, was a silent one. Strains of stories whispered in her ear as she touched each memory.

Here was her parents' wedding photo, which showed the red-haired Pat holding tight to his bride's hand. The photo was black and white, but Maureen had been told more than once the shades of red in her dark, unruly hair had been his gift to her, in addition to her green eyes.

Sean took after his father too, she knew: black hair and height he had not quite grown into yet. She grinned. He towered over her, and most of the nuns, too. Yet, while his father's eyes seemed to twinkle merrily in every photo, Sean's were more serious. Though kind, his blue eyes were always wary, as if he had to guard what was left of his family from the perils of the unknown.

The grin fled her face as the warrior flashed before her. Perhaps Sean was not wrong.

When she looked at her friend again, he had put away the family portrait and was looking at a snapshot of the two men in front of their plane – a Lancaster, Sr. Theresa said. Sean's father was from Scotland, heir to some estate near Inverness. He met Pat, a Westport native, at boarding school in England. As soon as Hitler invaded Poland, the friends enlisted together. Eventually, Pat became a pilot and Jamie his navigator. They had been in their third tour of duty when they died, and their medals rattled amongst their treasures.

She bit her lip and picked up a small photograph – the last one ever taken – of her mother. Five-year-old Sean clung to Katherine's hand, while Maureen whispered something in his ear. Mary had not survived her husband long, but before she succumbed to pneumonia, she named Katherine as Sean's guardian.

Sean rarely talked about Katherine. He said his memories of her were hazy. Maureen remembered, though. She remembered a tiny cottage near the sea, and the smell of bread baking. There was a warm sunny bit of floor where she and Sean played for hours, it seemed.

When Katherine died, they were already day students at the abbey's school. The Mother Superior – Mother Bernadette – had taken it upon herself to contact what family they had left and arrange for their care. Sean's great-aunt in Scotland and Maureen's paternal grandfather, a consumptive under the care of a specialist in Dublin, had been more than happy to leave them at the boarding school full time. The family trusts took care of the details.

Her hands started to shake and she discarded the worn, often-handled photos for the ones she rarely looked at: older photos, mostly forgotten. She searched to see if some forgotten man would stare at her from the shadows.

"Maureen." Sean laid a warm hand on hers. "I don't think he's in there."

"How do you know?" She pulled back to look at him, and he flinched.

She sighed and slipped the lid back on the box. She was angry – angry she could not remember more, and angry that there was no one to give her answers to questions she did not even know to ask – but it was not Sean's fault.

"I know, I really do, but I can't shake the feeling

that he's . . ." she paused. He would not – could not – believe her if she tried to explain.

"Related." Sean's eyes held hers, and his voice was nothing more than a whisper.

Or, perhaps he could. "We have to find him – go after him. Something."

"I don't think—"

"Sean, you saw him. You heard him, too – I know you did. These things shouldn't happen, but they did, and we have to go back there."

"Okay," he said quietly, halting her panicky babble. "It's okay, Maureen."

There were voices outside the common room. Sr. Theresa began to stir in her corner.

"Put these back and meet me outside the kitchen door after lights-out," he muttered. There was a smile lurking at the edge of his mouth.

She stared at him. He could not be suggesting what she thought he was suggesting.

"What, you think you're the only one who can break the rules?" His cheeks were pink. "I don't know who he is, but I saw him too. I felt his—his *call*. Besides, I can't very well let you explore the church alone, can I? Oi!"

She gave him a quick peck on the cheek and squeezed his hand before he could swat her away.

Sean laughed and let his accent broaden into the country burr they had grown up speaking. "Ah, go on with you – put these back before they think we're up to something, aye?"

Three

Maureen's green eyes glowed in the half-light as she sailed out of the kitchen doorway. Sean followed, feeling slightly sick. He listened to the night, and found himself holding his breath. He was waiting for an alarm to sound – an alarm he knew in his gut would never be raised. After his earlier daring, he did not know what to say. This had been his idea, but it was her show. What happened next was all on her.

The fieldstone church was separate from the rest of the abbey, and built at the top of a hill that commanded views of the surrounding countryside. It was a short trek, and they walked in companionable silence. As they crested the hill, the newly risen moon came out from behind low clouds. Its light threw into stark relief a circle of young oaks that would, one day, tower over the little building. Their branches strained towards the sky, and the moon painted them in silver.

It was eerie and beautiful, and not quite of this world.

He shook himself and reminded himself why they were here. This was no time to allow the power of the morning's vision to carry him away. He looked around for his friend.

She was gone.

The heavy oak door, the gateway to the church,

opened with a grating sigh of wood and age. Panic seized his chest. He nearly bolted until he realized it was only Maureen, opening the door. He wondered where she had gotten the key – or if she had a key at all.

He shook his head. Some things were better left unknown.

She motioned him inside with a jerk of her chin and closed the door behind him. He waited for her to lock it again, hesitant to step foot into the nave without her. She touched his shoulder lightly as she passed him.

"What are we hoping to find in here?" he asked. His voice bounced off the stones and he winced.

"I'm not sure."

There was no way that was true, but he followed her anyway.

"I thought we'd start with the altar – you know, by the tabernacle," she added as she glanced at him over her shoulder.

He stopped. "Maureen Clare O'Malley! That is sacred space – we can't search it. God resides there."

"Not tonight He doesn't."

His jaw dropped. She said it quietly enough that he could have ignored it – pretended like she had not just committed sacrilege – but he would not. He stopped in the middle of the nave and crossed his arms over his chest.

Maureen wandered to a stop ahead of him. He could not see her well in the dark – they should have brought torches – but he imagined she was rolling her eyes at him.

"I'm not planning on searching the tabernacle itself, Sean, just the space around it."

He said nothing and he could hear her shift her

feet.

"Look, it's mad, I know, but I just want to see if I can feel anything standing there, where he was."

Still he hesitated, but it was not her proposed blasphemy that sent shivers down his legs. Even at this distance, he could feel the sensation of power – ice-cold power – emanating from the space around the altar.

Maureen gnawed at her lip and debated grabbing Sean to drag him to the altar. He was bigger than she was, but if she grabbed him just right—

She froze. Waves of warning, the chills of the vision, skittered up her back. Her breath caught in her throat as the air itself changed tone, as though lightening had struck within the church.

"Maureen, step away."

Sean's voice was gruff and his face appeared paler than normal in the moonlight. Fear was staring out at her from the dark hollows of his eyes.

She wanted to do as he said, but she was frozen in place with her back to the altar. Mist had begun spilling in waves over the marble steps, pooling at her feet. The old pair of runners Sr. Theresa grudgingly let her wear were obliterated as the mist snaked higher and higher.

Her throat strangled a scream. The mist was going to swallow her if she did not move.

"Maureen!"

She did not know how much time had passed while she stared into the maelstrom of swirling mist, but Sean's voice cut through her panic. He stepped forward.

She tried to speak, tried to say his name, but her mouth refused to translate the screaming urgency in her head. She watched him reach for her. She wanted desperately to move, to take the three steps necessary to touch his fingers, but the terror that infected him had consumed her.

She managed to stretch out a hand to him. If he could just grab it, she might be safe.

Their fingers touched. Lights flashed and the air crackled around them. All was noise and light. And then, there was nothing.

Four

"Oh my God, Sr. Theresa was right, you are a Changeling," Sean muttered. He did not know how long they had been lying in the tall grass, staring up at the starry sky. Long enough to realize that this was not a dream.

The church had vanished, and there were no sounds but those belonging to the night.

No, not a dream, but a huge, hideous mistake. The world started to tilt at funny angles and he dug his hands into the thick, matted earth.

"Me?" Maureen sat up. He winced at her speed. "It wasn't until you touched my hand that anything happened." She gave him a half-hearted glare as she attempted to smooth the back the riot of curls that had escaped her braids.

"And what did happen? In case you hadn't noticed—"

"I know, I know. No church. Nothing."

Yet, that was not completely true. She turned away and scanned the darkened countryside. Sean followed her gaze and tried to ignore the prickling unease that danced up his spine.

The church itself was gone, but the tumbledown remains of a stone structure, overgrown with weeds, sat in the middle of where the building had once been. Surrounding them was a great ring of oaks, or rather, what was left of them. Someone had been at them with an axe; a few raw stumps gleamed in the light of a moon that had just crested the hill. Beyond the oaks, with their twisted branches, were other stands of broad leafy trees that extended down into shadow.

The abbey, its collection of buildings and the modern trappings of their tiny world, had disappeared – either because they had not yet been built, or because they had fallen to ruin long ago.

"Sean," she whispered, "I don't know how, but I think we're still here – still in Carrickahowley, I mean – but just in a different time. Does that make any sense?"

"No," he muttered. He sat up and rested his chin on his knees. "But I agree with you." Just saying it made his heart skip a few beats. What had happened to them? He shook his head and gestured to the sky. "The stars are the same – just shifted slightly, like the moon."

She glanced at him out of the corner of her eye. "It was just after being full when we left, and now it's barely a sliver. When did you start stargazing?"

"One of your books had a chapter on the constellations. I wanted to see if I could see the pictures – Orion's belt and all that."

She acknowledged this with a small smile. There were all sorts of books she managed to bring into the dorms – books Sr. Theresa would have confiscated, had she known.

He opened his mouth to speak and closed it again; there were no words to make this right. Maureen nodded – he knew she understood, even if she gave no indication she cared. How could she be so cavalier? They had just spun through a vortex housed in the church altar and ended up . . . here. Wherever here was.

He watched her meander to the edge of the hill.

His spot among the tall grasses was safe; he did not want to leave it, but she looked lonely standing out there, all by herself.

"You win," he whispered, too low for her to hear, as he joined her. She always won. Together they stood in silence and contemplated the deepening night.

"Sean, what are we doing?" Her voice was a hoarse whisper but after the quiet, it made him jump. "Why don't we just go back to where we–we landed and try to – I don't know – summon up the mist, or the feeling, or whatever it is?"

Without waiting for an answer, she grabbed his elbow and hauled him back to the centre of the oak grove.

They waited. The moon passed behind a cloud. Maureen clenched his hand at every shiver that shook her shoulders, but nothing happened.

Sean glanced at his watch and stifled a yawn. "Look, it's after midnight. It's technically a new day. Maybe it only happens on Sundays or during the full m—"

"Or maybe we're not really here? Maybe—maybe this is a dream, or we're delirious? What if we fell in the church and all this is just a hallucination?"

He stared at her for a long moment before shaking his head. She lifted a shoulder as if to say it was worth a shot, but he refused to laugh.

"It's just . . ." her voice was small and it trailed off as she turned from him to stare out into the distance. Words could not do justice to the emptiness, which grew deeper and darker with each passing moment.

"Maureen, did you know?"

As soon as the words were out of his mouth, he knew it was the wrong thing to say. She was always charging ahead, always wishing she was anywhere but where she was. Somehow, that wishing and dreaming always managed to land both of them in trouble – probably because he was always following. Saying 'no' to Maureen was not a strength he possessed.

Of course, the trouble usually meant they had to peel potatoes in the kitchens – or some specialized torture involving embroidery or silver polish – not time travel that left them stranded on the hill, year unknown.

"Did I know what, Sean?" she spat. "Did I know the bloody fog would swallow us whole?" The weak moonlight and unshed tears made her eyes shine as she glared at him.

"Did I know we'd be lost in time? Did I know we would be alone, with no answers? No way to get home? No! You saw everything I saw. I told you everything I knew."

He closed the gap between them and folded her into his arms. Her shoulders rose and fell as she took deep, shuddering breaths, but her cheeks were dry when she looked up at him.

"Sorry."

He held her away from him and gave her arms a squeeze. "Me too."

She nodded and made a face at him. He grinned, but as her eyes shifted to the landscape beyond him, he let his arms fall.

"I think we should try to find a dry spot in the trees and rest."

Even though sleep was tantamount to giving in, he nodded. It was the only thing they could do. Maybe daylight would bring answers – or better yet, perhaps daylight would bring them a way home.

Five

S ean woke with a gasp and a sickening heave of his stomach. The waking was so sudden, he forgot where he was. He forgot he had spent the night back-to-back in the dirt with Maureen. He forgot they had travelled through time – he even forgot they were now stranded. It came back to him in a rush and his stomach twisted even more.

Behind him, Maureen was stirring. He started to turn to her but she hit him and 'shushed' in his ear.

"Do you hear that?" she hissed.

His protest at being smacked in the shoulder died on his tongue. He closed his mouth and listened. There it was – the sound that first woke him.

"Someone's chopping down the trees."

Maureen nodded slightly. "Aye. I was having a nightmare and the noise blended with it, somehow. It woke me up."

Something about the shadows under her eyes, and the steady beat of a handsaw and axe made the hair on his neck stand. "I don't think we should be seen by whoever is up there – doesn't feel right."

She eyed him for a second – hunches and wild suppositions were her area of expertise – but nodded. "Nothing has felt right since yesterday morning. Let's get out of here."

They helped each other stand and quickly brushed off the leafy debris of their night under the stars.

Sean stretched and rubbed at his face. "If there's any civilization here at all, we'll find it closer to the bay. There's probably a road or path at the base of the hill – if we can get to it without being seen."

A shout and the ear-splitting groan of a monarch's fall overshadowed this last. They stared at each other as the birds jeered above them.

She took his shoulder and pointed to a gap between the trees beyond them. "That's an animal track – we can use that to slip down the side."

She was practically pushing him towards the trail, and he did not resist. They were silent as they attempted to thread their way through the forest as quickly as possible.

Just as predicted, the small wood ended at a rutted lane, which skirted the trees and headed off towards the unseen shore. Whatever lay beyond, it had to be more helpful than the wilderness around them. He only hoped that it would be friendly, too.

"Did you know the church was built on a fairy hill?" Sean asked absently as they meandered down the lane. The desire to find civilization was tempered by the fear of just what it was they were going to find.

Maureen glanced at her friend. His hands were shoved in his pockets and his shoulders hunched.

"I had heard something like that," she said. "Are you telling me you think fairies grabbed us and sent us hurtling through time?"

"No. Although, it's as good a theory as any, at the moment." He looked up and winked at her. She rewarded him with an eye-roll. "I was just thinking about what Sr. Theresa used to say about leaving out a bit of milk for the Good Folk and all that."

"Sr. Theresa also used to put a bit of 'cold iron' above our beds, to ward the little beasties off."

Maureen said it with a disparaging laugh, but a small tingle of unease played about her shoulders. Sr. Theresa was a funny sort – a jumble of contradictions. She was lean and stern most of the time, yet she was one of the few at the abbey who visibly enjoyed greeting the Lord, and the coming day, at Lauds.

They had been in her care for nine years, yet they only felt like a family when she shared her secret love: fairy stories. These tales were at turns whimsical and terrifying, and had no place as bedtime stories in a Benedictine abbey.

And they loved them.

Even so, perhaps the nun had been right to defy Mother Bernadette when she raided the kitchen to keep the Good Folk happy.

Sean seemed to be reading her mind. "Who knows? Maybe the iron would have worked, if we'd been carrying any."

She snorted and made a show of checking her pockets. "Oh aye, that explains it – I'm fresh out. What does our hill being a fairy hill have to do with anything?"

"There were still oaks on it – old oaks – and that ruin. There was a shrine there once, too. It was destroyed in the 1500s, I think – during the Reformation, anyway. I believe it was something about a host of 'devil-worshiping heathens, cavorting on the hill' under the guise of 'popery.'"

He looked up as she gasped – partly from shock and partly from recognition. The gnarled oaks around that old grotto of her vision creaked in her memory.

"Where did you hear that?" she managed to croak.

"Unlike you, I listen during class. Of course, no one ever mentioned the oaks. Maybe the reformers were right. No one built anything else on the hill till the Benedictines came and established the abbey."

"Next you'll tell me they salted the ground, too." She rolled her eyes. "All right, smarty-pants, when was the abbey built?"

"Sometime in the 1880s, I think."

Unbidden, her feet stopped moving and her heart started pounding. "That's quite the gap of time, between the 1500s and 1880." The meagre track ahead of her twisted and wavered in the early morning sun.

"It is." Sean grabbed her arm and forced her to keep walking.

"And they're sidhe mounds, not fairy hills – they mark where the Tuatha were led into the earth after the Celts won the land," she muttered as she allowed herself to be dragged along the bumpy path. There was no help for it but to keep moving. Panicking was only going to keep them stuck here – whenever *here* was.

"God, who was he?"

She did not need to ask who 'he' was. That another human – if the man was human at all – could use power straight out of myth to call to them in the middle of Sunday mass was as frightening as it was incredible.

Of course, she was the one who had listened – listened and followed.

Sean let go of her arm and jammed his fists back

into his jeans. "For what it's worth, I think we're closer to the 1500s. The ruins were pretty raw."

"Do you think he'll—?"

He cut her off with a sharp wave of his hand. In the silence, they could hear the creaking of a cart.

Maureen moved to his side and they stepped into the tall grasses along the path. There was not much cover on this stretch of the lane, but perhaps the driver would ignore them. They kept their heads down and continued walking.

Instead, the driver slowed.

"Dia dhaoibh. An bhfuil an beirt aguibh ceart go leor? Ar thárla rud éigin daoibh?" asked a voice behind them.

Maureen closed her eyes against the dread washing over her. "Oh no – we can't – Sean, my Irish is horrible."

"I wouldn't say it's horrible, lass. You've a bit of a funny way of speaking but I wouldn't say you're as bad as all that," said the old man as he pulled the cart up alongside them.

A shaggy pony, in no hurry to reach its destination, took the moment to munch the clover growing between the lane's tracks. The driver himself had a shock of white hair that hung in rough-shorn waves about his wind-beaten face.

They stared at him.

"That I understood," Maureen whispered. "Sean?"

"No idea."

She groaned but favoured the old man with her brightest smile. "I meant I sometimes have trouble out here in the west. We're from Dublin."

"Oh, aye?" The old man peered at her. "Is that where you got them clothes, then? Or were you robbed on the road?"

Maureen looked down at the jumper and slacks she had changed into before sneaking out of the abbey, and back at the old man. He wore a long, rough tunic, belted over a pair of leggings. The leggings, drab and stained, were tied close to his legs with long bands of matching fabric. The morning was cool yet, and he had a dark blue cloak draped over his shoulder. At least Sean was right about the time. They were definitely closer to the 1500s than the 1800s.

"We were set upon in the road – robbed, like," she said slowly. "We met some minstrels though, and they gave us a bit to eat and these clothes."

Sean snorted quietly and she bit her lip. Perhaps traveling minstrels was a bit much. The man in the cart said nothing; he just sat there looking at them with his head tilted to the side.

While she waited for his verdict, her stomach began to make demanding noises. It was well past her normal breakfast hour.

The old man grinned. "A bit, but not nearly enough, aye? Will you be heading to the stronghold then?" He gestured to the square block of a tower just coming into view.

Maureen exchanged glances with Sean. The stronghold was Carrickahowley Castle.

"I've an errand or two there myself – there's room here in the cart, if you're tired of walking. And, if you help me unload her, there might be a bannock or two in it for you as well."

They needed no more prodding and clamoured into the cart.

"That's fine, then – I'm Tomás by the way, Tomás Conroy."

Six

The sounds and smells of Carrickahowley Castle met them a good half-mile before they reached the stronghold itself. What was deserted in their time – with only the occasional fishing boat for company – was bustling with life. Nearly twenty ships filled the waters of the inlet, and the noise from their crews was rivalled only by a small market doing brisk business in the harbour. Overseeing it all was the stout stone tower. It glowered at them, even as it offered its protection.

Tomás manoeuvred his cart alongside a rickety dock and hailed two men standing close to the pier. They stopped their chatter and waved back. He turned to Sean and Maureen.

"Here we are. Hand those bundles off to young Owen over there." He nodded his head at the younger of the two men as he approached the cart.

They scrambled out, eager to repay him – for his lack of interest, and the ride. Tomas tied off his pony's reins and strolled over to the other man.

"No, that's all right, lass. No need to strain yourself," Owen said to Maureen as he took the sack of – well, of what, she was not sure. It was heavy, though. She handed it off and reached for a smaller pack.

"Ah now, you're a bonnie bit of a thing, but breeches or no, the lad and I can manage this." The young man laughed and sauntered off with two bundles under his arms. Sean looked at her and shrugged, but followed the other boy anyway.

She made a face and contented herself with unloading the cart and stacking its cargo close to the gangplank Sean and the boy had used to access a large ship. That was one mercy, at least. The gangplank was a flimsy thing, balanced precariously between the pier and the boat.

A shudder roiled her shoulders. Water, boats and swimming – these she did not mind. Heights, now? Heights made her legs weak.

She wrenched her eyes from the pier and the churning waters below to look at the ship. It did not look like any of the others in the bay – they were small and fit with rowers. This ship dwarfed its neighbours and sported two masts rigged with sails. She wondered if the ruler of the keep was also the one who had liberated the caravel from its rightful – European – owners, and slapped it with an Irish name.

She shook her head and returned to the bundles. Some were wrapped so intricately she could not resist the impulse to unravel a bit of the linen and spy their contents.

Maureen quickly put the wrappings back and returned to the cart for another load. It seemed Tomás was a skilled blacksmith – if the daggers were anything to go by. From the corner of her eye, she could see the old man and his friend talking. They had ceased to pay her any mind, so she hunkered down in the cart as close as she dared, and tried to listen.

"They gave me a fair story about being from Dublin and band of traveling minstrels, but I don't know that I've ever seen minstrels with costumes like that. The whole tale is a pack of lies, I'm sure. Have you ever seen travellers on the road as clean as them? Either they're runaways from some Lordling in Dublin or they're spies."

"Spies? You suspicious old git." The other man was laughing. "They'd be pretty bad ones if that's how they're turned out. What do you want me to do with them?"

"Take them to Herself. She'll sort them out one way or the other."

"You really think they're spies, Tom?"

"No." He sounded disappointed. "But if they are runaways, I'm sure she's going to want to know what strutting peacock she's going to have to contend with when someone comes looking for them. They're trouble, Liam, I feel it. And there's enough trouble lately without inviting more out of Dublin."

The other man – Liam – sighed. "But Tom—"

"Liam, they were heading this way on the main road. Now, I've been up, loading the cart since well before daybreak. Had they come from somewhere east of me, I would have seen them, or at the least, the dogs would have. But they didn't. Those two started somewhere close by and my guess is the hill."

"Ah now, none of your fool stories, Tomás Conroy. It's more like they came over land!"

"Maybe, maybe not. All I know is people have been saying the Good Folk aren't happy. Lots of lights, lots of noise coming from that hill of late. First, it was the wee shrine, and now they've taken to cutting down the oaks. It's the last straw, Liam O'Neill. Something isn't right. That Scot – the gallowglass with the learning Herself took on – agrees with me. And he's been to the Continent."

"Is this your plan, old man? Blather on about heathen nonsense until I agree to shove those poor wretches under Herself's nose?"

"And what's this, Liam O'Neil? Do you not trust my instincts anymore? Haven't I saved your foolish young hide more times than I can count before you lot cast me off?"

"Cast you—now, Tom, you know that wife of yours practically begged us to stop taking you out to sea."

She heard Liam pause and risked a peek in their direction. The younger man was shaking his head at Tomás and grinning sheepishly.

"Your instincts are fine, and I'll take those two to see Herself – but you'll have to come with me and explain it yourself." Liam paused and shifted to look at the caravel; Sean and Owen were headed back to the gangplank.

"They do look a bit too clean, don't they?" he mused.

Liam was right. Compared to him – or anyone else in view – she and Sean were spotless, a night spent in the dirt and leaves notwithstanding.

"Aye well, I'll take them, but before I do, there's the small matter of the Keefes we must discuss."

"Are you done, then?" Liam asked his brother as he and Tomás returned from their chat.

"Aye," Owen beamed. "Galen and the lads helped a bit."

Maureen rolled her eyes. The rowdy gaggle of youths that accompanied Sean and his new friend had made short work of her neatly piled bundles. After his first load, Owen had barely touched them.

"Well then, what are you waiting around here

for, Owen O'Neill? You've duties to attend to, do you not?" Liam arched an eyebrow at the young man.

Owen stuck out his tongue but scampered out of the way of the bigger man's reach and disappeared into the caravel.

"Tomás here is just after telling us your story," Liam said as he turned back to them. "Bit of bad luck, aye? Care to take a stroll with us? We've a mind to take you to someone who might help."

He did not wait for them to respond – or agree. Maureen shot a look at Sean and fell into step with the two older men as they led the way through the crowded harbour market.

It did not take long to reach the thatched hut abutting the base of the stronghold. Tomás stopped before it, with his hand on the plain wooden door.

"I've been remiss – I never caught your names. Who are you, then?"

"Sean McAndrew," Sean said. He held out his hand. "And this is Maureen."

"Maureen O'Malley. It's nice to meet you."

"Oh? Aren't you well-mannered?" Liam grinned and shook both their proffered hands. "Minstrels? Truly?"

"Only the clothes," Maureen replied with a small curtsey. "And a bit to eat."

He was watching her closely and she raised an eyebrow. The blond man with the weather-beaten face could not seem to help himself, and smiled.

"Aye, well then – you're an O'Malley? Would you be kin, then?"

"Kin? No. I mean—what?"

Liam and Tomas exchanged a meaningful look and she frowned.

"Are you kin to Herself? Is it why you're here?"

The big man asked.

"We aren't here for any specific purpose, and I claim kinship with no one."

Her voice was cold and her face tight. She saw Sean bite his lip but she did not relax her gaze. She did not like being baited into revealing information – especially when she did not have information to reveal.

Liam snorted. "Aye, well, whatever the reason, our lady, Grania, will sort you out." He looked over at Sean. "You know what I mean, don't you, lad?"

"I don't know about kinship, but I've heard of your lady," he answered slowly.

Maureen's mouth went dry and she stared at her friend. Grania. The woman Liam referred to as 'Herself' and 'our lady,' the owner of the stolen ship, and the ruler of the keep were the same person.

She mentally slapped herself for not making the connection. Of course, the last time she and Sean had talked about the woman, there was real scholarly doubt as to whether Grania Uaile – Grace O'Malley – Pirate Queen of the Irish Seas, actually existed.

Seven

Growing up at the edges of Clew Bay – shadowed by Carrickahowley Castle and Clare Island – it was hard not to have heard the tales of Grania Uaile. The woman was a pirate, an unspoken chief, and the mistress of several strongholds along the western coast, Carrickahowley and Clare included. No one seemed to care whether the woman was real or not, not when the idea of her was synonymous with Ireland – with freedom – itself.

Sean once attempted to research the woman, to see if there was any connection to Maureen's family. The nuns said Maureen's father had done some work himself, but his records were locked away in Dublin.

At first, Maureen had gone along with his search – listening to his findings and helping occasionally – eagerly enough. But when infamous ancestor turned into a possible fiction, the research lost all its appeal for her. It did not matter that Grania Uaile inspired poets and rebels for four hundred years; if she was not real, Maureen was not interested.

"Did you ever find out if my father's people were related to Grania?" she asked now.

"You do remember! Why did you act like that while we were walking, then?"

Liam and Tomás had left them alone in the

small room beyond the wooden door, while they presumably went to fetch their captain. Sweet rushes covered dirt floors and filled dim corners. Dust motes danced on the streams of light let in by the slit of a window close to the ceiling.

She rounded on him. "And let them think we're here to cause trouble with a pirate? Do you think I'm mad?"

"Do you really want me to answer that?" He rolled his eyes and she grinned at him.

"I overheard Liam and Tomás while you were loading the ship. They think we're runaways, or spies. It was a mistake to say we were from Dublin."

Muffled voices sounded beyond a door that led deeper into the stronghold. Maureen was looking at him as though he should know what she was talking about, but the sounds were distracting.

"Think, Sean. The submission of the nobles."

He bit his lip. King Henry VIII, and then his daughter, Elisabeth, had tried to bring the Anglo-Irish lords under the control of the Crown – to secure England's back door against Spain, as it were. But what did the Tudors have to do with a local pirate?

"Look, I don't have time to give you Sr. Theresa's lecture – if the stories about our host are real, do you think she gave allegiance to England willingly? Do you think any of the chiefs out here did? The Crown never stopped trying, though – still hasn't."

Sean closed his eyes. There was no time for Maureen's nationalistic speeches, either.

"Let me guess," he muttered, "Dublin is, at this moment, synonymous with the Crown?"

The noises beyond the door stopped; Maureen took his shoulders and forced him to look at her.

"Us being from Dublin might make us part of a plan to force Grania to submit—"

He groaned – what a mess – but Maureen continued.

"Or even more likely, uphold the terms of her submission."

"But we're not—"

"How is she supposed to know that, Sean? We're strangers here – Grania and her men can believe anything they want, and we can't prove a bloody thing."

"Well, I am glad Liam and Tomás did not waste my time with imbeciles."

The words that were about to come out of Sean's mouth choked and died. Maureen's hands dropped from his shoulders and together they faced the now-open doorway. A small, lean woman stood there, with Liam and Tomás just behind. Their faces were bland and their hands empty, but they held themselves taut and ready.

"But what is troubling," the woman continued, "is your grasp of the situation. You see, if you are not what Tomás and Liam believe you to be, but have such a clear understanding of the problems we face here, what exactly are you and why are you here?"

"Double agents?"

Sean closed his eyes. Flip, cheeky and nervy. He knew Maureen did not mean to say the words aloud – she *never* meant to say some things aloud – but the woman before them did not know that, nor did she seem amused.

Like Maureen, the woman wore men's clothing. She was wiry and weathered, as though tempered by the wind and sea spray outside her home. Short dark hair hugged her head in coarse waves and darker eyes regarded them steadily. She was no taller than Maureen, yet she dwarfed everyone in the room. Grania Uaile would not brook impertinence.

"Do you mock me, child? I know neither you, nor your supposed kin. Yet, you show a remarkable knowledge of me and mine."

"I never said I had kin. I merely gave my name." Maureen's voice was cool and Sean shook his head. She recovered well, he had to give her that – even if her recovery veered dangerously close to impudence.

"Indeed." Grania rewarded her with a slight bow of the head.

"It was your men who decided I was of interest – and not based on anything I said, either."

"Oh, who are you then?"

Maureen pursed her lips. Sean prayed she left 'minstrels' out of whatever story she decided to spin.

"My father was Patrick O'Malley, lately of Dublin. He died fighting on the Continent and my mother shortly after him. She and Sean's mother were good friends and Mother McAndrew raised us up until she passed last spring. We have no other kin."

"Even in our poor home, news of the Crown's difficulties out here reached our ears," Sean put in.

Grania turned her stony gaze on him. "Poor? With those hands and that skin? You can tell me a lot of tales, but poverty is not one of them."

He bit his lip and looked at Maureen. She ignored him and lifted her chin.

"I did not try to tell you we were poor, although there wasn't much left when Mother McAndrew died. Sean was forced to abandon his studies and I was almost compelled to marry the first man who could keep me, which is poverty of another kind."

Grania looked between them. Her face was unreadable, but Sean felt rather than saw her relax, if only slightly. Liam and Tomás had not, however, and he forced himself to stand still.

"Am I really to believe you two are simply runaways?"

"What evidence do you have to the contrary?" Maureen countered. "The suspicions of men who don't know us? I know they only wish to protect you, my lady – and they're good at that, obviously – but their fears are based on nothing we've said. Yes, we're from Dublin. Yes, we are runaways. But that is it. Had I known where we'd end up, I certainly never would have taken Tomás' offer of a ride, nor help him unload the daggers and the like onto one of your ships."

Sean coughed to cover a gasp. That was bold, even for Maureen. Grania did not acknowledge the challenge, but he did see a quick arch of an eyebrow. There may have also been a small twitch of the lips as the woman suppressed a smile. Then her steady eyes captured him.

"And you, lad?"

He opened his mouth to speak but found nothing of value was willing to come out.

"Uh, I just carried the crossbows. I don't know anything about daggers," he finally croaked.

Maureen snickered and elbowed his side.

"I mean, I—"

"No, please don't continue. Maureen O'Malley and – Sean McAndrew, is it?" She turned to her lieutenants. At a simple hand gesture, they relaxed. The two newcomers were no longer an immediate threat.

"Will you join me and the lads for a midday meal? I understand Tomás promised you bannock cakes in exchange for help."

Maureen grinned at him and they nodded together. The rules of hospitality being what they were, Grania's men were not likely to kill or imprison their mealtime guests – at least, not until the meal was over.

"Good. This way, if you please." Grania turned and led the company through the doorway into the stronghold itself.

Maureen tried not to groan when she saw the narrow flight of stone steps – steps without a rail – that hugged the outer wall of the stronghold. Grania and her men had already started the climb and Sean was behind, giving Maureen a tiny nudge. There was no help for it. She put a reluctant foot on the first step and tried to stay as far from the edge as possible. Heights were bad, but edges were worse.

Grania's pace did not falter as they passed the tower's first level, and then the next.

"Can you swear to me no one will be looking for you?" the pirate asked, keeping her back to them.

So intent was she on keeping her balance and not looking as the ground receded, Maureen nearly missed Grania's question. She wished she could see Sean's face, but knew that was the point of walking and talking – they would not be able to collude on a story. They were not out of trouble just yet.

"I can swear, if you desire it," she said.

Unbidden, the vision of the blue-eyed warrior – the impossible man who had led them to this place – flitted across her mind's eye. It was possible he was looking for them. They had followed him into the gateway, but they had no idea if he knew it – had no idea if, knowing, he would come for them. They were on their own.

The stair opened up on Carrickahowley's great hall. A fire flickered merrily, belching peaty smoke into the air. Stone benches flanked the huge hearth and the equipment of war, or rather, of the lady's occupation, hung on the walls alongside woven tapestries of muted red and gold.

Grania turned and stood before them, barring their entrance into the hall. She arched a single eyebrow at Maureen's lack of answer.

"I do desire it."

"Then you have it," Sean replied, his voice firm. Maureen had to fight to keep the wide grin off her face.

"Well, my – ah, 'double agents,' as you say – you know what cargo we carry, and you know what I am." Grania paused and looked at them closely.

They stared back without flinching.

"There's no glory being a ship rat, but it will keep you fed, and out of trouble. And you, Mistress Maureen, will not have to turn yourself out in skirts, nor bring misery to some poor lad as his wife. Will you trade that brand of poverty for training with me?"

Eight

"**M**aureen, I can't believe you got me into this." Sean muttered. He stood on the forecastle of Grania's flagship. It was a Portuguese caravel, which Grania had renamed the *Éadaí Baintrí – Widow's Weeds*. He liked the woman's sense of humour, but the people – enemies, rather – she attracted were not as high in his estimation.

The *Widow* and two other galleys in Grania's fleet had been on their way to Galway Bay to trade, but now he scowled across the iron-grey sea at a fast-approaching ship. The mood of the caravel and its crew was growing darker, louder and more frenetic as the other ship refused to raise a flag, despite its approach in open water.

He and Maureen had been Grania's ship rats for just over a month. All the downtime tales in the bunk suggested that ships with no flag usually boded ill – especially when they gave no indication they were going to divert their course to avoid collision.

Forget boding ill – Sean *was* ill.

"Oh? Who volunteered first when Grania asked if we'd like to join up? I do believe that was you, Sean McAndrew," Maureen retorted as she pushed away from the looming danger.

"Come on, we've got to help Owen with the gear down below. I'd put your leather jerkin back on."

She nodded at the crumpled vest he had discarded as the midday sun beat down on his chores in the forecastle. "Worst case, it'll deflect a blow or two."

"Aye, and delay my death by a whole minute or two." But he shrugged back into the jerkin, and tied it tight.

Maureen was outfitted in similar clothes, but despite her best efforts – dark hair wound close to her head and a smudge of dirt on her nose – to him, she still looked like the pretty convent girl who earned snickers when first introduced to the crew. She had begun to prove her worth, but looks were deceiving.

He knew she wanted carry a dagger on her leg and a blunderbuss at her hip, and command the same respect her pirate ancestor did. He also knew it would take more than a month to happen. Of course, considering how close they were to discovering a way out of 1584 – the year Grania's bard declared it the week before – she might just have the opportunity.

"We're not going to die." Maureen eyed him over her shoulder. "Do you honestly think they're going to let us anywhere near weapons? Or fighting? That'd be a great way for them to lose."

"Thank heaven for small mercies," he whispered as he followed her to the midsection.

A violent rocking threw them against the deck. Water shot through the air and up over the side of the ship.

"What was that?" he groaned, even as he dreaded the answer.

"A cannon ball, lad," Owen answered. His head popped up through the hatch. "You two, down here – help me with ours!"

"This day just keeps getting better," Sean

muttered. He bared his teeth in an attempt at gratitude as one of Grania's men pressed the hilt of a sheathed short sword into his hand. Maureen was equally equipped and right behind him as he slid down the ladder into the dim, low-ceilinged hull where Liam's younger brother was attempting to load the caravel's single cannon.

To his relief, he discovered purpose, and the constant need to move, replaced his grinding fear and panic. Time ceased as they laboured in the perpetual gloom below deck. They heard Liam and Grania shouting commands through the hatch while they scurried in the darkness.

"Why haven't they hit us, or us them?" he asked finally as he shoved another cannon ball in the rolling monstrosity that nearly took off his foot moments before. Naval battle tactics were still a mystery, but it seemed to him that two armed ocean-going vessels should be able to strike one another.

Owen stopped what he was doing and tossed his lank, dirty-blond hair out of his eyes. Sean expected the other boy to make some smart remark about wet-behind-the-ears recruits, but Owen barked a laugh instead.

"But no – you're right, lad. One of us should have hit *something* by now. They're deliberately staying out of our range, and aiming across us, not at us."

Maureen turned from stuffing rags into the cannon. "Isn't that what they'd want to do – keep us off guard so another ship could approach—?"

Liam popped his head through the hatch, cutting off the rest of her words.

"Roll that cannon to the starboard side, another ship is coming up fast!"

"It's a witch you are, Maureen O'Malley," Owen muttered as he hurried to heed his brother.

She rolled her eyes and helped him push. "It's what *I'd* do," she whispered.

Before they could move the cannon into position, there was a screaming rendering of wood and metal. The impact sent cannon and ship rats flying backwards. Sean hit the floor hard.

For a moment, he was blind and deaf. He scrambled unsteadily amid the debris until the sounds of metal clashing with metal filled his ears. He called to Maureen, but she did not answer.

Smoke stung his eyes and he spied the ruins of the lantern smouldering in the corner. He swore under his breath and rushed to stamp it out.

Owen groaned and crawled to his feet. "We have to get the cannon to the starboard side," he growled. "They're close enough, we'll hit them now."

"But Maureen—"

"Is fine. Owen is right." Her voice was coming from the other side of the hull. "I was just a little dazed. Come on, I'll help move that bloody thing!"

From the sounds above, Sean guessed the impact of the other ship had brought with it an attempted landing party. There were no more directions coming from Liam or Grania, but it no longer mattered. Owen, despite his teasing, kept them from tripping over their novice feet, and they worked tirelessly to force the other ship to retreat.

Whether ten minutes passed, or an hour, Sean did not know, but the noise above deck seemed to ease. He paused to look over at Maureen, who grinned back at him.

She was enjoying herself. Soot-covered and bruised, she was nearly gleeful. He smiled to himself as he turned to Owen to see if one of them should go up and take stock of the situation above. He was hoping Owen would volunteer.

The other boy caught the question before he could ask it.

"Aye, I'll go. We've nothing left for the cannon, anyway. No one expected a full-scale battle this close to home. When Grania finds out who did this, there's going to be a war-party for sure."

Before Owen was even halfway up the ladder, a large form filled the hatch, blocking the light. With barely a cry, the boy was tossed into the corner.

"Look at what we have here – it's a prize for ol' Davey then."

The words, garbled and leering, stopped Sean from trying to reach Owen's side. He stared at the shape but in the dark, he could see nothing but the dull gleam of a blade pointed in his direction. He pulled on Maureen's arm, to drag her back, deeper into the hull, but she resisted.

"He's English," she hissed as she pushed at him. Her knife was out and ready. "We have to get out of here."

Sean groped at his belt, desperate for his short sword. It was barely out of its sheath when another volley of cannon-fire rocked the ship.

The attacker stumbled down the ladder. Maureen ran at him, shouting and waving her arms.

Sean froze. He wanted to scream at her – stop her, somehow – but his body and mouth refused to obey.

The wicked iron in her hand flashed as she turned back to him.

"Come on!" She waved at him to hurry and his paralysis broke. He bolted, shouting nonsense, as the other sailor regained his footing.

They were almost up the ladder, almost free, when meaty hands grabbed at his legs. Sean's grip on the wooden rungs slipped, shredding his palms with tiny slivers, and he was falling.

He slammed onto the floorboards. For a moment, he couldn't breathe, couldn't see – couldn't even hear.

Owen kicked him in the ribs.

"Maureen," he managed to croak.

"Aye, that bastard took her."

Sean grabbed Owen's hand and let himself be pulled up. He thought he could hear Maureen shouting somewhere above.

He was up the ladder before Owen could even respond, and small knots of intense fighting greeted him on deck. It meant nothing to him – all he wanted was a dark head of coiled hair. He called for her but his voice was lost to the din.

He started for the starboard side of the ship, terrified he might see her trapped aboard the enemy boat, or worse, floating in the sea. But even as he moved, he spied her pressed up hard against the foremast. Whether she had taken refuge or been tossed there, she was safe for the moment. Her captor was too busy defending his life from one of Grania's men.

Cloak swirling and sword flashing, the man made his attack on the English sailor look like a graceful dance. Captivated, Sean wondered if this was the mystery gallowglass Owen kept mentioning – a mercenary supposedly on an errand for their captain.

Maureen shouted his name and the din of the fighting came roaring back. She was trapped, he could see now, hemmed in on all sides by swords, fists and bodies. Sean moved without thinking – it was the only way to reach her in time. He dodged a trio of men and bared his teeth gratefully at Liam as the other man dispatched his own opponent to make a small passage for Sean.

"Who is that?" Maureen asked when he finally reached her side. She jerked her head at the cloaked man.

"I don't know, but I think he saved your life. Come on."

"Get yourselves back below deck." The man had no need to shout – his voice carried over the din and would brook no disobedience. "It is not safe up here, and I cannot protect you both."

The English sailor lay face down not ten feet from them. Grania's warrior was standing over him, already searching for his next opponent. Sean could just see the man's stark profile before he rejoined the fray.

He needed no other motivation to move. Maureen's arm clasped in his hand, he pulled her. He was blind to everything except the promised safety of the hatch.

"I think not, my boy."

The voice that stopped him was mildly amused, English, and far too close. A burst of pain bloomed at his temple and Maureen's fierce cursing sang him into unconsciousness.

Nine

S ean woke to the stinging sensation of someone slapping his cheeks with a none-too-kind hand. Ammonia filled his nose, and he snorted and gagged.

"Maureen!" he shouted as his head cleared. "What happened? We were nearly at the hatch and someone—"

"Someone," a gruff voice behind him interrupted, "gave you a blow to the head and took her."

Owen was standing before him with a bag of salts in his hand. "Aye, I saw. It was another of the lads we'd taken on." He glanced at the man behind Sean. "What do you think, Dubhghall, is he going to live?"

"His head will hurt for a good while – here, chew on this." Working behind him in the shadows of the hull, the man named Dubhghall shoved something into Sean's open palm. He held it up to his eyes – it was a leaf of some sort.

"It will be bitter, but keep it in your mouth. Do not swallow the leaf – just chew it and hold it in your cheek. It will ease the pain."

Sean made a face. The leaf *was* bitter, but chewing gave him time to think. Dubhghall, he realized, was the man who had saved Maureen – saved her only so Sean could lose her again.

"And Maureen?" he asked. His voice was garbled as he talked around his medicated chew. "Is she going to live?"

"Maureen is gone," Dubhghall replied before Owen could respond.

The other boy glared. "You don't know that. Liam is in charge of the boarding parties. I saw her taken myself, and if she's there, they'll find her."

"If she's there," Sean echoed. "You said it was one of the lads who had joined – who?"

"He's a kinsman – one who claimed to be kin, at any rate. Galen O'Flaherty approached the captain right before she sent Dubhghall here to the Continent to bring back – ah, well, something of her Mam's that had been stolen, aye? That was just before you lot were brought on. Of course, Herself is furious. I wouldn't want to be near any O'Flaherty holdings for a while, aye?"

"It was a test."

"Kinsman? But Galen spoke English."

Sean and Dubhghall's words tumbled over one another, but Owen stared at Sean the hardest.

"How do you know that?" His eyes were narrowed and his lips formed a thin line. Gone was the wisecracking lad who had taken him and Maureen under his wing.

Dubhghall did not seem keen on elaborating, and Sean, not certain what the man meant, answered for himself.

"He said, 'I think not, my boy' right before he hit me – in English. I am from Dublin, aye?" He tried to keep his voice light, but Owen's face remained stony. "Of course, it could just mean he has some English as well, but—"

"So, were you in on it together? I should have known—"

"No!" He lurched to his feet and Owen's hand flew to his dagger. Sean reached for him – to stop him – but faltered. The room was spinning.

"Calm down, Owen," Dubhghall growled as he yanked on Sean's arm.

He allowed himself to be pulled back to the sacks of grain that had been his perch and immediately regretted it. Even as he helped him sit, Dubhghall was putting something damp and foul smelling above his ear.

He bit down on a yelp and ground his teeth – bloody thing stung. After several deep breaths, he risked a glance at Owen.

Dubhghall's word clearly carried some weight with the crew. Owen was still glaring at them, but some of the tension had left his shoulders and his hand was no longer on the hilt of his dagger.

"I've some English too, Owen – does that make me a traitor? The lad and lass were just unlucky. Galen was the sole one among us leading those ships here. He saw some sort of advantage in taking Maureen, but what that was, and what they will do with her, I do not wish to imagine."

"Neither do we," came Grania's voice from the hatch. She slid down the ladder, with Liam close behind.

"My lady."

Even without seeing the man's face, Sean could hear the respect for their captain in his voice.

"Master Dubhghall, glad I am to see you. I regret I could not greet you before you boarded." Grania inclined her head briefly. The respect was mutual.

She turned to Sean. "I am sorry, lad, but Maureen was not on either ship. Our attackers had longboats and eager rowers. The crew had already fled by the time we boarded, and Maureen was not among those they left behind."

He realized Grania's news only confirmed what he knew in his gut. "They took her with them," he said, his voice low.

"Aye, that may be. She was not among the dead, either, but we don't know why they took her – if at all."

She paused and an itchy heat began to spread up his neck. He must have grunted or made some sort of noise in his throat, because the captain spared him a glance and chose her next words carefully. "They may have misused her, or they—"

"By taking her, they've misused her."

Before he even realized what he was doing, Sean was standing again and his hands were in fists. Dubhghall tried to pull him back, but he wrenched his shoulder free.

No one said a word and his chest squeezed tight. "I – we have to find her," he said finally.

"She is bait, lad." Grania's tone was blunt – angry, even – but there was sympathy in her eyes. "I cannot control what they do to her between now and whatever scheme they have intended for her comes about. Furthermore, I have little inclination to see what that scheme is."

"Bu—"

"My lady Grania," Dubhghall interrupted. This time, his hand on Sean's shoulder was firm, and the fingers biting into his skin demanded his silence. "*The Widow* is in need of repairs and Galway is the nearest port. Would you allow Liam and myself to ask some questions of those who deal in these sorts of sordid dealings? Between the two of us, I am certain we can determine who might be responsible for attacking you."

Sean held his breath, almost afraid to hope. This was not just about Maureen – it was about discovering why a kinsman would turn traitor and lure attackers to O'Malley waters.

Grania flashed a grim smile at the man behind him and nodded once.

"Aye, do that. And you, Sean, are you able? Then go with Owen. There is work to do above deck. It will keep you from brooding. Liam." She turned to address her first mate. "I need you to direct the galley crews. Master Dubhghall, if you will join him and attend to any injuries, I would be obliged."

Grania was skilled indeed at injecting purpose back into her ship and crew; activity followed the sound of her voice, and her cohorts were eager to restore the fleet's routine.

Sean turned to Dubhghall, who was bent over a large chest. Its contents clinked and clattered as the man rummaged through it.

He cleared his throat. "Thank you. I don't—"

"You are welcome." Dubhghall did not look up, but his voice rumbled from the depths of the trunk. "I will do what I can to see Maureen is returned to us."

Impatient to follow his captain's orders, Owen nudged Sean's arm. He frowned but followed. There was work to do.

Ten

"Careful with that one. I nearly had to kill her to get her off the bloody ship – she bit me!"

"Oh, you poor thing, what do you expect, cavorting with pirates and rabble? Do you need the surgeon to look at you? Is it likely to fall off?"

Maureen kept her eyes closed listened intently. Both men were speaking English, but only one was familiar. Galen O'Flaherty was a crewman on Grania's flagship, and had been leering at her since he first helped Owen unload Tomás' cart.

"Bugger off, Jamie," Galen cursed. He sounded like a moody little boy. "Just make sure she's bound before she comes to. I'll not be the one responsible for her attacking the Governor of Connacht when he comes to inspect her."

The other voice did not say anything and she risked opening her eyes, just enough to catch a glimpse of her surroundings. She closed them again quickly as the tow-headed young man named Jamie approached her with rope in hand.

She was in what looked to be a part of a ship's staterooms. She was above deck, at any rate, and the room was clean, if spare. She choked down the nearly overwhelming urge to flee. Her head was fuzzy and her limbs did not want to cooperate. Even if she were able, she had been knocked about the head once already this day, and knew worse would be in store for her if she risked running and was caught again.

Jamie was gentle enough as he bound her arms and legs to the small stool where Galen had dumped her, and she suspected he knew she was awake.

"That should hold her – don't worry, Galen, you and Sir Bingham are safe from the wee lassie, now."

Jamie's good humour was interrupted by the clatter of boots entering the room.

"Galen O'Flaherty." The new voice was older – and cold.

Maureen held her breath.

"Not only did you not warn us Grania O'Malley's flagship travelled with two galleys, thereby outnumbering us, you also saw fit to snatch a wench in the woman's care, and expose yourself as a traitor in the process. That was not the plan, boy."

The drawled menace in the man's voice made her eyes snap open. She gave up all pretence of unconsciousness to better observe the emerging drama.

The refined voice belonged to an equally elegant man with brown hair and a well-kept goatee. His eyes, however, were two dark slits on his face and his breath whistled between bared teeth. This, she presumed, was the Crown-appointed Governor of Connacht.

Galen had straightened himself and stared ahead to avoid the governor's stare.

"Her name is Maureen O'Malley, Sir Richard. She is Grania's kinswoman."

"Oh, is she?" Sir Richard Bingham arched an eyebrow and regarded her for the first time. She tried not to flinch. "They share a family name, and that makes them kin – kin worth dying for?"

A bright red flush crept up Galen's neck and she smirked. The rat deserved everything the man threw at him – although, thank heavens it was Galen under Bingham's scrutiny, and not herself.

"I didn't mean to expose myself, but I had no choice. Your instructions said to find anything which might implicate Grania O'Malley." Galen pointed at her. "She and a lad appeared no more than a moon ago. Grania barely said two words to them before they were bound to her service. 'Tis less time than it took for her to take me on, I can tell you."

He was nodding vigorously, warming to his topic.

"All any of us knew was that they were orphans from Dublin. I thought their story funny. It sounded a bit like my own, and I thought conscripting a lass was curious. There were some who suggested she and the lad were spies."

Galen looked at Bingham with wide eyes. The older man made no move to interrupt him and he continued.

"Naturally, I thought you should know. When Davey boarded with the party, I asked him to storm the hold and snatch her. He did, but that damned Scot killed him. I had to act!"

"You had to do nothing!" Bingham roared. "You had to stay aboard those ships and guide Grania to me, not smuggle some chit off the boats because you took a fancy to her!"

"But her story—"

Bingham growled and struck Galen across the cheek with the back of his hand. The large glittering ring on his finger scraped along the boy's face.

Galen glowered at his attacker as he touched the angry red graze, but remained silent.

"Now then, girl, perhaps we should hear from you." Bingham brought the full force of his haughty gaze to bear on her and she froze. The blurry edges of her brain were suddenly sharpened with a fear she could taste in her mouth.

"You understand us, I presume? You have been following our conversation with enough interest, at least."

Maureen bit back her first response that she had no choice but to follow the conversation. Jamie had been gentle with the ropes, but she was still tied to the bloody stool.

Instead, she said, "Grania O'Malley is no kinswoman of mine. Sean and I are orphans. We found our way to Carrickahowley by accident." She was reaching for indifference but could not tell if Bingham was buying it. "The lad there is right. Grania's men did think we were spies, and she met with us – questioned us, like. When our answers proved satisfactory, she offered us a spot on her ships. I rather think she wanted to keep an eye on us, and seeing that one, I can understand why."

Galen scoffed and Bingham turned his fury back on the boy. "Shut up, you snivelling fool. I'm listening, and she might actually have something to say."

He motioned for her to continue.

"I am nothing to Grania," she stated, her voice flat. "But her boats? Those she cares about. An asinine attack like the one you just pulled, she cares about, but not enough to chase you. That is presumably what you had intended before Galen fouled it up? She wouldn't still be around to spoil your little world, Sir Bingham, Governor of Connacht, if she were so daft to fall for that trap."

To her surprise, Bingham laughed. "You insolent little cur. Grania wouldn't have had reason to know it was a trap if this callow young fellow hadn't taken it into his head to snatch you." He stepped closer to her, and she struggled to keep from shying away.

"It wasn't supposed to be me she was chasing, but the captain. Galen there was supposed to volunteer to go with her men on a little fact-finding trip once they put in for repairs in Galway. It was just possible that an unknown English mercenary such as our Captain Pennington might be enough to incite her rage. You are small enough for her to make an example of, understand?"

This last was said, with a nasty smile, to the stout man who now stood in the doorway to the stateroom. Next to Bingham, he was a drab, sallow creature. Pennington did not say anything, but he winced a little at his superior's implication.

"Captain Pennington here could lure her to Dublin, where there would be reinforcements enough to hold her. Then, I would have her, I would have her and damn the clans allied with her. They may still rebel, but they'd not have her ships."

Bingham shook his head and laughed at Galen. It was a sour sound, devoid of any humour. He took the boy by the shoulder.

"As it is, my half-wit spy who cannot follow orders had to expose the gambit and leave me with nothing!" His grip on Galen's shoulder tightened and he slammed his fist into the boy's face.

Maureen abandoned her bravado and turned from the spectacle, but not before she saw Galen spit a tooth onto the cabin floor.

"You said find something, find anything to provoke the bloody woman," the boy growled. "Well, I did. The lass is a kinswoman, and she will bring Grania to us – either her, or the lad who was with her. He'll not leave her behind."

"Aye, puppy love will inspire the boy to die rescuing the girl, but by all accounts he is not a pirate, you fool."

She could not take it anymore – she squeezed her eyes shut, but what she could not see, she could hear.

"You had to think for yourself, didn't you?" Bingham shouted as he delivered blow after sickening blow. Galen grunted and wheezed but accepted the beating with less noise than she thought was possible.

Seconds or minutes later – she had no idea which – the sounds of the attack finally ceased and she risked opening her eyes. Galen was huddled on the floor and Bingham stood above him. Captain Pennington and Jamie, forgotten in the nobleman's rage, were as far from Bingham as they could be and still remain in the room.

Her breath whistled harshly between her teeth. Sr. Theresa had taken a ruler to her hands more than once, and Grania was not a gentle commander, but she never once witnessed the kind of raw rage Bingham had unleashed on Galen. Even as she sat there, torn between screaming and cowering, the nobleman delivered a final, brutal kick to the boy's head.

Galen collapsed, senseless.

She groaned but refused to turn away again. Bingham glared down at his handiwork and motioned to Jamie with a casual wave of his hand.

"You – boy – whatever your name is, get this

worthless baggage out of here. Toss him overboard, but make sure he is awake before you do. It would be a pity for him to drown before he can tell that O'Malley woman what we have. Go!"

Jamie hurried to follow his orders and Bingham turned back to face Maureen. He stared her in the eyes and she stared back. His were empty, pitiless eyes.

"You are a brave one, girl. That is good. You had better hope you are wrong about Grania. You had better hope you, and her wounded pride, are enough to lure her to Dublin, or there will be no reason for me to keep you alive."

"My lord, is this wise?" Pennington asked. He was twisting his cap in his hands and looking between Bingham and Maureen.

"If the girl is a kinswoman, might it not incite the O'Malley woman to extraordinary measures? It's well known the only naturally womanly thing about her is her feeling for her family."

Maureen was still sitting in the corner bound to the stool. Jamie had left, dragging the bloody mess that was Galen behind him. She shifted to try to find a comfortable angle for her aching arms and shoulders.

Threats issued, Bingham was ignoring her entirely. He was doing his best to ignore the captain as well, much to Pennington's obvious dismay.

"Are you questioning me, Pennington? I am not paying you to question me."

Petulance crept into the captain's voice. "No, my lord. I'm merely attempting to gauge the danger to my men and the precautions we should take in order to ensure our voyage home is a success."

"You could pray, Pennington," Bingham muttered. When Pennington began a mewling protest – she suspected he feared the mottled mask of rage as much as she did – Bingham sighed. He looked more bored than annoyed.

"I do not deny Grania O'Malley is a dangerous woman, Pennington – all the more so because she is unnatural." Bingham turned to the porthole window and stared out at the sea.

"By all that is holy, she has fomented the rebellions of these lands for the last forty years," he continued. His voice sounded tired, as though this was an argument he had with someone – likely himself – many times. "She has at least two hundred men at her command, and a fleet twenty ships strong – a fleet, might I remind you, not sanctioned by Her Majesty, the Queen."

"Neither is this venture, my lord."

Bingham turned. His mouth was turned down and she thought she saw Pennington flinch. She did not blame him.

"Her Majesty has put me in charge, Pennington. My methods are my own and you knew the risks when you took my gold. Whether you survive it is up to your own wits and skill."

Maureen chewed her lip and watched the captain surrender his loyalty, and likely his life, to Bingham. There would be no help from that quarter, at least.

Jamie, the young midshipman, appeared in the doorway. "My apologies, Captain, but the men have retreated at your command, and the Irish are following with a landing party. Will you give the order to drop the longboats?"

"Aye, Jamie, do that," Pennington said. "Have

the Master at Arms fire a few shots across the bow of the flagship, too. That will give them distraction enough, and perhaps discourage the better of the two galleys from giving chase."

"Aye, Captain," Jamie bobbed his head, and made to leave.

"Boy, wait," Bingham called. "O'Flaherty – did you dispose of him as I asked?"

"Aye, m'lord – he's been tossed overboard. He was awake, but I'm not sure how long he'll be able to stay afloat if the Irish leave him in the sea."

Bingham ignored this. "They saw you, then?"

"Aye, m'lord."

"Good. Pennington, you give the order to flee. I want young Jamie here to deal with our cargo." Bingham nodded curtly in her direction. "Only, put a sack over her head. I do not want her making the crew nervous. She is not to be touched – yet."

$\mathcal{E}\textit{leven}$

"**I**s he alive, Liam?" Grania demanded, striding up to her first mate.

Sean and Owen paused in stacking the barrels that had overturned during the fighting. In the other corner, Liam was hunched over the form of a young man. The limp bag of bones was still dripping seawater all over the planking.

Sometime in the messy aftermath of the attack, Galen O'Flaherty had been plucked from the sea. Their captain had only just been notified he was aboard. She did not seem happy about it.

"Oh, aye, he'll live." Liam turned and straightened as well as he could in the cramped hold. "He's a bit the worse for wear – someone's fist had a go at his face and I think their feet got the rest of him. The lads tell me he was spotted but allowed to tread water for a bit before being brought aboard. Do you want me to fetch Master Dubhghall?"

"No. There are more vital injuries for Master Dubhghall to attend to." She gave the boy a disparaging look. "He'll live."

Liam dropped his voice. "With this lad in the water, m'lady, is it likely the lass—?"

"Don't say it, Liam." Her voice was soft and she glanced at Sean. He tried to look busy with the barrels but his stomach was churning.

"The lass may not claim to be kin, but I feel it in

my bones we are. She is a bold young thing, and proud – and alive. Tie O'Flaherty up and let him dry out." Grania paused and a slow smile spread across her face. "And make sure Cook prepares something toothsome for the men. They have had a day, aye?"

"Aye, my lady." Liam said as Grania slipped back up the ladder. He grinned and his big teeth gleamed against a face grimed with soot, blood and sweat.

"The lad will be ready to talk before sundown with that. Lads, take Herself's message to the cook. I'll bind our guest, here."

Sean led the way to the ladder, but he paused before climbing. Maureen was gone. It was his fault, and the boy who had taken her – had been following her with greedy eyes since the day they arrived – was sitting in the corner. Tied. Helpless. Just as he imagined Maureen was now. The urge to scream, to grind his fists into Galen's face, to do *something* was almost too strong to ignore.

He gripped the edges of the ladder until his arms shook and his knuckles turned white.

Owen nudged him up towards the hatch. "Don't try it," he muttered. "Let Liam have first crack at him."

Still, Sean hesitated. What would happen if he just grabbed Galen and shook him awake – shook him until his teeth rattled in his head?

A snarl passed over his face and Owen seized his shoulder. "You'll have your turn, but Liam is Grania's first mate."

The hand on Sean's shoulder squeezed until he unhooked his hands from the edge of the ladder. Owen nodded. There was understanding – commiseration even – in his eyes.

"My brother is kicking himself for letting Galen on board. We were taken in and nearly trapped. It's the risk we run, aye, but he likes to think he can protect Herself from it."

"I know." Sean sighed and rubbed the back of his neck as he stepped out onto the deck. He tried to muster a grin for Owen, but it came out more as a grimace.

"I just hope there's enough of him left when Liam's done."

Owen chuckled. "Don't worry – Liam is many things, but butcher isn't one of them. He knows how you feel. You'll have your chance."

"All right, lad – I need your help."

They were docked in Galway, and despite being granted permission by the Tribes to enter the city, Grania had allowed no one off the boat. The interrogation of Galen O'Flaherty was underway and their captain wanted to ensure no loose lips interfered with Liam's progress.

"My help?" Sean tore his eyes from the harbour and turned to the first mate. He was serving the watch, searing the image of every boat, every seaman, into his memory. Technically, his turn had been over long ago, but it did not matter. Maureen was out there somewhere.

"But is he—has he even started talking yet?"

"Oh aye, the rotten snake is talking, but only in English. I know a bit – but you have it, aye?"

Sean nodded slowly. "Aye – and so does Dubhghall. And he's a little more intimidating." He thought back to the image of the Scottish gallowglass swinging his sword in broad arcs as he fought Maureen's first attacker. Dubhghall was more than capable of scaring the truth out of their traitor.

Liam was already on his way back to the hatch. "Oh aye, he's scared of our Master Dubhghall," he tossed over his shoulder. "But you'll do one better, I think."

Sean hesitated.

"Come on, lad, I thought you wanted—"

"I do! But I'm not—" His face flushed. "I really do, but what if—what if I can't? Maureen—"

"You'll do fine – you've a connection to the lass. It will help, trust me."

Owen was waiting for them by the ladder to the hold.

"Stand watch, lad – barring fire, we're not to be interrupted."

Owen nodded and Liam disappeared into the hold. Sean had no choice but to follow.

The hold was dark and smoky, lit by a single lantern with dirty oil. Crowded by sacks, crates and barrels, Galen sat, bound to a stool. His head was high and his face – bruised and puffy – was defiant. Grania stood before him, her hands clasped behind her back, while Dubhghall paced behind, just beyond the muted light of the lamp.

"We've not hurt him," Liam said quietly. "Yet."

Grania heard her first mate and turned to them. "As much as I would like to beat the lad to a pulp for what he has done," she said in an undertone, "I don't believe it will help. Whoever is behind this is either more devious than we think, feeding us information through Galen, or holds so much fear over the lad that he will die before giving us the information we need."

"I'm hoping it's the former," Sean muttered,

trying to ignore his heart hammering in his chest.

Grania grasped his shoulder lightly. "You and I both, lad."

Sean met her eyes; they were steady, calm. He let out the breath he had been holding, and went to stand before Galen.

He was watching them with open curiosity and Sean wondered if he was afraid. He did not look afraid.

"I understand you'll not speak your native tongue," he began. Translating his thoughts into English was harder than he thought it would be.

Galen scoffed at this. "That I had to speak it at all was a pain I was forced to endure for this farce. My game is up, and so I will speak it no more. I feel no more kinship to the Irish than Her Majesty, the Queen, does."

"Ah, so O'Flaherty is just an affectation, then?"

"Ah, no," the prisoner echoed. "My name is indeed Galen O'Flaherty. However, my kinship to our fine captain and her first husband is rather suspect. But my – well, let us call him my benefactor – made certain it looked well enough should enquiries be made."

Sean arched an eyebrow at this but let it slide. Discovering Galen's real identity was a diversion. He focused instead on his flowery speech and the benefactor. There was pride in Galen's voice, but there was also hate.

"You speak rather fine. Your benefactor, as you call him, did you a disservice nearly letting you drown."

Galen shifted on his stool, grimacing slightly as his bonds chaffed at his wrists. Sean hoped Liam had tied the ropes tight.

"It's you lot who nearly let me drown."

"Hm. Seems to me, this benefactor was ridding himself of baggage he no longer required. I suspect, had you done your job, we would be on the trail of our attackers already. Instead, we're sitting in the harbour, stuck aboard our ship interrogating you, when all of Galway is ripe for our spymaster." He nodded at Dubhghall in the corner. Warrior, doctor, and now spy – he hoped Grania paid her gallowglass well.

"Thanks to you, Master Galen, we know it was a trap."

A bitter scowl replaced the pride in Galen's face, yet he still refused to speak.

"I think, Master Galen, you outlived your usefulness. I think, as you sit here bandying fancy words, you have outlived your usefulness to us. What's to stop me from telling my captain that we ought to do what your benefactor nearly did, and drown you in the sea?"

"Nothing, except the lass," Galen said quietly. His eyes narrow slits and his mouth turned down in a sneer, he seemed to be daring Sean to contradict.

"Aye, the lass. Maureen." Her name hung in the silence of the hold. Betrayed by the sound of leather and cloth, he knew Liam and the others had tensed behind him.

"She wasn't part of the plan, was she?"

Galen twitched and a dark grin spread on Sean's face. He suspected bringing up Maureen was a test; Galen wanted to know just how dear she was to them.

He bent low and brought himself close to Galen. He had the lad's attention now – had the entire room's attention. At the edge of his sight, he saw Dubhghall put a hand on the hilt of his sword.

Sean snarled and lunged. He grabbed the hair at the back of Galen's head and yanked it back. He was going to prove just how dear Maureen was.

His mouth close to Galen's ear, he hissed, "It appears we traded you for Maureen. It is a poor trade. Tell me why I shouldn't let them murder you right now? You don't think Grania has network enough to discover the whereabouts of one lass? A comely lass like Maureen gets attention, Galen – you know that especially, don't you? Even if she is hidden, those watching her will talk. Your benefactor cannot shut up all his men, all the time. I will find her, with or without you. Helping us, however, will prolong your miserable life."

He released the traitor and shoved him. The stool rocked and crashed back down again. Galen let his head fall forward with the movement and Sean fought the urge to plow his fist into it. Breathing hard, he got to his feet and crossed his arms, digging his fingers into his skin until he could bear the pain no more.

Galen brought his head up. The haughty defiance was gone – replaced by naked anger, and just the smallest hint of fear. "You'll find her, but will they follow?" He jerked his chin at Grania, behind him.

His composure was stunning. He had been trained well.

"Her life depends on them following. If it takes too long, he'll kill her, and try something else."

"Who is 'he'?"

Galen did not answer right away and Sean leaned towards him again, his hands in loose fists at his sides.

"We can't do anything, Galen, without knowing who we're supposed to be fighting. We can find out, but if we do, and it is not from you, then you have proven yourself worthless to us. Do something almost honourable with your short life and tell us what you know."

His words hung in the air – even the murky eddies of light from the lamp slowed.

"The English Governor of Connacht, Sir Richard Bingham, is the man behind the attack on Grania's fleet," Galen said quietly, his eyes focused squarely on his lap.

Sean heard the quick intake of breath behind him. The name was familiar to their captain, then.

"Why?"

"Now, that is a bit more obscure," Galen mused. He eyed Sean from beneath his brows. He could not seem to help his arrogance. "He's paid mercenaries from England to attack, cripple and flee. He hoped to anger our lovely captain into following the retreating fleet all the way to Dublin. There were meant to be more attacks along the way – to whet her appetite."

The boy grinned at this but Sean refused to be baited. The rest of the room waited in silence and he blessed their patience.

At last, Galen relented. "Once in Dublin, with enough support of allies there, Bingham reckoned he would have the grounds to imprison her, and whoever else he caught alive. Then he could take her misdeeds to the Queen. With luck, Grania would be tried and then hanged for her crimes."

"Why Dublin? Why not here – where he's supposedly this great governor?"

"Do you know nothing of what's going on, lad? Bingham is a new governor with unpopular ideas. He has allies in Dublin, but precious few out here. Grania, on the other hand, has little support within the Pale. However, she does command the loyalty of many of the Irish chiefs along the western coast. If he were to take her, it would have to be in open water or in enemy territory. He is not a dumb man, Sir Bingham. He knows his chances in open water – hell, you lot nearly took him down today."

"Which is why you took Maureen," Sean said slowly. "It stung, nearly losing today, didn't it? Your pride wouldn't let you stay, and Maureen must have seemed like handy ransom." Galen's plan was mad, but he could understand it.

"But Bingham wasn't happy, was he, Galen? Taking Maureen exposed you as a traitor, and nearly ruined it for him. That is why you're back here, and Maureen is there, on her way to Dublin."

Galen shrugged but remained silent. There was nothing left to say. Sean sighed and turned to Grania and Liam. The captain arched a single eyebrow and he nodded.

"I have the story – or as much of it as he has," he said in a language they could wholly understand. "It may be the best we can do. Can we discuss it elsewhere? I fear for his safety if I'm forced to stay in the same room with him for much longer."

A wry smile quirked at the edge of Grania's mouth as she nodded. "Indeed. Liam – my quarters. Owen?"

Owen's face appeared in the hatch.

"Lad, help Master Dubhghall attend to our prisoner. You will stand first watch over him. Dubhghall, join us when you are done."

"Indeed, my lady."

Sean followed Grania and Liam up the ladder. Owen gave his shoulder a quick nudge as he passed, whether for luck or sympathy, he did not know. Sympathy could wait – he needed the luck.

Twelve

"**I** am not a bag of goods for you to toss around at your pleasure," Maureen grumbled as she tripped over her own feet, again. Of course, the sack on her head and the ropes around her arms contradicted her. Jamie was leading her through what amounted to a labyrinth to her blind eyes and talking was the only way to dampen the panicky numbness that threatened to steal over her limbs.

"My apologies, your highness," the midshipman muttered as he lifted the bag from her head and balled it up in his hands.

Expecting the glare of sunlight, she squinted, but the small room was dark. It was night already, and she was on yet another ship.

"Welcome to the good ship *Excelsior*, miss. Here you will journey in style as we make our way to Dublin. For a prisoner of the Crown, you have been granted an excellent suite of rooms." Jamie waved an arm at the ornately decorated rooms behind him. "Of course, you will not make any use of them – my orders were to make sure you were bound and kept rather out of sight in this small corner of Sir Bingham's stateroom."

"You know, for a ship rat, you speak rather well." The snark of the jibe was lost somewhat, distracted as she was by Bingham's quarters and her own.

It was actually an antechamber to what she assumed was Bingham's receiving chamber. It was barely four feet wide and only about two feet deep. Sleeping would be awkward, but then, she was not sure she would be able to sleep, anyway.

No window, or hook for a lantern, relieved the walls. The only light to grace the room would come at Bingham's pleasure. Loathing aside, she hoped the Englishman would make frequent use of the room beyond.

"As do you, for a pirate," Jamie countered. He crossed his arms over his chest and tossed blond hair from his eyes. Despite the poor hygiene standards of the 16th century, the young midshipman was not hard on the eyes, nor did he seem to despise her – just his position as her minder, perhaps.

She met his gaze. "Indeed."

The midshipman snorted. He looked amused – annoyed, but amused.

"I'm not a pirate, yet," she amended. "No more than you are a mercenary simply by being a midshipman in Master Pennington's fleet. It is a trade like any other. Out here, Grania's occupation is a respected tradition – expected even, despite her being a woman."

"Respected? Certainly, for cattle-thieving natives."

"I've spent much of my life within your *respectable* world, Master Jamie. I will take Grania's over yours any day. At least she's honest."

She bit down on the words but they were already out. Why had she said that? Her real world consisted of the nuns and the other students at the abbey. Their piety was not dishonest – just not something she belonged to, or shared.

She did not belong anywhere, really. The whole country considered her parents' war record treasonous. People looked at her and Sean – whispered and glared – any time they went into town.

Was that why she had she followed that man with the wild blue eyes? For the promise of a place where she belonged? Even as she dismissed the idea – had been dismissing the idea ever since they stepped through the gateway – it settled into her chest like a warm spark.

Jamie and his ilk might scoff at her, but in Grania's crew, it did not matter if she knew how to embroider, or sit prettily in mass. Here, her wits were as valued as her ability to tie a knot in a rope. And if she could not scamper along the rigging like some of the other lads, it did not matter, because Liam would rather have her, and 'her canny mind,' at the prow.

She inhaled sharply and forced herself to focus. Jamie was still watching her – looking at her as though she were some creature, some otherworldly thing he had never seen before but might bite if he were not careful.

He was right, but he was also going to help her.

She lifted her chin. "What would you have me do, Master Jamie? Thank you for the bonds, which keep my honour safe, here in this tiny cell?"

Her honour – and the safety of her person – meant nothing here among Bingham's mercenaries, and she stifled a shudder at what it might mean if they loosed her among the crew.

"I am a prisoner, scorned because I stand with a woman who refuses to be cowed by the likes of your master. I am a native, aye, but my bonds still chafe."

Jamie clicked his tongue but the ghost of understanding flickered across his face. "It is a treacherous and deceitful game they play," he admitted softly. "Using you is dangerous, too. But they are my betters, and I cannot defy my orders."

His expression turned ugly and before Maureen could react to the change, he drove his fist into her middle with enough force to drop her to her knees. She gasped for air, and tried to roll away from him, but he was too fast for her. He kneeled beside her and with a deft movement, bound her like a pig – ankles to wrists – with barely enough rope between them to crouch.

Rage and terror squeezed her scream into nothing but a wheeze. Tears burned her throat and she bit down hard. Swallowing blood, she glared at him. She would not cry for him.

"You pathetic little boy! You are just as bad as the rest!" she managed to spit as he tugged on the ropes and tested the knots.

His movements were stiff and quick, and he avoided her eyes. "Orders, Miss," he muttered as he stood. He turned to leave. "I'll see what I can do about them."

The last was said so quietly, Maureen was not sure she actually heard it, but she filed it away in her memory anyway. She had underestimated his loyalties, but she would not do so again.

Thirteen

High above the hold, at the other end of the *Widow's Weeds*, were Grania's chambers. A long, sturdy table, strewn with maps, dominated the small cabin. Colourful hangings graced the walls, and hid, Sean suspected, the entrance to her sleeping bunk. This was their captain's inner sanctum, known only to trusted lieutenants such as Liam.

Idly, his eyes drifted over the maps. Even though the island's orientation was drastically different from the maps he knew from school, he still managed to place modern landmarks along the crudely detailed coast.

"Now, lad, what kind of tale did you manage to wring from that wretch?"

Grania faced him and he focused on her solemn brown eyes. They demanded his complete attention and he took a deep, steadying breath.

"You know Sir Richard Bingham, I understand?"

"Of course. My son Tibbot was raised in his brother's house – hostage for my good behaviour, such as it is."

Damn. That complicated things.

"I do not know Sir Richard personally, mind," Grania continued, "but I do know he is a mean little man with big ideas to bring us in line with England. He means to break the chiefs and their power, and he will not stop until the last of us submits. The Crown is more than willing to support him, too."

She swept her hand at her quarters, disordered still from the attack. "This was his doing?"

"Aye. He hired mercenaries out of England to attack your fleet as you made your way to Galway. They were meant to keep attacking you, encouraging you to follow. The idea was to lure you to Dublin—"

"Where I have few allies, and he could take me with the full measure of support from the Crown," Grania finished for him. "He has created a monster of me in his mind, and overestimates my desire for revenge."

"He must think your memory dim," Liam scoffed. "Never have we followed an attacking fleet so far afield, not when we have ready strongholds to withstand attack and siege."

Grania shook her head and paced along the length of the table.

"They must have realized they underestimated our strength. That is why they took Maureen, aye?"

Sean nodded. "Galen wasn't supposed to take her though, and Bingham was so angry, he ordered him sent back to us. I think his sole purpose now is to anger or frighten us enough so we follow Bingham, despite knowing it's a trap."

Her laugh was a sharp, mirthless bark. "That is quite the plan. Were the man not so hell-bent on destroying us, Bingham might have been someone I would want to know. As it is, he can rot in Dublin before I will allow myself to be drawn into his schemes."

"But—"

"I spent nearly two years in a Limerick cell, lad — I am not so stupid as to put myself in that position again, nor risk those who follow me. Without guaranteed protections from Her Majesty herself, I will not follow that madman into a trap. It is unthinkable. I am a pirate, not a champion. Maureen knows this, and so do you."

He suspected this would be her response, even without knowing she had been a prisoner once before. Grania was right; it would be a reckless and thoughtless gamble to risk the lives of these men in something so foolhardy, and yet . . .

"I do understand you, my lady, and I mean no disrespect." He grabbed the edge of the table and stared at it as he searched for the words that might convince her. The lines of the grain danced before his eyes.

"You say you are a pirate." His voice was quiet as he finally lifted his head and met Grania's eyes. "Yet, you fight to keep your way of life. You are a pirate who commands the loyalty of over two hundred men – loyalty and respect. But more than that, your kin, your neighbours – and even your enemies – bow to the power of this Pirate Queen."

He let the title hang in the air for a moment but continued before Grania could interrupt.

"You are a pirate who strikes such fear in to the heart of men like Bingham that, in their fear, they hatch a plot – worthy of a monster, aye – to snare you."

He pushed away from the table. He had the room's attention but he kept his eyes on the captain.

"You are not just a pirate, my lady Grania. You are an inspiration. You are that which embodies the spirit of this land, of a people proud and rebellious. You are Ireland, now and in the centuries to come, and you are that young woman's kinswoman, whether by blood or the tenacity and spirit that marks you both. You know it. I know you do."

Grania did not deny his accusation and he nodded.

"I know, because I am her only companion and now it falls to me to be her protector too. She, who always shielded me, needs me. It would be unthinkable for me not to ask your help, and furthermore, unthinkable for me not to follow her captors, regardless of your answer. You owe me nothing, and your refusal will not be looked upon as poor hospitality, but I will ask you none-the-less. Help me get Maureen back."

The room was silent. He could hear the sound of the harbour, the waves lapping against the side of the ship. He could hear the long intake of breath as Grania made to deny him.

She was staring at him, hard. Her mouth was set but her eyes – those frank brown eyes – were narrowed.

She started pacing the room.

"We do have permission to enter Galway proper," she said finally. "Bingham will have someone watching, you can be sure of it. He'll know when we leave and he'll be expecting something, no matter what subterfuge we employ."

It was not the refusal he expected.

It was bait.

Bloody pirate, he thought with a small grin.

"We should make his spies, and his fear of you, work to our advantage," he said. The edges of a plan were forming in his mind. "Do you have any ships, recently acquired, or someone with a ship who owes you a favour?"

Grania looked confused, but only for a moment.

A smile bloomed on her face and this time, her laugh was genuine. "Aye, I do. What do you intend? Shall we flee on a different ship, in the dead of night?"

"Not flee, no. Follow."

She scowled at this but Liam's face broke out into a wide grin. "He's right. It could work. Dubhghall and I will take Galen and identify Bingham's spies. We can ride over land to meet you down the coast as you make your way to Dublin in a ship Bingham has yet to mark as yours."

Grania frowned slightly but motioned for Liam to keep talking.

"We could send a coded message to Tomás. He can outfit a new ship with provisions and men who will take the *Widow* and her galleys home when the repairs are complete."

She looked at Sean as Liam finished, a single eyebrow arched. "You seem to have fired the imagination of my first mate, Sean McAndrew."

He bowed his head. "It was not me, my lady."

"Do not go by sea."

From shadow of the doorway, another voice added its thoughts to the fray. Dubhghall emerged from the dark, his cloak and hood drawn against the cool October night. Beads of water caught the lamplight.

"Do not mistake me. The idea is a good one, but we should not be on the ship leaving Galway for Dublin. Approach Dublin by land, not sea, and you will have the better of Bingham. You may succeed in winning the lass back without sacrificing lives."

Liam considered this. "We shouldn't risk sending the *Widow* back to Carrickahowley, then."

"Aye, Galen was honest on that point, at least. Maureen's life hangs on the idea that you will follow. Bingham will need proof to justify keeping her alive."

Sean nodded. Dubhghall was right, but the implications . . . no, he was not going to think about the implications. He looked at Grania and waited as she surveyed the room. The other men, those who knew her better, waited too. The air hummed with their eagerness, with their desire to take revenge and fight.

She completed a circuit of the room and stopped directly opposite Sean, the table between them. She rested her fingertips lightly on the wood and watched him for a moment before speaking.

"We will go," she said, her voice ringing in the waiting silence. "God help us, we will go."

His heart leapt. It was more than he had hoped to achieve, and yet, the responsibility for this adventure's outcome, for his comrade's lives, waited in the shadows of his elation.

"God help us," he echoed, nodding into Grania's stare.

$\mathcal{F}$ ourteen

The tentative flickering of a candle woke her. Its light was distant, and the carrier was moving slowly and silently through the outer stateroom. Nightmares had already forced Maureen towards consciousness, and now her eyes flew open.

Bingham had gone to his rest hours ago, and of the crew, only Pennington, his steward and Jamie knew of her presence on the *Excelsior*.

Fear of the reckless soul who would risk Bingham's wrath calling on her at this hour had her scooting as far into the corner of the small alcove as she could. She wondered if anyone would come to her aid if she screamed.

She looked around her bare corner for something – anything – to use for protection. Only an empty chamber pot remained. It was her one luxury, and now her only weapon.

She wrapped her bound hands around the cold metal and used the wall to help her stand to a crouch. She was not going to do much damage, hunched and hobbled, but if she kept to the darkest corner in her open prison, she might be able to surprise her would-be assailant. What she would do afterwards did not matter at all.

Candle and carrier crept ever closer to the alcove. She waited – barely breathing but with her heart hammering at her ribcage – to pounce.

At last, the candle and a cautious foot eased around the open doorway. She launched herself at the light, holding the metal chamber pot before her as both shield and bludgeon.

"Christ, girl – are you mad?"

Jamie moved just in time to avoid her attack. He swung the candle up and away from her as she came at him, and she nearly crashed into the opposite wall. Undeterred, she turned and faced him.

"What are you doing here?" she growled as she threw herself at him again.

He grabbed her, but her momentum dragged them both to the ground.

Tossed to a corner, the candle hissed as it went out and darkness descended again. She thrashed for a moment longer until the midshipman's hand clamped down on her nose and mouth, and the other tightened around her middle.

Between the fetters and Jamie's superior strength, she tired and stilled. There was nothing she could do, however, to stop her heart from banging at the walls of her chest. She resented its show of fear. Every deafening thud told her she was weak, powerless.

"Listen to me," Jamie growled in her ear. He loosened his grip around her waist, but did not take his hand from her mouth. "Have you no idea of the risk I'm running? Pennington has been watching me since Bingham tasked me as your minder. If he suspected any sympathy on my part, he'd take it up with Bingham, and then someone else – someone not nearly as nice as I – would be in charge of watching you."

She resisted a snicker at this and waited for him to finish.

"If I take my hand away, do you promise not to scream?"

She nodded, if only to find out what the midshipman intended. He slowly eased his hand from her mouth and helped her to a more comfortable sitting position.

Crouched, he peered at her. She glared back, silent.

A wry grin spread across his face. "Aye, well at least you didn't bite me."

"Yet. Depends on how you intend to be 'nicer' to me."

He ignored this and reached for the candle. He fumbled with something in his sleeve and the light flared to life.

She said nothing and watched the boy warily. He returned her stare for a moment and then offered up the candle.

The moon was nothing but a cool slice of silver again. It barely illuminated the outer room, let alone her small corner of it. The candle would be a warm and welcome friend.

"Is this it?" she asked, not moving. Her gaze flicked between his face and the proffered candle. It took all she had to resist the urge to snatch it from his fingers.

He frowned. "You don't want it?"

"I want it." She held out her bound hands. "I just want to make sure you're really going to give it to me."

"Aye, it's yours – I don't want you tossing your chamber pot at my head," he muttered. "I'm surprised they kept that in here with you – nasty weapon, that!"

She grinned and jerked her chin at the overturned pot that had rolled into the corner after he tackled her. "Not tonight – it's empty!"

He matched her grin and she relaxed slightly, even as she kept the candle clutched in her hand. Hot wax dripped on her fingers but she ignored the pain. The light was worth it.

"Besides, what need have I for weapons?" she asked with a shrug. "Bingham thinks me meek as a lamb. He was more worried about 'a filthy mess' too near his person than my access to potential weapons."

"Aye, well, it's not his first mistake on this voyage." The midshipman rose from his crouch. "And yes, that is it. You're a resourceful one, girl. I'm sure you'll find many a use for it." He tossed something in her lap. It was the flint.

"Keep them both well hidden. It shouldn't be hard, what with Sir Bingham's order against violating your person, but prudence in this case is wise, yes?"

"Thank you." Her voice was quiet and tight.

Jamie nodded and she blew out the light, conserving it, as he slipped out of the room and back to his berth.

She wiped at her wet cheeks and smiled wildly into the darkness.

It was not much. It did not mean Sean or Grania were coming to her rescue. It did not mean she could trust Jamie with anything but this one gift. He had tied her ropes tight, after all.

But ropes could also be burned.

She palmed the flint and tucked the candle in the waistband of her breeches and the modern conveniences of cotton and elastic underneath. Candle safe, she curled up on the tattered rug and slept.

Fifteen

Sean scooted closer to the low fire, grateful for its heat and light. The night was cold and like the rest of those in the camp, he had only his cloak for protection against the persistent drizzle.

It took three long days of riding – not to mention navigating the Pale at Kilcock – but he, Grania and Owen had arrived at the outskirts of Dublin that morning. Of the crew left behind in Galway, only Liam and Dubhghall had travelled inland, taking an alternate route to intercept Grania as she headed east. When the full group reunited the day before, Liam had informed his captain that Galen had been delivered to the O'Flaherty's, to see that justice was done. No one seemed willing to talk about what that meant, and Sean was glad not to know.

The men's horses – fast as they were – barely had a chance to rest before Liam and Dubhghall were off again to explore Dublin's harbour and identify Bingham's ship, the *Excelsior*.

Now, all five sat clustered about the fire trading jokes and telling stories – well, Sean, Owen and Liam were. Dubhghall was his taciturn self, and Grania alternated between listening appreciatively to her first mate and studying the flames that spit and sputtered in the rain.

"You have made certain Sir Bingham will hear of the *Venture*?" she asked, tearing her steady gaze from the fire to look at Liam.

Her thoughts were never far from her ships and crew.

Liam nodded. "Galen recognized one of Pennington's messengers – a lad named Nicholas who didn't know of Master Galen's disgraced status, aye? We took young Nicholas aside, slowed him down a bit and gave him some choice information. He'll deliver it fine – we paid him well for his trouble."

"Paid? Truly?" Sean whispered to Owen as the boy handed him a stick of roasted meat. He bit gingerly so the steaming meat would not burn his lips and tongue.

"Aye – in mead," Owen whispered back. "How else do you think they got him to tarry? He probably woke up a day later with the biggest head in Galway."

Sean started to laugh but Liam shot them a nasty look from across the fire. He bit his lip, grinned at Owen and the two returned to their supper, snickering.

"By this time to tomorrow, the messenger will be telling all those aboard Bingham's ship the *Venture* has reached Dublin, likely carrying the notorious feminine sea captain, Grania Uaile and her contingent of fierce wild Irish bandits." Liam grinned and paused. When no one clapped or cheered at his performance, he scowled.

"You lot make a terrible audience. Back home there'd be roaring applause at my story by now!"

Owen laughed. "Back home they'd be in their cups by now!"

His brother ignored him. "Aye, well, the *Venture* has her orders to remain just out of reach in open water. At midnight, provided she has not been engaged, she will begin the trip to Galway."

"And if she's engaged?" Sean asked.

"She'll still make her way to Galway, lad. She's a ship worthy to be Grania's flagship, were Herself not so fond of the *Widow's Weeds,* of course."

"Speaking of which, did the Lord of Howth come through with safe harbour?" Dubhghall asked.

While Dubhghall and Liam were in Dublin, Sean, Owen and Grania had skirted the city and ensured their escape route to Howth was secure. When Sean questioned why they were escaping to the north, when it would require they go past Dublin again to return to Carrickahowley, Grania had smiled. In light of Bingham's machinations – and through him, the machinations of the Crown – Grania wanted to have a wee chat with an ally: Sir Hugh O'Donnell.

"Aye, after some convincing," Sean muttered – if holding Sr. Christopher Lawrence, Lord of Howth at the end of a firearm constituted convincing. Some more of Grania's *business* dealings, apparently.

Grania smiled. "I don't have many allegiances this side of the Pale, but there are a few, so long as I am discreet."

"And speaking of discretion, my lady Grania—"

"No, Liam. Whatever it is, no."

"But how—?"

"Whenever you start something with such deference, I know I'm not going to like it. I have known you since you were in skirts, Liam O'Neil, and have had the honour of your allegiance these last ten years. Deference does not suit you. Speak plainly."

Liam sighed and looked at his captain ruefully. "Grania," he began again, "Owen will take the horses along the road to Howth at midday. It would make me – make us – rest easier if you were to go with him."

"Is this mutiny, or have I finally reached my dotage?"

"Neither, Grania, and you know better than to ask."

"Apparently not, Liam O'Neil. Never would I have thought my own men would ask me to hide, to allow others to risk themselves against a man who has named me the source of his woes – me and those he deems closest to me." She stood and Liam leapt to his feet after her.

Sean and Owen exchanged looks but settled in for the show. Even Dubhghall was watching the argument with interest.

"If you think me such a helpless woman, why do you follow my command at all?"

"Grania—"

"No, Liam. I appreciate you would rather be captured than allow me to fall into that man's hands, but was it not I who agreed to this scheme? I will stay away from the *Excelsior* because it suits our purposes, not because I fear for my safety or my life." Grania took a deep breath and held the eyes of each man around the fire in his turn.

"You and Dubhghall will slip onto the ship and I will guard the perimeter when Sean sets the charges on the explosives. Bingham will be expecting me, and if you must engage him, my absence may keep him off balance."

No one challenged her, but still, Sean shifted uncomfortably. The plan was to use the explosives – timed to the messenger's arrival – to cover Maureen's rescue and escape. Although he knew Dubhghall's concoction of powders would cause more smoke and noise than destruction, its use as a distraction bothered him.

His impression of Bingham was of a man pushed to extremes. Maureen was his prisoner. His entire body was tight with the fear of what the Englishman would do to her if spooked. He bit the sides of his cheeks and swallowed the last of his supper.

"Liam, I've been thinking," he began.

"Aye lad, you do that a lot."

Sean ignored this. It was not the first time his preference for words over swords had been noted by the crew. "Why the bombs? Why not just steal aboard at night and get her out — why the theatrics?"

"You think Bingham is a scared man, Sean, and I think he is too canny to be scared."

Liam wrapped his cloak close and eased back onto the ground before the fire. "He is too canny to leave her unguarded. And he is too canny not to expect something. We sent ships along and came by land to confuse him, to draw him out, and it is working. He is holed up on his ship, keeping Maureen close. We need something to divert his attention."

"The news of the *Venture*, plus a loud spectacle should do just that," Dubhghall added.

Sean did not doubt that — the spectacle was going to distract the entire city. "What about Maureen?"

"What about her, lad? She's a resourceful lass. She'll know what is happening, when it happens."

Sean bit his lip and marshalled his thoughts. It was important they believe him. "Aye, but would it not be better if her resourcefulness were used to our advantage? I want to send her a message."

"Oh, aye?" Liam snorted. "And get the lot of us taken in the process, I'd wager. Lad—"

"Do you know where she is for certain?" Sean countered. "Do you know the inside of that ship? You are good Liam, but you haven't eyes on the *Excelsior*. Let me be those eyes. Let me board the ship tomorrow – early." He looked at Liam, Grania and Dubhghall in turn. They stared back, but remained silent.

"Who besides Dubhghall here can speak English well enough to pass if you're caught? None, as I recall. I don't know how to fight well, aye? I was felled easily enough. Now Maureen is gone, and you are here, risking your skins because of it. Let me do what I can – let me be your eyes. They won't catch me and we'll be all the more prepared when the time is right for her rescue."

"And I will go with him, to make certain," Dubhghall said quietly but quickly to interrupt Liam's bubbling protest.

Sean fancied he could see the gallowglass' eyes staring at him from the folds of his hooded cloak, discerning his thoughts.

"I will make certain it all goes to plan."

"You will stick to the plan, lad – no heroics."

The company had begun to settle down for the night. Liam and Owen were tending to the horses and Grania was banking the fire. Sean was scouring the cooking pot when Dubhghall grabbed his arm from behind and spoke in his ear.

"I don't—"

"I know." Dubhghall's tone brooked no argument, and Sean did not doubt the ship's surgeon, assistant spymaster and all-around mystery-man *did* know he was entertaining ideas about circumventing Liam's theatrical display.

"Liam's plan is risky," Dubhghall continued, "and you have no desire to gamble with their lives any more than you have to. It is noble, lad, but it is daft and it will not work. Do as you said you would. Get a message to Maureen. Be their eyes and gather what information you can, and let me worry about tomorrow night."

Sean ground his teeth but nodded silently. Dubhghall released his arm and slipped away.

The plan. The plan might get them all killed, but Dubhghall was right and he knew his own odds were slim. As he settled down for the night, his head pillowed on his arm, his mind raced. The plan was all they had – all Maureen had. And it would have to be enough.

Sixteen

The *Excelsior* had made her temporary home in the crowded Dublin harbour where the caravel blended cosily with its fellows. Trading vessels from all over the known world were docked here it seemed, and Sean blessed that he and Dubhghall managed to blend cosily with *their* fellows, too.

Of course, he had no idea how many of the other vessels, loading and unloading their wares, were actually mercenary ships, ready to pounce on Grania's brigands should they be so foolish as to attempt a rescue.

He shook his head. That was enough of that kind of thinking.

"Are you ready, then?" Dubhghall's deep voice broke through his dark thoughts.

Sean glanced up at the man, shrouded against the driving rain that had succeeded last night's drizzle. With a nod, he squatted in the dirt and snatched a pebble. He put a hand to the neck cloth Dubhghall managed to procure the day before. All of the *Excelsior's* crew wore one, it seemed.

"Ready as I'll ever be," he muttered.

"Keep your head down and be quick. I will wait here, and provide . . . distraction should anything go wrong."

Sean nodded – ignoring the implications in Dubhghall's words – and set off in the direction of the caravel. Along the way, he spied a crate and grabbed it. It was empty, but he pretended otherwise as he fell in behind another two lads who were helping load similar crates onto the caravel.

Not looking at the dark waters far below the gangplank, Sean gained entrance to the *Excelsior*. He deposited his load on the deck before he could be tasked with taking it into the hold, and slipped behind the clutter of rigging and lines amidships.

From his hiding spot, he watched the ship – the way its sailors moved and talked to one another. He scanned the forecastle and aft, trying to discern where Bingham would have established his headquarters in another man's domain.

Would he have taken the captain's quarters for his own, or set himself elsewhere?

Nothing was coming to him, but he knew he had to move – he would be discovered soon. Before he could leave the safety of his hiding spot, however, a commotion rippled through the bustling deck. A man who could only be the captain – his cap and his bearing marking him well enough – was forcing his way past his men to the stern. He was visibly agitated and practically shouting at a lad on his left.

Sean did his best to remain invisible as they passed, and was rewarded with a snippet of conversation.

". . . Nicholas, we must bring this to Sir Bingham . . ."

The messenger. He was early.

Sean slipped behind them and watched as they disappeared into a passageway. He hurried to catch up and nearly yelped when he brushed up against another seaman coming from the opposite direction. Sean met the young man's eye and dropped his gaze quickly, muttering an apology. The blond youth said nothing, but continued to watch as Sean passed.

Trying not to run and call even more attention to himself, Sean kept his head down and followed the captain.

The seconds passed and no alarm was raised. He made it inside.

Increasing his pace, he hurried to keep Pennington and his companion in sight. They turned a corner and by the sound of the voices, stopped. Sean looked for an alcove or door – anything to disguise his presence should Pennington reverse course. There was nothing and he stood there, heart pounding, trying to split his attention between the way behind him and the voices around the corner.

Above the ambient noise of the ship, Sean heard the captain speak.

"You've done well, and you've earned that. Get your horse re-shod and disappear for a few days. I cannot say how this will play out."

"Aye, Captain – I'll do that. Thank you, sir."

Sean knelt and pretended to adjust the lacings on his shoes as the messenger passed. Nicholas paid him no mind; he was too busy counting the coins in his hand.

When the passage was empty again, Sean slipped around the corner. He could not see Pennington, but he could hear his voice. He edged closer to the open doorway of what must be Bingham's quarters. The two men were arguing.

". . . discuss this in front of the girl? Lest you forget, m'lord Bingham, she does speak English."

"My dear Pennington, are you really afraid of a little girl?"

Sean grinned and slid back around the corner. Pennington and Bingham should both be afraid of that little girl, he reckoned. They should be afraid of that little girl and those willing to risk everything to rescue her.

He was still smiling and contemplating his next move when he heard a sound that made his heart leap. It was Maureen, or rather, her laughter – her mocking, irreverent laughter – sounding from a room on the other side of the wall. She was close.

He bit his fist, the one clutching the pebble, and forced himself to keep silent. He wished he could simply call out to her. There was no doubt she would understand the tapping code they used to get messages to one another at school, but if she was not listening for it, she might miss it. If she was busy antagonizing Bingham and the captain, she might not hear it at all.

He put an ear to the wall – Maureen was silent but Bingham and Pennington seemed to be arguing some more. Just do it, he scolded himself.

He started tapping at the wall: *I am here. Tonight. Three bells. Be ready.*

Translating the message into their code was not difficult, but keeping it short was. There was so much he wanted to say. He waited a beat and repeated the message two more times. Maureen may not even be in a position to respond, but he ignored the anxiety clawing at his insides and waited just the same.

A thud reverberated through the wall and he jumped. He could not be sure if it was Maureen's answer, but it would have to do. To linger here was madness, and he had to warn the others that the messenger had already delivered news of the *Venture.*

"I'll come back," he whispered. "I promise."
With one last look, he turned and ran.

"I've reports, m'lord Bingham, from the harbour and from Galway," Pennington declared as he stepped into the small stateroom. Maureen sat in the antechamber, her bounds yet untouched by Jamie's gift of fire. She kept her head bowed and pretended not to listen. She was good at this act, having had lots of practice in the five days she had called this hole-in-the-wall home.

Although the *Excelsior* had docked in Dublin two days before, Bingham and his company of mercenaries had made no move to decamp for less cramped quarters on dry land. More of the great governor's paranoia, she suspected.

"And what do your spies have to say, Pennington?"

"Must we discuss this in front of the girl? Lest you forget, m'lord Bingham, she does speak English."

"My dear Pennington, are you really afraid of a little girl?"

"She's kinswoman to that pirate – I trust her not at all."

Maureen laughed.

It started out as a small chuckle, but she could not help it, and loud peals of laughter bubbled up. It was true; Pennington was afraid of her.

He was afraid of her and of the people who might, or might not, come to her rescue. She had not allowed herself to hope they would come, that Grania would find a way around Bingham's trap, or that Sean would come on his own. But something in

Pennington's stance, in the tone of his voice, told her he was afraid.

That meant only one thing: they were here. They had come for her.

The sound rippled out of her, at once relieved and mocking. They were afraid, and their fear made her strong.

"And here I thought you may yet be reformed," Bingham remarked in a low voice. He turned to her and she looked up at his reddening face. She refused to flinch.

"M'lord Bingham, forgive me, but this cannot wait," Pennington said behind him, his tone urgent. He reached out to put a hand on Bingham's arm.

She wondered at this small show of mercy. Rage had flickered across Bingham's face, the same rage that left Galen a bloody mess. Pennington was afraid of something, certainly, but he was more afraid of Bingham.

The nobleman shrugged off Pennington's hand as he turned from her.

"Go on," he growled.

Maureen abandoned all pretence of ignorance and listened intently as Captain Pennington relayed his news.

"A ship has been spotted in open water beyond the harbour. It's not one we identified as part of Grania's fleet, but it does match the description of a ship my man found quite interesting – a ship that docked in Galway Bay not four days ago. I believe Grania O'Malley is on that ship."

Pennington paused, but Bingham silently urged him to continue.

"Her flagship, the . . . *Eddy Baintree*—forgive me, m'lord, these Irish names are confounding."

Maureen grinned as the flush of embarrassment

spread over the captain's face.

"I'm told it translates to the *Widow's Weeds*. Regardless, the Tribes granted her flagship permission to dock five days ago, m'lord. My man said the *Widow's Weeds* and her crew remained docked for another two days whilst repairs were completed. In the meantime, another ship, an Irish galley called the *Feon* . . . the *Venture*, docked, traded and was gone the next morning."

"And what leads you to believe it is one of Grania's fleet – a trading galley is not unusual in Galway or in the waters off Dublin, Pennington. I trust this is not going to be a waste of my time?"

"M'lord, no one recognized the vessel, and none left the ship except to load supplies. Now, it could be they didn't have permission, but that there was no talk of it at all raised my man's interest."

"I see your point, Pennington. And it is your belief Grania and her men escaped your spies on the *Venture*?"

"Aye, m'lord – well, Grania at the least. I believe she left her first mate, that Scottish gallowglass of hers, and Galen O'Flaherty behind. They drew sufficient attention to themselves to cover the departure of the *Venture* – they were nearly expelled from Galway for their trouble," Pennington added dryly.

"The *Widow's Weeds* and its two galleys, when they left the next day, did travel towards Dublin, and I believe her men were on it. The seas have been calm and they should have no trouble making our waters by tomorrow at the latest."

Bingham walked away from Pennington to stare out the porthole into the harbour beyond. The captain followed, his urgency crumbling into fretfulness.

"Sir Bingham, should we not ask the magistrate to send reinforcements? The *Venture* and half of Grania's crew – at the least – are already here. Wouldn't it be wise to be prepared?"

"No, Pennington. Not yet." Bingham pulled something from his sleeve. "Give this to one of your messengers – have him deliver it to the *Riptide*. It is a small ship – fast – and it docked yesterday. They'll know what to do."

Maureen's heart sank. Of course – Bingham wanted Grania. He would be prepared for almost any eventuality.

"But my lord—"

"Pennington, you must understand. I will not allow that female – that pirate – to get the better of me. However, it is unwise to bring in the Crown just yet, even if they use only the Irish at their command in the fighting. Grania O'Malley must first be in my keeping. You knew this when I hired you. Backing out now will be to your detriment."

"Of course, Sir Bingham." Pennington turned to carry out his master's orders but paused at the doorway.

"One more thing, M'lord. If I may, I suggest getting *that* secured – below deck, if possible."

Bingham turned to look at her as Pennington gestured to her with contempt, but she ignored them. An odd thumping had started from the passageway on the other side of the wall. She almost dismissed it until she realized the sounds were not random noises but a rhythmic tapping, almost like—

"It looks as though they came for you after all," Bingham was saying. The calculated menace in his voice tore her from the thumping. She looked at him, terrified he heard the noises too, and understood what they meant.

Distract him, her brain screamed.

"Just as you hoped, my lord."

"As I hoped?"

Flustered, she failed to translate the message. It did not matter. It was Sean – it had to be. He was on the ship. Somehow, he was on the ship. Reckless with relief, she narrowed her eyes at Bingham and sneered.

"Of course you hoped – or did you think your plan would fail? It may yet, my lord." She barred her teeth in a mockery of a smile. "I highly doubt Grania O'Malley will make it easy for you to capture her. She will make you a laughing stock, Bingham – mark my words."

So intent was she on holding the governor's eye, she did not see him raise his hand.

"You are a reckless chit of a girl, and you go too far."

The force of the blow drove her head into the wall. A myriad of stars exploded before her eyes and the sting of his jewelled ring tore across her cheek. She stayed where she was with her eyes squeezed shut, and waited for Bingham to strike again.

But he did not. The clatter of his boots and the slam of a door told her she was alone. She sighed and put her hands to her cheek. It was bleeding but she did not care. They were here. She would have to be ready.

Seventeen

"So it's settled, aye? I will set Dubhghall's charges, with Grania watching the harbour. Sean and Dubhghall will enter the ship at three bells, during the changing of the watch. They've been on it once and it will be easier for them to infiltrate it under the cover of dark."

Liam took a breath and surveyed the small band in front of him. Sean did his best to stand tall, to be brave enough to be counted among those who would risk everything to thwart Bingham.

The news of the messenger's early arrival – and the need to change the evening's rescue plan – had been met with the fluidity and competence he had come to expect from Grania and her men. Using flames and smoke, Liam had warned the *Venture* of the likelihood of attack. They were confident her captain would avoid serious damage from her foes – be they the Crown or mercenary. As such, the *Venture* had new orders to hold off her pursuers until nightfall and then disappear.

Sean tried, but found tapping into Liam and Owen's excitement almost impossible. His brain would just not stop – delivering the message was only the first step and it did not guarantee success.

Liam continued to issue his commands. "Owen, if you do not see us by the setting of the moon, weigh anchor – and don't argue with me."

Owen's face was mutinous, but he did not say

anything to contradict his brother. Liam put a hand on his shoulder.

"If we are caught, you will want to be on your way to warn the rest of the crew. Make your way to Carrickahowley and send a message to Richard Burke – no use Herself having the Devil's Hook for a son-in-law if he can't get us out of a spot of trouble, aye?"

Owen flashed Liam a quick grin, "Aye, I'll do that – if I must. You lot better not fail. I would hate going with Tomás to Himself, cap in hand. Lady Margaret would never let us hear the end of it if her mam was in jail, again!"

"Well, it is lucky for you that I don't intend to annoy my daughter so," Grania said lightly. Her eyes crinkled at the corners. "If you think you would have a time of it, imagine the words Margaret would have for me."

Owen made a face. "I'd rather not, my lady. She may not have had your talent for the sea but you did rear her. It is said she has your knack for a choice word or two, aye? The Burkes are terrified of her!"

Grania snorted and Liam swatted at his brother's shoulder.

"Get on with you, lad." He turned to Grania. "It is well they are. If this doesn't go to plan . . ."

"It will go, Liam." Her tone was firm and Sean watched as she held her first mate's eyes.

"Aye," he said after a moment. "Aye, it'll go."

Grania squeezed his shoulder briefly before turning to Sean and Dubhghall.

"This rests on the two of you, now. We have made the plans we could, but in all likelihood, Bingham will see through our gamble with the *Venture*. I don't know what you will face on that ship, but you must be prepared to either fight your way out of there or sacrifice your lives." She said this directly to Sean and he looked down at his feet.

She was right. The thought had lurked in his mind since Bingham had made off with Maureen. He realized, as he stood among those who prepared themselves for this same fate every time they stepped out as members of Grania's crew, he was not worried about the fighting. He was worried they might fail.

In the end, if Maureen was not free, if she was used as a cudgel to beat the proud woman before him, then the fighting and dying were not worth it.

He took a deep breath and lifted his eyes to meet Grania's stare. He would make sure it was worth it.

"Aye, my lady Grania, we understand."

Dubhghall put a hand on his shoulder. "Although, we'll do our best to avoid it, aye?" Humour coloured the man's voice and he motioned to the sack slung across his back. "I have a few extra surprises should things begin to unravel on the *Excelsior*."

"I like the way you think, Master Dubhghall. I shall leave it to you, then." Grania turned to the rest of the crew. "You all have your orders. We're to be in the harbour before the sun sets – make haste."

"Get away from me, you—you son of a whore!"

"Jamie, get that wench below deck and be done with it – watch her feet, boy."

Maureen, curled in a ball, punched her feet out as far as they could go. Jamie dodged at the last moment and rolled to the side.

"Bastard," she hissed.

"I haven't any choice," the midshipman whispered as he lunged at her again. There was nowhere for her to go but she was going to inflict as much damage with her elbows, knees and teeth as she could.

At Pennington's suggestion, Bingham was having her moved. She refused to make it easy for him. He had ordered her tied up like an animal, and caused her to bleed. She was finished being his chattel.

In her panic, all she could think was if Bingham brought her to the hold, Sean would never find her – not in time, anyway. He would be an easy target for Pennington's mercenary guards, and she would be trapped here, forever at Bingham's mercy.

Jamie had his arms around her middle and she twisted in his grip, trying to reach his arms, hands – anything – with her teeth. She was snarling like an animal, but she did not care. They were not going to take her.

"Enough of this," Bingham growled. He succeeded in seizing her head with a rough hand and forced a soaked rag over her mouth and nose.

She tried to scream, tried to wrest her head away but the drug was too fast. Oblivion seeped into her limbs, and even as she struggled, she knew she was no match for it. Jamie's voice at her ear commanded her to sleep, and for once, she obeyed.

The seas were alight with flame and the sound of its hungry flame filled the air. The nameless ship beyond the borders of her sight was burning. Bingham was laughing. He was leering. He was taunting her as Grania rode away on horseback.

They were leaving her.

Escaping.

The ropes binding her were gone and she ran, but there was nowhere to go. The ocean itself burned. Only this floating prison was safe.

Behind her, the crew jeered and mocked. It could not be true – they could not have left her here. Even as the despair washed over her soul, she spied a tiny boat tossed about by the angry sea. Sean sat with oars clutched in his hands as he fought the waves.

The fire was closing in. He was not going to make it. She called to him and he looked up. His smile was the sweetest thing she had ever seen.

She reached for him, and he for her, as the waves of flame consumed their world.

"M'lord! M'lord Bingham! The messenger has arrived. He says – he says…"

"Out with it, man!"

"M'lord, it's the *Venture*, she's—"

Maureen gained consciousness with a terrible scream. It tore through the air and obliterated the messenger's words.

"Sean!" she cried. Tears were coursing down her cheeks. "Oh God, he's gone – they've left! We've lost—"

"It's the soporific, m'lord." Jamie raised his voice over her hiccupping sobs. He made to help her sit but she shied from him. "It must have given her fever dreams."

He wrestled with her a few seconds more but succeeded in getting her upright by pinching her hand and hissing at her under his breath.

"They're watching you – be quiet."

Glaring at him was the only answer she could give. The dreams – the all too real dreams – had left her wobbly and weak, but that was not her main concern. Her rope bindings were gone, taken from her sometime during her delirium. In their place were iron cuffs on her wrists and ankles.

She choked back the panic rising in her throat and took several gulping breaths, only to gag on the stale air and fetid stench of too many unwashed bodies in one room. She had to get out of here, but Bingham seemed to have moved his centre of operations below deck. Men bustled in and out, heedless of the prisoner chained in the corner. The sun was setting, casting hazy red shadows throughout the hull. At their centre was the nobleman. Pennington stood at his side accompanied by a young man, who waited impatiently to deliver his news and be gone.

With a curt nod, Bingham motioned for the boy to continue.

"M'lord." The messenger's voice was reedy and high. He was scared, as though her delirium had charged the very air. "It's that Irish galley, the *Venture*, sir. We've been informed she's managed to–to disappear."

"Disappear? A ship that size cannot disappear."

The boy glanced around the hold helplessly. Bingham ignored him; he kept his eyes on Maureen, instead.

"Did they say anything else?"

The messenger turned to Pennington. "Only that the *Riptide* was going to give chase and attempt to find her. If there's nothing by three bells, they'll return."

"Thank you lad – take this."

"Aye, Cap'n. Thank you, sir." The messenger

bobbed his head and clutched the coins in his hand as he fled the hold.

"I'm told she was a sleek little ship, m'lord." Pennington sounded almost envious of the Irish galley. "Under the right conditions, she could have easily escaped the ships sent to bring her in, even the *Riptide*."

"Under the right conditions, Pennington?" Bingham sneered at the captain. "Under the right conditions . . ." He trailed off and glanced around the room. His eyes returned to Maureen and drilled down into hers.

"It was a diversion," he said quietly. She stiffened at the deadly cold in his voice. "That pirate played us for fools!"

She opened her mouth to goad him, to tell him he had made it easy for Grania, but a series of deep, reverberating reports sounded from somewhere beyond the ship. They reminded her of the cannon fire during the battle on the *Widow's Weeds*.

"Watch her," Bingham growled as he turned on his heel and fled the hold.

Pennington started pacing, anger and fear at war in his face.

"What is going on, lass?" Jamie whispered.

"Even if I knew, I would not tell you, Master Jamie." She knew he had no choice but to obey Bingham's orders, but his concern for her did not make him trustworthy. It only made him dangerous.

Jamie looked at her for a moment more and she returned his gaze, an arrogant eyebrow arched at the question in his eyes. The midshipman shook his head briefly and returned to his duties.

Maureen rested her head on her arms and hid a

grin. The rest of Grania's fleet was safe, and they were coming for her. Bingham could rage all he wanted. Chains or no, she would be free of him and this ship before another day dawned.

Eighteen

Dubhghall and Sean slid quietly into the little dinghy. The first of Dubhghall's charges was set to go off as soon as they reached the *Excelsior*. Grania and Liam would then keep themselves busy looking like terrified bystanders and making their way to the second set of explosives, which would cover their escape from Bingham's ship.

Upon reaching the harbour an hour earlier, they discovered Bingham had ordered the *Excelsior* away from the dock. Anchored in the open water, it was accessible only by rowboat. Not long afterwards, they watched a messenger row out, presumably to deliver the news that the *Venture* had escaped from the nobleman's net.

"He knows," Sean whispered.

"Aye, canny man, Bingham." Dubhghall's voice was shaded with dark humour; despite the fear gnawing at his gut, Sean smiled.

"It changes nothing."

No one challenged him, and Grania clasped his hands in hers. "It has been my pleasure, Master McAndrew. Bring her home safe."

Now, bobbing in the harbour's choppy waters, hoods drawn against the day's incessant rain, Sean stared at Dubhghall.

"What is it, lad?" the man finally asked.

"Why are you doing this?" He stared hard at dim

outlines of Dubhghall's face, trying to discern something – anything – in those eyes that continued to evade him even as they stared back at him.

"You're not one of Grania's men," he continued. "I mean, you are, but you're a gallowglass – a mercenary. You have nothing at stake in this, and yet you risk your life with them – with me. Why?"

Dubhghall sighed and looked off in the distance. "Aye, that is true enough. Now," he added. His voice was a mixture of resignation and hesitation.

"Now?" Sean whispered to himself. Apprehension crept along his neck. He did not know if he wanted the man to continue. Whatever Dubhghall was saying, whatever it meant, it was bigger than this daring rescue.

"Aye, now. Perhaps it will not always be so. Perhaps, I feel responsible."

Startled, Sean's eyes snapped back to Dubhghall. The other man was still gazing out to sea. He barked a harsh laugh and returned his attention to Sean.

"Perhaps we have dallied here long enough and should see about freeing Maureen from this nightmare, aye?"

Sean was silent. The moment was gone, but questions crowded his mind. He bit down on his lip and continued to row.

"Aye, we should."

The passageway outside Bingham's stateroom was empty. The whole ship seemed empty and it made Sean nervous. It had been almost too easy to gain access to the ship. Dubhghall's skilful rowing, which allowed them to advance on the ship without alerting the men who should have been on watch, had gone to waste.

A mere smattering of crew lingered on the deck and none had taken any notice of them – not to stop them, nor to raise an alarm. Even so, he moved quietly through the ship's interior, wishing desperately that his heart would not hammer against his ribs quite so loudly.

Dubhghall was only moments behind him, having detoured at the hold to keep an eye on any reinforcements who might come up from behind.

"Don't do anything brave, lad. Get Maureen, and get out. If Bingham is there, wait for me. I shall be along shortly. Guards will be in the hold, and I would rather they not take us unawares."

Sean took a deep breath, handling the oil-filled vial and soaked rag the man had offered him before they parted. One touch with a bit of flame and it would smoke, burn and then shatter.

"Focus," he growled at himself. He sidled up to the stateroom's entrance and listened. No sounds came from within and he risked poking his head around the empty doorway.

It was empty.

Heedless now of Dubhghall's advice, he ran into the room, eyes searching everywhere. A massive desk was bare and an overturned stool had rolled into the corner. The quarters had been abandoned – and in a hurry, it seemed.

Sean spied an alcove to his right – a threadbare mat was the only evidence it had once been home to some hapless soul. Maureen was not here – but if not here, then where? A low, grinding panic started to fill his head and he stood in the middle of the room, frozen.

"You must be Sean," drawled an English voice behind him.

Something in the voice pierced his inertia. Drawing his dagger, he turned slowly to face the middle-aged man standing in the doorway.

His fine clothes, though rumpled and dirty, marked him as a man of distinction. His eyes however, belied the composure in his voice. They were constantly moving – searching his face and scanning the room behind him.

Sean had the sudden impression that Sir Richard Bingham – for this had to be the man himself – was a man unhinged.

"Is it just you?" Bingham gestured idly to the hallway beyond the stateroom with his drawn sword. "I must admit, I did not think you had it in you."

"Why is that, Sir Bingham?" Sean relaxed his stance slightly but did not take his eyes off the Englishman.

"You know who I am – how gratifying." The nobleman gave a courtly bow. "I am surprised because you are with that O'Malley woman. It amazes me that men and boys who would hide behind a woman's skirts would attempt to pull something off so daring as a rescue. Alone."

"Who said anything about hiding? Grania O'Malley is a leader – she inspires, as well you know, m'lord."

Bingham did not contradict him and a malicious grin took over Sean's face. Disgust for the man who had taken his best friend hostage trumped his fear.

"Aye, you know. You know because you have your own distorted, bitter vision of her in your mind. She's inspired you, but I'm not sure your impressions of her have any truth to them at all."

He paused and Bingham arched an eyebrow at him, but made no move to interrupt.

"How are you going to explain that to your superiors, m'lord? How will you explain that none of your delusions about us wild Irish have stacked up? Hiring out a mercenary fleet to capture a pirate who won't be baited, and who led your own men on a merry chase this afternoon, is not a promising start for Connacht's new governor, is it?"

Sean held up his dagger, pointing it at Bingham as if to emphasize his point.

"Besides, who said I was alone?"

This broke the snide smile on Bingham's face. He spluttered and tried to turn but found the pointed end of a sword pressed into his back instead.

"Very dramatic, lad," muttered the cloaked figure behind Bingham. Dubhghall jabbed at the Englishman with the sword, and forced him into stateroom.

"If you think this gives you the upper hand—"

"M'lord, it would behove you to keep your silence just now – lad, she's in the hold." The gallowglass motioned for Sean to join him, outside the reach of Bingham's sword arm. "I was able to clear the area before realizing Bingham was on his way to you. Get her, and get out!"

"But what about you?"

"I will follow. Just—"

The clanging of metal on metal interrupted Dubhghall's words. Bingham, taking advantage of the distraction, struck the gallowglass' sword with his own. Wordlessly, he danced around the warrior and taunted him with his blade. Dubhghall growled and pushed Sean out of the doorway before tossing his cloak to the floor.

"That woman is afraid to face me, eh?" Bingham sneered. "Well, how about I just cut through each man she throws my way until she is ready to fight? How many of you can there be?"

Sean fled the hallway as Grania's champion advanced on Bingham, but not before he heard Dubhghall's amused retort:

"How many of us are willing to fight for Grania? You may have to go through the breadth of Ireland to find out, m'lord – starting with me."

Maureen coughed and wiped at her stinging, watering eyes. Smoke filled the hull, but the quiet groans of the dazed crewmembers reminded her she was not alone – not yet.

It had happened quickly, almost too quickly for her to react. If she had not seen the cloaked figure lurking beyond the entryway to this section of the hold, she would have been dazed in the explosion of light and sound that followed. As it was, she had seen him, recognized his intent and been ready – ready for any indication her rescue was imminent.

She did not know if the lanterns had been shattered by the impact of the cloaked figure's fireworks, or if he had simply thrown them to the floor, but she blessed the darkness. Without a key to the irons about her wrists and ankles, she hobbled over the prone bodies of Pennington's crew, avoided the ones who were stirring, and made for the passageway. She would worry about the irons later – the man who had the key was not among the stunned crowd, anyway.

The bomb had gone off shortly after Bingham had stormed from the hold. She would never get close enough to him to get the key now, and had no desire to, unless it was to taunt him with a blade.

The idea made her grin with savage humour, but she pressed on.

Once in the passageway, she paused, uncertain of which way to go. Part of her screamed for freedom, but the men behind her would soon pour into the hallway, intent on fresh air and their assailant. Only Bingham seemed to realize Grania had not come to Dublin to engage his fleet, but rather to create a diversion to free Maureen. No one but the nobleman would be looking for her just yet, which made keeping to the shadows until she could find Sean the safer option.

Feeling her way through the gloom, she reached the stairs to the deck. Noises behind her told her the men stupefied by the blast were headed this way, as well. Their noise and the dark pressed in on her and she bit down on her panic. She forced herself to breathe, and to look.

Barrels peeked out of the shadows in the alcove under the stairs.

Her options dwindled as the noises grew. She eyeballed the space between the barrel and the alcove ceiling. There was just enough room. Cursing the irons and the sounds they made, she wedged herself in, turned her pale face to the wall and prayed.

The deck was crowded now with men, some of whom were still coughing and complaining. The captain and his mates were trying to organize the crew, but Dubhghall had hit them fast and disappeared too quickly. Wisps of smoke still trailed from the hatch, and the men were still dazed by the attack.

Sean tried to slip through the melee when he spied the young blond crewmember, the same lad he had run into that morning. The other boy caught his eye and nodded.

He sidled up to Sean. "She's down there, somewhere. She hid when your man's bomb went off. I don't know how, but she was ready."

His heart in his throat, Sean tried to push past, but the young man stopped him.

"You were with Bingham when the bomb went off?"

Warily, Sean nodded.

The young man put something cold and hard in his palm, pushed him towards the hatch, and backed away. "I have to call the guards now. I have a life—"

"Aye, we all have lives to lead," Sean muttered. "Good luck with yours."

He slid down the stairs just as he heard the young man's shout, calling what was left of the able-bodied crew to Bingham's stateroom.

The acrid smell of rotting eggs wafted through the warren of dark, low-roofed rooms that made up the hold of the mercenary caravel. Sean lurched forward and then froze. He had no idea where to start looking.

Maureen was nearly ready to untangle herself from her hiding spot when another volley of feet clattered on the stairs above her. Her heart thumped fast, almost in time with the sounds. She squeezed her eyes shut and waited for the newcomer to move deeper into the hold. Her arms, her back, her neck – all were aching and if she did not move soon, she was afraid she would never be able to get herself free of the cramped little hole.

The stranger checked his stride at the bottom of the stairs and stayed there. She cursed silently. She was not going to be trapped here. As quietly as she could, she turned, slid to the ground, and risked a quick peek.

Whoever he was, he was not keen on checking his blind spots. He was just standing there, dumb.

She launched herself at him.

Startled by the noise, Sean turned with his dagger drawn but at the sight of Maureen hurtling towards him, it slipped from nerveless fingers. He grabbed her and held on, hugging her with all the strength he had left.

"I knew you'd come," she breathed into his shoulder. She let him hold her for a moment more and then pushed at him with her bound hands.

"Took you long enough! Are you it? Can we get out of here?"

"Hold on, Maureen – we need to get those chains off, first."

"I'd like that very much, Sean McAndrew but they key is in Bingham's . . ."

The words died on her lips as he held up a small key. He cocked an eyebrow at her and she smiled wide.

"Where did you get it?" she asked as he attacked the shackles at her wrists and tossed them away.

"A crewmember slipped it to me – a friend of yours, perhaps?"

"Makes me kind of wish I hadn't bit him so hard."

He snorted and bent to undo the cuffs at her ankles. "I wouldn't worry about that." He grabbed his dagger and stood. "Your friend just called the crew to Bingham's stateroom. I've one of Grania's crew with me and I'm pretty sure he's fighting for his life right now."

"Come on, we have to go."

They took the stairs two at a time, but at the hatch, Sean held out his hand and peered through the opening. No one had remained to guard the hold, and he helped Maureen over the lip and onto the deck. He kept an arm around her shoulders, ready to guide her to the side where Dubhghall had tied the dinghy, when a terrific blast rocked the ship.

A physical wave of sound pushed them to their knees and they hugged the deck as debris rained down around them.

When they looked up, smoke was billowing from what had been Bingham's stateroom. The wind was rising and as the smoke cleared, Sean spied a single figure standing at the ragged hole, highlighted by the weak fires left in the wake of his explosion.

Sean stared at Dubhghall. The man was waving his arms and shouting at them, but the roaring in Sean's ears overwhelmed the man's voice. He knew he should move but he could not tear himself away. Even Maureen was gaping – the entire ship seemed to stop, hold its breath, and wait.

Fighting the paralysis, Sean watched Bingham and his men recover their senses and make for Dubhghall's position. Before they could reach him with their swords, the gallowglass jumped to the deck and rolled.

Bells began clanging. A second contingent, led by Pennington, ran past Sean and Maureen. They were nothing to the captain now, compared to the fight between Dubhghall and Bingham.

Pennington's men met Dubhghall as he struggled to regain his footing. It seemed they would swallow him, devour the lone warrior as Sean and Maureen stood by, helpless.

Without warning, they heard an inhuman roar – a great bellowing that seemed to make time stop. Dubhghall leapt to his feet. Teeth bared and black hair flying, he swung his blade. The first volley of Pennington's men scattered and fell back.

In the brief pause, his head snapped up and he stared at them.

The intense blue blaze of his eyes crossed the gap. Tattoos stood out starkly on the pale skin above his gauntlets as he held his arms aloft with his sword. For a brief moment, his eyes searched theirs. Silently, he begged them to understand, just as he had in the vision before the altar.

It was him.

He had found them.

"Go."

Nineteen

"He's gone then?" Grania asked. They had taken in the lines at Howth and were nearly an hour into their journey home. Sean and Maureen were in her stateroom, wrapped in blankets with tankards of ale before them. Maureen gripped hers with a tight hand and looked at Sean, eyebrows raised.

He knew she wanted to hear his side of the adventure while she had been cooped up on the *Excelsior*, and was curious about man who had flashed so brightly before them.

So was he, frankly.

"I don't know," he said quietly as he stared into his ale. He did not remember how they managed to get into the dinghy or row back to the relative safety of the dock, where another explosion had sent half the city into a panic.

"I could have sworn I heard a splash – a body-sized splash, aye? – in the harbour as we were rowing away, but I can't be certain it was Master Dubhghall."

Grania considered this in silence. He looked up at her and waited.

"It is a shame. I will miss the man, but I don't think he meant to return to us." The pirate turned and retrieved a small linen roll and a thick sheet of parchment, folded and sealed with wax.

"Sean, this is for you," she said, holding out the

parchment. He took it and slowly settled back onto his stool, his fingertips tracing the rough paper. A stylized eye stared at him from the black wax.

The roll was meant for Maureen, and she unwrapped it eagerly. Within it was a folded bit of paper – modern paper, not parchment. With a startled glance at him, she slipped it back into the protection of the linen.

"That was for you, specifically, Maureen. Dubhghall never doubted he and Sean would set you free."

Maureen looked over at her friend. He was clutching the parchment in his hand, waiting for the security of his berth to open it. Happy tears threatened the corner of her eyes but she blinked them back and grinned at her captain.

"Aye, my lady. Neither did I."

October the Ninth, Year of Our Lord 1584
Sean and Maureen,
By now, you may know who I am, but I doubt you understand it. It was not my intention to send you on this journey, and yet, it must now play itself out. You will have questions, and by the gods, I will do what I can to see they are answered.

I promised Sean I would see to your safety, and I have. Despite that she is a pirate, and now consummate enemy of Sir Richard Bingham, Grania Uaile is as good a protector as you could hope to have – for now.

I can do one better, but it will take time. I know you will not believe me, given the lives you could have here, but there is a place for you back home – back in your own time. It will need claiming, but you are strong, and claim it you will.

The full moon on the fourteenth of February, 1585, which is 128 nights from this evening's adventure, will take you home, if you time it right. Step inside the circle of oaks at the same hour you left, and none will be the wiser that you were gone - except yourselves, of course. There is no help for that, I am afraid.

Learn what you can between now and then, and take care of each other. I will remain always,
Your Friend,
Dubh
~ Maureen, your father gave me the letter. He asked me to send it to you. It was my failing which forced me to keep it until now. Read it, and share it with Sean. I hope it will bring comfort to you both.

Rebel

Dublin, 1916

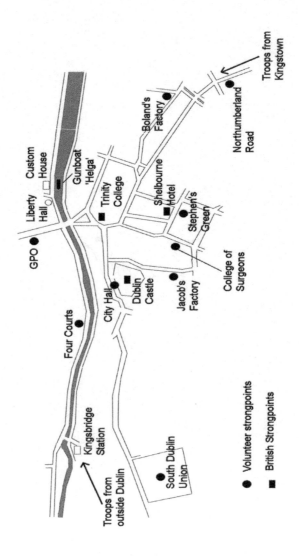

One

. . . We will be home soon – our tour is nearly up. You were not able to sit on your own when I saw you last, and now your mother tells me you run around – chasing the cat, the dog, Sean. Poor boy is going to have his work cut out for him.

I wish I could write more, but my time here grows short. In just a few short hours, we will be flying our last mission. Were it the last mission of this dreadful war. Know this, little one: we fight, not for England, but for the world. This evil cannot be allowed to flourish – it cannot be allowed to stamp out the hope, which lives in the heart of each man. Love keeps me strong, keeps all of us here strong, but it is the magic I see in your eyes – that pure child's gift to see wonder and beauty wherever you look – which gives me hope our efforts will not be in vain.

Keep that light alive for me, little one. Keep that love, that magic alive. The wonder of the whole world can live in your heart, if you let it . . .

Much love to you and your mother.
~Pat
March 29, 1944

Maureen folded her father's note. She had read it more than enough times to memorize it, but she never tired of tracing the scrawled letters with her eyes and fingertips. She had not realized how much she would miss the ritual of going over her mementos with Sean until they could no longer do it.

Dear as the letter was to her however, it did not mask the fact that her father's dreams for her were a bit loftier than those she had for herself.

She glanced at the muddy stable yard, strewn with straw and rocks, which seemed to multiply and grow in the muck. To her modern eyes, it was dirty, squalid. It was also the only place she could find some privacy. Hope, love and magic were lovely, but she was not sure she had time for them anymore. Using her wits to stay alive amongst Grania's pirate crew was sometimes the best she could manage.

"There you are – reading. How is it you read?"

She bit back a scowl. There went the privacy. She tucked the letter into the pocket she had sewn into her breeches and arched an eyebrow at Owen.

"There are a lot of things I can do that I'm not supposed to."

"Aye, like defy Grania's order to have your hair cut."

Her hand automatically went to the braids pinned at the back of her head. "I've no desire to look like a boy," she muttered.

When Grania had demanded she take a knife to her hair, to save it being caught in the rigging and lines, Maureen had refused. When Grania met her refusal with a blank stare – the woman was unused to disobedience – Maureen had declared she did not intend to earn a nickname like Grania's own: *Grainne Mhaol* – Grania the Bald.

Instead, she earned the moniker *Márín Mhiúil* – Maureen the Mule.

"You had no desire to muck out the stable either." Owen shoved the wooden bucket at her and nodded in the direction of the stables. "And yet, here you are."

She rolled her eyes and followed Owen. As penalties for defiance went, cleaning out the stables was not too bad, although she would have preferred to be part of the wedding feast preparations up at the stronghold. Aiden O'Malley – a farmer, not a pirate – had married his sweetheart, Ionia, earlier that morning, and Grania had offered the hall at Carrickahowley Castle for the wedding feast. He was kin, and Grania always did what she could for kin.

It took more than an hour, but the first four stalls were clean and scattered with fresh straw. Maureen brushed a stray curl from her forehead and stared at the remaining eight. A groan escaped before she could stop it.

"Ah, don't tell me the fearless *Márín Mhiúil* is daunted by a few itty-bitty horse stalls."

"Daunted? Certainly not, Sean McAndrew." She turned to her friend with a grin. He was leaning against the stable doors, smiling. "When did you get back?"

"Just now." He pushed himself forward and snagged the wheelbarrow on his way to one of the dirty stalls.

"How'ya lad?" Owen called. He leaned on his shovel and tossed the perpetually-too long shock of dishwater-blond hair out of his eyes. "Back already – Did Tomás have Grania's order ready, or was it a social call?"

"Ah, you know Tomás. Any call is a social call. Maire had to shoo us out of the cottage just so she could get ready for the feasting. Liam is taking care of loading the *Widow*. He sent me to check on you two."

"Check on us?" Owen grunted. "Did he not think we'd be up to our work?"

Sean rolled his eyes and traded a grin with Maureen. "Ah no, I think Liam just remembers you nodding off a wee bit during watch last week."

Which was the reason Owen was also cleaning the stables.

"It's not my fault he put me on the late-night watch four nights in a row." Despite his grumbling, Owen gave them a wink and returned to his work.

"And so Tomás is full of stories today?" Maureen asked. She shovelled manure into the wheelbarrow and tried to remember to breathe through her mouth.

"As always."

"The hill?" She kept her voice low. Any mention of the hill, outside of Tomás' wild stories, made people – Owen included – nervous. Its lore went deeper than simple superstition, and the fire that destroyed the shrine was recent history to them.

Sean nodded. "More oaks."

It was all he needed to say. When they arrived in 1584, someone had been in the process of taking down the oak grove, one tree at a time. Whoever it was – and 'Englishmen' was the common answer people spat out – had kept at it during the six months since they had been in Grania's company.

Maureen imagined the dead and dying giants lying amid the weed-infested remains of the grotto and shivered. The locals were not the only ones who were uneasy on the hill. She wondered how she would manage to sit through the mass now, knowing what she knew. If everything worked according to plan – according to Dubh's plan – she and Sean would find out soon.

It was February 14, 1585.

"Do you think going to the feast tonight is really a good idea?" her friend asked as they shovelled the last of the manure into the wheelbarrow. "We'd be cutting it awfully close."

"We could always stay."

He snorted and turned to her. "What is it about this place – this life – that has you so enamoured? I thought we agreed to follow the plan. Dubh—" He faltered on the enigmatic warrior's name.

"Dubh has not returned to us," she hissed. "If it's so important we go back to our own time, don't you think he would be here to make sure we went?"

"Maybe he is."

"Maybe he didn't get away from Bingham." She walked beside Sean as he pushed the laden wheelbarrow out of the stables. "Our good governor is not a nice man, Sean. I'm lucky he didn't give me much thought beyond being a pawn to lure Grania into his trap. You saw what he did to Galen."

"I did."

She shrugged. "Then you know what he's capable of. Dubh—"

"You didn't know him. He would have been able to get away. I know it."

"Well, I don't. And I don't know if following his plan is really in our best interest. I'd just feel better if he were here, going through it with us. I feel like we're running at the hill blind – I like to see what's coming, Sean."

"What's coming is a great big load of trouble, and you know it. We can't stay here, Maureen. Opportunistic pirate or canny businesswoman, the English see Grania as a rebel. We've been lucky these last few months."

"Speak for yourself." She smiled to take the

sting out of the words. Both of them had worked hard as crewmembers in Grania's fleet. Regardless of whether they were Grania's kin or not, they had earned their captain's respect through gruelling labour and steadfast loyalty. It was the least they could do after the pirate had saved Maureen's life.

"Look – I know we have to go back. I don't like it—"

"Do you think I do? Do you think I want to go back to being an altar boy and boarding school brat after all this? It's just, he told us to go. The same way you knew we had to follow him, I know we have to at least try to follow his plan."

His cheeks were wind-burned and peeling but that did not account for the flush that crept up his neck. She put a hand on his arm; it was taut with muscle that had not been there six months ago.

"Okay," she said quietly as his breathing evened out. He had her there – he had followed her into the void on nothing but a hunch. As much as going back to the abbey galled her, she owed him the same trust.

He looked down at her through black hair that had grown shaggy in their time among pirates. He preferred it shorter, but Owen once teased him that he kept it shorn so close to his head, he was certain to be mistaken for a monk. Ever since, Sean had let it grow.

They brought the wheelbarrow to a stop just before a large dung heap. Maureen wrinkled her nose and helped Sean hoist the awkward contraption to allow the mess from the stables to roll out and onto the heap. To think the stable hands did this every day.

"As for leaving tonight during the wedding celebration," she continued, keeping her voice light, "can you think of a better time to slip away? Everyone will be so busy feasting and carrying-on they won't be paying any attention to us. I've already packed my things."

She nodded to the pile of stones intended for fencing, just beyond the dung heap. Her pack was within easy reach, tucked in a small gap.

"Things? What things are you packing? We didn't come here with anything."

"My clothes? As charming as these breeches are, I'm not sure Sr. Theresa is going to let me wear them on Saturdays."

Sean looked down at his own loose hose, bound to his legs with strips of cloth, and nodded. "Just so long as that's it."

She finished unloading the wheelbarrow. "Well, a few mementos . . ."

"Maureen."

"What? It's just a few bits and bobs – things to remember our time here." Was it her fault she had done a good job at helping Grania in her chosen trade – and been well rewarded for it?

He rolled his eyes. "So long as it's small. We have to walk to the hill, aye? I'm not carrying your pack if it's too bloody heavy for you."

"Very funny." She made a face at him and he snorted.

"Oi, are you two done nattering?"

Owen stood at the stable doors, his hands on his hips. "Sean lad, if you're going to help, then help. Mistress Maureen was faster when she didn't have you to smile at. I'd like to have a bit of roast mutton at the feast, not the scraps from whatever's left!"

"Aye, Mammy!" Maureen called merrily.

Wheelbarrow in hand, she made her way back to the stables. Owen was grinning at her as she passed and she gave him the benefit of a quick curtsey. She was going to miss him – she was going to miss all of them.

Two

"*I* *have loved you forever, your heart mine to keep – yet beyond me you step, waking all those who sleep . . . The wind whispers your name, and the mists do speak to me. Faceless phantom, wanderer, king, you beg of me always, wait.*"

"What is she singing?" Maureen asked Maire Conroy, Tomás' wife. The woman was dabbing at her eyes as Ionia O'Malley, Aiden's new bride, sung a sweetly melancholy song.

"Ah, it's an old song of her clan – she's a Scot, you know. They sing it at the wedding feast."

"It sounds sad."

"It is a bit of a sad tale, but lovely." Maire was smiling wistfully in her husband's direction. "It's a tale about a princess and a warrior – theirs is a love so sweet and strong, it lasts throughout time. She's saying she'll wait for him, forever, though fate is cruel and hides him from her."

"Och, aye – 'tis sweet enough. There are bits about heather and mountains, love and betrayal, even a bit of war and treachery thrown in – just what you want to sing at a wedding. Those Scots are a funny lot, aye?" Owen snorted and nudged Sean.

"Go on with you, Owen O'Neil." Maire swatted the boy and he waggled his eyebrows at Sean and Maureen.

"I think it sounds lovely," Maureen insisted, even as she covered her mouth to hide a smile. The tune was lovely, but other than that, she thought Owen was right.

The song ended and Owen left to search out more of his roast mutton, while she and Sean were caught up in a group of avid listeners around Liam. The elder O'Neil launched into a tale of Grania's great daring during a surprise attack from the Keefes, a neighbouring clan. It was a fun story, and one she had not heard before, but she could not let herself enjoy it. It was not easy to say goodbye, but pretending they could stay was almost worse.

Sean broke from Liam's pantomime of swimming through dangerous waters and caught her eye. He arched a single eyebrow and she nodded.

"Are you leaving us then?"

"My lady," Maureen breathed. She turned from the stairwell and met the curious brown eyes of her captain. Sean had gone five minutes earlier, and was probably already waiting for her by the stable yard. "I wasn't feeling well. It's a bit warm in there, aye?"

"Aye, you do look a bit flushed, but that is not what I meant." The corners of the pirate's eyes crinkled with a smile.

Maureen chewed her lip and Grania put a hand on her shoulder. "I always wondered how long you two would stay. You have a place here if ever you need it, or want it."

"I do want—" She stopped herself. She wished they were closer. She admired Grania and they respected one another, but that did not make them close. Grania was the captain of the fleet, and the title alone kept them apart. The woman had more to do than see to the care of two whelps who were too old to need it.

She took a deep breath. "Thank you, my lady."

Grania let her hand drop. "Was Tomás right, then? Were you some Lordling's offspring looking for adventure?"

"I thought Tomás believed us to be spies."

"Oh, he had many theories – you were at once spies, changelings, and baseborn issue who would bring the likes of Christopher St. Lawrence down on our heads, again."

The stories about the Lord of Howth had been true, then – no wonder Grania had to threaten him with bodily harm in order to ensure their safe passage from Howth.

Maureen tried not to smile; that was her favourite part of Sean's story of her rescue.

"Not I, my lady – I'm sorry enough you have Sir Bingham to cope with."

"My troubles with Bingham were not your doing, lass. You were simply convenient." The pirate shrugged. "At least now I have the measure of the man."

Word of the sweeping changes Bingham intended to make had already reached their backwater stronghold. Measure of the man, indeed.

"We aren't some Lordling's children, legitimate or otherwise. We gave you our oath, and meant it, but . . ." Maureen hesitated.

"You belong somewhere else." Grania was searching her face and she nodded.

"Then I hope you find where that is. I wish you Godspeed, Maureen O'Malley." She held out her hand. Maureen took it and Grania pulled her into a fierce hug. "May He grant we see each other again on the other side."

Words stuck in Maureen's throat but she managed a watery smile as Grania released her. The older woman was smiling as she turned her towards the stair, and allowed the dark to swallow her one-time charge from view.

The moon should have been high in the night sky, but low, heavy clouds hid her light from the earth below. Maureen held the torch aloft as they made their way to the hill on foot.

"Remind me again why we didn't borrow the pony cart? I told you Grania stopped me, right? She would understand."

"Because she doesn't need more stories of mysterious goings-on," Sean muttered. "Imagine how that would look – we disappear and the pony cart is stranded at the base of the hill."

"It wouldn't be stranded. Grania's ponies are smart – like as not, they'd meander to Tomás' homestead."

"Perhaps, but people would still talk. Don't forget, it was the stories of the hill and the Good Folk that destroyed the shrine."

"It wasn't stories, Sean. It was fear and politics that destroyed it."

He rolled his eyes. "Perhaps, but we don't need to make more trouble for Grania, aye?"

Maureen grumbled but he could hear the smile in her voice. He linked his arm in her free one and took a deep breath of the bracing night air. The hill was not far now, and they covered the distance in silence.

As the path turned a familiar bend, his step slowed. The leafless trees danced in the breeze and cast eerie shadows in the torchlight. He shivered with a cold that had nothing to do with the February chill. There was an otherworldly power here, one they could somehow wield. He hoped Dubh was right.

"Let's not linger," Maureen whispered. "Dubh said we needed to step in the circle at the same time we left – I reckon we're close to that time now. If we don't leave now, I'm afraid I'll never get the nerve to go near the hill again."

He was glad the dark hid the surprise in his face. They still shared that, at least. He squeezed her arm and they stepped onto the path up the hill together.

Sean gestured for the torch as they reached the top of the hill, and Maureen handed it off with some reluctance. Under its glare, she could not see the details of the ravaged grove. She remembered her daydream, so long ago now it seemed. She remembered how the gnarled oak branches had waved in the breeze, their circle protecting the lonely shrine – a hermitage maybe, for a warrior-monk with tattoos snaking up his arms.

Without the torch, she could see what had become of her dream. There were still some oaks left, but the gaps between them were noticeable.

She stared at the holes. The night seemed deeper there, as though the holes swallowed the torchlight and left an endless nothing in its place. She pulled her cloak tight and watched Sean pace the perimeter to examine the fallen timbers. They had not even been used for firewood.

"Sean, I . . ." Her voice failed her. Fog trailed at his feet as he walked. Even as he paused and looked at her, it bloomed larger. Wisps of white wrapped around his legs up to his knees. The crackle of static buzzed in her ears.

He was staring at her, but he had not moved.

He needed to move.

She wondered if that was how she appeared in the church: unaware of the tremor of light and sound surrounding her, oblivious to its menace. Then, she remembered the feel of it, remembered how the terror slammed into her body and made it nearly impossible even to breathe.

Rational thought fled her mind and all she could think to do was to keep him close. She raced to his side and held tight to his arm before the mist reached out to claim him for itself.

Three

Sean gulped at the air as the world formed itself around him again, solid and cold. Jagged lines of light echoed across his closed eyelids and the smell of lightning burnt his nose. He did not recall the vortex being so violent the last time.

It was almost as though — but no, that was impossible. Yet, it had seemed as though something had snatched them from the hill and pushed them through the gateway, against its own volition.

He shivered. It was cold in the church, colder than it should be, for August. And that was where they were supposed to be – August 31, 1958.

But they were not.

It was not a logical deduction, but rather a feeling – a remembering – of an otherness, which had clung to him for weeks among Grania's crew. It had pitched his awareness at the oddest moments, as if he had moved too fast. It was a feeling difficult to forget, and now it was making the gorge rise in his throat.

He shook his head and forced his eyes to open. The building was dark and they were sprawled, not about the altar platform as he had feared, but up against the spindly wooden guardrail. Maureen's hand was still clutched around his arm. Her eyes were closed but if she slept, her dreams were chaotic. Her forehead was creased and her mouth turned down in an angry frown.

"Ah sure, I told myself, the church will be a mighty fine place to stay the night. Not a single soul comes up here but the old dears at the abbey, but no – what are you lot doing here?"

Without thinking, Sean scrambled to his feet to stand before his friend's prone form. He was not a good fighter, but thanks to Owen, he could hold his own – for a little while at least.

"Show yourself!" Fists held high, he watched as the wraith in the nave slowed to a stop. He thought he saw the stranger grab at something and he lunged just in time to get the beam of an electric torch in his eyes.

"Sean, what–?"

"Ah now, lad – there's no need for that. I'm not going to hurt you."

Maureen and the young man's voices collided in Sean's brain and he crumpled to his knees. The floor tilted under his trembling hands but he held on. The power of the gateway still lingered on his skin, but he marble was solid and cool.

Maureen was at his back, her hands on his shoulders.

"Are you okay?" she whispered.

"Are you? It's not . . . we're not *home*."

"I know." Her voice was barely a whisper and she pinched him as she glanced meaningfully at the boy standing over them. He was watching them from under a shock of sooty hair that fell in a heavy wave over his forehead. His eyes were wide and there was a small smile at his mouth, as though he could not help it.

He held out his hand.

"I'm Gerry – Gerry Ballard. Sorry I startled you. I'm not supposed to be here m'self."

Sean took the hand and allowed Gerry to pull him back to his feet. "Aye, well – it looks like we're in good company, so."

"Where are you headed?"

"Dublin."

Sean turned to Maureen. Her ability to slough off the gateway, the travelling through time, the *otherness,* defied reason. She looked back at him but lifted an eyebrow in Gerry's direction. The boy was watching them. Her outrageous response to Gerry's question was going to have to wait.

"I'm Maureen O'Malley," she added as she held her hand out to the boy. "And this is Sean McAndrew. It's nice to meet you, Gerry."

"Likewise, lass. I'm off to Dublin, too – there's a race on," Gerry said amiably. He tucked his torch under his arm and sat in the pew. "It's not an official race, what with the war on and all, but the prize is grand enough, if I win. Da doesn't like me racin.' Would rather I put myself to simply repairing bikes instead of scaring me Mam with all this racing nonsense, as he says."

Sean glanced at Maureen and she wiggled her fingers ever so slightly to let him know she had heard it. War. As if the bright beam of the torch had not been hint enough.

At least it was the 20th century.

Sean had no idea how to respond to the boy's life story – even Maureen seemed at a loss – and the three of them stared at each other until Gerry broke the silence.

"Look, I don't bite. I just wanted to make sure it was kids and not vandals in here."

"Get a lot of that out here?" Maureen swept her arm wide at the simple church.

It was not a home to reliquaries or gold. That

sort of finery was kept in larger churches on less confused ground, Sean suspected. He wondered if the nuns knew. He wondered if they ever suspected the abbey was home to a different – older – power, one born in the very bones of the land itself.

Gerry was laughing softly. "No. That's why I knew I could have some fun with you. It looks as though you fell – are you all right? What's taking you to Dublin?"

Her mouth popped open but nothing came out. Sean watched her search for an answer with his own grin. He just hoped it would be better than the tale of minstrels she once spun for Tomás.

"Us? Oh, we're all right. I mean, yes I fell – we were messing and fighting over the torch. I—I think it rolled over there and broke, though." She waved a vague hand at the pews just beyond the guardrail. "We're heading to Dublin to find work, maybe help the war effort. We're orphans, aye?"

He peered at them from under his bangs. "Are you from the school, then? How old are you – 15, 16?"

They nodded silently. Gerry made a face.

"Were they going to make you take the cloth? No wonder you're running away. I don't think I know a single person who's been in school after 15. Of course, I haven't been to school since I was 10. Da needed me on the farm. My sister might stay longer – so long as Mam stays well."

"Your name sounds familiar," Sean said slowly as he tried to filter Gerry's barrage of words. "Is your sister at the abbey?"

"With me Mam and Da still living?" Gerry laughed and Sean mentally kicked himself. Carrickahowley Abbey had been an orphanage once – before a wealthy patron had endowed it as a boarding school for his errant offspring.

"Ah, I know you're just messin'. She goes to school in town – little place, nothin' so fancy as this."

Sean nodded and looked at Maureen. She slipped a hand over his and he met her eyes.

"Trust me," she whispered. Her eyes were clear – more than that, they were excited. He frowned, but nodded.

"Gerry, I don't suppose you'd like company on your way to Dublin?"

"And weren't you just readin' my mind?" Gerry jumped up from the pew, a wide smile on his face. "Can you ride a bike – a motorbike, like? I have my own, but I have another one I'd fixed up and hoped to sell in Dublin. Except, I'd have to cart it all the way, and that will take the better part of a week. If you two can drive it, we'll be in Dublin tomorrow – Wednesday at the latest."

Maureen caught Sean's eye and winked at him. Both of them could ride – if just barely.

One of the young priests who had spent the summer travelling the parish had taken it upon himself to teach Sean to ride his motorbike. Maureen, not to be outdone, had 'practiced' driving, too – at night, after curfew. The nuns had caught her at it, of course, and her midnight revels had earned her nearly a month in the kitchens.

Sean looked back at Gerry. The boy was bouncing on the balls of his feet, waiting for their answer.

He had no idea why they were going to Dublin. There was no reason for them to leave the church, let alone the hill. Leaving was not going to help them get home to 1958 – that was Dubh's job. Dubh was supposed to find them, was supposed to get them home.

Maybe Maureen had been right. Maybe they should have stayed with Grania.

The thoughts jabbed at him as they chased each other through his head. He ground his teeth into his lip and looked at the boy, whose anticipation was a palpable thing.

"We can both ride. If you'll have us, we'd love to join you."

Four

Maureen blew on her fingers and tried to tuck her cloak tighter around her body. Sleeping on one of the wooden pews in the church was better than being exposed to the blustery February night, but without a fire, it was still cold.

Thanks to a day-old broadsheet in Gerry's back pocket, they knew it was February still, but February in 1916. Seeing the date, Sean had turned a faint shade of green. He had tried to catch her eye but she had ignored him. She already knew it was 1916 and she knew who Gerry was, but she was not surprised he did not. Sean had not spent the summer before studying the various failed rebellions that marked Ireland's history. He had stocked shelves at the tiny shop near the inlet, instead.

She heard Sean stirring and sat up. There had been no time, and no opportunity, to say anything beyond 'goodnight,' after agreeing to join Gerry on his way to Dublin. The boy had gushed that it was going to be great fun, assured them his Aunt Jenny would be more than happy to put them up and maybe even find them jobs, and then insisted they go to sleep so they could be out early enough – before the nuns made their way to the church for Lauds.

His enthusiasm left her breathless.

"So, are you going to tell me why we've agreed to set out for Dublin at four o'clock tomorrow morning?"

She grinned in the dark. Gerry was snoring so loud there was no reason to keep their voices down, but Sean was whispering anyway. Wrapped in her cloak, she waddled over to his pew.

"You know the plaque in the old cemetery – the one on the angel?"

He shifted to give her room to sit. "The war memorial?"

"The same. It lists all the local lads killed in 'valiant battle' – some of them weren't from the world wars, though. Some were from our own conflicts."

"Ah, right – our honoured dead."

She ignored the sarcasm in his voice. "I was curious, so I looked up the names of the boys who hadn't died in wars. Gerald Ballard was one of them."

Sean took his time responding.

"That's where I recognized his name – Maureen, he died in the Rising."

"I know. On April 26, 1916, to be exact."

"We have no business going to Dublin with him." He was making no effort to keep his voice low now, and she winced as it bounced off the stones. "It's bad enough we agreed to go in the first place, but now? This is mad – what were you thinking?"

"Sean, listen to me. That boy there, the one who snores and talks a lot, the one who has an Aunt Jenny, a young sister who might get to finish her schooling, and a mother who falls ill far too often, is going to die in two months. We're going to stop him."

She took a deep breath. The words had spilled

from her mouth, almost unbidden, and Sean was holding his head in his hands. He was right: it was one thing to head to Dublin a few months before a revolt, but quite another to stop someone from dying in it.

Yet, if she were right, they would be able to send Gerry home well before April 24, when the Irish Republican Brotherhood, led by Patrick Pearce and James Connolly, would attempt to liberate Dublin and the rest of Ireland from British rule. They would fail. After a five-day siege of Dublin – five days of rioting, looting and death – the British Army would succeed in forcing the ringleaders of the rebellion to surrender.

By mid-May, the leaders would be dead – executed following secret military trials. The revolutionaries were not popular with the rest of the nation until they died. Once dead, they became martyrs. Forty years later, Ireland was divided and men still died for their fight. Just a month before she and Sean passed through the gateway, two men had sacrificed themselves with Pearse's nationalistic poetry on their lips.

She shivered and Sean looked up from his hands.

"What about Dubh?"

"What about him?"

His mouth popped open and her cheeks immediately burned with guilt. She had not forgotten about the man – far from it – but he had failed them. They were alone. They always had been, and it was time they started making their own way in the world. Wishing and waiting was not going to serve them anymore.

"He's not here," she added. "Something went very wrong and he wasn't there to make sure we made it home safe."

"What if he doesn't know yet?"

"Doesn't know? Last time he had been a member of Grania's crew a good six months before we even arrived. How could he not know?"

Sean looked like he wanted to speak, but closed his mouth and stared at her instead. She shrugged. It was an honest question.

"I felt something in the mist," he said finally. "It felt like something pushed and pulled us through the gateway. You felt it, too—I heard you. You said something just before we went through. Right as you grabbed me you said, 'They can't have you.' I don't know what you meant, but what if 'they' have him? What if he's trapped?"

The memory of her terror nipped at her shoulders. She rubbed her arms and stared at the tight weave of the cloak as it stretched over her knees. There was nothing she wanted to – or could – say about the threat within the gateway. It was horrible and beguiling all at once. It wanted them – wanted to *own* them.

She forced her mind to go blank. She could not think about it. Not now.

"What if he just doesn't care?" she muttered.

"You don't believe that. He saved your life – he cared."

"Fine – I'm sorry." A quiet snort in the darkness told her he did not believe her. "Right. Say I'm wrong. Say something has him. How is staying here going to help him – or us?

"How does going to Dublin help us?"

"I don't know." She rushed on before he could interrupt. "Have you ever met the Ballard family?"

"No."

"Neither have I. When I asked around, I found

out their farm is abandoned. Some even say it's haunted. Gerry left behind a family – people who mourn him. We know what that's like. Wouldn't you spare them, if you could?"

Sean's silence made her wince. It was true, though.

"He doesn't sound like a rebel," he said finally. "Gerry didn't even flinch when you said we were going to help the war effort. He wants to race, build his bikes – help his family. Why was he in the Rising?"

"I don't know – personal accounts were reserved for the leaders, aye? Maybe it was his Aunt Jenny, or one of his racing friends? I just – I don't think he should die in that war."

"That doesn't mean we should die in his place. I don't believe either, even if you do."

She let this slide. She believed in freedom. Their fathers had died protecting it. Politics, revenge, the things men died for in border skirmishes between the Republic and Northern Ireland, were not her ideologies. Ireland, or part of it, had earned its statehood. Nationalism, the pride in – and unity of – the nation trumpeted by heroes like Patrick Pearse, had died in the politicking of the Civil War.

"We won't die, Sean. We were pirates for six months. I think we can handle Dublin."

Sean's laugh seemed to burst from him. Gerry's snoring stopped abruptly and they held their breath in the thundering silence that followed.

The boy grunted once, twice. The pew creaked as he shifted in his sleep and resumed his nighttime symphony.

"This is mad," Sean whispered into the night.

She waited, afraid to say anything to influence him one way or the other.

"It's mad, but I'm in." He grabbed her hand and squeezed. "God only knows how long we'll be stuck here – and someone has to keep you out of trouble."

Grinning, she squeezed back. "Speaking of not getting into trouble – we're going to crash Gerry's bike if we don't get some sleep."

"We're going to crash Gerry's bike anyway," he muttered.

"We are not – you'll do fine." She touched his shoulder lightly as she went back to her own pew. "Of course, if he's too busy taking us to hospital because you managed to drive us into a wall, he'd be safe from the Rising then, too."

Sean's laugh was dry and she smiled sleepily into the night.

Five

Draped in a dark cloak, he marched across the plain. Mag Mell, the Plain of Joy, was desolate. For countless years, the air had hummed with the living beauty of this place. Now, no tree, no flower, no blade of grass marred the emptiness. The air was heavy and filled with fog. It shifted with each step he took. There was no moon, no sun – no point of reference – only the mist. It was alive with light and movement, revealing his way even as it sought to disorient him.

Dubh walked faster. His stride carved a path through the haze. Though he had lost count of the mortal years that passed since he last came this way, he remembered. He remembered the cave – a mere speck on the horizon – and he remembered the girl.

She was waiting. Her golden hair was twisted in tight braids, and within its intricate weave were glimmering stones. Bits of magic that looked like flowers, but sparkled when she moved, crowned the head that barely came to his chest. Niamh had grown to womanhood in his absence, and she was waiting for him.

"Dubh Súile." At the light-hearted chime of her voice, the mists bloomed with colour: golden yellows, blues and greens drifted in the current.

"Mistress Niamh." He bowed low, his deep voice humble.

"You have been gone many days, good sir."

"Too many," he replied, unable to hide the smile in his voice.

Her lips twitched with an answering smile and she gestured for him to enter the cave. He hesitated. His teeth ached with the dissonance leaking from the craggy stone face, but the high-pitched whine must be worse for the sprightly Fae woman.

She lived here, she told him long ago, to keep those she cared about safe. He had refused to enter then, had walked away from her cause.

Niamh held his gaze now and he nodded once. With the slightest bow of her head, she turned and led him through the cave network until they came to a small but cheerful room, carved right into the rock.

It was spare and indirectly lit by four small orbs of light, tucked in the corners. Vibrant hangings, woven by her mother, graced the walls. A few, he noted, were newer. He suspected these were Niamh's own work.

"You have improved." He pointed at one whose tones of rose, gold and blue twisted a pattern, which shifted as he watched. It trapped him in its weave as it whispered its story. He tore his eyes from it; he had no time for the tales it could tell.

"Sit Dubh, please. Glowering at the tapestry will not help you find your young mortals any faster."

"So you know?"

"I know, and I am not the only one. It was a physical thing for us, your waking."

"You were aware of it, even in here?" The cave, it was said, blocked the mists, and with it, the wild magic of the Fae – of the Tuatha Dé Danann who resided within the Faerie realm of Tír na nÓg.

Niamh smiled. "You never did understand why we retreated here. These walls are only a shield – the discord you feel is the bending of perception. It prevents those who would focus on us from seeing us. A gateway between Faerie and the world of man cannot be opened here, but our own magic – what is left of it – remains." She waved a hand at the ever-shifting hangings and he nodded. The ache in his teeth was gone, but the prickle of magic, separate from the mists, remained.

The young Fae smiled as she saw the understanding in his face. "It has been so long, Dubh. We thought them all gone from your world – thought you were the last one. He controls it all now – except them. Except you."

"And you."

She accepted this with a nod of her head. "And me."

The quiet command in her voice sent shivers up his spine.

"Then you know what happened? You know what I did?"

"Not the whole of it, no. I know she woke you – woke you when most of us thought you beyond waking. I know they passed through your gateway – moved bodily through, as you did so long ago. I peered through the veils you put up to protect them from the king."

She let the words hang there and Dubh cringed. There were rules in place, governing the Changelings and he should have brought Maureen and Sean to Tír na nÓg to face the king as soon as he realized they had followed him through the gateway.

But knowing who they were – whose children they were – he could not risk it. He would not threaten their lives in such a way.

"Why did you leave them? You worked so hard to protect them, and then you just left them, Dubh."

"They did not need me – they were safe with Grania. I only wanted to get them home, to their own time without calling the mists – without calling his attention to them."

He had tried to employ old human magic by using the phase of the moon to access the gateway between the worlds – the worlds to which, as the descendants of man and Fae, they were heirs.

It should have worked. Maureen and Sean had not stepped foot in Faerie, which meant they should have been able to go home – to the same time they left it – but something had gone terribly wrong.

"Once they were among their own, I would have gone to them and explained. My presence among Grania's people would have stirred too much attention – there and here. You know that, Niamh."

"And now?"

"They are lost. I watched over them – I am not cruel. I waited for them on the other side, in their church, but they never arrived. I felt them move through the gateway, but I do not know where they exited—"

He tried to control his voice, to slow his words, but his heart was beating too fast. He had travelled in their shadow and protected them from those in Tír na nÓg who could see between the realms. He knew he cared too much, and it clouded his reason.

He looked up at Niamh and made his face bland under her scrutiny.

"You should have stayed," she scolded. "You did not know they were cutting down the trees on the hill?"

He started to protest but the words died on his lips. The trees – no, he had not known.

"If you insist on using human magic, you must abide by its rules. By the time they returned to the oak grove, more had come down. The circle was not powerful enough and their journey was interrupted."

The enormity of her words and of what he had done swelled before him. It was foolish to suppose the king would be unaware of their passage through time – even if he could not see them, Nuada Silver Arm would have been able to feel them.

Dubh had failed them, just as he had their fathers. "I have to find them."

"You do. He will act soon."

It was not the words, but the way she said them.

"Are you afraid for them?"

"Much has changed."

That was not an answer. "Not much. Mag Mell was barren when I left, and stands much the same now."

"Mag Mell was the first to fall."

He sighed. Arguing with Niamh had always been pointless. "When last we spoke, you could barely utter Nuada's name without spitting, and you had no thought but to hide yourself and others under the guise of safety. The mortal world was never your concern. What has happened?"

"The mortal world is still not my concern – although it will be consumed with darkness should he be allowed to pursue his path. They must return home – safe – before Nuada can use them – and use them he will. They have the power to destroy everything."

He ignored this last bit of dramatics. The history

of the Tuatha Dé Danann and the Changelings was a long one. He may have been the last in generations, but he was by no means the first. Despite the war that had given Nuada Silver Arm the throne, destruction had never been the outcome of the meeting between Changeling and Fae.

"Do you know where they are?"

Niamh nodded. "Indeed, and getting them out now will not be easy."

"You speak in riddles."

"Aye, you taught me well, Master Druid." Her laughter was merry and Dubh allowed himself to smile.

"They feel it, you know – the magic," she continued. "They feel it even more than you do – you came to us when man still believed in Faerie. They grew up under newer gods – sterile and chaste. The power, latent in their veins, leaves them breathless, and I think in some ways, a little reckless."

Absently, he nodded. He grew up with the magic of the old religion in the very air he breathed.

"They are in a time of great upheaval – they arrived at its eve. It is 1916 for them, and they know it. They stumbled from the gateway and ran into a young man named Gerry Ballard. Master Ballard was meant to die in the Easter Rising."

"Meant to die? Has something changed already?"

Niamh stared at him. "How do you think I found them so quickly? Why do you think I want them gone?" She paused. "How much time do you think has passed since they travelled the gateway?"

At her words, his stomach dropped.

"I walked Mag Mell," he whispered. "I did not wish to call attention to myself by drawing on the mists."

"You forgot your own tales, Master Druid – do you not remember that for a night spent in Faerie, six months shall pass for man?" She giggled. "I see the Faerie Sleep yet weighs heavy on your senses. You walked the Plain and time passed in the mortal world. Time passed for them."

"And in that time?" He ignored her merriment; he had no patience for her Fae sense of humour. "What has happened?"

"Maureen recognized the young man as well. She decided to help him, see to it he lives. They are in Dublin, and if I judge her correctly, they will participate far more than Master Ballard ever did."

"Have they traded places?" He could barely get the words out before another horrible thought chased them. "Did Nuada send them?"

"It is likely." Her face hardened and her tone was clipped. "They have already worked themselves into the fabric of history, Dubh Súile. You will have to do the same. Remember, things must be taken and given in equal measure. Make sure you know what is meant to happen."

"I will – and I will take care it does."

Niamh was not finished. "If you want to protect them, protect what is left of their timeline. Make sure they are safe – hide them if you must. He tried to destroy you, once – nearly succeeded, too. He will do it again, and he will use them to do it."

He cocked his head at her. The urgency in her voice had nothing to do with Nuada, her father and king, and the man she had been fighting for as long as he could remember.

She smiled in the face of his confusion. "You do not know who they are." It was not a question.

"Of course I do. Their fathers—"

"That is not what I meant. She woke you – do

you not know why? It is not merely because she is her father's daughter."

He stared at her. The guilt for their fathers' deaths in man's last great war lay heavy in his heart.

Her eyes drifted to an intricate weaving in progress on her loom. A colourful array of filaments and ribbon, faintly glimmering, etched a labyrinthine design across its surface.

"Your threads have always been linked," she whispered, "but this time is locked. You cannot step around them as you did with the pirate. Their path is yours, now."

"How?"

"You know how. It is in the bloodlines."

"But we are not – they are not . . . That is impossible." His voice was louder than he intended, and she arched a pale eyebrow at him. His eyes fell before she could see the shame and regret in them.

"I have no kin to carry my name. Those I loved are all gone, dead so long not even history remembers their deeds. No one remains to tell those stories, now."

"Except you."

"Do not mock me. I am not fit to sing their songs anymore."

Niamh reached for him. "I do not mean to taunt you with riddles, my friend. You know what they are – they are kindred souls, Changelings, like yourself. That is all you need to know."

He searched her face and she smiled. It was small and beautiful.

"Do not slip from us, Dubh Súile. They have need of you – I have need of you. It is time."

The words left him cold. She had warned him of this, years ago, before he retreated from the worlds.

He had not wanted to face it – had not the courage to face it. Nuada Silver Arm was king, emperor, god of Tír na nÓg, and there had been peace for a thousand years.

Yet, if Nuada was responsible for Sean and Maureen's presence in 1916 – if the king had placed them in the path of the coming whirlwind, as he had their fathers – then it was indeed time.

"I will see to it."

The Fae woman nodded. He grasped her hand and lightly brushed his lips across her fingers. Raw power tingled at his lips and he smiled.

He needed no guide to find his way out of the caves. The mist beckoned to him from the Plain and he allowed himself to answer its call.

He stepped into the open and willed the raw power of Tír na nÓg to surround him. It coiled about his body. It draped him in white and he threw back his head. He begged it to swallow him, to hide him from the view of those who were watching as he summoned more. At last, he moved within a towering white wall of deafening noise.

A low rumble of thunder sounded and the wall fell away. Mag Mell was empty once more.

Six

It took them two days to get to Dublin. Engine trouble on the spare bike stopped them for a full afternoon, and they had to trade chores for a hot meal and a night in a drafty barn. Yet, the woman of the house was kind enough to send them on their way the next morning with bread and cheese. They made the feast last until they could make it to the Mallory Boarding House, run by Gerry's Aunt Jenny.

Gerry was full of stories of his Aunt Jenny. Up until her husband had died the winter previously, she would spend several weeks of the summer months at the Ballard farmstead. Now, she let rooms out of her house and attempted to manage the small shop she and her late husband owned.

"I'm sure she can use the help in the shop," Gerry said to Sean as they walked their motorbikes – engines silent – along the pavement. Aunt Jenny lived a few miles from the city centre. It was a secluded little neighbourhood, complete with its own park, and its residents would not appreciate the noise.

Sean nodded absently. Shop work would be handy; they were going to have to find a way to support themselves while they were stuck in 1916. Maureen had confessed to bringing – and losing – a few gold doubloons. It was just as well they were gone, he thought. He and Maureen would probably have been fingered for stealing if they had tried to sell them.

"And I'm willing to wager she'd want your help in the house, lass."

"I'm not very good at the domestic side of things," Maureen warned.

Gerry did not seem to hear her as he slowed to a stop before a set of steps, which lead up to a three-story townhouse.

The house, and its fellows, was nestled in quiet enclave that was once prosperous. Lace curtains hung in the front windows and a tangle of ivy clung to the brick face. Yet, the windowsills sagged and sloughed their paint into the driving wind. The brass knocker was shiny with use but the tall black door was scuffed and dull.

"I'm sure you're grand, lass," he said at length. "Aunt Jenny will sort you out. This is it – stay here with the bikes. I think maybe I ought to do the talkin'. Aunt Jenny is lovely, but she's not expecting you."

Sean and Maureen exchanged glances and hung back with the bikes while Gerry went to attack the knocker.

A small woman came to the door and immediately bundled the boy up in a huge hug.

"Gerald Matthew Ballard, what the devil are you doing here?" Her voice carried far as she switched to upbraiding her nephew. "Oh, you bold thing! Your Da is already after sending me a telegram letting me know you'd legged it. He's that mad at you, lad."

Gerry ducked his head and Aunt Jenny peered at them over his head. "And who are you then? Did you help this young rascal flee in the night?"

"These are my friends, Aunt. They're looking to

find work in the city and offered to help me drive the bikes here so I wouldn't have to use Da's cart – he should be happy about that."

"Oh aye, you just left it at the abbey, I hear. What were you doing there? Not chasing after fairy stories I hope."

She waved at Sean and Maureen to come forward. "Ah, you frozen darlings, come in the house – imagine, riding those bikes in the cold. The lot of you are mad. We'll have us some tea and you can tell me all about it."

"Lemon or honey, lad?"

"Black, please."

"I'll take honey," Maureen chimed in.

Mrs. Mallory had bustled them into the drawing room despite their road-weary clothes. It was clearly the company room, full of what looked to be the woman's prized possessions. A small tintype of a man – likely her dead husband – stood on the mantle beside a carriage clock that chimed the hour. It struck four as she set a small table with the tea things.

Jenny Mallory was a slight woman who shared her nephew's fragile features. Her fading blond hair was pulled into a modest bun at the base of her neck, and her clothes were neatly pressed, but old. A smile creased her face, but watchful eyes peered at them from behind a pair of wire-rimmed spectacles.

"And you, Master Gerry, will take a bit of both, aye?" she asked now.

"Aye, thank you, Auntie."

Mrs. Mallory pinned her nephew to his seat with

her pale eyes. "None of that sweet talk until you can tell me why I shouldn't send you straight back to your Da. What were you doing up at the abbey – and why are you here now?"

Gerry made a face at Sean and Maureen and took a deep breath before launching into the tale of their meeting.

"That doesn't tell me what you were doing there at that hour," she declared when he finished. "You could very well have left the farm early enough for your Da not to catch you – he's up close enough to Lauds, himself."

Gerry blushed and looked down at his hands.

"Well, you know the stories, Aunt."

"Oh Lord, you were chasing after fairy stories – and fairy gold too, I expect. What is the matter with you, lad?"

"Fairy gold?" Sean asked with a big grin on his face. Maureen shot him a look. They were supposed to be students – orphans – from the school. They should know the stories.

Gerry saved him. "Ah sure, the nuns don't share those kind of tales, do they? A terrible pirate queen once ruled Carrickahowley, aye? Some say she hid her ill-gotten treasure of Spanish gold on the hill. It's said a small bit of it was unearthed when they were building the abbey. Every couple of years they find more – just when they need it, like." He shrugged. "Some even say the Good Folk took it and dole it out, so long as the nuns behave themselves, and leave a bit of milk and bread now and again."

"Spanish gold?"

Maureen froze. From the corner of her eye, she could see Sean looking at her – drilling holes in her head with his eyes – but she kept her gaze firmly on Gerry. That was where her doubloons had gone: they had been scattered about the hill during her mad rush to Sean's side. She hoped Tomás told some fine stories after they left – they had certainly given him enough material.

Even as she avoided her friend's gaze, another thought dawned on her: they had also given Sr. Theresa reason to defy common sense – and Mother Bernadette's edict – and leave the kitchen's scraps out for the Good Folk.

Sean was never going to let her live this down.

"A load of nonsense is what it is." Mrs. Mallory's tone was brisk. "And what in the world were you doing looking for Spanish gold – John Ballard isn't so hard up for money, is he?"

"Oh no, Aunt. My bike money does well enough for Da, but I thought I could bring it to you – pay for my keep and help you, like. But then I found these two, and I knew I didn't need it."

Gerry's face broke into a lopsided grin while his aunt's thin lips disappeared into a tight line.

"And what makes you think I need your money, lad?"

"Well, you . . ." Gerry faltered and his grin crumbled. "I mean, it's just that you haven't been down to see us since Uncle died. Da's been muttering something about them Fenians and I just thought you were maybe in a spot of trouble up here."

Mrs. Mallory stared at her nephew until his eyes fell to his lap.

"Is that what you thought, Gerald Ballard? Stick to racing your bikes, and don't worry your head over me. 'Them Fenians.'" Her lips twisted into a sneer. "You know nothing of the world, lad. No wonder your Da is sick with worry."

Maureen's eyes darted from Gerry to his aunt while Sean studied his hands with intense interest. Fenians were the men and women who struggled for Irish independence – sometimes no matter the cost. Some people liked to think of them as low-class rabble, while others thought they were heroes. It seemed Gerry's father was in the former camp.

Gerry squirmed under his Aunt's pride. "I'm sorry, Aunt. I just—I just wanted to help. Mam misses you. But I forgot about the money as soon as I heard Sean and Maureen here wanted to come to Dublin. If you'll take them on, you could come down again this summer."

The stiffness in Mrs. Mallory's shoulders relaxed slightly and she gave her nephew a small smile. "Ah, well . . . It's hard to argue with that." She patted his hand. Gerry's relief was nearly palpable. "We'll see what we can do. For now though, we're going to write your parents. Why didn't you just tell them you were racing?"

"Da doesn't like it – says I'm scaring Mam to death."

"Sure, if the consumption doesn't take her first. You will be the death of my sister, Gerald Ballard – running all over God's creation the way you are." She shook her head. "When is this race?"

"Saturday next. I came in early to see if I couldn't shift the other bike to pay for my entry fee."

"Well, let's see what we can do to help with that. I know a few lads around here who might be in need. Now, come on all of you – let us get you washed up. You smell of the road and my boarders aren't keen to share their table with tramps, aye?"

Seven

Help them.

Maureen's eyes snapped open. She had the bedclothes clutched tight in her hands and her breath was coming fast. It rasped loud and ragged in the silence of her tiny room.

Mrs. Mallory had found them each a corner to call their own. Hers consisted of a small cot and washstand in a windowless little room in the attic, while Sean slept in the old carriage house. Both had once been servants' quarters, but she and Sean were the only servants in residence, now. Whether or not they stayed depended on an interview in the morning.

She stared into the dark and waited for her breathing to slow. The dreams. She had been having them since they first passed through the gateway. At first, while they stayed with Grania, they had been blurry, indistinct but menacing. She never spoke to Sean about them – could barely stand the feeling of them, let alone speak them aloud.

Besides, talking about them, probing them deeper, might give them more meaning than they ought to have. They were just dreams.

Except now, they were different. Darker. Just thinking about them made the palms of her hands sweat. They still made no sense, but now she was running around in them, starring in them as a bewildered, terrified wanderer.

Tonight, she had been chasing after a man – well, she thought it was a man. It was a figure ahead of her, cloaked in shadows and mist. Muted screams and snarled curses hounded her and open flame flickered just beyond a rickety barrier. She choked on the smoke as she ran. Whether she was trying to stop the figure, or find him, she was not sure. She did know, without her help, he was going to walk into something horrible.

"Help them."

The echo of the dream's demand shot adrenaline through her veins and her heart banged painfully against her ribs. She sat up and snatched a small tumbler of water from the washstand.

She wondered if it was Dubh, if he needed their help. But no – there was no way for them to help him. He was far more powerful than they were. Besides, how could they help him if they had no idea where he was?

The command niggled at her.

Gerry did not need their help anymore – he was as good as gone once the race was over. Thanks to the argument between him and one of Mrs. Mallory's boarders, a teacher employed at the school where Patrick Pearse was headmaster, it was clear Gerry was no supporter of 'them Fenians.' How Mrs. Mallory had originally managed to get her nephew involved in the Rising – if she had at all – was a mystery Maureen was glad she no longer had to unravel. He was safe now.

Sean had watched her all through dinner – watched her even as she watched Gerry and his aunt – as though he were waiting for her to do something, or give away some secret. She wanted to tell him Jenny Mallory's politics did not matter –

they did not have to get involved in them. They were not trading Gerry's life for their own.

No matter how compelling the cause.

Maureen bit her lip. What if that was it – what if it was the Rising?

The cot had no headboard and she leaned against the wall. The chill damp soothed her heated skin.

Help them? No, it was unthinkable. So many things had gone wrong in the build up to Easter. The Rising had been doomed, almost from the start. No matter how much it tugged at her heart, it was too late to help them.

Wasn't it?

Sean wandered through an empty field. A low mist mired his steps and the hum of too many voices filled his ears. In the distance, flames licked the sky. He was searching for something. He had no idea what, but he suspected he would know when he saw it – if, in fact, he ever did. His feet ached and he was so weary. He had been searching for days – for years.

Forever.

One voice grew in intensity over the others.

"Help them," it demanded.

Sean shook his head. That was not what he was looking for.

Louder this time: "Help them."

"No," he whispered into the heavy air.

The voice hissed in his ear. He stumbled and nearly fell.

His eyes flew open. The dark of the carriage house swallowed him and he opened his mouth to scream.

"No mam, no porridge today."

The scream collapsed into a shuddering sigh. Gerry was talking in his sleep. Gingerly, Sean sat up – he had no urge to wake his new friend. With waking would come questions, and he had too many of his own to make up answers for Gerry.

The never-ending barrage of questions had circled his brain as he fell asleep, and now that he was awake – fully and horribly after the nightmare – they attacked him again. Questions like, why Maureen had really brought them to Dublin. He feared, from the moment he saw the date on the broadsheet, she had her own reasons for coming to the city.

How many times had she talked to him about the Rising – about all the risings, and how they could have made a difference if they had succeeded? How many times had she gone on about nationalism, argued with no one in particular about the causes of the violence in the North? Even though she claimed the Civil War had stolen the nobility from the fight, the Rising, which had paved the path to the war, and independence, was an ideology for her. It was practically a belief – her own religion.

Even he had to admit the Rising was the culmination of Grania's fight. It represented everything he had said to convince the pirate to defy reason and chase after Bingham. He scoffed at Maureen's zeal, but he did not deny its power.

It was a power that would one day topple an empire. One day – but not today. Today, Maureen's heroes were destined to die.

He sighed and stared at the grate. It glowed faintly with dying embers. The dream still snatched at him. It was not the first dream to wake him in the night, but it was the worst. It reminded him too much of the menace lurking in the gateway core. Its directive nagged at him, too. Help them? He had no desire to help them. He had no desire to change history any more than they already had.

Sparks danced in the air as the coals shifted and settled. There was nothing to do but stay close to Maureen's side and hope Dubh found them before the Rising began.

Dublin was about to burn. If they were not careful, he was afraid it would be Maureen lighting the match.

Eight

"What are we doing here, Maureen?"

"We've been over this." She checked the annoyance in her voice when she saw Sean's face. He looked tired. "We're standing in for Gerry – we're saving his life."

"By putting our own at risk?"

"How exactly are we doing that?"

"You saw Mrs. Mallory yesterday when Gerry mentioned 'them Fenians.' She looked like she was mad enough to spit, which tells me she's one of them."

She nodded. She had come to that conclusion herself. It still did not mean—

"And then there's her choice of boarders – that teacher works at Patrick Pearse's school, Maureen. That's awfully telling."

"So her being a nationalist makes it her fault her nephew was killed?"

He looked at her and rolled his eyes. "You said it back in the church. He's no believer, but he is devoted to his family. If he stayed, and she told him to jump, he would – without any questions."

She acknowledged this with an impatient shrug. "Sean, even if it was Mrs. Mallory's fault Gerry was killed, do you really think she's going to trust two runaways the same way she does her nephew?"

She jerked her chin at Gerry who was, at present, arguing with his aunt. Mrs. Mallory was insisting he give the teacher, Peter Donavan, a discount on the spare motorbike as a favour to her – to make up for the argument the night before.

Mrs. Mallory was a far better negotiator than nephew was, it seemed. Gerry's lower lip was sticking out and Maureen suspected a pouty capitulation was in the offing.

"Fenian or no," Sean whispered, his voice harsh in her ear, "I think she would have tried to protect Gerry. We're orphans. She owes us nothing."

Sean was right. Mrs. Mallory did not owe them anything, but neither had Grania. Yet, the pirate still took them on, and risked much to foil Bingham. She did not have the same confidence in Mrs. Mallory, but the prim proprietor of the Mallory Boarding House was their best – and only – option.

"Sean, the doubloons are gone, which means we have no way to keep ourselves while we wait for Dubh, or more likely, figure out our own way home."

"He'll come for us. I know it."

She bit back a hasty reply. His blind trust was baffling, but she was not going to argue with him. There were more important things at stake.

"In the meantime, do you fancy begging for food? Or sleeping rough?" She asked instead.

"No."

"Neither do I. We don't have letters of introduction. We don't have a family. We don't have anyone but Gerry and Mrs. Mallory. And I'm not going back to Carrickahowley to sleep in someone's barn."

They stared at each other without speaking. Before the silence could grow into an insurmountable thing, she grabbed at his hand.

His sigh was heavy and resigned. "You'd tell me if you were planning something, wouldn't you?"

"I've never not told you. Didn't I tell you when I planned to distract those merchants so Liam could take a peek at their ship to see what they stole from Grania?"

"Yes."

"And didn't I tell you when I wanted to stay out all night to see the meteor shower?"

"You did. Dragged me with you, too."

She smiled. They had both gotten into so much trouble with Sr. Theresa – and Mother Bernadette.

"And didn't I tell you about a vision I saw in a church, of a man who asked me, without words, to follow him into the void?"

"Aye, but about that one, Maureen – can we not do that again?"

There was a smile on his face finally, and she gave his hand a squeeze.

"I shall do my very best."

"Will we get breakfast then? I don't fancy sitting down with Mrs. Mallory on an empty stomach."

"Aye. She's nice enough, but do you get the feeling she's, well . . ."

"Watching? All the time?"

She snuck one more glance at Gerry and his aunt. It seemed a truce had been declared.

"Quite."

"So, my girl, what is it you do?"

"Do?" Maureen started at the question. How was she supposed to answer that?

"Yes, do – what are your skills? Please tell me the Benedictines taught you something useful." Gerry's aunt was peering at her over her spectacles.

"Keep in mind, I don't hold with truancy, lass. So, give me a good reason why I should take the two of you on."

"Well, I've spent quite a bit of time peeling potatoes."

Sean snickered and Maureen gave his side a quick jab with her elbow. She had not meant to say that, but at least peeling potatoes was better than 'pirate.'

"Ah, a bit of a trouble-maker then?" Mrs. Mallory was smiling.

"I wouldn't say that, but I think perhaps I've overheard Sr. Theresa calling me an unruly imp from time to time."

"Is that so? And would you bring chaos to my home then, too?"

"Oh, no – at least, I would try not to."

Not to be left out, Sean added, "Don't forget the silver, Maureen – she polishes that well, too, Ma'am."

"Ah well then, at least you can be trusted – if you were truly bold, you'd never be allowed near the silver."

Maureen smiled. She had not thought about it that way. She wondered what Sr. Theresa's insistence that she endure countless hours of embroidery meant.

"Tell me, do you have as much experience peeling potatoes, young man?"

"A bit." Sean shrugged. "Usually, I was too busy with chores or stocking shelves at the local shop."

"Indeed." Mrs. Mallory glanced between them. Her face was smooth, unreadable.

"Tell me this, then: can I rely on you? You won't be running off to join England's war any time soon, will you? I recall Gerry mentioning it."

"No Ma'am. We told him we might try to find some way of helping, but well, that was before . . ."

Maureen's voice faded as Sean pinched her hand. Almost too late, she understood his caution. Mrs. Mallory had not come right out and said she was a nationalist. Presuming too much was dangerous.

"Before?"

"Before we realized our help was needed elsewhere," Sean put in.

"I see."

"If you can find use for us, we'd be much obliged."

"Well lass, I can see you two have been raised right. Normally I'd need a letter, or some other form of recommendation, but as you hitched a ride with my feckless nephew in the dark of night, it's likely that is out of the question."

She stopped and looked at them for a moment. Maureen clenched her hands to stop from filling in the silence.

The woman nodded. "Yes, raised well – you can keep your own counsel, and you're discreet. If anything, taking you on means I will cease to run afoul of my sister's husband every time my nephew decides to get it into his head to run up here to help me."

Mrs. Mallory stood with a small sigh. "I can offer you three shillings a week, plus the room and board. You'll have Sundays to do as you please, although I do expect you to attend church with me."

Maureen opened her mouth to agree but paused and snuck a glance at her friend. Sean gave her a quick grin and nodded. She did not need his approval, but she wanted him with her on this.

"Agreed."

"Good – we'll start right away. Sean, I'll have Gerry take you down to the shop. My man there will show you 'round the place." She looked them over and clucked her tongue.

"Maureen, where on earth did you get those clothes? Have you no frock? Ah, well – never mind. We'll all go down to the shop – maybe we can find you something more suitable there. Let us be gone then, aye?"

Nine

More than a week had passed since Gerry won the amateur's motorbike race but it was finally time for him to yield to his father's repeated demand he return home.

Mrs. Mallory had cooked up a fine meal the night before, and they all said their goodbyes, but Sean still rose with Gerry at dawn to help him load his pack with provisions from the pantry. They walked the bike to the street, which was quiet in the early-morning chill.

As they approached the Mallory front gate, Gerry turned, hesitated for just a moment and then stuck out his hand.

"You'll take care of them – Aunt Jenny and Maureen – won't you?"

Sean cocked an eyebrow as he took Gerry's hand.

"Of course, but what—"

"Aye, well – I'm not as blind as Aunty likes to think. I know something's coming."

He bit back the urge to deny Gerry's claim. It was easier to pretend nothing was wrong, and he and Maureen were simply biding their time until Dubh found them.

"I almost wish I could take the two of you with me. It's mad, like. I brought you here – thought you could help to get her away from the city a bit, but it eats at me. When I tried to talk to Maureen about it . . . well, that one – just look after her."

"What did you say to Maureen?" The words came out too fast and too loud. Sean took a deep breath. It was no business of his if Maureen and Gerry had private conversations.

"Ah, it was just herself making sure I was set to go – that Dublin was no place for a lad like me. Now, what do you think she meant by that?"

"She meant exactly what she said, likely. She doesn't want you mixed up with your Aunt's dealings."

"Well if that's the case, it's not a place for the two of you, either."

"No, it isn't."

"But she believes in it, doesn't she."

It was not a question.

"Yes."

"Then do as I asked. Take care of her – take care of each other. Don't—" Gerry paused as he searched for the words to say.

The last of Sean's irritation melted. Gerry was a good lad, honest. He was glad the Ballard family would be able to stay together.

"Look, if it were me, I would have to help – she's me mam's sister, aye? You're grand and all, but you're not family. You don't owe her anything." He searched Sean's face and shrugged. "Something big is coming. You shouldn't be here when it happens. Get her out before it's too late."

Mrs. Mallory turned from the kitchen window and looked back to Maureen. "He's off then. Wee Ger – I'll miss him, but I'm glad he's going home."

"Truly? You didn't want his, um, help?"

Mrs. Mallory laughed. "Gerry? Help? I'm not sure what you mean, Miss. He's a good lad – bit of dreamer like my sister. His father, now he is a sensible man."

The older woman came into the small room off the kitchen where she kept her laundry and mending. With a sigh, she sat next to Maureen and took up the socks she had been teaching Maureen to darn.

For whatever reason, the nuns had decided that as the granddaughter of the Honourable William O'Malley, Maureen would not need to know how to darn socks – embroider, yes, but darn the socks that so often got holes as she traipsed about the wilderness of Carrickahowley? No.

Mrs. Mallory, of course, believed otherwise. Considering, in 1916, her grandfather had only just been called to the bar, Maureen was forced to agree.

"Any other father would send his boy to the city and make a man out of him, but not John Ballard," Mrs. Mallory continued. "No, he thinks his son would fall in with the wrong people – would be too susceptible, too eager to help his kin." Her voice was faintly mocking.

"John knows what's coming. Knows and doesn't care so long as he and his can prosper out there. He thinks they're safe." Mrs. Mallory made a disparaging noise and looked at Maureen over the tops of her spectacles. "He's not safe, not really, but I'm glad Gerry has gone back to the farm. It would kill my sister if anything happened to her son."

"Why isn't he safe?"

The older woman searched her face. "Why did you tell Gerry you were coming to Dublin to help the war effort?"

Maureen shrugged. "We didn't know who he was – or what he was doing in the church. It seemed a safe, neutral thing to say. I didn't tell him which war, after all."

"Do you see this as a war?"

She did not have to ask what 'this' was, but she did struggle over what she knew of this time, what she believed, and what she knew was coming – not only in a few months, but also in the years that followed. Was it a war?

"Yes."

"Why?"

"Because England will never let Ireland go – not willingly." Maureen took a deep breath and fought the tremor in her voice. "Because self-determination must happen. Because we must have an identity of our own and because the Crown will not grant us these things without a fight. We have to earn them, even if it means war."

Her words hung in the silence that followed.

Mrs. Mallory pursed her lips. "Your talents were wasted on the potatoes, lass."

Maureen grinned.

"So she always told the nuns, but would they listen?"

"Sean."

He leaned against the doorway, his arms crossed over his chest. She wondered how long he had been standing there, but even as she thought it, he smiled at her. Not too long, then. She let her breath escape through her teeth and held up her sock.

"Mrs. Mallory is teaching me to darn socks."

He cocked an eyebrow at the mess in her hands. "Is it supposed to look like that?"

"No." Mrs. Mallory took the sock and tossed Maureen a new one to practice on while she ripped out the botched stitches.

Maureen grinned sheepishly and he let out a throaty chuckle. "Remind me not to get holes in my socks. You'll have to forgive her, Mrs. Mallory – many of Maureen's talents were wasted on the potatoes, but the more womanly crafts were not one of them."

Maureen made a face at him; he laughed even as Mrs. Mallory clicked her tongue at them.

"I can see that. Don't worry yourself, lad. We'll get her ready to run a home soon enough. Now, how about I put the kettle on and we can have a cuppa, aye?"

He stepped into the small room to let the older woman leave and collapsed into the spindly chair she made vacant.

Maureen put the socks down with a sigh.

"That bad?"

"No – yes." She shrugged and looked at him. "I don't know. Is Gerry off, then?"

"Aye."

"I know you think we ought to go, too."

"No. No I don't."

She opened her mouth, ready for the argument, but stopped. "You don't?"

"No." He lowered his voice to a whisper. "Not while there is still a chance he could come back if something goes wrong. He's cannier than his aunt thinks, but you were right to keep him out of this. I know I don't . . . *understand* this like you do, but you were right. I just wish – I just wish we could stay out of it, too."

"You can, Sean."

He raised an eyebrow at her choice of words and she hurried on.

"I can't sit here and do nothing – how could I,

knowing what we know? And—" she paused. "I want it, Sean. I want to feel it, and I want to belong to something greater than us. Can you understand?"

He stared at her, a look of helplessness creeping over his face. "I don't – I . . ." He ran his hand through his shaggy black hair and glanced around the small room. "What can you actually do?" he whispered.

She winced at the fear in his voice and glanced at the doorway. Mrs. Mallory was just beyond, waiting for the kettle to boil on the range. This was not the time or place to discuss it.

A single eyebrow raised, she looked pointedly between him and the doorway again.

He nodded and tapped the arm of his chair lightly with his finger.

Sunday. The park.

Ten

"**M**aureen, did you know meetings go on in that little room off the kitchen?"

"Are they any different than the meetings in the sitting room?" she asked.

She kept her voice pointedly low and Sean grimaced slightly. It was Sunday – despite the biting March wind, there were still plenty of people milling about the small neighbourhood park.

"No."

The gravel crunched underfoot as they meandered along the park's manicured paths. The wind found the gaps in Mrs. Mallory's hand-me-down coats, and Maureen pulled hers tighter across her chest.

"Then it doesn't really surprise me." She looked up at him and he rolled his eyes with a wry humour he did not feel.

"You know," she continued as he grabbed her arm and tugged her close to his side, "I think the boarding house is some sort of training ground. Mr. Donavan has been bringing lads round every Saturday since we got here."

"Oh that's just lovely, that is."

It had only been two days since their chat in Mrs. Mallory's kitchen, but he suspected his friend had used the time to develop a plan he knew – just knew – he was not going to like.

"Think about it like this – the closer she is to the

conflict, the better I will be able to help."

"Help?" His voice squeaked on the word but he made no effort this time to lower his volume. "Why are you helping? We've saved Gerry's life. We don't need to do more."

"You're right – we don't, but I do."

"This is crazy, Maureen. What can you do for them that would make any bit of difference?"

"We know things, like Casement's failure with the guns from Germany, and MacNeill finding out about the whole thing and calling it off. Look, I think we have information that could help. What is wrong with wanting to give them a fighting chance?"

"And warning them about Sir Roger Casement does that?" Casement had managed to procure guns for the rebellion – and a ship to transport them – from the Germans, but the British had intercepted the ship before it was able to land. Casement had been arrested and the guns themselves had been scuttled, along with the ship. There was nothing Maureen could do to stop it.

"Yes."

He rolled his eyes. Of course she thought differently. "Maureen—"

With a soft hiss, she yanked her arm from his grip. The wind whipped at the curls that had escaped her braids and narrow green eyes glared up at him.

"We can't stop the Rising – no one could stop it – but we can give them something to hold onto. The news about Casement split the support for the Rising right down the middle. Telling them now – if they believe the information – would give them a chance to re-group, to strategize. We can help them."

Her choice of words sent a cold shock of dread down his spine.

Help them.

"No, Maureen. No. We can't help them."

"Why not?' She sounded genuinely confused. "What if they succeed, here? What if—"

"What if, nothing. Do you hear yourself? What if we don't exist in a future where they succeed? What if our fathers don't meet our mothers?'"

Her face flushed, but she made a disgusted sound in the back of her throat.

"Maureen, what you're suggesting is crazy."

"Crazy to want freedom?"

"Crazy to think that just because some rebels are able to kill more people today, that the killing will stop tomorrow."

Even as he spoke, Maureen's expression hardened and she arched an arrogant eyebrow at him. He clenched his teeth. They were just flinging words at one another. She was going to do this – help them – one way or another. It did not matter what he said.

"I can't stop you, Maureen. I know I can't – never could. But can I ask you to do one thing?"

She eyed him with the faintest air of distrust. He cringed inwardly but pushed on. "Keep us out of it. There is nothing you and I can – or should – do here."

"But, how can I—?"

"What's the line you were throwing at me, back when we were at school? 'It will be said that our movement was doomed to failure. It has proven so.' They know they're going to die."

Her eyes were bright and she blinked. "But they fight anyway," she whispered. "You're leaving out the rest: 'Yet it might have been otherwise. There is always a chance of success for brave men who challenge fortune'."

It was less the words and more the way she said them that made the small hairs on his neck stand on end. She wanted it. Damn common sense, she did not just want to help them – *she* wanted to challenge fortune.

He could not stop the jittery, frustrated words that tumbled out of his mouth. "Don't you understand how dangerous this is? This isn't a game. It's not some directive, either. God, Maureen – I think there is something bigger than us, bigger than Dubh, and bigger than this damn revolt at work here. I don't think it's a nice something, either. It's bad and it wants us. I–I don't want to die."

This last was whispered and she grabbed at his hand. Angry words died in his throat as she held herself close to his side.

"I did not drag you to Dublin to die in Gerry's place, Sean McAndrew. I have no intention of dying – nor allowing you to do so."

"Then do you get some sort of thrill from defying fate?"

She snorted. "I know there's something in the gateway – something that wants us. I could feel it behind Dubh when we first saw him in the church, and I felt it pulling at us the last time we went through. But, I don't see what it has to do with the Rising. I think it has to do with Dubh, and he's not here. The Rising is – it's here and it's now. They need us."

It was always going to come back to that – to helping them.

"I wish we'd never met Gerry – never promised ourselves we'd keep him alive," Sean muttered, even as the words filled him with shame.

"You don't mean that."

"I do." He looked up. Maureen was searching his face, looking for something – his acquiescence, his good humour – anything but what he knew she saw.

"I don't," he added. "I—I don't know anymore. There's no escaping this, is there?"

"I don't think so." Her voice was quiet, and her eyes slid from his.

There was no escaping it, but maybe he could temper it. He had to try.

"Fine. Help. But promise me we won't get directly involved – no fighting, Maureen."

She was silent. He held his breath and waited.

"I promise."

It was barely a whisper, but she had said it.

He nodded his head and steered them towards the entrance of the park. It was enough.

Eleven

"Thank you for seeing me this afternoon, sir."

"Ah, there's no need to salute me, son – sit. Aye, just put those on the floor."

Dubh leaned his walking stick on the desk and slid a haphazard stack of papers off the only other available chair in the small office.

"Commander Connolly, it's a real honour to meet you, sir," he said as he eased himself down.

"Likewise, Captain Doyle."

Dubh opened his mouth to protest but the short, stocky man with brown hair and guarded brown eyes held up a handwritten letter and waved it before his face.

"Yes, I know about you, man. You've a great friend in Liam Mellows. I've never heard him speak so complimentary of anyone – what did you do? Bribe him?"

James Connolly chuckled loudly and Dubh smiled. Bribery would have been easy. It had taken him over a month to ingratiate himself with the Irish Republican Brotherhood and their military wing, the Irish Volunteers, in Galway. It was April already and the time in Galway had given him the opportunity to study what was happening, become part of the fabric of the Rising as Niamh had instructed. It had also given Maureen and Sean time to work themselves deeper into the conflict.

He just hoped it was not too late.

"Ah, so he was as good as his word then – he did threaten to send a letter ahead of me."

"And a glowing one it is, too. He says we're to put you to good use."

Dubh nodded. He gestured to the walking stick. "I'm not as spry as I once was – took a ball to the knee in the Cape, but I manage just fine for all that. Hard to keep an old warrior down, aye?"

"You were in South Africa? Truly?" Connolly looked at him again, obviously searching for other signs of age. The Second Boer War had been over for fourteen years.

"Aye – fool eighteen year-old that I was, rebelling against me Da. I enlisted in time for Lord Kitchener's campaign. Permanently soured me on His Majesty's forces, if you understand me, sir."

"I do – nasty business, what happened out there." Connolly clicked his tongue. "Warrior, hm? Well, we're glad to have you. Have you a place to stay? I've a few safe boarding houses."

"Thank you, sir, but I have a place. I simply wanted to present myself and let you know I am at your disposal."

"Thank you, Captain. I'll bring Mellows' letter to the council meeting tomorrow. As far as I'm concerned, we're lucky to have you, but a few of the lads will want to give their stamp of approval, aye?" Connolly stood. "Have you eaten? There's always a few lads in the canteen who would be more than happy to trade stories with you, I'm sure."

"I'd like that."

"Grand – I'll take you myself and grab a cuppa while I'm at it."

The single cup of tea had turned into a morning of war-stories, with each man trying to top the tale of the last. As Captain Doyle, Dubh entertained a constantly rotating stream of men in the canteen for two hours after Connolly left him to attend to his own business.

Connolly's absence suited Dubh just fine. He was not here to curry favour with the would-be leaders of the Irish Republic. He did not intend to interfere with the Rising, either by helping it or by derailing its leaders' plans.

No. All he was to do was remove Maureen and Sean from this time, and do so with as few ripples and reverberations to the timeline as possible.

Again, he cursed his stupidity, which had brought him to this point. He cursed his caution and the need for secrecy. He cursed Nuada and his edict, which had forced him to hide those like him – kin of a sort – lest all of them suffer the king's wrath.

He and his walking stick thumped along the hallway, grim thoughts chasing one another, until he came to Connolly's office. The door was ajar. He had thought to offer the man a final farewell, but the sound of conversation crept out through the crack.

"How can you be sure she's telling you the truth, Jenny?"

"I can't, but at the same time, do you know many people privy to Casement's plan?"

There was silence in the office. Dubh held his breath.

"No. She told this to you, herself?"

"Not in so many words, no. Listen James, I don't understand it myself, but she's been at it for weeks – dropping hints, like, and saying things she shouldn't know."

"And you're certain she's not playing you?"

"I wish I could be sure, but I cannot think that the Brits have wee spies infiltrating our ranks. They've too much to contend with in Germany to worry themselves about us. Those two aren't what they say they are, but they're not spies, either."

"You say your nephew found them?"

"Aye. He brought them up as help for me – as if there aren't enough hungry mouths in Dublin looking for work."

She snorted lightly and Connolly made sympathetic noises of agreement.

"I took them on, though," the woman continued, her tone brisk. "I don't doubt they're alone in the world, but they carry themselves well. The boarders like that sort of thing. I was in service, mind, before I married Mr. Mallory. Miss Maureen is as fine a young lady as I've ever seen, and the lad, too."

"And? Come on, Jenny, out with it."

There was a sigh. "I want her – both of them – to come here. I caught them arguing in the garden the other day. She knows something more – more than Casement, mind – and the lad doesn't want her to share it. All the same, I can see *she's* keen to tell me. I don't understand it. I may never understand it, but there's a light in her eyes, James."

"And coming here will what, scare the information out of them?" There was laughter in Connolly's voice. "I can try, but it sounds like the lad might be a bit of a problem."

"He may be at that. I have him in the shop now. O'Toole is there, watching him."

"He'd be better off at St. Edna's or here, where we can keep an eye on him."

"Ah, James – she's very protective of him. Splitting them up may backfire. Let me bring them to you first. See what they have to say."

"That's fine, Jenny. Pearse will be in for the council meeting tomorrow. Bring them 'round an hour or so before and we can all have tea together, aye?"

"That'll be grand. Thank you."

There was movement from within and Dubh darted down the hall and out of sight.

It was already too late. Niamh was right. He could no longer simply snatch them from this time. They had changed too much already and now he had to make sure their history played out as it should.

What was it Niamh had said? The time was locked. Things – lives – must be taken and given in equal measure. She told him he knew what would need to happen, and he did.

The leaders of the 1916 Rising must die, and it meant seeing this battle through to the bitter, bloody end.

Twelve

"Grab your coat, lad – we've an appointment in the city. Declan can manage the shop this afternoon."

Sean shot Maureen a quick glance but she motioned for him to grab his overcoat. Mrs. Mallory was already outside the cheerful cobalt storefront, fussing with its white bunting.

He untied his apron and tossed it to Declan O'Toole, store manager at Mallory's Dry Goods, and followed Maureen.

The tram ride was too short, and too loud to say anything to one another. Instead, they slowed their steps and trailed behind Mrs. Mallory as she led them through the throngs of people crowding the streets on this blustery Saturday afternoon.

Sean hunched his shoulders against the wind. "Do you know where we're going?"

"Headquarters I think – she mentioned tea."

"Headquarters?"

He looked up and scanned their surroundings. His skin prickled, but not with the cold. Liberty Hall was ahead. He had seen it when the nuns took them to Dublin the summer before. At the time, it had been empty – evacuated – and slated for demolition, but Sr. Theresa had regaled them with tales of its former glory. Once it had been known as the Northumberland Hotel, a chic nineteenth century city-centre guesthouse, only to be taken over by the nationalist movement. Eventually, it would house the Irish Citizen Army, a socialist and militaristic group headed by a one James Connolly. Connolly had recently joined forces with the Irish Volunteers – joined forces to plan a revolution.

"What do they want with us?"

Maureen did not have a ready answer and he rolled his eyes. "This isn't exactly what I would call not getting involved, you know."

A full month had passed since their walk in the park. Except for his birthday, which had featured a loud argument in the back garden, they had spent the better part of that month trying – and failing – to avoid the only thing that seemed to concern Maureen: the Rising. It had been a lonely month, one full of night terrors and daytime worries. Where was Dubh?

"We're not involved," she countered. "We may just be going to have tea."

He snorted. Not bloody likely, he wanted to say, but did not. She was already annoyed with him for putting a stop to her idea of letting someone know about the weapons in the Trinity Arts Department.

"Look, I just told her enough to make her believe me. Small bits of information, things only someone involved would know."

"And now they want to know more – want to know how you know, aye?"

Her face blanched. "She's not a bad woman, Sean. I just don't think she trusts us."

"There's no real reason for her to," he hissed. "And don't you dare pretend you aren't even a little excited."

Maureen had been staring down at the pavement, her lips a thin line but now the corner of her mouth lifted in a small smile. "And you're not?

How many people back home can say they've met with the leadership of the 1916 Rising – and sat down to tea with them?"

"Not many – not many still living, anyway."

"Right – and don't look at me like that. We'll still be living when all of this is done."

He looked ahead to where Mrs. Mallory was waving for them to catch up.

"I hope so, Maureen."

Mrs. Mallory ushered them into what was arguably an office. There was a desk, a few chairs and a bookshelf. Yet, most of the surfaces, including chairs, were covered with documents, maps, scraps of paper and pamphlets.

A young woman had taken their coats and announced them to the room's occupants. Two men – one tall, his three-piece suit slightly rumpled, and the other shorter and stout, with round glasses jammed on his nose – stood as they entered.

"Mrs. Mallory, it is good to see you again," said the bespeckled gentleman.

Maureen glanced quickly at Sean. They knew what James Connolly looked like. They had seen his picture more than once in their history books. But flat, black and white pictures, and dry pages of type were nothing compared to the man himself.

The gentleman next to him was the headmaster of St. Edna's, a poet, and member of the Irish Republican Brotherhood: Patrick Pearse. He offered his hand to Mrs. Mallory and though his greeting was congenial, he looked at all four of them with obvious scepticism.

"Well let's not stand on ceremony, Pearse – everyone – sit, please. Tea?"

"Thank you." Mrs. Mallory turned to Pearse. "Did Connolly fill you in on our conversation yesterday?"

"He did, but I would rather discuss it without these two present, if you don't mind," he said with a quick nod at Sean and Maureen.

"Ah Pat, look at 'em. You're training lads younger than these two at St. Edna's."

"Aye, but they've been vetted. We don't even know who these two really are."

"I can help you with that, Mr. Pearse," Maureen interrupted. Sean had guessed it accurately during their walk, but then, she had as well – a week ago. She knew at some point, Mrs. Mallory would need to validate Maureen's information. She would have said something – even included Sean in the hatching of the plan – only, she wished he wouldn't look so—so scared and angry all the time.

It had taken her the better part of the week to think up some reason for how she knew the information she had given Mrs. Mallory. As excuses went, hers was weak, but she had relied on the woman wanting to believe her more than cold facts. James Connolly and Patrick Pearse might not be so easily fooled.

"My name is Maureen O'Malley and this is Sean McAndrew. Before they died, our mothers worked in a Big House near Newport. We were raised there before we were sent to the abbey – but we weren't at the abbey for nearly as long as Gerry believed," she amended, looking directly at Mrs. Mallory.

The woman smiled as if this confirmed some suspicion on her part.

"We didn't exactly grow up with a great love for the Empire – no one in the family did. I'm not sure why. I do know that there was always someone about, talking about Home Rule and then the Free State – talking about plans and whatnot. I picked up a few things – learned to listen. When we were sent away, I convinced Sean we had to do something about what was coming. Happening upon Gerry was just a lucky chance."

"But why are you here now?"

She opened her mouth but before she could think of something to appease the suspicion in Pearse's face, Connolly interrupted.

"They're here because I asked them to be." The man was no longer smiling – but neither was his face as guarded as Pearse's was. "And I asked them to be here because the girl has information we'd like to hear."

She ground her teeth into her lip. There was little else she could say without them thinking she was some kind of witch – or crazy person. Besides, Sean was listening and she had a promise to keep.

"I'm not sure what else I can tell you that I haven't already told Mrs. Mallory."

"Then perhaps we'd just like to hear it from you." Connolly kept his voice bland, but firm.

Maureen glanced at Mrs. Mallory.

"You know, about the *Aud*," the woman prodded.

Maureen arched an eyebrow. "The *Libau,* you mean?"

Sean inhaled sharply and Connolly's attention shifted to him.

"You disagree with this, lad?"

"I'm no loyalist, if that's what you mean. I know what's at stake. I'm just – I'm not . . ."

"You're not a warrior, then – is that it?"

"Warrior," Sean echoed.

Chills raced up Maureen's neck. Connolly's choice of words filled her mind's eye with images of a cloaked warrior, framed by fire – a warrior who battled an army with only his sword so they might escape harm.

A warrior who could not – or would not – help them now.

"No, sir. I don't think I am."

Maureen put her hand on Sean's and glared at Connolly. There was no shame in not fighting. The other man shrugged.

"Enough of this." Mrs. Mallory's voice sounded tired. "Tell them what you know, lass. There's no room in my place for people who can't be useful."

Maureen's mouth fell open with shock and she stared at Mrs. Mallory. The other woman's face twisted and her lips formed a thin line.

Too late, Maureen realized her error. Mrs. Mallory was risking her reputation with the rebel leadership by bringing them in. If Maureen proved uncommunicative, then the woman's place within the Rising was open to question. Mrs. Mallory had given them a roof over their heads, food for their bellies and meaningful work, and in return, Maureen had taunted her with titbits of information she could not substantiate. Shame flushed her cheeks and she dropped her gaze from Mrs. Mallory's care-worn face.

Sean opened his mouth but she squeezed his hand.

"It's alright – let me. We agreed to this, remember?" she whispered, and, not waiting for him to respond, she turned back to Pearse and Connolly. "Mrs. Mallory is right. I do have information. Your plans to get weapons from Germany are not going to succeed."

"Is that so? And just how is it you came by this information?"

"I can't tell you, but it is the truth. If you don't do anything, on April 20, you'll remember this and you'll know. Warn Roger Casement to make sure the *Libau* has a radio – don't change the date for the pickup in Kerry – do something."

She looked between Connolly and Pearse. They stared back at her, their foreheads creased in mirror images of confusion.

"It's too late for that, lass. Casement left Germany yesterday – and the *Libau* a few days before him." Connolly turned to Pearse. "It would be like that damn fool not to have a bloody radio on the ship," he muttered. "Don't tell Clarke."

He turned back to Maureen. "Is that all you have, then?"

Too late.

Connolly's words echoed in her head. It was too late. Too late.

She cursed herself – she should have known it would be too late, but the despair clawed at her anyway. Their failure was her failure now.

"What else would you have me say?"

Mrs. Mallory stood. "It isn't all she has. I heard them one afternoon, out in the garden, arguing about Trinity. Tell them, girl. I cannot protect you now if you won't cooperate."

"Now you listen here!"

"Sean, no!" Maureen grabbed at him as he lurched to his feet. "We don't have a choice anymore," she hissed. "You were right. It wasn't enough."

He had railed at her that day in the garden, nearly begged her not to give them access to more guns, and she had let it go. It was his sixteenth birthday, after all.

"Nothing will ever be enough for them." He

gestured to Mrs. Mallory. "She says she can't protect us now – but who will protect us if you do tell them, Maureen?"

"We'll protect each other." She gave his shoulder a squeeze. It was what they had always done, and nothing was going to change that. "Besides, you know what's at stake."

Confused, Sean's gaze shifted between her and Mrs. Mallory, until at last Maureen saw the spark of understanding kindle in his eyes. It was not too late for Gerry to come back to Dublin to help his Aunt if she needed it. It was not too late for the boy to die in the Rising.

He relaxed in her grip and slipped away from her as soon as she let her arms drop to her sides. Connolly coughed noisily into a handkerchief and she turned back to them with a lifted chin. Her argument with Sean was none of their business.

"I can tell you Casement is planning to go to go to McNeil as soon as he lands in order to convince him to call off the Rising, and from the perspective of arms, he isn't wrong. You don't have near enough firepower to go against the British war machine."

"What are you saying, lass – is Casement a turncoat?"

"You can't possibly believe this, Connolly. The chit is mad."

"You're not listening to me." Maureen overrode Pearse's protest. "Even without Casement, Eoin MacNeill will try to shut you down. With the *Libau* sunk, and Casement arrested, he will succeed. You will change the date for the parade movements from Sunday to Monday, and the country will not rise as one. You need firepower. You need to convince him."

"She's not mad. She's a witch," Connolly

whispered as he stared at Maureen.

There was awe in his voice and Maureen allowed herself a small smile.

"Listen to her, Pat. She knows."

"She's a spy of some sort – she's playing us."

"I'm not. There is a weapons cache under the Arts Department in Trinity College. Send someone to check it out."

"Oh, certainly – so your bosses can nab one of us."

"I didn't say steal them in broad daylight," Maureen snapped. "Send someone to check. Keep us here until you can liberate them."

The two men exchanged glances.

"It can't hurt, I suppose," Connolly allowed.

Pearse nodded, but his expression was dark. "Fine. You will stay here until the weapons are secure, however."

Ignoring the flutter of nerves in her gut, Sean's glower, and Mrs. Mallory's tense expectation, Maureen nodded in agreement. "We'll wait."

"Is this what you wanted?" Sean growled at Maureen after the door to the small sitting room closed with a soft click. Mrs. Mallory had left them to wait until Pearse and Connolly could confirm the guns were where Maureen said they were. And just in case they decided to disobey orders, a key turned the lock with an obnoxious rattle.

Maureen did not answer his question.

"Is it?"

"What else could I do? You heard her. . ." her voice trailed off.

He wrapped his arms around himself. He had heard Mrs. Mallory and he could not stop shaking, even as Maureen's fingers touched his upper arm.

"What is going to happen to us?" He hated how plaintive – how weak – his voice sounded.

"Nothing." She shook him gently. "Nothing, Sean. They didn't believe me."

"Connolly did. And when they find the guns in Trinity, they all will. Oh, God." He could not continue. The implications of their teatime chat with the Rising's leadership raced out before him and he covered his face.

"Look, you said no fighting – I'm not fighting. I'm just giving information."

He uncovered his eyes. "Aye, information we're bloody hostages for."

"Now you know how it feels."

"Maureen, that's not what I meant."

She was turning from him. It was the closest she had ever come to talking about her time on Bingham's ship, but already her face had closed down.

"Forget it – I didn't mean anything."

He cursed under his breath and put a hand on her shoulder. "Promise me, Maureen."

She jerked herself free. "What do you want from me? I already—"

"Promise me, again."

Her lips twisted into a brief snarl and the air turned thick with anger, but he ignored it. He was not going to surrender – not this time.

"Promise me we won't do this. We will not fight. This isn't our war – it's not our time. We shouldn't be here and we shouldn't be helping. I can't believe I let you—"

"Let me? Who are you, Sean McAndrew, to be telling me what to do at all? I don't need your permission and I certainly don't need to promise you anything. I'm giving them a fighting chance. I'm giving them something to hold on to when everything else starts to collapse. That's it. It's hope."

"It's a nightmare. And it's one that will destroy a lot of people before it's played out."

"Then leave," she barked at him.

He stepped back, as though her words had slammed him in the chest. "Leave?"

"Yes. Leave." She was fighting tears now. "Make sure Gerry stays at home. Then you'll both be safe and you won't have to worry about what's happening here."

Her words spun around him like angry magpies and he stared at her.

"How could I leave?" he asked after what seemed like ages. The flush of anger was still high on her cheeks and the tears glittered unshed in the corners of her eyes. "I don't have a home without—" His breath caught in his throat. "We might never have a home if we don't get out of here, but I'm not leaving you here, with them."

She sniffed and brushed at her eyes with the back of her hand. "You make them sound like monsters, Sean. They're not. They're just men."

"All the same, I'll stay."

"Good – that's good." She looked up at him and gave him a half smile. When he did not answer it, she shrugged. "I wasn't planning on doing more, you know. I made a promise not to get us involved, and I won't. But, I'm not leaving, either. I want to see them proclaim the Republic. I want to hear it from Pearse's lips. I want to remember this – take it with me. They'll fail. They'll die, but I want to remember."

"And when it's done, will you be able to leave it?"

he asked. He didn't know if he wanted to hear her answer – or if he would believe her if she said 'yes' – but he had to try. "Truly? Will you be able to leave?"

"And go where?"

"Back to Carrickahowley. I've money saved for tickets." Maureen opened her mouth to speak but he rushed on. "Gerry will help us – I know he will. We won't starve, and we won't have to sleep rough."

"But, what would we *do*?"

"Live a life. Even if Dubh never finds us, we can have a life there, I know it."

She stared at him for a long time, searching his face. He did not know what she found there but after a few breathless minutes, she nodded.

"I promise."

Thirteen

He found her in the garden. The guns under Trinity had been liberated, and safely brought to headquarters. After a day and nightmare-plagued night rattling around Liberty Hall, he and Maureen had been allowed to go back to the boarding house. Of course, Connolly had looked as though he would rather keep a close eye on them himself, but Mrs. Mallory assured Connolly they would be safe with her.

And safe they were, but it was a hollow victory. Despite Maureen's promise, despite the seeming understanding they had come to, she would not look at him, let alone talk to him. She avoided him when she could and Mrs. Mallory took care to keep them busy enough that it was the following Sunday before they could find time enough to talk without the woman overhearing.

Of course, he and Maureen had spent the better part of the month not talking, but after their argument at Liberty Hall, he thought he would scream with all the things they no longer said to one another.

He watched Maureen trail her fingers along a peeling trellis overburdened with old vines. Her face, once ruddy with health and good humour, contrasted starkly against the nimbus of her dark curls. She seemed to shimmer in the damp air, as though she were one of the Good Folk – as though she were about to slip from sight and into that other, unseen world.

He cleared his throat.

She looked up and quickly shoved her hands in her pockets. The untidy patch of new green snatched at her feet as she made her way to him.

"Talking to the garden, were you?" he asked by way of greeting.

Head cocked to the side, she regarded him for a moment. She no longer shimmered, but there was something distant about her – as though she were still wandering beyond him.

"No," she breathed. "I – I was thinking."

"About?"

"You – this place. Dublin." She shook her head. "You were right. They won't stop asking me questions. It's like I'm some sort of pet soothsayer."

He had to clench his teeth to stop the automatic 'I told you so.' Recriminations never seemed to work on Maureen.

"Haven't you done enough?" he asked instead.

"I don't know."

She finally looked him in the eye. There were dark circles under hers, and they seemed almost too green – too bright.

"I just don't know anymore, Sean."

The prickle of nameless dread swelled and heat flamed his cheeks but he forced himself to keep his voice even. "Maureen, what if they're meant to fail? Have you given any thought to what our world will look like if they win?"

She flinched. "I'm afraid of what our future looks like if they keep fighting – fighting like they're doing in our time. What if winning now stops all that?" Her voice was no more than a whisper. "I keep – I keep hearing this voice that tells me to help them. No matter what I do, it keeps insisting."

"A voice?"

"Not all the time – just in dreams." She looked at him. "At least, I think they're dreams."

"You too?"

They stared at each other. He supposed he should be relieved he was not the only one visited by visions of destruction night after night, but instead he simply felt empty.

"I've been having them for a while," she admitted. Her voice was small, defeated almost.

Sean grimaced slightly. Maureen had been carrying this for far too long, and he had not noticed – but then, neither had she. "Me, too."

"Since Grania."

He opened his mouth and closed it again. His had only started once they arrived in Dublin. He wanted to ask her what happened in her dreams, but already she was turning from him.

"Who do you think . . .?" It was harder to ask than he thought it would be.

"What?"

He clenched his fists and forced the words out. "Well, I just thought maybe Dubh was responsible for them – mine, anyway."

The laugh caught in her throat and he winced. He hated the derision in her voice any time they talked about the man. He hated the fact that, as time went on, and they remained alone in a city on the brink of revolution, he began to share her contempt.

"I think," Maureen began, a small smile lighting up her face, "sending us dreams would be even more obscure than pretending to be a gallowglass and letting us swab the deck for a month while he travelled the high seas on some adventure for our captain."

Sean thought about it and shrugged. "Not really."

Her lips twitched. She started to nod and giggle, and an answering laugh bubbled in his chest. They stood before the wild garden as peals of mirth shook them to their knees.

They held onto one another until tears poured down their cheeks. She told him about the dreams, about the horror she saw. She told him how it made her feel – as though she had to do something – anything – to make the anxiety go away. He told her about the desolation he saw and the endless searching in a night filled with noise.

They did not agree on what the dreams meant.

He wanted to protest, wanted to insist they must mean *something*, but as her face gave way to the exhaustion hiding just beneath her laughter, he retreated. She had given him her promise to leave the city. It would be over soon; he could let it rest. Yet, even as he relented, his heart pounded with the same sickening urgency.

The Rising was only a week away.

Fourteen

"Sir, I have a special delivery here for you." Dubh patted the courier's sack slung across his shoulders. Sir Matthew Nathan was the Under-Secretary for Ireland, head of the British Empire's administration in Ireland, and his office in Dublin Castle was as tidy as Connolly's office in Liberty Hall was disordered.

Sir Nathan glanced up from the handwritten letters stacked neatly before him.

"You're not the regular courier – what happened to Samuel?"

Dubh saluted smartly. "I have clearance from London, sir, and was tasked with delivering this missive, along with my new orders."

Sir Nathan regarded Dubh above his spectacles, actually looking at him this time and taking in his officer's uniform. "At ease, Captain . . . what's this say? Captain Doyle McAlister. Irish?"

"No, Sir." He held his arms stiffly at his sides. "My mother's people were, but I was born and raised in Inverness."

"Indeed. Well then, let us have it."

Dubh handed off the typed note from Room 40 of Her Majesty's Admiralty. It referenced a Sir Roger Casement and an arms shipment due to arrive in Ireland in three days' time, on a steam ship masquerading as the Norwegian cargo transport, the *SS Aud.*

"Who gave this to you, Captain?"

"I'm not certain, Sir Nathan. It came through channels, but I was never told its provenance."

Sir Nathan grunted and pushed away from his desk.

"This note is next to meaningless unless I can determine its validity. What are they thinking up there, sending me dates for a bloody rebellion without putting some sort of authority on it?"

"Sir?"

"Never mind, Captain. Where are you meant to be stationed?

"I was told to report to a Col. Cowan, sir."

"Well, do that then. This," he waved the nondescript typed note in the air, "no longer concerns you. Good day, Captain."

Dubh saluted and slipped out of Sir Nathan's office. He had read that the man would not seek, nor be granted, authority to do anything about the note until it was too late, but it was a start. At least now, the British were on their guard. At least now, there was a chance at making sure next week's events played out according to history's plan.

Fifteen

Maureen hovered in the drawing room, her feather duster poised above the carriage clock. Mrs. Mallory was in the kitchen, arguing with her afternoon guests. She had not seen them arrive, but she knew their business was likely rebellion-related, and it was not good news. The words "*Libau*" and "sunk," reached her ears through the two walls separating them from her.

The dusting forgotten, she slipped into the hall. There had not been time to warn Roger Casement or the crew of the *Libau* that the British had discovered their ruse, but Thomas Clarke had ordered a group of men to wait at the rendezvous point yesterday. As she listened in the hallway, she understood these men had met with disaster on the road – a car crash.

Her heart thudded loudly in her ears with a mix of exhilaration and fear. She had hoped the weapons under the Trinity Arts Department would prevent the frightened chaos that originally followed the sinking of the German steamboat and its cargo three days before the Rising.

Perhaps, as Sean said, it was as it should be – even though the thought made her throat tighten.

"Jenny, the *Libau* is gone. Even with the guns under Trinity, MacNeill has cancelled the movements for Sunday. Pat sent me down here with a summons. She and the boy have to come to

Liberty Hall."

"What, for more information? I don't think she has any, Willie."

"Aye, well Pat thinks otherwise. He also has more than a few questions about how the British discovered the shipment."

The duster clattered to the floor and Maureen brought her fingers to her mouth. Spies. Trinity notwithstanding, they still thought she and Sean were spies.

A harsh laugh sounded from within the kitchen.

"You must be joking. They've been in my care for these last two months. They're quick, respectful and keen. Whether they know more or no, they're not spies."

"I'm just following orders, Jenny – they have to come."

Maureen froze as Mrs. Mallory and Patrick Pearse's younger brother, Willie, opened the door into the kitchen.

"Maureen, there you are." The woman flashed Maureen a big smile and pretended not to notice she had been eavesdropping. "Come along, lass – we're going to headquarters. We'll collect Sean on the way."

Mrs. Mallory elbowed her way through the crowd of men camped in the hallway outside Connolly's office in Liberty Hall. An ominous undertone had overtaken the general din of the Citizen Army headquarters.

Maureen tried to free her arm from the woman's grip, but Mrs. Mallory was not letting go. Sean trailed behind them, flanked by Willie Pearse.

There had been no time to answer his confusion when they collected him from the shop. Mrs. Mallory and Willie had been too close behind for anything more than a breathless hello and instruction to grab his overcoat.

A tall, thin man, with his full brown beard mussed and suit rumpled, burst from Connolly's office. Angry words followed him out.

"Damnit, man! We have to risk something if we're ever to bring the world's eyes on us – if we're ever to get the foreigners out of Ireland!"

Connolly and Pearse appeared in the doorway. Connolly's face was pale but for the bright red spots on his cheek, and he held onto the doorframe with bloodless fingers.

"Another time, Connolly. We aren't ready," Eoin MacNeill said over his shoulder. His tone softened briefly. "I'd rather wait another year than kill a thousand men in a futile attempt. Casement is in jail. We don't have enough guns, even with the arms from Trinity. They have the advantage. They know."

"Aye, they may. But Eoin, what is the price of freedom?"

"Not unarmed boys, Connolly. Not if I can do anything about it."

MacNeill pushed his way through the crowd and Connolly stared after him. His shoulders slumped slightly and all those gathered in the hallway held their breath.

No one spoke. No one knew what to say.

With a snarl, Connolly hurled himself back into his office. Maureen heard the thump and clatter as the contents of his desk were tossed to the floor.

Still the group did not disperse. Pearse stood where his comrade had been and caught his brother's eye.

It was the only warning they had. Willie grabbed Sean's arm and pushed Maureen ahead of him. Mrs. Mallory, making small sounds of annoyance at Willie's back, was close behind.

Connolly looked up as they entered his office. His face was dark and he had been muttering to himself as he stood amid his own disarray. He glared at each of them until his gaze came to rest on Maureen.

He rushed at her with a roar and grabbed her by the shoulders before she could even flinch. "You." He gave her shoulders a shake. Hard eyes bored into hers. "You knew this would happen."

"Aye. I told you it would happen," she snapped.

"Can we stop MacNeill?"

"Short of shooting him? No."

Connolly chuckled and released her. "I like how you think, lass."

"Thank heavens for small mercies," Maureen muttered. She rubbed her arms where his fingers had bit into them and glared at him.

"Is there nothing – nothing at all – in that wee canny brain of yours that will help us?"

"I've already told you."

"What, about Casement?" This was Pearse. He stepped around the debris of strewn papers and the spilled inkwell. "The lads in Kerry are keen to rescue him."

"Are you mad? He's in the Tower."

"Maureen."

Sean tried to push around Mrs. Mallory but Maureen caught his eye and shook her head.

"Aye, she's right. Trying to rescue Casement at this point would be suicide." Connolly scribbled something on a scrap of paper and handed it off to

Willie. "Give this to Clarke. If he questions you, tell him I said it to you all – the Kerry lads are to do nothing."

Willie nodded smartly and hurried from the office. As soon as he was gone, Connolly rounded on Maureen again.

"Is this it, then – is there nothing you can do that will give us the advantage? Nothing to prove that you didn't feed our information to the British? I hear Casement only managed to get us 20,000 rifles. It isn't much, certainly, but it would have helped."

"I am not a traitor," she snarled. "I just saved the lives of the lads who would have gone after Casement. The British knew about the shipment because they intercepted messages from the German Embassy in the States. The Brits don't like having their ships sunk by German U-boats, so I'm pretty certain they were paying careful attention. More than you lot seem to be."

"Now, you listen here, you—"

"Connolly, leave off."

Pearse pushed himself between them and Sean was there to cup her elbow as she stumbled back. She looked at him and tried to muster a smile of thanks but he was not looking at her. His eyes darted around the room. He was watching, waiting.

Connolly glared at Pearse. "You're the one who thought she might be a traitor."

"If I were a traitor, would I kill you off by inches like this?"

Both men turned to stare at her. She gazed back, eyebrows arched.

Pearse acknowledged this with a brief bow of his head. "Indeed. If the British really knew what we were after, they'd have arrested all of us as soon as the ship sank."

"They may yet, Pearse – oh no, not because of the wee spitfire in our midst. Calm down, lad." Connolly waved a dismissive hand in Sean's direction and turned back to Pearse. "Let MacNeill call them off. Let him think he's won. Then we'll tell them ourselves to stand to arms on Monday."

"It is a holiday," Pearse allowed. "We'll still have a captive audience, and the army will still be caught unprepared."

"Right. They may know we're up to something, but they don't know where, and they don't know how."

Pearse did not respond right away and Maureen held her breath as he glanced about the room. He looked at them all in turn, but his eyes were far away.

"Aye," he said finally. "Call the rest of the council. We'll have to mobilize runners to get the word out, but it can be done."

Sixteen

Maureen woke with a gasp, drenched with sweat. She clutched at the thin quilt and tried to get warm, tried to stop her body from quivering with the memory of the dream. It was as she told Sean; they never truly left her.

Hands reached out to her from the mists, beseeching. Whole scores of people drifted in a plain, weeping and crying out. Yet others were angry and ran up against what seemed like a wall of soldiers. Men shouted words she did not understand and the sound of marching feet soon began to bellow in her ears.

The land itself was torn asunder, and it filled her with anguish so deep she thought it would consume her. She could have healed the rift, if only she knew what to do – but now, it was too late for her to do anything. She had already promised to leave Dublin after Pearse issued the Proclamation. She had promised to give it all up and build a life in the country – promised to wait for a saviour she feared would never find them again.

Tears streaked her cheeks. They were fruitless tears, but she let them fall. Her heart ached for the people she could not help and she wept for the men she knew would die before the day was over. She wept until the sky lightened, stained faintly with pink.

Empty of anguish – empty of everything except

a distant sort of interest – she watched the sunrise. It was Easter Monday. It was time.

"What is this? What's happening here?"

"Maude, get a load of this rubbish."

"Mum! Look!"

Maureen smiled as the young boy tugged on his mother's coat and pointed at the two flags hoisted on the General Post Office's flagpoles. One was the familiar green but the other sported blocks of green and orange separated – united – by white.

In the street, Willie Pearse was growling at passers-by as he tried to set up a barricade. The rebels inside knew the British Army would come. They knew the barricade would not hold, but it did not matter. They would defend it until they could no longer stand.

She passed out the last of the notices proclaiming the new provisional government of a free Ireland and made her way through the press of bodies to Sean. He insisted they mask themselves in the middle of the crowd – it would be easier to slip away – but he still did not look pleased. She knew he did not understand.

"They only let a few of the people inside the post office go, Maureen."

"There weren't too many people in there to begin with. They'll be all right." She linked her arm through his and squeezed.

Pearse and Connolly emerged from the building to stand on the portico. Willie stopped complaining and saluted his commanders. At noon, they had stopped traffic while leading 150 men from Liberty Hall to the post office. No one knew what to think of all the commotion and a sizeable group had gathered before the massive columns of the Georgian building. The two men chatted quietly and the stocky leader of the Citizen's Army stood off to the side while Pearse stood between the columns to address his fellow citizens.

"Irishmen and Irishwoman: In the name of God and of the dead generations from which she receives her old tradition of nationhood, Ireland, through us, summons her children to her flag and strikes for her freedom . . ."

The ache in Maureen's heart refused to go away. Her promise to Sean was a promise to hide, to allow part of her spirit to wither away and die. How could she leave these people? How could she leave this fight? Yes, Sean was right – it was late to stop the British from coming and too late to stop the looting and the death of innocents.

It was also too late to stop the flame of nationalism from spreading across the city, and then the country, as the Rising's leaders were executed one-by-one.

Too late.

It was not too late.

She knew what the Volunteers could do – should do – to survive, to delay the surrender, to challenge fate.

She slipped from Sean's side and began to push her way through the crowd.

He was right behind her. He grabbed her arm.

"What are you doing? Where are you going?"

She stopped and stared into his eyes. "Saving them."

"No!"

"Let me go." She yanked her arm from his grip and started to run. Pearse was finished reading the

Proclamation. The Rising had begun.

"You cannot be serious. You're allowing this?"

"She was rather convincing, lad." Pearse handed a slip of paper off to Willie and focused on Sean. "And I'm surprised you're not there with her. She could use your help."

"She could use yours, too. You sent her alone?" Sean tried to keep his voice low, to keep from screaming.

When Maureen slipped away from him, he had been too shocked to do anything, too shocked to fight the crowd and too shocked to move.

And, in his shock, he had lost her.

She had enough time to explain to Pearse and Connolly that Dublin Castle was relatively undefended, and only Sir Mathew Nathan, the English Under-Secretary for Ireland, and two other officials, were in residence.

He arrived in time to hear her tell them that if Seán Connolly, captain of the regiment tasked with the mission to take the Castle, would only press his advantage, the Rising could disrupt communications between Dublin and England.

He stood by, helpless, as Pearse and Connolly sent her out into the city to intercept Seán and his men. She fled with barely a look at him, to prevent the squad from retreating, as history remembered.

"Lad, I can't spare anyone. Near one thousand Volunteers defied MacNeill, but we need more. The Four Courts are secured, and there are lads in St. Stephen's Green. Those, along with the group at the factory, should give Maureen and Seán some protection while they take on the Castle. I wish I had more to send, but I don't. I don't even have enough to secure the ports or the train stations. The British will come, but this might hold them off a bit longer."

"You're just delaying the inevitable!"

"No boy, we're testing their resolve to destroy their own city," Connolly put in. He grabbed Sean's shoulder and with a rough hand, turned him around. "What are you doing here, boy? Didn't you say you weren't a warrior? Get yourself somewhere safe and stay there."

"That's what I was trying to do before Maureen went tearing off. Before you sent her—"

"Even if I were so inclined, there's little I could do to stop Maureen. Nothing you could do, either. You've two options, lad. Join us here, or find some place to lick your wounds."

Sean rubbed his shoulder and watched Connolly walk off. Pearse spared him a brief shrug and moved on to the group of lads building the barricades.

His chest was tight, and their words buzzed in his ears like so many stinging bees. He spun around.

Help. He had to get help, but there was no one.

Maureen had been right about that. They were on their own – had been from the start.

He stood on the portico and glared out at the people still wandering in the street. This was madness, but he was not going to lose Maureen to it.

He started to run. If he was fast, he could still collect her and get out of Dublin before the Army closed down the city.

Seventeen

Seán Connolly, a stage actor and now Captain in the Irish Citizen Army, silently motioned for his men to follow him into Dublin Castle's guardroom. Maureen hung back. Even though the three men stationed within were only eating their lunch, all she had to defend herself with was the knife Grania had given her and a sidearm she did not know how to use.

She had joined the group at the castle just as Captain Connolly was considering retreating to City Hall. His explosives were wet, and he had no idea that the rest of the castle was practically empty.

He met the messenger and his new orders – to press the attack – with scepticism, even after the guards proved easily subdued.

"Are you certain the rest of the castle is unguarded?" Captain Connolly's face betrayed a heady mix of emotions, from distrust to exhalation.

"Yes." Maureen made shooing motions towards the castle proper. "This room is secure – you need to contain Sir Nathan." The Under-Secretary had to have heard the shooting – he was probably already calling London. They had to act.

"Right. George, take yourself and five men and keep an eye on the courtyard. Tom, get Chris and mind the entrance to the state apartments. Once we're certain the castle is empty, and Nathan secured, we'll reinforce all the gates. Now, lass – where is Nathan?"

Everything froze as the words 'I don't know' echoed in her head. Before she could utter the damning admission, the sounds of a scuffle brought them both to the hallway.

"Surrender or we will take measures to secure this building."

She peered around the captain's arm. Three men – their well-tailored suits rumpled and sweat-stained – stood in the hall brandishing brave words and fists. The man in the middle immediately caught her attention. His gaze was dark, but his high forehead smooth, as though he were only slightly perturbed at this affront to his authority.

Sir Nathan. It had to be.

"Maureen!"

She tore her eyes from the Under-Secretary to see Sean attempt to push his way through the crowd of militants blocking the hall. The rest of his words were lost as the sound of a hammer being cocked echoed in her ear.

She could not see who it was but she knew, if a shot was fired in the crowded hallway, things were going to get ugly – uglier than they already were – fast. Dublin Castle was within her grasp; it had to be taken at all costs.

Captain Connolly had his hands on her shoulders in an attempt to pull her out of the burgeoning melee, but she locked her knees and wrenched herself free. As she broke from his grip, she shouted at Sean to stand back. Her sidearm found its way to her hand and before anyone registered what was happening, she took hold of the barrel and clubbed the Under-Secretary in the head. He stumbled and dropped to his knees. His friends, too stunned by her attack, stared at her.

It was distraction enough. The rebels seized the other men and wrestled them to the ground as Maureen stood, numb, over Nathan.

It was done.

Dublin Castle was secure.

"Maureen, what are you doing – what have you done?"

"Done? Nothing. I'm taking a stand. They need our help."

"No, they don't. Helping them changes things, Maureen. You're talking about changing history in real ways – not just a bit of information here or a hint there."

"But Sean, think about it." Her eyes were bright and a beautiful smile lit her face.

It terrified him and made him want to cry at the same time.

"If we help – if they succeed – maybe there won't be a civil war. Maybe partition won't happen. Maybe—"

"Maybe we won't live to find out," he spat, not even trying to keep the scorn out of his voice. "Helping them destroys our world. That's what the dreams meant. You know it."

"I don't know what those dreams meant, and neither do you. Get off your high horse. It's time to believe in something."

"I do."

"And what's that? Preservation? Of what? Our world, the one where we're orphans, controlled by nuns, the state and people who don't know us? No, Sean. This is more than that."

Sean growled and pulled at his hair. "Maureen, you don't believe that. Think of Sr. Theresa. Think of all the people who love you."

"Don't you dare throw Sr. Theresa at my head. This has nothing to do with her."

"You aren't listening to me. You want this for you, but this isn't about you. This is about our families – our grandparents. Would you stop a moment and think what doing this is going to do to them?"

"Sean, it's different. This is politics."

"No it isn't, Maureen. Politics, war – it has a personal effect. This is personal. It's personal for me. You promised me."

She paused for just a moment and he thought he saw her eyes flicker with emotion. Regret? Confusion? He didn't know, but it wasn't his friend who started at him through those green eyes.

"I know, Sean. And I'm sorry."

He did not believe her, but he had no chance to challenge her empty words. She drew away from him as Captain Connolly approached them, a folded paper in his hand.

"Maureen, I need you to deliver a message to the GPO. We're secure here. George will tell you the password on your way out." He looked pointedly between Maureen and Sean as he handed her the slip of paper.

Maureen nodded smartly. "Certainly, Captain."

Sean followed as she headed into the courtyard and grabbed her elbow.

"We need to get out of here."

"I'm not going anywhere. I belong here – they need me."

"For what? Message running? Supplies? Oh, aye, I can see you're quite the important personage around these parts."

She took no notice of his sarcasm. "Look, this may not be your fight, but it is mine. The longer they're able to hold out here, the more things will change. I feel it. I know it."

"You're delusional, Maureen. I can't stay here. I can't watch you do this." He turned to walk through the courtyard alone.

"Sean . . ."

He turned. Hope flared in his chest and died when he saw her face.

"I tried, Sean. I tried to be quiet. I tried for your sake. But I can't – I won't."

"I'm not asking you to be quiet, Maureen. I'm asking you not to die. I'm asking you to think about what you're doing."

"I have."

"There are other ways."

"No – not for me."

He had lost her.

Numbness swept over his body. He heard her words, knew what they meant, but he could not muster the energy to combat her mindless belief. Nothing he could say – nothing he had been saying for nearly three months – would change her mind. And he could not follow her.

"You know if you do this, the army will round you up with the rest of them – if you aren't killed first."

"No. I'll get out before they do."

"Where will you go? Mrs. Mallory's isn't safe."

"No, but other places will be. What about you?"

She was saying goodbye.

"I'm getting out. I can't stay here – the army is going to lock this city down and I don't want to be trapped here when they do. I'll telegraph Gerry when I get to Kildare. He knows. I told him we – well, he'll have a place for me, anyway. I'll wait for you there."

Maureen nodded and squeezed his shoulder. Then she was gone, her message – her mission – clutched in her hand.

Maureen bit the insides of her cheeks and tasted blood, but at least the tears did not fall. She did not know what she had expected Sean to do. He was right, of course. He had nowhere else to go in the city and Mrs. Mallory's boarding house was not safe. Nowhere in Dublin really was.

George muttered the password at her and she slipped out onto the street. As soon as his back was turned, she started to run.

She dodged small knots of loiterers who were beginning to rumble darkly and darted past anyone who looked official. She ran until she could no longer breathe – ran as though the image of Sean standing there alone chased her. She ran and left him, and the debacle at Dublin Castle, behind.

She crossed the Liffey but ducked into a lonely alley, safe from prying eyes, safe from Sean's reproachful stare. She leaned her head against the cool brick of the wall behind her and let the tension of their argument seep from her skin into the damp cobbles beneath her. The decision had been made and worrying about it now did no one – not Sean, not the rebels – any good. Sean would be safe with Gerry, and when this was over, she would join them. She would make it up to him, somehow.

With another deep breath, she rubbed at her face and lurched to her feet. She had a message to deliver to Pearse. And after that – after that she had to warn the lads in St. Stephen's Green that the British were going to try to drive them out by sniping at them from the roof of the Shelbourne Hotel.

Sean walked slowly, and let his feet lead him where they would. He knew he should get out of the city, and yet he could not bring himself to feel the necessary urgency.

He passed Stephen's Green and nodded to the Volunteers stationed there. A few of them recognized him from Liberty Hall, and did nothing to stop him as he slipped into the park. All he wanted was a quiet bit of green in which to think.

"God, what happened – why didn't she listen?" he muttered to himself. He knew the answer: the call of this madness was too loud. Maureen could hear nothing above it.

"Then make her."

Sean spun. He knew that voice.

A man was standing behind him, leaning on a cane. A low cap shadowed his face, but neither cap nor cane could hide the man's eyes or his voice.

"Dubh."

"That's Captain to you, lad. Captain Doyle. I was with Pearse and Connolly during the proclamation – followed you to the castle, aye? Why did you not stop her?"

The words touched the dread clawing at Sean's throat. "Stop her? How could I stop her? A speeding train couldn't stop her, now."

Dubh started to speak, but Sean's flood of panicky words would not be stopped.

"If you saw us, then you know what happened.

She's helping them and she's refusing to leave – she's so deeply enmeshed in this that there is no talking to her, no reasoning with her."

"Because you insist on using reason."

He snorted but Dubh grabbed him by the shoulders before he could turn away.

"Listen to me, lad. This is not a reasonable war. These men and women are full of emotion and passion. They sing about martyrs and blood sacrifice. This is danger, and love, and Maureen is throwing all she has at it. Use it. Speak to her. You are stronger than this."

Sean pulled himself from the man's grip and stumbled backwards. He spread his hands out in front of him, wishing they held some answer. Speak to her? Maureen was past listening.

"I lost my chance."

"No. Fight for her, not with her."

"But what can I do?"

"Only you know her. Only you." Dubh broke off and made fists with his hands. "I cannot do this. None of us belong here, lad."

All the questions Sean wanted to ask, like where Dubh had been the last three months, died in his throat. The man sounded scared. Even heading towards Bingham's boat, Dubh had not been scared.

"By the gods, there is so little I can do. Make this right, Sean, or lose her altogether."

Eighteen

"Young man, I understand Dublin Castle is under the control of the rebels. They already repulsed the men I sent out from Richmond Barracks and now those lads are holed up in City Hall," Col. Cowan remarked dryly after Sean was ushered into his office by an aide. The aide stood smartly by the door until dismissed, and even then, Sean suspected the heavily muscled young man was not far from his commander's door.

The Colonel's office was an oasis of calm from the chaos reigning in Dublin. It was a lean, spare centre of command, much like the man who sat behind the desk. He had a large map of the city spread before him; crosses and circles marked different groups and locations. Surrounding Dublin Castle, Sean spied a heavy circle and signs that could only represent the British Army.

"And while I would like to believe you," the Colonel continued, "I have a hard time swallowing the idea that Sir Mathew Nathan is still alive in there."

"He makes a good hostage, Colonel." Sean inclined his head respectfully. The British Army probably did not need his help, but they had it anyway. Maybe he knew a few things they did not. Maybe . . . maybe he could help.

"I'm sure you've noticed the Rising is spread a little thin. The rebels have less than one hundred men in there. I think it was luck and some quick planning that allowed them to hold off your troops, but they barely have enough to guard all the entrances. They're especially weak here, and here."

Sean pointed to the other areas of the map and noted with a small twinge of pride that one of his suggestions did not have the marks of a known location.

Col. Cowan folded his hands over the map and looked at Sean. His eyes were tired but his face betrayed no other weakness. Two days into the uprising, the Volunteers and British Army were entrenched in their respective – strategic – positions. The British had managed to isolate the rebel unit within Dublin Castle, but little else had gone according to history's plan, insofar as Sean could tell.

"Why are you telling me this, boy? Or rather, how is it you've been allowed to tell me this?"

"I'm not feeding you bad information, Colonel, if that's what you think."

Honesty was best. It was his only defence – the only thing he knew to do. Dubh had not been exactly forthcoming with advice.

Yesterday, after collecting him from St. Stephen's Green, Dubh had led him through the quickly deteriorating city. Riots and looting – neither having anything to do with freedom or nationhood – had broken out throughout the city. They watched in the shadows as grown men and boys hurled rocks, bricks, bins – whatever they could find – into store windows to liberate food, clothes and the occasional bauble. They tore once-cheerful bunting from storefronts and burned it – a small stab at victory as British artillery rumbled through the streets.

He and Dubh turned from them, and Sean could have sworn he heard the big man whisper, "It is as it should be – gods, forgive me."

It was nightfall when they reached a tiny warehouse outside rebel and British traffic. Even so, Dubh would not rest. He was headed back out into the city, but before he left, he gave Sean one command: stop Maureen – and through her, stop the rebels.

Maureen was right. Dubh was not in the rescuing business.

At the thought of Maureen, his stomach twisted a little bit more.

"Fight for her," Dubh had said. He did not know how to fight, but he did know walking into Dublin Castle and demanding she stop – or worse, taking her against her will – was the last resort. Besides, he had already tried that and it had not worked out very well. Forcing the conclusion of the Rising, ending it as recorded in history, was his only option. That meant giving His Majesty's Royal Army a little help.

It had taken a full day for him to gather his courage and waltz into the barracks closest to Dubh's warehouse. He did not have any courage left – or Maureen's ingenuity – to make up stories for Col. Cowan.

"You're bringing in more field artillery, correct?" Sean asked instead of answering the Colonel's question. "You know Liberty Hall is empty, right? Oh, no, you didn't know that." He bit his lip and hurried on.

"You've already surrounded the Four Courts and the post office with big guns, so keep that up. Those are their biggest strongholds. There's more, but I'm not sure you'd believe me."

Col. Cowan raised his eyebrows. "I'm not certain what I believe, young man. While I appreciate your information, you still haven't told me why."

"I don't know myself, Colonel. It's just something I thought I had to do." Sean clasped his hands behind his back and stood tall. There was nothing else he could tell the man without further altering the outcome of the Rising.

"Just, please, send men in at those points I showed you. Bombard the castle with the artillery, and you'll likely be able to take it back."

Col. Cowan eyed the space between him and the door. Before Sean could react, the Colonel had called to the aide, stationed, as Sean suspected, right outside the door.

"Lad, I don't think you ought to go anywhere. With this kind of information floating around your head, I think it best we make you our guest. Just until this thing blows over, of course."

Sean snorted. "Guest? Or Prisoner?"

"That is up to you."

He eyed the aide. He was a big man – at least Sean's height and probably twice as wide. Struggling would be pointless, but he still had to try.

"I helped you." He pounded his fists on the Colonel's desk and the aide's meaty hands bit hard into his shoulders.

Col. Cowan put up a hand and the aide eased his grip.

"Precisely. Don't think I don't appreciate it. Would you rather be out there? It's going to get ugly."

"It's already ugly, Colonel – but you have to stop it. Keeping me isn't going to help you do that!"

"I disagree." Col. Cowan stood. He nodded to the

aide. The hands were back, gripping harder this time. "If you think of anything else that will help us with your Fenian friends, you'll let Pvt. Howell here know, so we can make note of it for your file."

"They aren't my friends – I just told you . . ." The words faltered and died as he stared at Col. Cowan. No one knew he was here. Dubh was in the guise of an insurgent, doing his part to help balance Maureen's madness, and Maureen thought he was headed to Carrickahowley.

The Colonel regarded him for a moment, his face a smooth mask.

"Private, don't put him in the general lockup – put him in one of the solitary bunks. If he is a traitor, I don't want the other rabble doing him harm." He looked back at Sean. "It's dangerous out there, lad. I'm doing you a favour."

Maureen kept to the shadows as she made her way along the quay. It was well past midnight and the gunship, which had been pounding the post office since dawn, was silent now. There were still soldiers about, however, and a contingent awaited her – or anyone like her – at the mouth of the bridge. She had no choice but to cross the Liffey; she needed to warn them.

She held her breath as a small squad of men passed her and prayed her cap kept her pale face hidden. There was no moon, but the city was on fire and an unnatural light filtered through the streets. She was not certain, but she believed it was early on Friday morning. Despite all she had done, the Rising was close to collapse.

Far from giving the army pause, taking Dublin

Castle and managing to hold on to St. Stephen's Green had lent the whole uprising a new sense of violence. In her forays to gather food and information, she discovered the raids on suspected sympathizers had started in earnest three days before. The army's hostility – even against innocents – was already turning some enclaves against them. Civilians were hurt, some dying, and people were going hungry. She missed him, but she was glad Sean had escaped the city when he did.

Beyond the bridge, and leading up to the post office, the streets were deserted. Firelight and shadows played across the destruction. She shivered and ran the rest of the way to the barricades; they were still in place at least. She did not have the password, but she would bully her way in if she had to.

No one even asked for the password – she was pulled in and surrounded immediately by men and voices.

"Lass, what's happening – have you news?"

"Did you see the horses out there? I did that."

"Shut up, Danny."

"Are you mad, woman, crossing the river? The area is crawling with soldiers." This was Connolly, sitting on a dirty mat on the floor while his secretary wound a bandage around his ankle. Joseph Plunkett lay next to him, coughing blood. They were dying, but there was still a spark in their eyes. They had not given up the fight.

"I wouldn't be a good scout if I let something like a regiment of soldiers stop me in the dark, now would I?" Maureen tossed at him. "And yes, Danny, I *smelled* the horses. The stench might do better than those barricades to protect you."

Pearse advanced on her. He looked tired but

pleased.

"We heard about the Castle. Captain Connolly was a brave—"

"Seán Connolly was a fool and got himself killed," Connolly muttered from the floor.

Pearse ignored him. "Did you join with Mallin's men at the College, then?"

"Aye, sir. The artillery was too much for us. Mallin sent me with a request for orders." Actually, the Countess Markievicz had sent her. Maureen had spent the last two days in that lady's company. She reminded Maureen of Grania – sharp tongued and sharp witted, but devoted to her cause, and those who flocked to her.

At least the Countess would still be alive when all this was over.

Pearse was shaking his head. "I have none. I was hoping you had another trick up your sleeve."

He put a hand on her shoulder. The suspicion that once marked his face was gone. She wished she could give him something for his hope and faith in her, but she had nothing left. She shook her head.

"Ah, well. Tell them to dig in." He pointed a finger at her. "No surrender – what is it Willie?"

Willie Pearse hung onto his brother's arm, breathless. He was a mess. Blood oozed from a cut on his forehead and burns glared angry and red on his hands.

"It's the fires, Pat. They've spread to the roof. We're working to contain it, but if we can't . . ."

Pearse swore loudly. "They'll be able to let the fire do their work for them – they can just pick us off one by one as we try to flee."

"Why don't you just tunnel into the next building?"

Pearse stared at her and his face broke into a huge smile. "Brilliant girl!" He turned to his brother. "Willie, take a few lads and have them start digging – I don't know what you should use, improvise lad!"

When he turned back to her, Pearse's eyes were alight with a desperate hope. "Thank you. Now, get back to the College, if you can. Do what you do best, lass, and inspire Mallin – remember, no surrender!"

"But—"

She wanted to warn him it was not safe, that they should do something – anything – to forestall the surrender, but he was already gone.

"You shouldn't be here."

It was a deep whisper at her ear and Maureen spun, startled. Blue eyes glared at her from a Volunteer uniform.

"You."

She had only seen him once, in the flesh, and it had been through flame, smoke, and terror. But it was him. It was Dubh.

He grabbed her arm and started walking.

"It's a death trap," she protested, her voice barely above a growl. She tried to wrench her arm from his grasp as he dragged her to the back of the post office, but she might as well have been pushing against a brick wall.

"I need to get them out of here – they'll die. They'll all die!"

He turned to glare at her. "Do you think your death will change any of that? I need you to come with me. Sean is missing."

Nineteen

"Tell me you've discovered something."
Maureen stood in the entrance of Dubh's safe house – a derelict warehouse near the quay, which had escaped the notice of the British, so far.

Dubh nodded and stood before her. He arched an eyebrow. "Are you going to let me pass?"

"Have you found him?"

"I found him."

"Where?"

Dubh looked pointedly at the room behind her and she moved aside. He was silent as he walked the length of the warehouse. She followed closely, careful to avoid the sword sheathed at his side. She had thought it was a cane, at first, until she had brushed up against it accidentally and heard the song of metal rattling against the scabbard.

A scream bubbled in her throat, but she clenched her fists and waited as Dubh tossed his cap on the table tucked under the sloping roof. The warehouse was small and bare but for the table, chair and sleeping pallet he had managed to scavenge. It was a bleak, damp, miserable little place, and it smelled rank.

It matched her mood perfectly.

He turned to her. His blue eyes were dark in the pre-dawn gloom and his face bland. "Sean is currently in the company of Col. Cowan of the

British Armed Forces—"

"In the company of, or a prisoner?" she demanded as her hands slipped to her throat. Either way, it was bad.

"A little bit of both, I believe."

"Why didn't you let him leave the city?" she railed. "He was going back to Carrickahowley – he would have been safe!"

"He would have been safer if you had listened to him," Dubh snapped. He turned from her and leaned his arms against the table. He had rolled his sleeves up to his elbows and a stylized serpent wound down to wrap itself around his wrists and hands.

"Sean went in to stop you – to fix this – and he was detained, for his safety and for questioning. Whatever the reason, they have him."

"What are they planning to do with him?"

"Not let him go, certainly, but I don't know the specifics. It was not wise to get too close – not in this, at any rate." He gestured to his Volunteer uniform.

She looked at him and not for the first time, considered the enigma that was Dubh Súile – or Captain Doyle, as he was calling himself, this time.

Despite the sword, the long black hair clubbed at his nape, and the serpents coiling around his forearms, wrists and hands, he had a way of blending into his surroundings as though none of these were the heralds of a man who did not belong in the 20th century. He *was* Captain Doyle, and Captain Doyle had worked tirelessly to aid the rebellion's efforts at the GPO. Were the man to don a Royal Army uniform, she suspected the effect would be the same.

Maureen shook her head. It was too much. She

had to act, but the clarity – the certainty – that drove her through the beginning of the Rising was gone. She had known what to do then, had known how to help.

"We need more information," she said finally. "I don't suppose you have a British uniform stashed among your things here, do you?"

"I may – what do you have in mind?"

His words were a punch to the gut. How long had he been in Dublin?

"You–you're unbelievable, yet no one doubts you, ever. Grania confided in you – she trusted you. Sean trusts you."

"And you?" His face was faintly mocking.

"I don't trust you at all," she tossed at him. "But helping me now might be a good place to start."

"What makes you think I want to earn your trust? The responsibility for this lies with you, Maureen."

"I know that," She released the chair with a snarl. It rocked back on two legs before coming to a rest. "And I will fix it."

"How? Would you save them all? I do not believe you will be able to."

"I'll worry about that when the time comes. For now, we're going to pay a visit to Col. Cowen."

Dubh sighed and held her gaze for a moment longer before nodding. "Aye, there is a chance . . ." He looked her up and down. "Find a frock, lass. The less you look like a bloody revolutionary, the better."

She looked down at her torn trousers. The rolled cuffs were coming undone and there were tears at the knees, caked with dirt, soot and blood. She did not remember falling, but her clothes told another tale. They were Sean's actually – she had borrowed them. At the thought, her throat tightened.

"I don't have one," she said, her voice small. "My clothes are at the boarding house – oh, Dubh, Mrs. Mallory!"

"You have more to concern yourself with than whether or not Jenny Mallory is safe." His voice was just above a growl.

"Is she?"

He stared at her for a long moment before answering. "I saw her briefly at the Mount Street Bridge. She and the rebels were doing well, but I think the army has since taken it over. I believe she fell in the fighting."

Maureen took this in with a deep breath. At least the woman had died fighting for something, but still—

"Poor Gerry. He was so fond of her – she was family." She looked up. "She wasn't a bad woman, just driven."

The hard lines of Dubh's face softened. "She was, but she would have gotten him killed. You saved his life. Remember that."

Maureen turned from him. That victory mattered less now that Sean was a prisoner.

Dubh put a hand on her shoulder. "Can you wait here a bit longer? I will find something for you to wear."

He did not wait for her to respond. By the time she turned around, he was already at the warehouse door, ready to disappear back into the besieged city.

Twenty

"What is happening? What are you doing?"

"The Brigadier has ordered you to a more secure location."

"Secure? So I'm truly a prisoner now." It was not a question. It had been two days since Col. Cowan had invited Sean to stay 'safe' at His Majesty's pleasure. Two days holed up in a solitary room in the barracks, where he did not know the fate of anyone or anything. Two days of imagining what was going on beyond the barracks door.

Col. Cowan did not answer him directly. "The Brigadier seems to think it's dangerous to keep you here. Insurgents are making inroads in this area, and if word gets out we're holding you here – well, we don't need the extra bother, do we?"

"Then let me go!"

The Colonel dropped his gaze. "I cannot. I am under orders. You are to be tried with the rest. You know too much."

Sean tried to breathe but all the air had gone out of the room. The initial rounds of court-martials following the Rising meant certain death. Almost all of them had ended with execution.

"How?" he croaked. "I have done nothing to indicate I took up arms against the Crown. I tried to help you."

Col. Cowan paused and raised his eyes to Sean's

face. The man was as controlled as ever, but Sean thought he saw a flash of sympathy in the Colonel's eyes.

"I did try to explain that, but things have gone quite beyond my control – not that they were in my control to begin with. The Brigadier seems to think you know too much for you not to be involved in some way."

"Yes, as a traitor. That is a special kind of punishment all by itself."

The Colonel said nothing to this and Sean snorted. He held out his arms. "So, will you clap me in irons then? Do it – take me away."

"Are you ready?"

Dubh held out a drab overcoat and helped Maureen into it. The faded floral dress he found her was too big and she flatly refused to wear the bonnet, but at least she had combed her hair and washed her face while he had been out in the city, gathering more information.

"Let's go." He put a hand to her elbow and started steering her towards the door, but she pulled against him.

"Wait – would you tell me what's happening instead of barking orders at me?"

"Sean has been moved. We have to go."

"Did your commanding officer tell you that, then?"

He looked down at his Royal Army uniform. "I did not speak with the Colonel, but his aide was aware of the situation."

"Who are you?"

Her voice was bitter and edged with the faintest touch of hysteria. Dubh closed his eyes and strove for calm.

"I am a man." He knew his voice sounded tired but perhaps it was what Maureen needed to hear. "If we had the time, I would explain all to you, but we do not. I walk between the worlds of man and Fae – the Good Folk, aye? I have been in Dublin, attempting to fix your . . . your mess for three weeks now, but it seems you are far more skilled at wreaking havoc than I thought."

"Three weeks?"

He winced as the panic in her voice edged higher.

"We do not have time for this."

Arms crossed over her chest, the girl glared at him. "Make time."

"Maureen, Sean is in trouble," he growled. "I have a meeting with the Brigadier set up to try to have him released, but he needs to know we are trying." He put his hands on her shoulders and looked her straight in the eye. "He needs to see you."

"Where were you?" She yanked herself from his grip and pushed at him. "We were waiting for you! Three weeks you've been here? Why didn't you come for us?"

A mottled flush covered her cheeks and she looked like she did not know whether to scream or cry. He sighed and reached for her but stopped short of trying to grab her again. She was not going to be pushed.

"I could not. I just – I just could not. I made a mistake. I am here now, however. We will fix this, together."

"How?"

"I'm working on that part, but I need you to work with me. Trust me."

He waited as she searched his face. She nodded once and let him take her arm.

"Come, we shouldn't keep the British waiting."

"Thank you for bringing her in. Pvt. Howell here will escort her to see her brother." Col. Cowan dismissed Maureen and his aide with barely a look in their direction. "If you can wait a moment, Captain, I'll walk with you to the Brigadier."

"Certainly, Sir."

Dubh saluted smartly and Maureen fought to keep from rolling her eyes. He was good at what he did, but she was not supposed to know him. She was the meek sister of their prisoner.

"The less attention you draw to yourself, the better," he had instructed. "You do not want them to see you – not really."

"Is that how you do it?"

"Yes." He had looked down at her and smiled. "Most of the time. Sometimes people see me truly."

The words had made her shiver. They still made her shiver.

"Miss? This way, please."

She left Dubh to his machinations and followed Pvt. Howell into the holding cells.

"Boy! Oi, wake up. You have a visitor."

Sean heard the Private but could barely muster the energy to rouse himself. Visitor? No one knew he was here. He raised his head from where it had been resting on his knees.

She was standing behind Pvt. Howell, hovering there as though unsure where to put herself. A rush of bitter relief coursed through him. At least Maureen was alive.

He hauled himself up from the dingy floor as she rushed to his cell.

"Thank God you're alive," he whispered after their guardian moved back along the hall, to give them the illusion of privacy.

Maureen stopped short of grabbing his hands. He clung to the bars and searched her face. She barely looked like herself. She had scrubbed her face clean but he saw scratches amid her freckles and a smudge of dirt she had missed. But the biggest difference was her eyes. They were guarded – haunted. What had she seen out there?

"Sean." Her voice was thick and hoarse. Her mouth was open as though she would say more, but nothing came out. She grabbed the bars then and rested her head against them.

"Sister dear, it was good of you to come."

She looked up. "Is it true? Are you going to be court-martialled?"

"They're considering it. I'm an interesting character, you see." It was not easy to keep the resentment out of his voice.

"I was brought in by, um, an officer – he's having a chat with Col. Cowan and the Brigadier. Maybe if I – if he talks to them?"

"I don't know if talking is going to help anything."

"Captain Doyle is awfully persuasive." She said it with a small smile and her eyes lit up – she looked a bit more like herself again and he sighed.

Dubh's assumed name gave him a little hope, but he knew he could not rely on it. Nothing had gone the way it should.

Tentatively, she touched his hand. "I – I am so

sorry, Sean. I should be in here, not you."

Her apology sounded flat to his ears. "But you're not. You're out there – you're the one they trust. You're the one who has to end this."

"We're working on it."

He nodded. He did not know what to say to her. Dubh told him to fight for her, but he did not know where to begin. It had been so clear when he stepped into Col. Cowan's office, but now everything was in shambles and a war was raging outside that might kill them all.

"No matter what happens, Sean, I will get you out."

He glanced up and down the hall at the other holding cells. The barracks were far more secure than Bingham's boat had been, but she had put her faith in him then. He did not know if he could trust her – not really, not again – but she needed to believe he did.

He grabbed her hands and pulled her close. "I know you will, Maureen. You'll think of something." He kissed her forehead and gave her a little push back. Her mouth was set and the scared little girl who had walked into the barracks was gone.

"I will make it up to you," she whispered. "I promise you, I will. Be ready."

Capt. Doyle and Col. Cowan saluted the Brigadier.

"Gentleman, please sit. I haven't a lot of time. I hope this is quick."

"I understand you have a young informant locked up. May I ask what you intend to do with him."

"Pardon, Captain?"

"Brig. Lowe, please excuse my boldness, but after the mess with Bowen-Colhurst and that Skeffington fellow, is it wise to keep the lad?"

"What do you know about Skeffington?"

Dubh raised his eyebrows and gave the Brigadier a look that said, 'enough.'

Two days earlier, Capt. J.C. Bowen-Colhurst had gone mad and ordered the murder of Francis Sheehy-Skeffington and three other men. The Army had arrested Skeffington as an enemy sympathizer, much like Sean. Had the man been participating in the rebellion, it could have been understandable – but just barely. As it was, Skeffington was a known pacifist, who opposed the Volunteers' plans, and had only been attempting to restore something resembling order. He had been trying to help, and had been shot in the head for his trouble. The army had its back up against the wall, but killing civilians was not going to help.

"That it will be damn difficult to cover it up – excuse my language, Brigadier."

"Bowen will be dealt with. I can't have the boy taking what he's seen here to his Fenian friends."

"But a court-martial?"

"Orders, Captain. All those detained are to be tried. This is out of my hands, gentlemen. Gen. John Maxwell is already on his way to take command. I hear he is to be made Military Governor, as well. Maxwell is a formidable one and I'll leave the details of cleaning up this mess to him."

Dubh stood – he had the information he needed, but it would not hurt to try. "Why is this necessary at all, Brigadier? I know the lad – he came here of his own will to help. This is not the way to repay him."

Col. Cowan stood with Dubh and put a hand on his shoulder, silently asking him to wait.

"Brig. Lowe, I am inclined to agree with the Captain on this. The boy may know more about some of the planning that went into this, but nothing that can help us now. Surely we can recommend—"

"Because of the circumstances of this week, and because I need every man I have, I'm going to overlook this insubordination. There is nothing more I can or will do for one boy when this city is on the verge of collapse." The Brigadier's face was flushed and he moved to the door to show them out.

"Very shortly this will no longer be my concern and I'm not going to interfere with Gen. Maxwell's actions. He will have questions for the boy. Now, was there anything else, Captain?"

Dubh opened his mouth to speak, and closed it again. He saluted his superior officers and retreated from the barracks. He could only hope Maureen felt like following his instructions and was waiting for him at the warehouse.

Twenty-One

"We'll have to break him out. I have an idea."

Dubh opened his mouth to protest but the words would not come. The air shimmered before him and the hiss of magic – magic not of his doing – filled his ears. Time's revolutions slowed until the flicker of Maureen's eyelid would seem to take an hour.

A voice, silky with menace, slid into his mind.

"I knew you wouldn't be able to stay out of human affairs, Dubh Súile."

Dubh went cold at the words. Nuada Silver Arm, King of the Tuatha Dé Danann, had found him. Dubh had known he would not be able to hide from the king for long, but he had hoped to ensure the safety of his charges before confronting him.

"What do you think you will be able to accomplish here, Dubh Súile? This time is locked, and this war will have blood – whether it is the boy's or the schoolteacher's blood matters little."

"It matters to me, my lord. It matters to a young woman whose life is in my keeping."

"Hm. Such pretty words. Do you know what you do, my son? Do you think you can defy me?"

"Defy you? Did you wish their deaths in a time different from their own? Did you wish to see them stranded? Did you wish to unsettle the balance you have worked so hard to maintain?"

"You tempt my anger, Dubh Súile."

Laughter bubbled in Dubh's chest. "It was you, my lord, was it not? Did you send them the dreams, then?"

Before flinging himself at the British, Sean had told him about the nightmares he and Maureen had suffered. Dubh had been happy to let the boy believe he was responsible for them, that he had imbued them with some esoteric meaning, but it was a lie. For that kind of magic, he needed to be in Faerie – and he had been too busy becoming part of the fabric of the revolution to fuss with their dreams.

"Sean you could not touch, though you did not stop trying, did you?" He stopped and grinned. "But Maureen – yes, you almost had her. She is strong, though. If you claimed her, it would end badly for you. She is as strong as any you have tried to destroy."

"As strong as you, my son?" Scorn dripped from Nuada's words.

"Stronger, but she does not know it. You will never have her."

"I would not be so sure. Their war is not over, yet."

Nuada chuckled softly. Dubh clenched his hands at the sound.

"There it is," the king hissed. "The doubt. Good. Know this: they both have their uses. He waits, he watches, and that girl – well, you may be right, but even you do not know what she is capable of. She will need taming, that one."

"She is a human, not a pet, Nuada."

"Where has your deference gone?" Nuada's voice was a mockery of sorrow. "Besides, there is little difference between human and pet, Dubh Súile.

Why do you think I keep you around?"

The king did not wait for a reply; he slithered from Dubh's mind as quickly he had come, and the magic faded from the air.

"I said, I had an idea."

"They will have to surrender."

Maureen stopped pacing and looked at him. "Surrender? Why can't we just break Sean out of the barracks now, before they take him to Kilmainham?"

She shoved her hands in her pockets. She had mended her trousers; even too big and dirty, they were better than the dress Dubh had procured for her. "Then we can leave and let this rebellion implode on itself, like it's supposed to."

"Break him out? Have you any idea how dangerous that is? What if we are caught or attacked? Do you really fancy taking a man's life?"

"If he threatened mine."

"You have no idea what you are saying, lass."

"I know I'm going to get Sean out of there, no matter what it takes." She spun on her heel and put some distance between them. Dubh's presence was as overwhelming as it was comforting, and she hated the wise, knowing look in his face.

"I don't think that is what Sean wants."

"Bugger what Sean wants."

"I believe that is what got you into this situation in the first place."

His tone was dry and she snarled at the wall before turning back to him.

"And I will make it right. Are you going to help me or not?"

"Believe me or no, lass, violence of the sort you are risking is the last resort. Had I believed for a moment that Bingham would have allowed for a trade, or allowed you to leave, Sean and I would have worked to secure your freedom that way. Brig. Lowe and Gen. Maxwell are not Bingham. They are reasonable men fighting an unreasonable war."

"But you heard Pearse – no surrender."

"And who is to blame for that?"

She rolled her eyes. "Don't try to put that on me. They would have thought to tunnel through the buildings without me. Where do you think I got the idea from?"

"Time and history are funny things, lass. You know they did it – but did you get that knowledge from books, or because you were responsible for it?"

"You're talking in riddles." She knew she sounded peevish, but she did not care. "I helped the Volunteers obtain the weapons at Trinity. I helped them secure Dublin Castle – for a little while, at least. I did that, and it wasn't in any history book I can recall."

"And now they won't surrender. 'There is always a chance of success for brave men who challenge fortune' – right, Maureen?"

The rumble of his deep voice was faintly amused and she glared at him.

Dubh shrugged and continued. "The history you know was established by those left alive – how many people knew about Trinity?"

"Lots of people. There was Mrs. Mallory, Pearse, Connolly and Clarke – and he had to tell the Council. Plus, the lads who fetched the guns."

"How many of them were alive after the Rising?"

"One, maybe two – MacNeill, I think."

"And the Castle?"

"Seán Connolly was shot trying to take City Hall – he was raising the flag when they got him – and the others . . ." She did not want to say the others were probably going to die or be sent away for internment. Even as she thought it, she looked up at Dubh. He was watching her, waiting, it seemed.

"You mean—?"

"It is embarrassing, what you lot were able to accomplish. It is embarrassing how you forced a great nation to fire upon one of its own cities, and lay it to waste in an effort to defeat you. You changed more than you realized. It is time to end it."

"End it?" she breathed. His words had rekindled a desperate hope. "No. Imagine, Dubh – if that much really did change, imagine what they could do if they lived."

"No!" He slammed his fist on the table, and she jumped. "No. Nothing good can come from this."

"So, you want me to sacrifice those men?" She was not going to back down – no matter how fierce his glare.

"They are prepared to die, but Sean is not – nor should he have to. His life is at stake, Maureen. He knows nothing that will help the British, but if this goes on any longer, they will feel compelled to take action – any action. Without the surrender, there will just be more death."

"What does Sean's imprisonment – or freedom – have to do with the surrender? What is it, some sort of trade?"

The tattooed warrior stared at her. He did not say a word but his eyes were searching her face. She wondered what she said.

"It is a negotiation," he answered finally, his voice quieter. "Imagine how different it would be if the rebellion was under control, and the leaders were offering up their unconditional surrender. Sean would be a small thing next to Pearse and Connolly."

"You negotiate with them, and you're going to bring a lot more attention to yourself than I think you're willing to do. Not everyone is going to ignore those tattoos or that bloody sword."

"No one else sees them." He looked at her. Again, he seemed to be begging her to understand, and again, she just did not.

"What do you mean?"

"You see me – both of you see *me*. No one else does. To James Connolly, I had the credentials to be what he wanted me to be – a comrade. Col. Cowan was no different. But you – it does not matter how I wish you to see me, you see what I am, the man I am – the man I once was."

"I'm sorry." The words slipped out of her and she did not know why. Yet, even as the ache in his voice made her want to cry, she clenched her hands. It did not matter what she saw, or who Dubh was. It had nothing to do with the Rising, or the fate of its leaders.

"So you negotiate. Why? Because they're reasonable men?" She snorted. "Reason has nothing to do with what's coming. Reason isn't going to be what court-martials and executes fifteen men – men I've stood with. Five days, Dubh. That is all they have left."

"I thought you wanted to save him, Maureen. I thought you wanted him to believe in you again."

She grabbed the edge of the table to keep from slapping him. Who was he to throw Sean in her face? He was the one who had been in the city for three weeks.

"I will save him," she said, her voice barely under control, "but I won't sacrifice the men who could really lead this country in order to do it."

The roar that erupted from Dubh's lips hurt her ears and he moved too fast for her to react. He grabbed her by the shoulders and put his face close to hers.

"Do you not understand, you feckless wee chit?" he growled. "They are already dead – their martyrdom is what this country needs, now. Sean helps no one if he is dead."

He stopped and pushed himself away from her. She stared at him, shaking, but kept her mouth shut.

"Help me help Sean, Maureen. You were right. It is a trade – it is his life for Pearse's life. You must give one of them up. Do not let them use you or Sean. It is a life wasted if they do. Let it go, lass."

He stood there, practically panting, and she stared at him. His words made no sense. Her imagination was too full of visions of a different – united – Ireland.

What was the price of freedom? Connolly had asked the question. Sean had asked it too, and it screamed through her head now, obliterating all else.

She turned from Dubh, away from his words and his eyes. She started pacing the warehouse, but it was too close. His presence filled the space. Unwittingly, she began to run – fleeing his words – but they chased her.

Let it go.

There was no escape. She burst through the door and landed in the muck outside. Her fists beat at the ground, and she cried out with a rage so deep it tore at her throat.

Let it go.

"No," she whimpered. But it beat at her.

Let it go.

Her fists stilled and she crumpled in the mud. Large shuddering breaths shook her as the tears flowed unhindered and with them, the last of her resistance.

She wanted to live. She wanted to fight – for freedom, for peace, and for life. For a life. She remembered Sean, so hopeful they could exist in this time if they just relied on each other and stayed out of the way of history.

"Let it go – let *them* go."

The words were now her own. Her own voice spoke to her from the depths. She looked out into the deepening twilight and swiped at her tears.

A trade then, not a rescue. The air seemed to shimmer as she breathed out the last of her hopes for the 1916 Rising. It was over.

Dubh was behind her – she could feel him. He leaned over her and offered his hand. She looked up at him for a moment and then took it. She would do it.

Twenty-Two

"What do you mean, 'no'?" Maureen tried to keep her voice quiet, but failed.

The grocers around the corner from the GPO – the new headquarters – was packed with weary men, most of them suffering from wounds and smoke inhalation. Connolly barely acknowledged them, but she and Dubh had managed to convince Pearse to speak with them in a small office in the back.

"Connolly and I talked about it when he passed the command to me. There can be no surrender. They'll have to take us themselves. We will go down fighting."

"Commander," she said pointedly, "You've made your stand. There are people out there dying – innocent people. More of them will die the longer this goes on. Do you want that?"

She searched his face for some indication he understood, or cared. Pearse looked back at her confused, as though his favourite pet had bitten him.

"Sean was taken, and it's my fault. I betrayed a promise to him, to help you. Believe me, he doesn't want to die." She paused and spread her arms wide to indicate the store, the men – the burning city. "He didn't want this. He would rather live. He would rather be far from this and live in peace."

"Then he is already dead. There will be no peace

so long as—"

The sharp crack of her hand across his flesh silenced him. Pearse stared at her as he cupped his cheek with a tentative hand.

"That is why you failed." Her voice was low and harsh. "Angry boys die for your vision, your lie. Sean will not be one of them. You don't deserve his sacrifice."

The man's shoulders started to slump and his eyes searched her face. She forced herself to meet his gaze and he shook his head.

"My lie? You believed me once – begged me to believe you. How can you say this? Where has your passion gone? You gave us – gave me – hope."

"It's over now. Stop the fighting and let people go back to their lives. End it."

"Was it you?" Pearse snarled as Dubh put a hand on her shoulder.

Dubh pinched her and she bit back a hot denial.

"Let me," he whispered, and he moved in front of her.

"It is disheartening, isn't it? When they grow up – stop believing the fairy tales we tell them?"

"Freedom is no fairy tale, sir. As a Volunteer—"

"Freedom of the kind you are selling is. Oh, I admit this Rising, this flag you planted, will do its job. It will spur a nation." He paused and spoke so quietly into Pearse's ear that Maureen had to lean in to hear him.

"But it is your deaths – the secret trials, the executions – that will really move things along."

Pearse tried to free himself, but Dubh dug his fingers into the other man's shoulder and forced him to stay.

"What are you saying, man?"

"Maureen did not want to tell you this, and even

if she did, you would not have believed her. The ringleaders will die – must die. It is written." He pulled back and stared hard at Pearse.

"Do you want to have this revolution succeed or fail? It is your head they want, not Sean's. Your death, your sacrifice, will mean so much more. Die this day, Patrick Pearse. Trade your life for his."

Maureen held her breath and ignored the shivers of otherworldly premonition racing up her arms. Pearse's face seemed to be at war with itself as anger and hopelessness gave way to the glow of inspiration.

"So, I'm not to lead the Republic after all."

"No, you'll take your rightful place – a place you are much more suited for."

"What is that? Traitor to the Crown?"

"No. Martyr. You said once that this is a blood sacrifice. You were right. By paying the ultimate price, you will force a nation to stand and demand freedom, self-governance and the right to make its own mistakes."

"But she said they still fight."

"The Irish were never a peaceful people, Commander. One day, however, they will learn to keep company with themselves."

Pearse nodded silently and Dubh released his shoulder. The Commander looked at Maureen and held out his hand. It was a truce, an understanding. She grabbed it.

It was a pledge.

"You have courage and spirit, lass. Live for me. Carry your vision of peace to the future." He grinned ruefully and touched his cheek where she had slapped him. "I think I would like to live on in your eyes."

Her throat closed on the words she did not know

how to say and she nodded instead. Pearse squeezed her hand and turned away.

"Why did you step in? I thought I had to convince him," she asked as she and Dubh watched Pearse go back to his men.

The warrior put a hand on her shoulder. "You had to be the one to end it – and you did. You inspired him and to stop him, Pearse had to see you withdraw from the fight. I merely inspired him in a different direction."

Maureen took this in silently and the hand on her shoulder squeezed gently.

"Now, find a corner to sleep in. You have been running around this city trying to save everyone since before the dawn."

"What about Sean?"

"He is safe for now, lass – probably asleep himself. I will go to the Brigadier to arrange for his release." Dubh nodded at Pearse, squatted over Connolly. They were arguing.

"I am about to convince the Commander of the British Forces in Ireland that the only way to obtain Patrick Pearse's surrender and end this madness is to release a 16 year-old boy who should never have been detained in the first place."

Maureen grinned. "Give 'em hell."

Twenty-Three

Dubh collected her in the early hours of Saturday morning. She was still groggy from lack of sleep, but she begged him to let her watch.

"You are torturing yourself, lass."

"I know, but I need to see it end. I need to see it end the way it should."

They made their way to a relatively safe vantage point to watch Pearse order the ceasefire and deliver his surrender document. The two-day leader of the proclaimed Irish Republic walked with his head high. He was beaten, but he would never bow, and in his heart, he would never truly surrender. Neither would Ireland.

Tears rolled down her cheeks as she watched. Dubh was wrong. It was not torture, not really. It was history, and she would witness it.

Dubh slipped a hand in hers as Pearse was led away. The receiving officer read the document to the gathered crowd. Maureen did not need to hear the words to know what it said.

In order to prevent the further slaughter of Dublin citizens, and in the hope of saving the lives of our followers now surrounded and hopelessly outnumbered, the members of the Provisional Government present at headquarters have agreed to an unconditional surrender, and the commandants of the various districts in the City and County will order their commands to lay down arms.

It was over. It was time to go home.

"I hope you'll forgive me," Maureen said lightly as Sean walked towards them under the watchful eye of Col. Cowan. "I tried for a grand rescue but he overruled me." She jerked her head at Dubh, standing at her side.

"No pyrotechnics?"

"Not even a firework."

"Just you, then."

"Just me." She reached out her hand.

Sean took it and held it tight. He knew the terms of his release, knew who had been rounded up that noon and who would soon face the firing squad. He knew what it had cost her.

The leaden ball of doubt, which had been sitting in his belly since the Castle, slowly began to melt. He pulled her into a tight hug.

"You are more than enough."

"We need to hurry – stay together, and stay close to me." Dubh tossed the words over his shoulder as they ran along shadowed alleys. He was leading them out of the city, but had not told them why.

There was no time – but he put too much effort into securing Maureen's soul and Sean's life to stop now. He could not, not when he was so close to understanding who they were, and what they meant to him.

His breath panted in his ears as he jogged the narrow streets. If he could reach a clearing – a bit of green away from curious eyes – he may yet get them to safety before Nuada attempted to claim them.

"Where are we going?" Maureen demanded. He looked back at her and caught the rebellious frown on her face. He cursed inwardly.

"Maureen, come on." Sean pulled on her arm to no avail.

"No. I have done enough running. The Rising is over. We're safe – safer than we were. What is all this about?"

"You will never be safe if I do not bring you home, now."

"Not until you tell me—"

"Fine!"

They flinched from him and he swore under his breath. He grabbed them both by the shoulder and attempted to compose his face – soften its stern lines. The trouble with Nuada was his fault, not theirs.

"I am sorry. We need to be away from here, away from *him*—"

He broke off as a stinging sensation bit the skin of his palms. He gritted his teeth and tried to continue. "I swear to you, I will tell you everything, but not here."

"Who is this 'him'?" Maureen demanded.

A burst of wry humour – Maureen's single-bloody-mindedness was a curse as much as a blessing – wove through his irritation and mounting fear. The stinging had reached his fingertips, and was spreading. They had to move.

"*He* is the threat you felt in the mist – don't ask me how I know. We are the same, you and I. I know you felt it – both of you. Nuada is looking for you. He will claim you if I do not get you away—"

He broke off as a scream wrenched itself from his throat. His knees buckled. He crumpled to the cobbles as the searing pain of a thousand bolts of lightning ripped through his body.

"Dubh!"

His hands still clung to their shoulders and they stumbled to their knees in the effort to hold him as he collapsed.

Maureen's eyes were wide as she looked frantically from the fallen warrior to Sean. "What are we going to do – Sean!"

His strangled cry cut her off. Sharp pinpricks, stabbing and insistent, attacked him along the outlines of Dubh's fingers where they still clung to his shoulder.

Nausea and pain radiated from the warrior's hand, through Sean's body. He struggled to speak, to warn Maureen, but he could not form the thought in his head. He clawed at the air as a shudder tore through him.

"No!" Maureen caught Sean's flailing hand, but he had already gone limp. "Sean, no – what am I supposed to do?" Her voice sounded far away, even to her own ears.

The weight of everything – of the Rising, of her betrayal, of the surrender – crowded around her, and she cowered on the damp cobbles. All she could do was clutch both Sean and Dubh to her, despite the tiny shocks of electricity that skipped across her skin wherever they touched.

A hideous listlessness stole over her limbs, dulling her to the pain that grew as the seconds ticked by.

Light flickered and then flared to life, radiant and terrible at the same time. It arced between all three of them, and over them. It surrounded them in a bubble of blinding light.

The wind rose and howled in her ears. It slashed at her face, her clothes and hands. The world spun out of control and they were caught in the maelstrom. Maureen struggled to hold onto Dubh and Sean, even as the earth fell away.

A vast nothing swallowed her terror. It swallowed the light and the air. It swallowed sound and her ability to scream. Then a horrible laugh, howling without mirth, filled her ears. Underneath it, there was a voice.

It whispered to them, cold and deadly.

"Welcome to Tír na nÓg."

King

KATIE SULLIVAN

One

Silence.

It beat at her. Tiny movements bombarded her. Breathing hurt her ears, so complete was the absence of noise.

Maureen opened her eyes. This was no dream – no nightmare to be avoided by deeper dreaming.

Nothing met her gaze. The darkness was absolute. Her shriek rose from deep within her soul. It shattered the silence and broke the bonds that kept her still.

"Sean!"

He woke with a start – he was in a crouch, breathing deep draughts of air, before he could even form a conscious thought.

Then he remembered. They had been in 1916. He had been released – court-martial avoided – and the Easter Rising had been put down. Maureen had traded the lives of the leaders for his and come out of the uprising unscathed, with Dubh.

Dubh.

Dubh was gone, Maureen was hysterical somewhere close and they were alone. Again.

"Maureen!"

At the sound of Sean's voice, Maureen stopped screaming. She heard him slide along the floor of their – what was it, a prison? A cage? Whatever it was, she heard him and reached for the sound.

Their hands touched. She was trembling and she held on to him to stop the shaking.

"What happened, Maureen?"

"You're asking me?" A bubble of hysterical laughter threatened to escape. "You were there, you felt—"

"I don't know what I felt."

"Yes, you do." Maureen took a deep breath and eased herself into a sitting position. "Think. When Dubh was—was struck, he grabbed us. We touched him."

"There was a shock," Sean said quietly, "like a current of electricity – and pain." His voice dropped even lower. "So much pain."

Maureen nodded even though he could not see her. So much pain. "There was light, and noise, too, after—after you collapsed. It blotted out everything. And then, there was nothing." She shook her head and tried to pierce the darkness, to see, but it was absolute. "It happened when Dubh touched us. It was him."

"No. He couldn't have meant for this to happen. I heard him scream – I saw his eyes, Maureen. It was—"

"Horrible," she finished with a shudder. "I didn't mean he brought us here – he was trying to protect us. I know that. But he was the conduit – and he is in danger, now. We are all in danger."

She kept her voice quiet – gone was the

shrieking terror. In its place was a cold, sinking kind of understanding.

She knew their opponent.

"Maureen?"

"He said it – and you knew it first, back at the church." She squeezed his hand. "We're there – that voice." She shivered as she allowed the memory to slip through her. *Welcome to Tír na nÓg.*

The words were familiar – the words were myth – but the voice had stalked her dreams and clouded her mind. It had not made her betray Sean, but it had allowed her to fool herself into thinking she was not choosing an ideology over her best friend's life.

"What—?"

Laughter drowned out Sean's words. It started out slow, but grew deeper and louder until it screamed in their ears. It teetered on the edge of hysteria. Underneath it lurked a dark, self-satisfied tremor, which was almost more terrifying than the barrage of noise.

"Welcome, children!"

Together, they scrambled to their feet.

"Show yourself!" Maureen called.

"Who are you to demand such boons from me, girl?"

"I hate it when people call me 'girl'," she growled. "Who are you to keep us here?"

"Nervy, always so nervy," Sean muttered. His voice was amused as he said it and she clutched his hand. It was good to be at his side.

There was no response to her demand – not a verbal one, at least. With aching slowness, the darkness eased and revealed their prison.

It appeared to be a crystalline box, but even as they watched, the walls melted until nothing but mist drifted at their feet. Maureen looked up. They were at the very centre of a cavernous hall. The ceiling disappeared into a milky ether above them and bare columns framed open doorways on either side of the narrow room. Veins of iridescence writhed along the walls and floor, whispering with the memory of life.

Without knowing why, Maureen thought she should know this place. In her memory, ancient trees creaked in the breeze, and she shivered.

The only thing similar to the grove in her vision was the mist. It was everywhere, dancing in wild patterns across the floor and gathering in harmless pools at the corners of the hall.

She watched, entranced, as it snaked around their feet, and she understood. The mist had been the darkness. It had muffled all sound until there was nothing.

At her glare, it shifted violently and flickered red.

"Ah, just when we thought your kind gone from your world."

The voice – the same voice that had whispered in her dreams and cackled as they were torn from Dubh's side – came from behind them. Maureen stiffened but forced herself – and Sean, glued to her side – to turn slowly.

The speaker was small. He looked human, but every sense at her command said he was not. He seemed to be made of the mist. It swirled at his hem, slithered up his arms and draped his shoulders in muted shades of green and blue.

He extended his hands towards them.

Sean stiffened and stepped in front of her. "Who are you?"

There was a faint smile on the man's face. "Who

I am would mean nothing to you, I fear."

They gaped at the stranger as he drew into himself and appeared to change. He grew taller and his shoulders broader. His robes took the form of a fine linen tunic, embroidered with threads of gold. A simple engraved circlet crowned his white-blond head.

"Do you know me, now?" His voice was deeper, and his language was ancient.

"Crown or no, I know only that you are mad," Maureen answered, her tongue fumbling over the words. It was an older form of Irish than what she had been taught – older than what she had spoken in the company of pirates.

With a ripple of the mists, the visage of the warrior-king disappeared, and the sprightly man glared back at them.

"I am Nuada, King of the Tuatha Dé Danann, and ruler of Tír na nÓg. You are in the keep of Findias, and you will give me reverence, Maureen Clare O'Malley."

"Nuada Silver Arm?" Sean gasped.

"You know me, then? I'm gratified."

"And what would the illustrious King of the Tuatha Dé Danann want with two orphans?" Maureen tried to keep her voice light. Trapped, attacked by light and sound, and presented with a mythical Irish king, it was not easy.

Nuada chuckled. It was a rich, throaty sound. "I want you to choose, of course."

"Choose?" Sean's voice verged on hysterical. Maureen squeezed his shoulder but he ignored her. "You—you snatch us from a Dublin street, imprison us, and now we're to choose? Choose what?"

"Life: yours, or his."

The king's arm shot out and three figures

emerged from the emptiness beyond the hall. Two men – slightly built and clad, not in the drapery of their ruler, but in a simple black uniform of slim suits and soft-soled high boots – escorted another at the point of what appeared to be spears. The prisoner was bound with the mockery of chains that clanked as he walked.

It was Dubh.

Shoulders back, the warrior stared ahead. Shaggy strands of jet-black hair had escaped the bindings at his nape. His sword was gone and his clothes were mussed, but he held his head high.

Watching him, Maureen found herself standing taller.

"What is this, Nuada Silver Arm?" Sean demanded, as if the ancient title would make the king human.

Nuada did not answer right away. He held Sean's gaze in his, and his eyes flashed an eerie silver. They were empty eyes, pitiless. Those eyes had never been human.

"This, Master McAndrew, is what happens to those who defy me."

He gestured to Dubh's jailors. At their king's silent order, they jabbed at the warrior behind his knees. He grunted with the pain, but refused to crumble to the ground. Instead, he knelt slowly, his back straight.

Nuada strolled over to Dubh and stood before him, waiting.

The warrior acknowledged no one.

The king snarled and reached into his robes. "This is what happens to all those who would dare break my commands," he called out. "This is what happens to those who would journey beyond their own time."

Nuada's arm whipped out and he struck Dubh with a fist clad in metal. Blood leaked from his lip, but he did nothing to stem its flow. Still, he did not look at the king.

Maureen and Sean drew even closer together. Nuada turned back to them.

"You will choose, my children. You will choose who dies this day, and who lives. Make the choice – it is Dubh Súile, or it is you. Someone will pay for these crimes."

Two

The mists shifted and eddied, slowly coalescing into the form of a slim young woman. She drifted gracefully as she advanced on the jeering denizens of Tír na nÓg, who were gathered at the dais outside Nuada's stronghold. Guards took no notice of her, and stragglers at the edges of the crowd seemed not to see her. She slipped through the mob as though its anger, its frenzied emotion, passed over her and shielded her from their senses.

Sean struggled as he watched her progress. She drew him, even as his eyes tried not to see her. The sensation was what he imagined seasickness to be like and he leaned into Maureen. She was standing next to him, and like him, had her arms bound behind her back. She stared ahead, defiant, as if the hate seething before her meant nothing.

"Nervy – so nervy." This time, the words were shaded with pride. She twitched slightly beside him and he knew she had heard him. "So, what do you think that is?"

Sean's whisper jolted Maureen from her reverie. Nervy was not exactly the word she would use to describe the sickening terror that had dried her mouth and had her heart racing in her chest, but at his question she tore her eyes from the horizon to look at her friend.

Dear as Sean was to her, she would have preferred to keep her eyes on the horizon. There was a dot out there. What it was, she did not know, but it was stationary – blissfully and delightfully still – and she was using as her anchor in this land of perpetual motion. Even the air in Tír na nÓg seemed to ebb and flow with the emotions of its inhabitants. Without the dot, she thought she might start to scream again. Scream and never stop.

"What?"

Sean jerked his chin at the crowd, and with deep reluctance, she allowed her gaze to follow. She sensed, rather than saw, a ripple of movement. Something – or someone – was slipping through the sea of pale, angry faces.

Her eyes kept sliding away from the movement and she tried looking at it from the corner of her eye. There it was – a woman.

"I see her," she breathed.

Her excitement was short-lived. The woman stopped and gazed directly at them. Whatever Sean was going to say died as a gurgle in his throat as the woman's eyes – bright silver beacons – held his.

Look elsewhere.

Her voice hissed in their minds, heavy with warning. Maureen resisted the urge to roll her shoulders as the voice tickled her awareness. It was so similar to the voice that haunted her dreams.

I mean you no harm, but you must not see.

They did as she asked. Together, they shifted their eyes to the horizon.

"What was that?" Sean muttered.

Maureen opened her mouth to respond and

closed it again. She had no idea.

They had not yet answered the king's demand to choose between Dubh and themselves. Nuada had not allowed them to answer, and she suspected he loved a show. Their choice would be meaningless without an audience.

Choose.

The allure of the king's words – the sickly-sweet assurance that what he demanded was the right thing – pulled at her, but she knew better now. His spell over her was broken, and her mind was her own. She shut out his voice, and ignored his demands. She would refuse to choose.

Dubh was not going to die because of them.

"Maybe she's here to help," she whispered finally. She looked him in the eye. "Whatever happens, we are not going to let Nuada do this – Dubh is not going to die, and neither are we. We will not choose."

Sean's face broke into a broad smile and he laughed. "I know – but thank you for giving me fair warning this time."

She answered his smile with one of her own. There had been no time to ask his forgiveness, no time to tell him anything. But his smile told her he knew. There would be time for the words later.

The noise from the crowd swelled and the smile slowly fled her face. There was a growing undercurrent of excitement, a heightened awareness amongst the people. She looked to the other side of the platform. Between them was a wall of guards, but Dubh took no notice of them, nor of the sea of howling faces throwing jeers at him.

The dais outside the immense face of the king's stronghold looked as though it was a common gathering ground. Beyond the dais, beyond the assembly of strange faces, were clusters of small buildings – like so many rough-hewn boulders – tucked along the craggy walls of the keep.

She had never given much thought to the myth of Tír na nÓg, let alone wondered what it would look like. Even so, the Land of the Young inspired images of a leafy, sun-dappled grove, or something drawn from Ireland's most remote, magical places, where the souls of her forebears remained, forever young.

Whatever Tír na nÓg was supposed to be, this was not it – a barren land, filled with hard, jagged edges. A land that seemed devoid of all life but that which jeered at her now.

The crowd's excitement reached an uncomfortable pitch. The wall of guards parted and Nuada drifted to the front.

"I call to you, citizens – Tuatha Dé Danann, hear me!"

His people roared.

The king raised his arms above his head and looked like he would absorb the wall of noise, as though he fed off their adoration and need.

"I present to you three enemies of this land. One, we looked upon as our champion, and the others are those who would bring Tír na nÓg to ruin."

The clamour rose again and Nuada glanced back at them. The glittering hatred in his eyes made Maureen move even closer to Sean's side.

The corner of the king's lip curled as he spied the movement but he said nothing and turned back to his people.

"I am not heartless, citizens. I know these orphaned humans – wards of an institution that has demonized us and reduced us to caricatures – could not have known that by using the gateways, they were breaking a peace nearly two thousand-years strong. They did not know. The first time." He put his hand up to stem the crowd before it could find its voice.

"The first time, I would have allowed them to go free, but of course, they could not leave well enough alone. They used our power again, and this man, our defender, Dubh Súile, helped them do it!"

The fury of the Tuatha Dé Danann – the people descended of the goddess Danu – buffeted the stage. Their passions were rising and Maureen bit her lip to quash the panicky thought that Nuada might not have as much control over his people as he thought.

"Nuada!"

Dubh's voice was loud and strong. It overrode the crowd's furore and silence fell.

The king glared at his captive.

Speak! You know this man. He will throw himself on his sword to save you from making the choice. Speak now. Divert the king.

The voice's urgency sent chills skittering up Maureen's arms. She glanced up at Sean. He nodded back.

Speak now!

"Nuada, you lie to your people!" Maureen shouted the first words that came to mind.

The king glanced at her. The menace in his face had shifted to something darker. She stifled a shudder and called up the memories of their time in 1916. They felt distant, as though years had passed instead of just a few hours.

"You knew we travelled through the gateway, Nuada. You knew!"

He said nothing. The people were whispering now – pointing at her and at the wall of mist behind her. From the corner of her eye, she could see it begin to rise and shift with the rhythm of her words. Where once the crowd's tumult had stained it red and black, the mist was now clean and bright.

She took a deep breath and stared into the sea of Tír na nÓg's citizens. This realm of Faerie may not be what she expected, but just by being here, she shared some sort of kinship with them. She had to.

She braved their frenzied emotion and spoke to them.

"He knew – he spoke to me! He walked through my dreams and showed me what to do – gave me visions of grandeur, which spoke to my darkest heart. He used me to help war and hatred fester in my world."

"And we went along with it," Sean added.

She flashed him a grateful smile. He had not been a willing participant in her schemes, and his support now meant everything to her.

"Maureen and I were lost and alone," he added. "We didn't know who to trust, but Dubh tried to guide us. He is your champion yet!"

The crowd was silent. The mists towered, nearly as tall as the keep. They roiled and shuddered with light and the faintest hum of noise.

Nuada stared at them, his lips twisted into a silent snarl. He started walking towards them, the gauntlet slowly coalescing over his arm. Sean and Maureen stood before him, pressed together but unbowed.

The king raised his arm and still they did not flinch.

His face was flushed. His arm hung in the air,

the menacing fist gleaming.

Maureen stiffened but the fist did not fall. What was he waiting for?

All was still, yet the air was thick with whispers. Beside her, Sean shifted. At the edge of her vision, she saw him turn his head. It took all her effort to tear her eyes away from the king, but she followed the direction of her friend's gaze.

Dubh was gone.

The spell broke.

Everything came rushing back, slamming into her in an explosion of sound and movement.

The king's arm fell without hitting its mark. Words seemed to fail him and he erupted with a howl of thwarted rage. With a flick of his wrist, he signalled for the guards to surround her and Sean. They had no time to react before the guards hauled them back into the stronghold.

Looking back, Maureen saw Nuada lift his arms and summon a great hazy wall to hide himself from a people denied their spectacle.

Three

"**N**iamh, that was too great a risk!"

"Do not presume to tell me what risks I take, Druid." Niamh glared at Dubh, her silver eyes hard and cold. Gone were the bits of magic and elaborate coils that once adorned her hair. Under a hooded cloak, she had wrapped the plaited coil around her head as a shining blond crown.

Anger and fear warred with each other in her elfin face, and he bit back sharp words. "Thank you for setting me free," he added meekly.

Niamh had used Maureen and Sean – used Maureen's natural inclination to argue and Sean's near-blind defence of his friend – to distract the king. Gateways were woven points between the worlds, and between points within Tír na nÓg itself. The more masterful the weaver, the easier it was to seemingly appear and disappear at will.

While Niamh was a particularly gifted weaver, her father was equally as gifted in other, more dangerous, magics. Her trick would only work once; Nuada would protect his prisoners – his new pets, Dubh suspected – better next time.

Nuada's daughter matched the placating tone of his words. "I know you fear for them, but we have time."

They were back at the cave, safe for the moment. Natural flame torches flickered above their heads as they stood at its mouth and watched the fog drift in harmless eddies. Sentries – Niamh's handpicked guards – stood silent in the shadows behind them.

Niamh pulled him away from the cave mouth and led the way to a high-ceilinged cavern. A table and benches carved right from the rock filled the space. She gestured for him to sit.

"The people will be angry," she continued. "Maureen spoke to them, and they heard her. She spoke a truth, and the mists responded. It will be difficult for them to deny a thing they saw with their own eyes. She is too young yet to know how to manipulate the people as Nuada does. He was not expecting that."

"But for that, she will be punished."

"Yes, she will."

"She is a human, Niamh – she is not trained as I was, and she is no warrior."

Her laughter was as sweet as the chime of tiny bells. "In that, you are wrong, my friend. Maureen is a great warrior, although, she will not take up arms again."

"Spell-weaver." His voice was low but Niamh's head snapped up and her eyes glinted with emotion that sent chills down his arms. Spell-weavers told the tale of their people – past and future – in their weavings. It was whispered by the fearful that spell-weavers could create the future with the weaving, instead of just record it.

"Did you know we are outlawed, now? The spell-weavers were the first of the guilds Nuada destroyed. He fears that bit of future-sight necessary for the weaving. The old works were burned not long after you and I parted ways. What I saved here is all that remains. It is as though he were erasing our story."

The intricate pathways of the unfinished tapestry within her chambers danced in his memory. It called to him – not as the Druid or the warrior, but as the bard. It spoke to him as the man who used to tell tales by the fireside, who carried the stories of his people in his heart and mind. Áine and Niamh's weavings were a powerful reminder to that man. They echoed through the once-locked chambers of his heart where those tales resided, and awakened memories he thought gone.

The man Nuada had become was right to be afraid of those weavings.

"Have you looked into their future, then? Are our threads still linked?"

"You know better than to ask me that, Dubh Súile. You have the future-sight yourself, and it is a power you will have to learn to wield again if you are to help us."

Heat spread across his face. He had not attempted to peer into the future since the fates had stripped him of his love, years before he became the plaything of Nuada Silver Arm.

"You know nothing of it."

"Do I not?" Her voice was as cold as the silver in her eyes. "You are not the only one who has been forced to forsake what you love in order to live."

He looked up from his hands. Her cheeks were stained faintly with pink and there was a spark kindling in those eyes. She was right. Now was not the time for tale-telling and weavings. She was dressed for war and had no need of the bard. She needed the champion.

"Then perhaps it is time we were honest with one another. You told me before that the Faerie Sleep weighed heavy on my senses, and you were right. Speak to me, Niamh. Help me understand the rage I saw outside the keep. What has happened here?"

She took a breath and appeared to be weighing her words, choosing them carefully. "Those who pledge themselves to the king do so at the cost of their magic. Those in his service may use their gifts as called upon, but it is only a favoured few. Even the Seers rest, dormant, until he summons them."

Ah. The Seers. They were the elite guard – not the men who had jabbed at him with their spears, but warriors true. In their ranks were the best of all the guilds – the weavers who could see far, the healers who could revive even those thought lost, and the magicians who could draw the mists into the most intricate of designs. Seers could read the mists, and see into the souls of those around them – even peer beyond the veil between Man and Fae.

They had been his teachers once. That they slept spoke volumes of the control Nuada wielded over the Fae.

"We are fading," Niamh continued. "Without the weavings, without the guilds, we have allowed ourselves to forget we were once glorious with wild magic."

"Is that why only the king remains unchanged? The rest look as though they could pass through the world of men unnoticed."

Now he understood why so many had felt his waking. His magic was unbridled – free – just as Nuada's was.

Niamh nodded and gestured to her own colourless robe. Its creation was a manifestation of her power, yet it dampened her natural magic, visually and metaphysically. It had also allowed her to approach the keep unnoticed.

"It takes an effort to appear this way. It keeps the people occupied and in return, he feeds us spectacles as a panacea to the beauty we once created. In this way, he controls us – keeps us safe, he says."

"But Niamh, that was his promise. He broke from his brothers in order to separate Faerie from the world of man."

She acknowledged this with pursed lips but kept her silence.

"Your people have long memories, Niamh. That promise won him the war."

"I thought it was you who won his war for him."

He gritted his teeth. Niamh had been young in the last days of the Fomorian War – but not too young to remember what her world had been like before the sons of Manannán mac Lir tried to tear Tír na nÓg asunder. And not too young to accuse Dubh of putting a tyrant on the throne.

Bres, Balor and Nuada each had a different vision for the realm left to them by their father. Chance brought Dubh to Nuada's stronghold instead of the camps of his brothers. Even so, the king had been the best choice. Bres and Balor had wanted to bring their war to man.

"Niamh, he watched men drive his people out of the world. Do you blame him for wanting to protect what was left?"

"But at what cost? You have seen Mag Mell. You have seen the keep at Findias and the people. We are dying. All that remains of our former beauty and power is your grove."

"And this cave."

Her mouth popped open to protest and closed again.

He smiled. "You are a canny woman, Niamh

Golden Hair. When we last spoke, you told me why you retreated here, but you did not tell me all."

The more time he spent within the earthen network Niamh and her followers called home, the more he understood. She told him the walls were a shield, which bent the perceptions of those who would search them out. She told him, too, that a gateway could not be opened within the cave – but that was not entirely true.

The cave itself was a gateway. In it lived an older power, a remnant of Nuada's forbears and a portal to deeper magics.

She regarded him with a small smile. "I was not yet sure I could trust you, then. You had been gone so long."

"Trust has not been easy since Áine passed beyond us."

Niamh's mother had been a balm to the ragged spirits that lingered after the Fomorian War. Her passing had left an empty space in the hearts of many – and a bitter enmity between two of those who should have worked together in her name. He and Niamh would need to start trusting one another if they were going to rescue Sean and Maureen – if they were going to survive the reign of her father.

"No, it has not." She bowed her head. "The curses I flung at you when you denied the rebellion were sung in grief."

He snorted. Her curses, telling him he would rue the day he denied her, had still been ringing in his ears when Nuada had snatched him from the Plain and thrust him into the twentieth century of man. At the time, he had considered bearing witness to Patrick O'Malley and James McAndrew's deaths a prophesy fulfilled. Although Niamh eventually rescued him, he continued to deny her cause. He retreated to his grove and let the wheel of time pass him by.

He took the young woman's hand. In his paw, it was as slight as a child's.

"And I have forgiven you that grief. I shared in it. Áine was my mentor, too, and I should have stood up to Nuada when she passed. Instead, I retreated. Like a coward, I hid."

"I never believed your sleep to be the act of a coward, Dubh Súile. Did you not once sing of the sleeping kings, who will rise when the need for them is greatest?"

She was smiling and he shook his head at her. "I am no king, Mistress Niamh."

"Are you so sure? You, who is a great leader of men?"

Shivers of old prophesy ran along his spine. "I have heard those words before."

"Then it is time to heed them. The mists are rising, dark with malevolent power. Not enough of us can hold the beauty of a flower in our memory, and now the green things are gone. Tír na nÓg is dying. Even out here, away from his influence, the most I can create is my work and the butterflies in my hair."

"And even those are gone."

"Today. But soon they will be back – forever, if we can manage it."

"What do you want me to do?"

"Help me, Dubh Súile. Help me make a war."

Four

The massive double-doors to the keep slid shut with a well-oiled sigh. Nuada turned to Maureen and Sean. His face was dark and his eyes empty of all but rage as they zeroed in on Maureen.

"How did you do that?"

"I don't – do what?" Panic made her voice high and she searched the open hall, as if it would have an answer that would satisfy the king. "What did I do?"

He ignored her. "Take the boy back to the cell. You – come with me."

Sean roared and tried to tear himself from the guards' hands. They were ready and held him fast.

"No, wait! What did I do?" Maureen's voice was shrill.

Sean caught the calculation under the king's seething anger and stopped struggling.

"Stop, Maureen. It's okay. Don't let him—"

His warning was cut short as one of the guards struck him in the chest with a club. He doubled over, gasping for air, and glared up at the king while Maureen shouted and fought with the men who held her.

Nuada's eyes flashed and at a silent command, three of the guards began to pull Sean back while three others attempted to drag Maureen in the opposite direction. Her howling protests followed him out of the hall until they were silenced with a sharp cry.

Something snapped in his head and Sean wrenched himself free from the guards. If they hurt her—

He started to run but the guards were too fast. They grabbed him and he fell to his knees. Hands were in his hair, pulling and on his arms, squeezing. Again, a guard struck him. Sean spat in his face and kicked out with his feet.

"Do it," he growled as the guard brought the club up to swing one more time. "Because I'll keep fighting. I will never stop fighting."

"Now, my dear – why don't we try that again?" The king nudged Maureen with his foot.

The guards had tossed her to the ground where she tumbled and rolled. The fall hurt, but she was glad to be rid of their touch. The sensation of it made her stomach roil, as if the power within the gateway was concentrated on the Fae's skin.

She came to a stop at the foot of a high, stepped platform. Carvings covered the surface. Ogham, runes and other ancient scripts of forgotten peoples glowed, as if the dead words were alive with light and magic. The echoes of lost language danced before her eyes and murmured secrets in her ears.

"Try what?" she gasped finally.

"That little trick you pulled at the dais. Do it again."

"I don't know what you're talking about."

"You do – you made the mists boil with your righteous indignation. Your truth." He spat the words as if they were something ugly. "At one time, only your learned mystics could call the mists and make them bear witness to their words. Even Dubh Súile does not presume to use them against me, in my presence."

The king paused and waited for her to speak, or perhaps do something. She stared at the platform, silent, and he laughed.

"I was right to choose you."

"You chose me?" The satisfaction in Nuada's voice made her sick. She turned to face him.

"Those dreams – so whichever of us listened to you was the winner?"

The mists were building. Her arms tingled with the faintest kiss of electricity.

"And what would you have me do for you, now that I have this dubious honour of being chosen by the great Nuada Silver Arm?"

He said nothing and she glared at him. The air crackled, and the cool breath of wind touched her fevered cheeks.

The king smiled. It was a cold, thin smile. "Oh, yes. Very strong."

Maureen gasped. She could feel part of her awareness surge into the mists, as if they were an extension of her very being. She could taste her terror on her tongue and feel droplets of rage bead on her skin.

"No."

The breeze dropped until the living fog barely stirred across the floor. Tears, salty and real, slid down her face.

"I don't – I won't be your tool anymore."

"You will. You will learn."

"And if I don't?"

"You will die."

The storm rose again, hissing this time with sinister intent. It slammed into her, the hate a physical thing that attacked her from within.

Her shriek rent the air and Nuada laughed.

"Yes," he whispered. "You will learn."

"What is he doing to her?"

Sean sat, crumpled in the corner of his prison. The guards had met his bravado with restraint. They had felled him with a solid blow to the back of the knees and a follow-up to the gut before dragging him back to the remote hall that housed his cell.

He knew there was no escape – he had given the shimmering wall a kick as soon as they had released him – but at least he knew what kind of weapons were at the Fae's disposal: spears and clubs. There was the magic, which he could feel lingering in the mists, but only Nuada and the nameless woman who had spirited Dubh away seemed capable, or willing, to use it outwardly.

The guards were stationed at either end of the cavernous hall, and just outside his cell was a man, slim and short. He puttered at a table arrayed with bottles and crumbling scrolls.

Sean held his ribs. The man's stature did not matter. Even if he appeared unarmed, he was as dangerous as the rest of the Fae. Perhaps he should be glad the little man was ignoring him.

He cleared his throat. "I asked, what is he doing to her?"

The little man sighed. Doctor, wizard or what, Sean did not know; he appeared to be a quaint country gentleman in his vest and shirtsleeves. Wispy brown hair was brushed back from a high forehead and wire-rimmed spectacles perched on the bridge of his thin nose. Pale blue eyes regarded him with mild curiosity and exasperation. He looked like a human, but the flicker of magic, just perceptible as a layer over his body, said otherwise.

"Moulding her," the little man said finally. "She is powerful. You both are, but she is unpredictable."

Sean could not argue with that but it failed to make him feel better. He shook his head and rested it against the wall. "What are we? Who are you?"

"You are Changelings, and I am Dian Cécht."

"A pleasure, I'm sure," Sean grunted. "What are Changelings?"

Dian Cécht sighed and turned to face Sean fully. "I am not a schoolmaster, young man."

Sean said nothing and the little man relented. "Fine – bloody nuisance you are, blundering out there without any knowledge at all. Changelings are the last of the descendants of man and Fae. We thought he was the last one."

"Who?"

Again, Dian Cécht looked at him as though he should know, but relented when Sean shrugged.

"The Black Eye, the Defender of the People. He granted Nuada victory in the Fomorian War."

"Fomorian – against Balor?" Sean blurted.

While Maureen spent time studying Ireland's failed revolutions, he contented himself with tales of her former glory – myths and stories from her heroic past.

The Fomorians, led by Balor, had made Ireland theirs before the advent of the Tuatha Dé Danann. After much war, and with the help of the god, Lugh, Nuada Silver Arm, the king of the Tuatha Dé Danann, eventually defeated them. There was more to the story, he knew, but that was the simple version. Sean looked at the little man and wondered if he should know who he was.

Dian Cécht nodded. There was a small smile on his face. "Against Balor – and Bres. Some say Bres tried to remain neutral, but such was the war between the brothers that none could stay out of it. The Four Cities were nearly brought to ruin. Findias, the keep here, is all that remains."

Brothers? This was not the story he had read. Of course, the old tales had said Tír na nÓg was beautiful – populated by gods and heroes. It was meant to be magnificent and crowned in glory, not desolate and cowering in fear.

"Who was right?"

The little man shrugged. "Who is to say? It waged for years. Nuada argued we should remove ourselves entirely from the world of men – guard the gateways. He said humans were too primitive, and their Changelings too dangerous. New gods brewing, he said, and man had no more room for us."

"But I don't understand. Our stories say Nuada Silver Arm was a king – a High King of Ireland – who ruled over the Tuatha Dé Danann nearly four thousand years ago. You speak as if this is recent history."

Dian Cécht abandoned his scrolls. He touched the crystalline wall and moved through it as though it were simply a curtained door. Sean did not know if he should be flattered with the attention or chagrined, because he was no threat to these people.

"We don't exist within your plane – your reckoning of time is far different than ours." He hunkered down in front of Sean and began touching his ribs with a gentle hand. Sean braced himself for the pain but found, as the man continued, the pain was lessened.

He was a doctor, then.

"We retreated from your world before the war ever began, but our connection to it did not die. The Changelings remained and through them was a tremendous potential to manipulate the world of men. Nuada saw the danger and brought it to a stop. Dubh Súile helped him."

Sean's eyes grew wide. "Dubh?" Of course, the last of the Changelings! Human, like them, but different. Older. Powerful.

"He came to us – passed through the gateway, body and soul. He was one of the few ever to do so. He knocked on the door to the keep and offered himself first as a wright. Nuada told him we had one of those. Then he said he was a smith."

"And you had one of those, too?"

"Indeed."

"And next, did he say he was a harpist?"

"You've heard of the story before, then?" The doctor smiled.

It was genuine and Sean answered it with a grin of his own. "They tell us Lugh helped Nuada defeat the Fomorians."

"Lugh was Dubh's title for a while, though the king called him his "Black Eye" – the one who could see far, the one who would protect us from the poisonous eye of his brother, Balor."

Sean arched an eyebrow. The Eye of Balor was meant to be a weapon, which would kill all who looked upon it.

His companion continued. "Dubh Súile had the future-sight, but refused to use it, you see. Balor, like many of the descendants of Lir, had the future-sight as well, but Nuada claimed it would corrupt all who believed in it. Dubh became his mascot – the crippled Druid who would learn from us while letting his earthly power dwindle."

"So that is the world Nuada created when he won? It's a world of dying magic." Sean's chest was tight. The idea filled him with inexplicable grief.

"He asked us to believe in him. And we did. We believed in his peace. A day lasts so long here, and we do not die as you do, but we do know how to inflict considerable pain. Imagine those endless days filled with war, pain and fear."

"Was it worth it?"

The doctor looked down at his clothes. "I glowed once. And there is magic in the mists – not just rage. There is magic in our souls, too – a power greater than the mists, which we can find only with deep searching – deep training. But there is uncertainty there, and passion, too – all the things that bring us closer to man, to you."

Sean fell silent. He could see the power's allure, and the danger, too. He had watched it in Maureen. Dubh had not been asking him to save her from the Rising, but to help her save her own soul, and keep it strong.

"She has that power – and I couldn't protect her."

He had not meant to say it aloud, but it was true. Between them, Maureen was the gifted one – he could feel the currents of emotion around him, but he was at a loss to harness it as she could. He looked at the little Fae man and shrugged.

"I think you're wrong – I may be a Changeling, but I'm a sorry one. I can't use it."

"It is not just flashing lights and spectacle. It is here." He poked Sean in the chest.

Tingles of raw magic crawled across his skin and Sean had to force himself to keep still. Despite his protests and the desire for peace, the doctor had not given up all his power. Still, he marched to Nuada's tune.

"You felt that, did you not? I am not wrong. You simply require teaching."

"And who will teach me? Him?" He jerked his chin at the hall beyond his cell. "No thank you."

"Peace is seductive, boy, but for it to last, it must be controlled. Fear is a great weapon of control, when wielded with skill."

"And Nuada wields that weapon well, doesn't he? He'll wield her well, won't he?"

The doctor did not respond. The silence was too much and Sean kept talking just to keep from crying.

"What happened to the others?"

"The other Changelings?"

"You said we were the last."

"They are born, to be sure, but man has done much to destroy them. Those who managed to send out their souls in search of us either drew away once they found us, and the emptiness here, or went mad. Never were they allowed to roam free, as Dubh Súile was."

"Then how did we—"

"You saw him in his grove – it's the one place that is of our world and yours at once, and it is his alone. She woke him – or perhaps together you woke him. You created the bridge through the worlds, but you did it drawing on the energy of his grove, not here."

"Is that why – it is, isn't it?" Sean gasped as the answer hit him. "He was there already, in 1584, a full month before us. That's how he did it."

"Indeed. He knew to be there for you and make sure the ripples your *otherness* caused did not reach us here, or disturb those who met you there. I'm certain he had plenty to do, in that case. Despite your foolish protests, you are as powerful as he was – maybe even more so."

Sean resisted the urge to roll his eyes. "How is that?"

"He was born to see magic – he studied as a Druid and trained in their deepest secrets. You – you two were not. Yet, here you are."

"How do you know so much about him?"

"I was an acolyte to the guild of healers during the Fomorian War. Dubh Súile took me under his wing and guided me through battle. He nurtured my talent and brought me to the king. He found a place for me here."

The doctor rose to his feet and stepped out of the cell. The wall formed behind him again, as solid as ever.

"Yet, you would let the king kill him?"

"Who has Nuada killed? No one – Dubh Súile is free."

"We aren't."

"You are not my concern."

Five

At first glance, the great hall seemed empty – stark, just like the rest of Tír na nÓg – but as the guards marched Sean through it, iridescent balls of light, tucked in the corners, flared to life. Nuada lounged on a raised throne, aloof from the spectacle that played out below him.

Maureen was on her knees. The braids she had pinned to her head in Dublin were tumbling down around her shoulders, and damp tendrils stuck to her cheeks. They were wet, but from tears or sweat, he was not sure.

He pushed against the guards, but they held him fast.

"Let him go." Nuada's voice sounded bored.

He was at Maureen's side in an instant. He gathered her up in his arms and wiped the hair out of her eyes. They were shadowed with deep circles. He opened his mouth to speak, but she glanced at Nuada and gave a slight shake of her head.

"Ah, that's a good girl – no need to talk about me as though I was not here, yes?" The king drifted down from his throne. "Come, let us eat and talk."

Three servants had appeared, each armed with a tray. Food – it appeared to be food – was piled high. Glistening grapes and berries crowded thick slabs of meat and wedges of cheese.

Sean scowled as his stomach betrayed him with a growl, but neither he nor Maureen moved.

Nuada clucked his tongue. "Come now, help her sit, boy. I fear she is unused to rigorous training."

"Training?" He forced himself to focus on the king's words instead of the bribe of food. "You call this training? I call this torture."

He held out his arm but Maureen waved it away and stood on her own. She smiled at him but it turned into a grimace when Nuada laughed.

"Torture? This? It seems man truly has become weak over the centuries. That is too bad."

"I thought you believed us always to be weak," Sean countered. "Was that not why you took your people out of our realm?"

The king snorted. "I see Dian Cécht has been telling tales while he kept you company, my boy."

"He did not tell me nearly enough." He and Maureen continued to ignore the food and instead, sat on one of the low benches arrayed before the throne. There was no thought of escaping. Nuada could overtake them in an instant, and the guards were still there, hidden beyond sight, with their clubs and pointed spears.

"Well then, I shall fill in the gaps – you shall see how congenial I can be."

Maureen let out a wheezy laugh and Sean frowned.

"I'm okay," she said as she patted his hand. "I'm just . . . just winded. He hasn't touched me – not physically."

"You see, she is reluctant. I thought perhaps if she had you here, if you knew she was safe, she might be more cooperative."

Sean had no idea how to answer this and he stared at Nuada as the king drifted towards his throne, a single tray in his hand.

"Eat – no? Hm. Suit yourselves. You will need to

before the day is out. See, I am a benevolent master. Changelings do not often have so much choice."

"And just what are Changelings?" Maureen asked. Sean opened his mouth to answer – to share the doctor's words – but the king overrode him.

"Your Sr. Theresa called you that, did she not?"

Maureen started and Sean looked between her and the king. Could Nuada pull knowledge from their heads, or had Maureen mentioned it during her so-called lesson?

"Leave Sr. Theresa out of this," she hissed. "She is no concern of yours, Nuada Silver Arm."

The king laughed. It was not a pleasant sound. "Foundlings and changelings, am I correct, Master Sean?"

Sean opened his mouth to speak but closed it and drew Maureen closer to him as if his arm could protect them from the king's mental probing.

"She was not wrong, although you people have twisted the word – as you twist everything my people left you." Nuada sneered. "Your stories say a Changeling is a Fae child, secretly swapped for his human counterpart. When the simple folk of the village discover the swap – because a child is ill, bad, or *other* – they lock them away, ostracize them, or simply kill them."

"Once that was true, but no longer. Science—"

"Do not speak to me of your modern magicians, boy. You are Changelings, but you are not children of the Fae in the strictest sense of the word. You are what is left of the meeting of man and the Tuatha Dé Danann. You carry within you a lineage of a great people, driven from your lands – driven from your very dimension – by invaders, by men and their gods."

Images of battle-scarred warriors fighting for the lush green of Ireland flashed through Sean's mind. Hidden, safe in a magical fog, were the Tuatha Dé Danann, led by Nuada Silver Arm. Despite himself, he shuddered. Maureen looked at him and nodded. She saw it too.

"Horrible, is it not? You are safer here – we could make a place for you. I have been offering Maureen that choice, but you see how she resists me."

"First you threaten us with death and now you extend your hospitality?" Sean barked a mirthless laugh. "No wonder she resists. You are mad, Nuada."

"And yet I know you are too dangerous to roam. You have too much power and the gateways would be a sore temptation to you. You are still human, after all. The choice I give you is the only one I can give you."

"By what right do you have to kill us?" Maureen asked. She pulled away from Sean and straightened her shoulders.

"It is what we do with your kind. You humans were never particularly bright – violent, yes, but certainly not bright. Sadly, you seem to have grown more ruthless as the centuries have passed."

Nuada sighed with deep resignation, but Sean could not tell if the emotion was a mockery or not.

"Of course, I would rather you live here, with us. Why do you think I work so hard to help you learn? To have two of you, born to the same generation – in the same town, no less, and reared together? It is kismet."

He eyed them from the throne. Neither one moved. Whatever he saw in their faces, it made him scowl.

"Oh, for the love of Danu, eat. Eat or I will force you to eat."

Maureen hid a smile; the king was irritated. Good. He was easier to withstand when he was angry.

She leapt to her feet and grabbed at a bunch of grapes. They felt real, at least. She popped them into her mouth.

"You will not touch either one of us," she said, talking around them as she chewed. Nuada made a distasteful face and she grinned at him.

She tossed half the bunch to Sean. He was still looking at her as though she was damaged and she waggled her fingers at him to let him know she was fine. Whether he saw it or not – or believed her – was another thing entirely.

"It may be kismet, but it does not give you the right of life or death over us," she added.

"And how would you stop me?"

"You said yourself we are strong. Perhaps we are stronger than you are. Perhaps we can truly be Changelings and strengthen your bloodlines."

"Blasphemous child." Nuada's face was growing darker and she knew she was risking his ire. "We need not your strength. I want you here so I may control you. We risk much with you running around out there. I would keep my people safe."

Maureen laughed. Sean nearly choked on the grapes in his mouth and turned wild eyes on her.

"Are you afraid of us, Nuada Silver Arm?"

"You do not know what true fear is, Maureen Clare O'Malley."

Sean pulled on her shoulder. "Are you trying to

make him angry?" he hissed in her ear.

She nodded ever so slightly.

"He'll hurt you."

She wanted to tell him he was wrong – that she could try to use the power against the king, because he *was* afraid of them, but Nuada was watching. She just squeezed his hand.

Nuada was not just watching, he was laughing. "Listen to the boy. There is no reasoning with me, and I will hurt you, but not if you work with me, my dear."

His voice sounded like honey. He had already tried that tactic and failed. Maureen slit her eyes at him and bit her lip. Perhaps, she thought, this time Nuada should think he had won.

"If you taught us your history – the stories as they really are, not the myths we've come to learn – we could be your bridge."

"Maureen, what are you saying? You'd work with him, after what he's done?"

She ground her teeth in frustration; Sean did not understand. But then, how could he? She had blocked him from her heart just as willingly as she had let Nuada in.

"Your Maureen is never done bargaining," Nuada called. "She bargains her soul for your life, for Dubh Súile's life. To have such an advocate. It must make you feel weak, boy."

Sean looked at her and she saw the understanding dawn in his eyes.

"No," he said quietly. "It makes me lucky."

Nuada's mocking laugh filled the great hall. "Lucky? You are naive. Show him, girl. Show him how you would bargain for them. Would you not do anything to save your friends? Prove it."

Before the king was even done speaking, hands

reached down to grab them. Maureen struggled briefly but the guards were too strong, and held them both fast.

Nuada approached them – approached them as the fabled king. He towered above them, his face terrible and beautiful all at once. His silver gauntlet flashed as it rose to strike.

"Sean!"

Maureen lashed out with hands and feet, even her teeth, as three of the guardsmen dragged her from Sean's side. At the centre of the room, secure within their grip, she could do nothing but watch as Nuada taunted her friend with glancing blows from the gauntlet.

But Sean did now bow under the king's rage. Instead, he was looking at her. His blue eyes were wide with fright, and something else – something darker, something she recognized as kindred.

Defiance.

The king struck him again, harder this time, and Sean sagged against the guards who held him.

Maureen forced herself to stop struggling. "Nuada, stop!"

The king turned to her, the mockery of a smile curving his austere lips into a snarl.

"Make me, Changeling."

The wind rose.

"Maureen, don't give in to him!"

"You will stand with me, girl, or he will die. You know how to unlock the power in your soul – do it."

"No!" She fought the panic in her voice. Too late, she understood. Pain had not worked to the king's satisfaction, so Sean was the next best teaching tool.

"You're stronger than this," Sean called. "Everyone keeps telling me just how strong we are.

Prove it. Don't be his plaything."

"Strong?" Her laugh verged on hysterical. "I'm the one he nearly destroyed. He touched your mind, too, and you denied him. You stood up to him. I barely could."

"And now?"

She felt Nuada's fingers lace their way through her mind. They brought with them searing, blinding pain.

"I don't know – it hurts so much, Sean. Everything hurts." Her voice sounded small in her ears, and she hated it.

"You have yet to feel pain, my dear." Nuada struck Sean again.

His knees buckled and he fell to the ground. The blows continued to fall but he took them silently.

A wordless scream tore through her, but Nuada just laughed. He raised his silver-clad arm again.

The scream turned to words, words she did not understand. The mists began to rise. Her hair whipped her face, stirred by a maelstrom that surrounded only her.

Sean lifted his head. He looked at her and tears began to run down his cheeks. "Maureen. Don't do this. Don't give in."

She held his eyes. "He'll kill you."

"No, he won't. I believe in you." His voice was no more than a hoarse whisper but it carried through the throne room. "I believe in you. You are better than he is – but if you give in now, he will make you his. He will destroy your soul. Promise me."

She stood at the eye of a hurricane, breathless, waiting. His words echoed in her ears.

Promise me.

"Don't ask me to sacrifice you."

"I'm not. I'm asking you to live, free. Promise

me."

"Free," she echoed. Her arms faltered and dropped.

"You will never be free," Nuada growled. "You will always be different, you will always be other."

"But I will not be subject to you."

The wind eased and then died. The roiling mass of red and black mist dissipated until it wafted in small, harmless clouds in the corners.

She took a deep breath and waited for the king's rage – his retribution.

He began to clap.

"That was beautifully played. I am impressed." He laughed at her stunned face. "Oh, don't look too surprised, my dears. I would not have been king long if I had not learned to anticipate the fickle natures of men."

He gestured to the guards. They pulled Sean up from the ground and hauled him to Maureen's side.

They let his arms go free and he wrapped them around her. For the first time in what seemed like years, she yielded to the embrace and rested her head on his shoulder.

"I don't feel so well," she whispered.

"After all that, I'm not surprised." He tried to laugh but it faded into a weak wheeze.

"No – different." Her eyes were losing focus. She began to fall. He grabbed at her, stumbled, but managed to ease her onto the floor.

He was on his knees, cradling her, but all he wanted to do was lay his head on the ground. It took all the energy he had left to focus on the king.

"What—what have you done?"

It was all he could manage, and as the dark closed in, he could have sworn the madman smiled.

Six

"Where are they, Nuada?"

"Such disrespect, my child. What happened to 'my king,' or 'my liege?' I would even settle for 'your highness,' or 'your majesty.' You sound like those disrespectful children when you speak like that."

"Enough. I did not come here to bandy words with you."

"No? Then why grace my door at all? Are you here to heal the breach between us?"

Dubh stood in the shadows, just outside the entrance of the throne room. Behind the guards and unseen by the servants, he dug deep into his training to keep himself hidden. While the Seers had finessed his knowledge, helped him adapt to the constant intrusion of the mists on his awareness, the Druids had been the first to teach him to blend in with his surroundings – the Druids and the hunters.

Even so, he lacked the native ease of bending the perceptions of others around himself. Despite Niamh's impertinent distraction, beads of sweat were already forming on his forehead in his effort to maintain the shield.

"You know why I'm here." Niamh sounded bored. She played her father well, Dubh thought. She wanted to push Nuada to his most arrogant – push him so he might divulge his plans for

Maureen and Sean, while Dubh searched them out.

Dubh had not pointed out that capitalizing on Nuada's hope Niamh might 'heal the breach' between them by submitting to his will was a cunning she had learned at her father's knee.

"Hm. I thought as much. Are you really so concerned with those mortals, my dear? They are alive – safe even – but I will not tell you where. Unless of course, you wish to tell me where you spirited Dubh Súile?"

Niamh snickered.

"Indeed. I knew I would regret allowing him the grove, but the hope he might prove to be other than what I expected was too tempting." The king laughed at himself.

"Dubh Súile's grove may be outside my sight, but I have men upon the Plain. In fact, those Seers still loyal to their king have been released. A gateway cannot be called into being without my knowledge. There will be no escape for you – you must know that."

"You would awaken those whose power you fear? Is war your desire, Nuada?" Niamh's tone was arch, but there was a warning in her words. "The last time the gateways were watched with such scrutiny, your brothers were deposed and you were placed on the throne. I would take care, lest it becomes a prophesy."

Nuada laughed again but Dubh was not fooled. Niamh had finally opened his eyes to a realm of dying magic. To unleash the Seers was the act of a desperate man.

"And who would depose me?" Nuada was asking Niamh. "You? My dear girl, I think not. Go back to your weavings – yes, I know you have defied me. That I let you live shows my mercy."

"Mercy?"

Niamh's voice cracked on the word and Dubh winced. Her composure was slipping. Of course, the king had always known exactly how to provoke his daughter.

"You are a tyrant and a fool, Nuada. You risk the people's anger with their presence – better than I ever could. You've slandered your champion – what makes you think the people will accept your new pets?"

"They are stronger than Dubh, and they must be contained."

"Ah, I see – you would neuter them. If they come under your heel, the truth of what the girl said will be rendered moot, is that it?"

"You always were a bright one, Niamh. It's such a pity you fight me. We could do great things together."

"You know I'll never join you."

"You are stubborn, like your mother."

"Leave my mother out of this. Her passing is on your hands, Nuada."

Dubh held his breath at the raw outrage in her voice. She was risking much in coming here. Now it was his turn, and the minds of his fellow Changelings were his quarry.

Niamh had accused him of failing them – failing to teach them – and it was true. They had heard her – obeyed her, even – during Nuada's spectacle outside the keep, but in all the months of chasing them through time, he had never attempted to speak to them. It was finally time to try.

He sent out his awareness to probe the stronghold's secret places. The king's prisons were mental as well as physical. Walking through their walls was impossible unless one had the proper words. These were cells of Nuada's making, and only the king would have the means to open them. Accessing the minds of those within the cells was another matter, however, and even then, it took concentration to navigate the labyrinth of spells and detours Nuada had created around them.

He was ruthless, and dangerous, but the king was not stupid.

Dubh quieted his mind until there was nothing but him, Maureen and Sean. One by one, he filled the space with their banter and smiles, with the rages and tears he had witnessed in these past months of dogging their steps and fighting for their souls. He used the knowledge of them to cut a swathe through the labyrinth. It was crude – human, Nuada would say – but effective.

He sighed as they appeared. They were mere pinpoints of light, but it was enough. He reached for them.

They could not answer.

His face flushed and he struggled with a rage so deep it threatened to shatter the safeguards protecting him. They were alive, but they travelled beyond his reach.

Nuada must have fed them. Food from the king's table was often laced with magic, but only at the high feasts. To hear Niamh tell it, there had not been one of those in many moons, but the lack of merriment in his hall had not deterred Nuada from pushing his devilry on Sean and Maureen.

The Faerie Sleep had claimed them. It was, perhaps, the only way to control them.

Dubh shook himself free of the grip of blinding emotions and shifted his awareness back to the throne room.

Nuada and Niamh were shouting at each other.

"They will either become my new champions, or they will die."

Niamh stifled a crude laugh. "You would risk their deaths, my lord? You are not exempt from the havoc that would create – the changes it would mean. You know who they are. You know—"

"Do not presume to tell me, Niamh Golden Hair, what havoc I will wreck. What of you? What will this – your defiance – do to our world?"

"Save it."

Nuada laughed. The mirth drew deep from his belly and the sound filled the cavernous room.

"You know nothing, you wee chit of a girl. I do not deny he is powerful, but would that I had never granted Dubh Súile access to Findias – never accepted his help. He turned the tide of our war against Balor and Bres. He allowed me to take my father's crown, but at what cost?"

Niamh made small noises to interrupt her father, but Nuada pushed on.

"I do not care to have the spectre of his power hanging over us. He retreated and we survived. When he woke, he went, not to me, but to the Changelings – his brethren." The word sounded foul on Nuada's lips.

"He allowed them to pass through – he took no notice of the rules we have in place here, and gave little regard to the training they would require."

"It was an accident, my lord!"

"Ah, there it is – the respect. You know he did wrong, do you not?"

"Perhaps," Niamh allowed.

Dubh winced.

"But meeting that wrong with one of equal – nay, more devastating – power is certainly not warranted."

"Only when you have been monarch for as long as I have will you be able to tell me what is warranted and what is not. And by the gods, that day will not come soon."

"But death? They are rash, I grant you, but Dubh Súile has power here, power he does not wield." Niamh's voice was rising, and her anger stirred murmurs in the air.

"I have seen who they are, Nuada Silver Arm. I have seen the place they take in the web of history we have woven here. Their death means you risk defeat at the hands of Bres and Balor. Would you destroy all you have built in order to neutralize his power?"

Her voice rang in the silence of the hall. Neither laughter nor mockery met her words. Careful to keep his mental shield in place, Dubh stepped closer to the throne room's entrance. Niamh's words were powerful, and he would see Nuada's face as the king attempted to combat them.

"You are not the only one with future-sight, daughter. I know who they are. The descendants of Domnall mac Aindriú have spread throughout the world, and are strong indeed."

Dubh stared at them. Salty trickles of sweat stung his eyes and blurred his vision. Domnall mac Aindriú was the name of his son, and his son had died as a babe in his mother's arms.

"Then why?"

Nuada brought the full force of his steely eyes to bear on the woman before him. Niamh did not cower.

"You are too ready to assume I would destroy them, Niamh. I would control them – contain them. I will not have their strength used as a bludgeon against me. I will not risk their power becoming so great that this world, and our people, rely on their capriciousness to save it. Not again."

Dubh closed his eyes and allowed Nuada's words to flow through him. Now was not the time to avenge the life he had lost. Now was the time to free them all from the tyranny he helped to create.

Keeping Sean and Maureen as pets might break their power, or it could force it to grow so deep and potent that their revolt would destroy Tír na nÓg and the Tuatha Dé Danann. Dubh slipped from the keep with Niamh's final words for Nuada ringing in his ears.

"But who will save it from you, my lord?"

"Who are they, Niamh?"

They lingered in Findias – in the home of one who kept close to the king, if only so he could protect the interests of the king's daughter. Miach was the son of Nuada's physician, Dian Cécht, and a healer himself. He would have to go into the king's service soon, or forswear his gifts. He looked at Niamh with hope shining in his watery blue eyes.

Niamh nodded to the young man and he silently retreated from the subterranean chamber. It was safe from prying eyes and ears, he said.

"They are the descendants of Domnall mac Aindriú—"

"How can that be – I was told . . ." Dubh's voice broke and he put his head in his hands. "I was told he was dead – dead with his mother while I fought Nuada's war."

He never spoke to anyone in Tír na nÓg – not even Áine – of his life among man, before the Fomorian War. That world was closed to him, and thinking about it was like poking at a sore tooth, painful and impotent. But now, with Nuada's words – with his son's name – hanging in the air . . .

"I returned to them, you know," he said, as if Niamh's silence was an irresistible summons to unburden himself of the truth at last. "I returned to the world of man after the war was ended. None of my kin lived, and had not for a very long time."

"How many years had passed?"

"Sixty. Sixty years, gone." He could not keep the bitterness out of his voice, and stood as if to escape it.

"I returned to Tír na nÓg and unleashed my fury on Nuada. He was newly crowned and feeling benevolent. He let me rage, but told me I could not return to them – could not save them. He told me my time in the war barred me from their lives."

He stopped and looked at her. "They were past saving, he said. And then I knew: there was nothing left for me in the world of man."

"And so you made a trade?" Niamh's voice was soft but he winced at the implication. "He offered you immortality – a life of learning and magic here as consolation for the life with them?"

"I could not have had a life with them. We were at war – the Cruthin and the Northumbrians. My father, brother and I led the mac Alastair clan in battle and were captured. Our people thought us dead, and my love, Mairead, cast aside our bond to ally with my rival, Mártainn mac Aindriú. She secured his men for the war, to see to it that our deaths were not in vain. His warriors saved my life. When we returned home, Mairead begged me to understand – to stay as a bard at Mártainn's hearth – but I could not. The child . . ."

He trailed off. His cheeks burned with shame.

"You do not need to explain yourself to me." Niamh smiled softly and reached for him.

He stared at her hand as it rested on his. She may not need his explanation, but part of his own heart did.

"We were on the march more than a year. Mairead had a babe in arms when we returned. He carried Mártainn's name. I did not discover he was my son until the night she begged me to stay, instead of going to Ireland." He sighed. The grief and pride lingered like ghosts in his heart. No amount of wandering could banish them.

"I couldn't stay. My pride would not allow it. I disappeared after that. I roamed Ireland for years – I tried to lose myself."

His laugh was harsh in his ears and he felt Niamh flinch slightly.

"It worked better than I imagined. I vanished. The bards say when word reached my kin, and Mairead heard of it, so wild was her despair she threw herself off the ridge that guarded our lands. Their songs chronicled her heartbreak and prophesied my return. It was said she waited for me between the worlds, and would use magic of her own to call me home again. They said one day, we would be as one."

He blinked back tears. "Of course, I heard these tales sixty years later, and it was not true. They were gone – Nuada said Domnall perished with her. I searched the mists for them, but I could not find them. I did not understand my power here well enough to build the gateway necessary to find them before they perished, either – not without becoming hopelessly lost."

He stopped. There were no more words to his story, no more words to recount his failure, but

Niamh kept her hand on his and brushed it ever so lightly, as if weaving an invisible web of wellbeing over it.

"He lied about Domnall," she said finally, her voice low and strained. "He lied about so many things – he lied to keep you here." She looked up at him. "Much has been stolen from you, my friend."

He looked into her face and saw a tear sparkle on her cheek. He smiled faintly and brushed it away. "And much has been given in return."

"Enough?"

Dubh let his sight wander beyond the room, beyond Findias and the realm of Faerie.

"That Domnall and Mairead live on in Sean and Maureen . . ." He sighed and allowed his child to die all over again, but this time as a man, surrounded by children of his own. "Then it is enough. They are worthy descendants."

There was no sympathetic smile or understanding on Niamh's face as he said this. Once more, the unfinished tapestry flashed before him. It writhed and twisted along the pathways of its tale, just as the realization of all the things Niamh knew and did not say slithered through his gut.

There was more to the story.

"Who are they, truly?"

"Did you never wonder what it was about them that woke you?"

"Maureen called my vision to her. She was the one who pierced the veil to see me – no one from the world of men had done that in over a thousand years." He shook his head at his foolishness. "I could not help myself. I had to reach out to her. I had to be seen. That was when I realized it was both of them. But she saw me, first."

"The girl with the green eyes." There was a smile in the Fae woman's voice.

"So green – like my mother's eyes."

"And her mother, before her."

Ice threaded through his veins and he jerked his hand back as though he had been stung, without quite knowing why.

"Your mother was *other*, was she not?" Niamh asked, standing. A secret, cunning smile had slipped over her face, and it made the hairs rise along his arms and neck.

"Other?" Other was the word used for those Changelings – like himself, or Sean and Maureen – who ventured to other times. They possessed a strangeness, a slight discordance with those around them. It took craft and guidance to overcome that other-ness, and though he wished to deny it, his mother never had.

"My mother was no Changeling."

"It is said," Niamh began, taking no notice of his growing discomfort, "when Manannán mac Lir still walked among us, our magicians could summon the souls of men – Changeling or not. They would call them across the boundaries between our worlds to do the magician's bidding. Knowledge and other boons were exchanged for this, but it was still considered a dark power. It was one Bres and Balor coveted, and one banished with the war."

Dubh nodded. The deeper magics were ancient, and perilous in the wrong hands. Nuada exploited that fear.

"A few mortals in the Isles learned this power. Their Druids kept it secret – only those highly trained in the mysteries even told of its existence. When invaders with new gods came, they attempted to destroy the priests – so horrified were these Romans, they could not allow the knowledge to exist. Yet, one of the priests escaped and she passed the knowledge on. It survived in this way – one dying mystic telling his or her student, and so forth – until the day came that it had to be used."

"Are you saying—" He stopped. He was not sure he wanted to know what she was saying.

"Did anyone ever tell you how the Fomorian War began?"

He shook his head. He had entered it in its final days. In his need to stay alive, he had asked very few questions.

"That power, wielded only once by humans, started our war. Nuada was stunned – terrified of the consequences and for once, truly remorseful at the cost. The woman called through the centuries was, as you say, no Changeling, and her presence upset the balance of power in a small clan of men. It is said that she saved them."

The bards refused to sing of the treachery that brought his clan – the mac Alasdair clan – to the brink of ruin. They refused to pass on the secrets that nearly destroyed his mother, and balked at telling the tale of how his father became a leader no one thought him capable of becoming.

"She did." The words were wrenched from him, but Niamh took no notice.

"I'm not sure how she survived – it was only her soul that crossed the gateway, mind. It must have been a valiant soul."

"My mother was a queen."

"Her mother before her could have been a goddess, and she raised her daughter well."

Dubh stared at her. There was no falsehood in her face, no manipulation.

"In the coming years, there will be a child.

Maureen, at least, must leave here."

"Maureen." He stared at her. His head buzzed with the dissonance of her words even as he acknowledged the truth in them.

"It would be well if it was both of them, but I cannot see all."

He held his arms close to his body and stared at the floor. Slowly – so slowly – he allowed himself to accept the truth of her words. Even as he did so, a horrible thought forced him to speak.

"Does Nuada know?"

"A child bred in captivity would be a useful tool. Perhaps his goal is simply to have a tame Druid instead of a crippled one."

He ignored the jibe. "He was so horrified by that one act he would manipulate it into happening again?"

"Part of me wonders if he regrets letting the old magics slip beyond his grasp."

He accepted this in silence. She put a hand on his shoulder and he forced his gaze outward, forced himself to look at her. She waited for him to speak.

"Long ago, I gave my oath to protect Tír na nÓg. I will do all within my power to uphold my oath." He stared into her eyes – those silver eyes deep with compassion, and bright with fire. "But if it comes to it, I will bring all to ruin to keep them safe. The line of Domnall mac Aindriú will be his tool no more."

She nodded. "I will call the people. It is time to gather."

Seven

S ean whimpered. It was a small sound. It was nearly lost amid the harsh noise filling his ears, but it was the whimper that woke him. The whimper voiced the fear, which had settled deep in his body and stolen his strength.

Yet, he could not remember why.

He knew where he was. He knew, too, that Maureen had collapsed in his arms as they battled a king. An impossible king. A High King of Tara, according to the legends. A lunatic, according to his own senses. No, he had not been frightened then.

He had been angry.

He opened his eyes. Before him was not the slow rippling of Tír na nÓg's mists, but a wall of blinding hate. From within its depths, hands reached out to snatch at him. Faces sneered at him, and voices shrieked.

He squeezed his eyes shut. It couldn't be real. Why were they attacking him? What had he done?

The kiss of a thousand whispers brushed his skin. He was no one, they said. He was powerless. He was weak.

He began to whimper again but stopped as hands grabbed hold of him. They were not whispers or phantoms. The hands were real and they were slapping him. They were pestering him to wake up.

Wake up! Of course. It was a dream. All he had to do was wake up, and it would be over.

Sean opened his eyes.

Monsters stood before him – ghastly aberrations with familiar faces. They cavorted and gestured to him. They laughed at him behind clawed hands with too many fingers and open wounds. Eyeless heads mocked him and huge empty caverns pretending to be mouths laughed at him.

His wordless howl joined them in a hideous symphony. It rose into the gathering gloom, and did not stop.

Maureen felt hands grab at her. She wanted to struggle, to keep them from touching her, but she was too weak. She could barely turn her head. A shout lodged in her throat, and came out as a sigh instead.

She remembered the throne room where she did battle with a fable – a fable who wished either for her capitulation or for her death. Neither option pleased her, so she defied him. With the strength of Sean's belief in her, she refused to allow Nuada to use her any longer.

And still, she was overcome. She had collapsed and the magic of Tír na nÓg had swallowed her whole – aided, no doubt, by the sleeping agent Nuada had slipped into their food. It had swallowed her and she could not move. She could not move and she could not see.

But, there was no reason to move. Nuada would never allow them to leave. Dubh had been spirited away and they were alone. They would always be alone.

Tears began to leak from her eyes and blanket her face with their wetness, but she made no move to wipe them away. It was no use. They had tried, at every avenue, to make something good come from this disaster – this nightmare – that had begun that night in the church. And at every turn, one more thing had come to tear them apart.

They would never be whole, would never be safe. Even worse, everything they cared for was at the mercy of a maniac who would use what he could to ensure their submission. Of this, she was certain. Nuada's wrath would destroy everything she and Sean touched, and they were powerless to stop him.

The darkness seemed to deepen.

The hands were back – those pesky hands that wanted her to move. Did they not know how tired she was?

She protested and it came out as a pathetic mewling. The hands forced her to sit. Muffled, as if from far away, someone was screaming. Part of her shied from the sound, but another recognized something in it, something familiar.

"Too much," a voice was saying. She could not place it. It was not the fable's voice and it was not Sean. It was—

"Can someone please stop his screaming? What was Nuada playing at giving them only the food laced with the Sleep? We will be lucky if they are sane when they wake. I may need you to call the other healers."

The voice moved away from her. With tremendous effort, she brought her fingers to her eyes. Her lids were squeezed shut. She needed to see. Her breath came fast and heavy until she remembered how to open them.

Slowly – so slowly – her rational mind freed itself from the grip of the king's poison. All was dark around her, dark and empty, but she knew it was not. The voice she heard – an exasperated voice of reason – was somewhere close.

Then there was the screaming. It was coming from Sean. As soon as she realized it, the muffled screams became a howling that beat at her brain.

The darkness had to go. As her mind cleared, she focused on her desire to see. She closed her eyes again and took air deep into her lungs. The heady swirl of her thoughts stilled. She called to the mists, to the whispers that haunted them. She entreated them to fall away and allow her to see.

When she opened her eyes, the room was clear. The mists were hers to command.

"Do you remember when Tír na nÓg lived, green with promise? Do you remember when human bards declared this land a paradise, a land where no man died, hungered or fell to frailty? Would they even recognize us now?"

Niamh stood before her army with Dubh beside her. He had abandoned the shadow of his cloaked hood and donned the regalia of the warrior. His chest plate – forged by Tír na nÓg's talented smiths during the war against Bres and Balor – glowed in the light reflected from the torches.

Too young to join that battle, Niamh had no regalia, but that did not stop her from rallying her people. She was a shining beacon in the growing twilight.

Hundreds – not just those who had first allied themselves with the king's daughter – had come from what was left of the Four Cities of Tír na nÓg to present themselves in Mag Mell. Niamh's words, her weavings and her tales had drawn them to her, but more importantly, the purity of their world, harboured within her soul, called to them and demanded they rise.

They would stand with her. They would stand with her champion.

"We create our surroundings, and led by this king, we are stranded in a desolate, angry world. The time will come when the mists will act as a maelstrom and wipe this place clean. I fear for us when this happens."

"What would you have us do?" called a voice near the front. The crowd parted and the owner of the voice stepped forward. It was the silversmith, Credne. His brand marked Dubh's breastplate and he was happy to see the talented man was yet alive. So many that he had known had passed rather than be a part of the world Nuada created.

"You, Master Credne? I would have you open your forge and stoke the fires once more."

"And I?" This was a woman. Macha had been a handmaiden of the Queen and was a princess in her own right.

"Macha, you once taught us all to laugh and sing. You crafted songs for love and battle, and I would have your beautiful voice sing us to victory once more."

"What about us?" a chorus of men and women called. Miach stood in their midst.

"Healers, you will attend to us – you will mend our bodies and our souls."

"My lady." It was a small voice at the centre of the crowd. The mass parted and a young child – who could not be old enough to remember when tales were sung merrily at feasts – came forward.

She was pale and slight, and a wash of fair red hair fell down her back. In her hands was cupped a small but radiant bit of magic. She stood before them, her eyes cast to the ground.

Dubh knelt at her side. "What is it, child?"

She looked up at him. Her eyes were the faint green of a misted hill. She was a child of the magicians.

Niamh knelt too and held out her hands. The child gently released her prize.

It was a flower. It was more real than anything Niamh wove through her hair, but it shared the same shimmer of magic.

As they watched, it bloomed in Niamh's hand. It opened, petal by petal. Its pale outer leaves gave way to a blushing heart. Its perfume scented the air and Dubh inhaled deeply.

"It was a gift, my lady, crafted by the beloved Queen Áine. We kept it hidden and safe so the memory of her magic would remain. It is now our gift to you, her daughter, Niamh Golden Hair."

Niamh gave the young girl solemn nod, and rose. She held the flower aloft, for the company to see.

"Who here has yet the memory to create a flower of such beauty?" she asked. The company was silent.

"We have been apart, afraid and alone, for too long, my friends. Our memories and our songs were banished when the enemy was defeated. In victory, we allowed ourselves to be cowed."

Turning, she passed the flower to the security of Dubh's hands.

"By standing aside and allowing the silence to grow, we allow a greater harm to be committed. Dubh is not our enemy and the children in Nuada's keeping have done nothing to us – save awaken the memory of what we once were.

"War is coming, and today we will stand firm and claim the Changelings as our brethren, as once we claimed Dubh Súile as our own."

Dubh cradled the flower and called on his training. Once, he had walked with the magicians, the healers and the weavers.

In his mind, a young vine, wet with dew, wove around the flower. It formed a living garland, studded with delicate flowers and budding leaves. He breathed life into the image and it grew heavy in his hand.

A golden vine, its bud and flower adorned now with precious stones, circled Áine's flower.

It was a crown fit for a queen, and he set it on Niamh's head.

The company roared.

Eight

Maureen's breath came fast. The mists had obeyed her. They had obeyed her without desperation or fear. They had obeyed a simple entreaty and a desire to see.

She was almost certain it was something Nuada did not want her to understand.

In the opposite corner of the cell, Sean was holding himself tight, but his shrieks had subsided to whimpers. She started to crawl to him. Something in the haze had amplified the narcotic in the food, and with it gone, the terrors it held for him slowly eased.

She stopped. How had she known that?

Whispers. Whispers in the mist.

Nuada had taught her too much.

"How did you—?"

She turned at the voice. A short, gentlemanly-looking Fae stood just beyond the walls of her cell. Pale eyes peered at her above spectacles. She wondered if he needed them, or if they were just a mirage – part of how he believed he ought to appear to her.

He smiled at her. "You are a clever one. I am Dian Cécht, healer to the king. He is right to try to tame you."

"He can only tame that which he can catch," she countered. She took her friend's shoulders in her hands. His eyes were bulging and his mouth was stretched wide with horror.

"Sean. Sean – it's me."

He made no response, but his hands batted at her and caught in her hair.

"Sean – no, stop!" She looked up at the doctor but he was watching them with detached amusement.

She made a rude noise in her throat and gave Sean's shoulders another shake.

This time he fought back and she did the only thing she could think of to break the grip of his Faerie-induced hysteria.

She slapped him. "Sean Robert McAndrew, stop this. Now."

He stopped. His arms fell limp to his sides and he stared at the space beyond her with his jaw slack.

"Sean? Can you hear me?"

He nodded slowly, still gaping into the distance.

"Focus on my voice. Whatever you're seeing, it isn't real. You need to wake up."

Blinking back tears, she gathered his hands in hers while he struggled to master his grip on reality. A quick glance at Dian Cécht assured her he was not going to attempt to stop her. Far from it – he, and the guard who had appeared next to him, watched with interest.

"Sean, come back to me. Please." Her voice no more than a whisper, she rested her head against their entwined hands.

After what seemed like ages, Sean began to speak.

The words were so faint she had to lean in to hear him. "What? What did you say?"

"*Márín Mhaol,*" he repeated, his face empty but for a small, wistful smile. His eyes searched the distance, as if remembering.

"Your hair. Grania wanted to cut it but you didn't want to be bald – Maureen the Bald. You wanted to be free, rebellious hair and all, so you were Maureen the Mule."

He finally focused on her and his smile bloomed wide. He captured one rebellious curl within his fingers.

"I should have stood with you. You didn't need me, but that didn't matter. I forced you to choose and I was angry when you chose to be free."

He shook his head when she would have interrupted and clung to the curl to keep her close to him.

"I know Nuada was in your head – but even if he hadn't been, you believed so much in what freedom could mean. You believed to the exclusion of all else and I didn't understand. It hurt – God, it hurt – but I still should have stayed. No matter what, I should have stayed. I should have stood up with you when you defied Grania's edict to cut your hair, too. I was afraid – you're so strong and I'm just—"

"My heart and soul." She put a hand over his mouth to stem the flow of his words. She did not know what to do with them.

"What did you see in your fever dreams?" she asked instead.

Sean looked at her for a moment and she was afraid he would slip back into the terror.

"Monsters," he whispered. "Faces I thought I knew, but twisted and ugly. They were mocking me, pulling at me, shouting at me with words I couldn't understand. I – it was horrible, Maureen. Everything I thought I understood – it's all wrong. All of this is wrong."

"It is." She rested her chin on his knee. "Do you

know what I see, every time I've been drugged?"

"Every time?" he mouthed with an arched eyebrow. He shook his head.

"Nothing. I'm alone. They drugged me on Bingham's ship, and when I woke, I nearly ruined your attack because I was afraid everyone had gone and I missed your message. I was afraid all of you failed and I was alone." She shrugged and gave him a half-smile.

"Here, I was alone in an endless darkness. Every time, all I love and care for is gone and there is nothing. This place terrifies me because the nothing is so close. What we see is pulled from our hearts and minds – the magic, the peace and the horrors all come from in here." She pointed to his chest.

"Part of my strength comes from you, Sean McAndrew."

He brought the captured curl to his lips and let it slide through his fingers. "Then I am yours to use as you will, Maureen O'Malley."

A gentle cough sounded from the corner. The guard was standing at attention as a section of the prison wall dissolved. Dian Cécht stood before it, waiting.

"This is touching, truly, but I have orders to bring you before Nuada. I suspect you've another trial by the masses in store."

"Because that will be so bloody useful," Maureen muttered. She was going nowhere near Nuada unless it was to drive a knife into his empty heart. Standing on a platform, a prisoner, while the Tuatha Dé Danann raged at her for being human? While Nuada tore down Dubh in order to make room for his new pets? No. It was not going to happen.

She slipped her hand into Sean's. Slowly, they stood. She looked at him and he nodded. She could summon the mists – and so could he. Both of them had suffered the hidden horrors of this place.

Maureen poured what she knew into the mist. She beseeched it to help – to guard her and Sean from those who would threaten them – to wash clean the lies Nuada had created.

The faintest chime of bells told her the magic in the mist had listened, and agreed.

Faint drifts swirled at Dian Cécht's feet and rose, caught in the updraft from the wall of heartbreak and agony building behind Sean and Maureen.

Hand-in-hand, and standing perfectly still, they glared down at their captors. The light flickered and winked out. Their hair lashed at their faces as the living wall of mist roared past them. It filled the hall and shot through the corridors beyond.

The guards fled, but Dian Cécht remained. As the tumult subsided, he stood staring at them. His glasses had melted from his face.

A tear slid down his cheek. It glittered.

"We're supposed to look like this," he whispered, looking down at the tear as it splashed on his hand. The spot was nearly iridescent.

"We were beautiful once – even during that endless war, we could create magic. We shined brightly, once."

Dian Cécht's shirtsleeves and vest gave way to robes of blue and green, glimmering in the watery light left in the wake of Maureen and Sean's storm. Mist curled at his hem and slithered up his arms, harmless now. He looked up at them. Wonder was at war with prudence.

"Go." He nodded at the empty hall. "With power

such as that at your command, none of us will stop you. He might, but we cannot."

"Help us."

Dian Cécht had gone back to studying his hand. He looked up, amused.

"I just did. Go."

Nine

"**M**aureen – slow down. Where are we going?"

Sean pulled on her arm and she slowed to a walk. Nuada's stronghold was a labyrinth, an empty, deserted labyrinth, and so far, they had simply been following the trail left by their living wall of nightmares.

"I think it's leading us out – to the doors."

"It?"

"The mists – the whispers in the mist." She bit her lip. "Can you hear them?"

He paused and the faintest hum of otherworldly voices brushed his skin.

"Yes – I think. It's faint." It was an instinct, hearing them, just like knowing Maureen's intent back in their cell. The storm they had set into motion was leading them, yes, but to where?

And when they got there, could they stop it? Or would it peter out on its own? How could they call such a thing into being without knowing how to control it? If it wreaked real damage, then the allegations cast at them would be true – this time.

He ground his teeth and forced the questions and fears into something coherent, something useful. "When we get to the doors, what will we do? Nuada will be waiting for us."

It was hard to imagine the king – who could pick their thoughts like so many ripe berries – did not know what had happened within his keep. He would have to be waiting.

"I know." She paused and looked at him. "I – maybe we should find another way out, find a place to hide. Something."

They stood in the middle of the passageway. All was silent. Even the whispers had subsided.

"Where do we go from here?"

She looked at him for a moment, at a loss for words. They both knew he was not talking about the stronghold. She opened her mouth to speak and that was when they heard it: the familiar howling of wind gathering force. The threads of magic and emotion were coming together and weaving a web fierce enough to bridge time, create havoc or simply hide a few wanderers, lost and alone.

And it was not of their doing.

Sean spun with Maureen in his arms, and together they dropped to their knees. The mists surged around them and his mouth filled with the tang of metal.

Time lost meaning as they crouched amid the storm – it could have been seconds later or an eon when a tattooed arm reached through the vortex and pulled them into an oasis of relative calm.

Dubh's cloak was gone and his black hair flowed loose over his shoulders. He wore a simple tunic covered with a silver breastplate, and at his hip was the sword Nuada had taken from him.

Even without the circlet of gold atop his head, Dubh Súile looked every inch the warrior-king Nuada had tried to emulate.

"I thought you had gone," Sean managed to whisper.

"I left a few things behind." Dubh's face broke into a broad grin and he squeezed them to him.

"Here we planned a grand rescue for the two of you. I should have known you would not need it – not anymore."

"All the same, it was lovely of you to stop by." Maureen freed herself from his embrace and nodded at the passageway. "We think Nuada's that way – is there another way out of here?"

Dubh shook his head, kept hold of their arms and started walking. The large double doors to the keep were just around the corner.

"The king and his guardsmen are at the dais. Of course, they are also somewhat preoccupied with a small rebellion."

He stepped over the remnants of Nuada's sentries. The men lay curled on their sides. It looked like they were sleeping.

"Did you . . .?"

"No, although they will have sore heads when they wake. I'll not take lives needlessly when there is still a chance Nuada will step down."

He moved ahead of them and put a hand to the carved door. On the surface was etched a pictorial history of Tír na nÓg. There was even a panel featuring a wild-haired man offering his many services to the king, in exchange for succour. Later, that same man, clad for war, stood victorious at the head of an army.

Dubh touched the pictures briefly and looked at them over his shoulder. His face was unreadable. "It is a small chance, but Niamh wants to give him the opportunity to see his folly. For all her ire, she is hopeful."

He gestured to them. "Brace yourselves. Her people demanded an audience at the dias to give me time to distract his forces inside and find you. We must go."

"So hopeful, you attacked Nuada's front door," Sean muttered. He did not ask whom Niamh was – the image of the silver-eyed woman who had rescued Dubh flashed before his mind's eye.

"Well, hope needs inspiration, as it were." Dubh gave them a wink. "She gained access to the keep last time with subterfuge, and such tactics would not work a second time."

He drew his sword and threw his weight against the doors. They yawned open and what was left of his wall of mist rippled out before them.

Night had descended on Tír na nÓg.

Nuada stood on the dais, surrounded by broken glow-globes. Their incandescent light threw sparks into the air and surrounded the king with the illusion of fire. The platform was clear but for another form – a woman. On her head was a simple golden crown that writhed in the flickering light.

The rest – Nuada's guard and Niamh's army – had arrayed themselves just out of reach. They were a neat line of bodies encircling the pair, and separating them from the rest of Findias. All of them were silent.

Nuada turned as they spilled out of the doors. He appeared unarmed, but Maureen knew he was far from helpless.

"These are your champions?" the king rasped. Contempt twisted his features. "A spent warrior and two children?"

"Is that truly what you see, my lord?" Niamh's voice rang clear in the night. "You've spent much time telling us not to believe what we witness with our own eyes. I see a warrior, scarred, yes, from battles he never expected to fight. I see a man who has returned to us stronger than he ever was as a callous youth." She bowed her head in Dubh's direction and he nodded back.

"I see a man who once gave his oath to protect our world, and who would do all in his power to keep it. I see two children – our descendants – our legacy to the human world. I see a story of the wonders they will accomplish waiting to be told. I see the gateway to other worlds in their eyes, Nuada. I see them as our forebears once did, when they acted as guides and soothsayers to the humans on the other side."

"Folly!" Nuada's bellow overrode all else. "You would have us be slaves to their constant questions – their puerile fantasies of violence and lusts! I will not have it!"

"What can you do to stop it? You cornered them and they discovered something no other human untrained as they are has ever discovered."

"What's that? Love? Mistress Niamh, you are naive."

She laughed and the sound of tiny bells filled the air. "Far from it, my lord king. They found power in the fears and horrors you pulled from their souls. They defeated you, using your tricks against you. They had the choice to either succumb or rise. And they rose."

"Who is defeated? Me?" The king's harsh laugh carried far, distorted and buoyed by the mists. "Because my house-guard, who have not seen battle for an age, allowed you and your tricks to pass through? This is madness! That you expect to win by these false arguments tells me you are yet unready for the rigors of rule, Niamh. Go home." He gestured to the crowd. "All of you, go home."

No one moved and he glided closer to Niamh, his voice low. "I will show you good faith, my dear. I will dismiss my guard – even call off the Seers – if you send these poor people home. They are not ready for war – they are relics of a dead age. Let them live out what is left of their lives in peace."

"My lord, you are the relic," Niamh whispered. She bowed her head in mock reverence.

"Do you reject my truce?"

Her eyes blazed as she lifted her head.

"No."

She brought her hands together, and in a flash, she was gone. The mists did not even ripple to betray her presence there at all.

Nuada blinked owlishly at the spot where his daughter had been. His mouth opened and closed but nothing came out. He spun and directed his energies to the crowd.

Nuada watched in mute rage as one by one, her army disappeared. Each figure seemed to wink out of existence as though it had never been there to begin with.

"He was not expecting that," Dubh muttered. A white mist had begun to pool around them as he murmured lost words of a dead language. As his voice rose, so too did the mist.

Maureen's hand clutched at Sean's arm. "Are we going to disappear too?" she asked. Sean could not tell if it was fear or excitement shading her words.

"No. We are going to run!"

Ten

"We must keep going – Maureen, come along."

"I have been tossed around, drugged, tortured and bound," she muttered as she slowed to a stop. "I need to catch my breath."

She rested her hands on her knees drew air deep into her lungs. Fleeing Findias had been easy. Niamh's disappearing army had caught the king unaware, and Dubh's white fog only added to the confusion. They had a good head start, but as the warrior kept reminding them during their gruelling march across the vast emptiness he called Mag Mell, it was not enough.

Dubh opened his mouth as if to protest and she glared at him. He shrugged and dug into a pouch at his side. From it, he pulled three small cakes – like bannocks or hardtack – and passed them around.

Maureen looked between him and the cake with an arched eyebrow.

"It is not laced with the Faerie Sleep, lass. We've a long walk ahead of us and I've no desire to carry you both."

Sean unwrapped his and took a bite. "It's good, Maureen. Eat it."

She made a face and tested a corner, watching Sean and Dubh as she did so.

"That's a good lass. Now, if you don't mind, we can chew, talk and walk at the same time. We must make haste."

"Care to explain why we're running pell-mell all over a land where everyone else seems content enough to appear – and disappear – at will?" she asked. She and Sean flanked him and lengthened their stride to keep up with the tall warrior.

"What you saw at Nuada's stronghold was an illusion. No one was there but Niamh, and even she was not where we supposed she was." Dubh smiled thinly to himself. "She was at the edge of the city, hidden by those who keep their loyalties a secret. It is dangerous to live within Findias and not support the king, but a few do. They will keep her well hidden until the keep is free of eyes. She will meet us."

"Meet us, where?"

"Our final destination is my grove, but despite Nuada's promise to call off his guards, it is likely watched. Instead, we make for a cave at the edge of Meg Mell. It will hide us well." Dubh paused and looked down at them. "I warn you, the cave lacks a certain harmony. With your newfound awareness, it will be jarring to your senses, but you must enter it."

Sean snorted. "This is supposed to be harmonious?" He waved a hand at the fog-shrouded plain.

Dubh ignored the question. "We will be safe there. Many in Tír na nÓg avoid it – it acts as a ward against the mists, and gives off waves of older magic, magic which grates at their senses, especially now." He gestured to the barren landscape. Nuada's rule had weakened his people.

"And the cave – it hurts them? It will hurt us?"

The warrior stared ahead without speaking for a moment. "Hurt you? No," he said finally. "You may find it uncomfortable at first, but you will get used to it. It blocks magic as much as it is a source of its own – and there is a chance, but no, you are not ready for that, yet."

Maureen stopped walking, her words stuck in her throat. The adrenaline from escaping Nuada's control was wearing off, only to be replaced by the realization of what had happened to them.

She had only just managed to gain a shred of control over the mist. To plumb the depths of her own nightmares, and send them out as a weapon, was a desperate act – one used blindly. Before she willingly traipsed deeper into the hell that was the supposed Faerie realm, she wanted more answers.

Sean must have seen the look on her face, because before she could stomp and argue about it, he slipped from Dubh's side and took her hand in his.

"I can't do this," she whispered. "It's too much."

"I know this isn't fair," Dubh growled. "It isn't fair what happened to you – it isn't fair that I let you step into the gateway without guidance and it isn't fair that I kept myself from you." Regret flashed across his face, shaded by something else – something deeper, kinder.

"I had been apart from man for so long – I did not know how to react to kindred souls. My only thought was to protect you once I realized you were in danger. I can right that wrong – I will show you how to cope with what you are, to accept the magic in the mist and discard the things that do not serve you. I promise you this. But first, we must reach the cave before Nuada finds us."

When she did not say anything – she was too busy fighting the urge to scream – Sean squeezed her hand.

"Maureen, he has a point. Believe me, I have no desire to enter that cave – not with *this*." He gestured to the mists floating on the current of air. "But I have even less desire to be a captive in Nuada's keeping again. We should go."

She looked into the warrior's brilliant blue eyes. In them was a plea, the same unspoken plea to understand that had reached out to her during Sunday mass, and she was overcome with the same need to find him. Above all else, she knew they could bring – no, had to bring – this man peace. She took a shaky breath and forced the fear – the questions – back.

"All right. But I'm holding you to that promise. Teach us, tell us who you are. You've kept far too much secret from us, Dubh Súile."

His white teeth flashed. "Spoken well, Maureen Clare O'Malley – and I promise."

He turned, and they ran.

"So, this cave," Sean called as they hurried after the warrior. "Won't Nuada have it guarded if it will work for your purposes so well?"

Maureen fancied she could hear the clank of armour in the mists trailing behind them. She knew it was only her imagination but she quickened her step to keep up.

"This is why we hurry. It is an open secret that the cave was Niamh's home after her mother, the Queen, passed from this world, but it is a shunned place. Because the mists don't work within its walls, the magicians had to step outside, sit exposed in Mag Mell, to cast the image of her warriors at the keep."

"She risked a lot to do that – you are not ready for war," Maureen muttered. Niamh's rebel forces were better prepared than Pearse's revolutionaries had been, but that did not mean they would win if they attacked Nuada now. "And it certainly looked like her performance was a declaration of war."

"She did risk much." The warrior looked at them. "You are important."

Sean rolled his eyes. "For what, their war?"

"No. Not because of what you can do, or what you are. You are important to me. Niamh rescued me so Nuada could not use me against you. It was not my intention to leave you in his keeping, nor did I intend to leave you in 1916, but sometimes things do not go as I plan. I am a mortal man."

"Aye, but from when?"

"That is a good question, lad, but one I will only answer when we are safe. Come, we are close, but we should run."

"We were afraid you'd been captured."

Dubh pushed Sean and Maureen into the cave ahead of him, and spoke to the sentry in the shadows. "No, my friend. We are simply mortal and slower to move."

"Aye, I've heard that is a problem amongst your kind." There was laughter in the sentry's voice and Dubh chuckled gamely.

"Any word yet from Niamh?"

"I have far less difficulty traveling Mag Mell at speed." Niamh emerged from the shadows. "The courtyard cleared quickly after you escaped. I was able to leave rather sooner than we thought. Nuada didn't follow you, however."

"So all that running, for nothing!" Maureen leaned against the wall.

"No, not for nothing, my dear. The king has some trick planned. It is better that you are here, where we can protect you. Have you fed them, Dubh?"

"Aye, the cakes were warily accepted."

"They'll need more. I hear they washed the stronghold clean with a wall of anguish. Nuada dosed them badly with the Faerie Sleep. Too many terrors were born in that and they used it to fuel a mist so strong—"

"I know, Niamh, I was there." He made his voice bland to soothe the panic in the young woman's voice.

"No, Dubh. It washed the compound clean." She stared at him, emphasizing each word. "I saw those who were caught in it as they stumbled out the door. They shimmered."

He had seen it. Nuada's drab minions had glowed, their magic returned to its natural state. Niamh's concern went deeper than Sean and Maureen's ability to fuel the mist and deconstruct magic.

"What are you saying?"

"I'm saying they've spent a bit of energy here, and it needs to be replenished before they return home. Recall what happened to you, Master Druid. They have a future there. They need to go back – this place is not for them, not yet. No more than that pirate ship."

"What is she saying? We can't go back if we tap into our powers here? Is that true?" Maureen looked from Dubh to Niamh. She could not believe she was even thinking it, but she wanted to go home.

"Of course you can go home, lass." Niamh arched an eyebrow at Dubh and turned to Maureen. Her face was relaxed, but tension still crackled in the air.

The Fae woman took her arm. "We simply need to feed you – restore your strength. Time moves differently here. Were you to go home in this state, you would collapse. I don't think you want to scare those kindly ladies who care for you, do you?"

"No." The word slipped out slowly. What were they not saying? She looked at Sean. He bit his lip and shrugged.

"Right, then – come with me." Niamh guided them deeper into the cave. Veins of metal and rough jewels sparkled dimly in walls lit not by the glow globes of the keep, but by natural fire torches ensconced above their heads.

As Niamh's cheerful but innocuous patter continued, Maureen managed to breathe out some of the tension she had been holding. Despite Dubh's warning, the absence of magic was soothing, once the high-pitched whine seeping from the cave's rough-hewn walls subsided.

"There is food and drink, and I promise you, none of it will cause the confusion, or pain you experienced in Nuada's house. His hospitality is lacking."

Maureen rolled her eyes. 'Lacking' was an understatement.

"The Faerie Sleep – was it Nuada all this time?" Sean asked as the tunnel opened up into a large cavern.

"Was Nuada what, lad?"

"We have old stories – warnings, really – of what you call the Faerie Sleep. Eating from the Good Folk's feasting table would entrap hapless mortals in the realms until they became hopelessly lost. Years could pass while they wandered."

Dubh snorted. "Aye, that sounds about right."

"Well, was Nuada king when Oisín passed

through here?" Sean stopped walking. The answer did not matter – not really. His conversation with Dian Cécht had already proved the mythology he thought he knew was true, but only to a certain point. Still, part of him needed the knowledge – needed it to make sense of what had happened to them.

"I heard he ate and drank in Tír na nÓg for countless days and nights. Though he fell in love with a beautiful Fae princess – even acted as her champion – he decided to return to his people. When he did, he discovered three hundred mortal years had passed."

"Oisín?" Niamh glanced at Dubh, a half-smile on her face. "He is the son of Fionn mac Cumhaill, is he not?"

"Time moves differently here," Dubh replied, pushing them forward into the cavern.

Maureen snorted. "So you keep saying."

"I'm certain Oisín will find his way here eventually, if that is how your tales tell it, Sean McAndrew." Niamh kept her voice low and soothing, but this time there was an edge of humour to her words. "And yes, Nuada may yet be king when those things happen – or *was* when they *did* happen. Tír na nÓg exists outside of time. In stepping foot in our realm, you too have stepped out of time. That is why you must eat – replenish yourselves."

She gestured to a table and cushion-covered benches tucked into a corner of the cavern.

Dubh approached the table first, and selected what appeared to be a small scone. He arched an eyebrow at Sean and Maureen and popped it into his mouth.

"See?" he said around the crumbs. "I am as

human as the two of you. There is nothing for you to fear within these walls."

"Are you really as human as Maureen and I?" Sean asked as he approached the table and selected a slab of bread. Maureen slipped behind him and reached around for her own morsel. He glanced at her and then eyed the couch behind them. She nodded and they sat. Together they watched Dubh as he tried to form an answer to Sean's question.

He eased himself slowly onto a covered stool. It placed him lower to the ground than them and he looked up to meet their eyes.

"I was born to a mother and father – a human mother and father – just as you were," he started. "But when I was born, older gods held sway with our kin, and it was understood I had a gift worth developing. I am a mortal man, but those who better understood the nature of the Changelings honed my talents. I could have spent my life in the world of man, and died there, had it not been for an accident."

Sean absorbed this and dissected Dubh's words. Barring the accident, he had told them nothing new.

He was a man, and his tattoos spoke of a less-than-modern time – the people here called him Druid, after all. Even Dian Cécht had told him more about Dubh than Dubh had.

"But who are you, really? Why could we see you in the church? Why—?"

"You promised you would tell us," Maureen chimed in, "that you would teach us."

"And he will," Niamh declared. She retreated from them and stood at the mouth of the cavern. "I will confer with my people – we must decide how best to deliver you to Dubh's grove. Talk and rest. I will fetch you when it is time to leave."

Dubh nodded at her retreating form and turned back to where Sean and Maureen waited for him to speak.

Eleven

I was born Dubhshìth mac Alasdair. Your scholars call my people Picts, but we knew ourselves as the Cruthin. I was a prince of my people and a warrior. The sons of Alasdair, my grandsire, ruled an area north of what is now Inverness, near Loch Ussie. They commanded many men and cattle. We played a part in the machinations of kings, but your scholars know little of us now. I fear we are imaginary creatures to you, painted with woad, and savage in our rituals, but we were a proud, courageous people once.

When I was born, nearly seven hundred years after the birth of the Christos, the old gods still found favour with my clan and those who held our allegiance. I was raised to be a Druid – from the time before my birth, it was known. Prophesy uttered on the eve of a great calamity foretold I would see far, lead men and devote my life to the gods.

At seven years of age, I left my home and trained in the Druid grove where my father's status – and the priestess's prophesy – mattered little. I was a novice like all the others and I spent nine gruelling years in study. However, unlike my fellow students, I was at once bard, astrologer, genealogist and arbitrator. My people knew me to be a Druid, but the Druids knew me to be a Changeling. I was a vestige of the Old Ones, born with magic they left behind in my blood. I could sing at the clan's hearth, or I could confer with kings and guide their wisdom. All avenues lay within my soul, but it was for me to choose.

I did not stay in the grove as they had hoped. They wanted me to lead the Druids, but I left that role to my uncle. Instead, I returned home to counsel my father and soothe rumours of war. Once there, I fell in love and took a wife, Mairead. The war we tried to avert came to us anyway.

I lost much in that war: my father, many brave comrades and my beloved. That it liberated our southern brethren from the Kingdom of Northumbria was a sorry consolation for me.

Rather than face the emptiness of home, I made my way to Ireland and wandered for several years as a bard – telling tales for a warm hearth and bowl of mead. Eventually, I came upon an aged man in the west, a man many whispered was an old Druid – a powerful one. He made his home atop a hill in a remote corner of Connacht, where none would go. The people of the area told me it was a sidhe mound, where the Tuatha Dé Danann had been led after the Milesians made Ireland their own.

I knew this man must be powerful indeed to live side-by-side with the Fae, so I went to him. I went to absolve myself of the guilt I still felt at the death of my father, and the loss of my Mairead. I went to rediscover the powers I had given up in my grief.

As it was, I found Nuada Silver Arm.

Deep in a meditation guided by the old man, I called a gateway to me and entered. That gateway delivered me to Tír na nÓg – Findias specifically. I had stepped into the middle of a civil war, and to stay alive, I had to convince Nuada he needed me. Calling upon stories I had known since I was a child, I curried his favour. I pretended to be the god Lugh. It worked.

In the end, I won him the throne. I defeated his brothers, Bres and Balor, in the Fomorian War. In return, he allowed me to live.

I was in my twenty-fifth year when I went on pilgrimage into the sidhe mound, and I spent many days in battle. A day here is a year in the world of men – but how long is that day? I know not, but when I sought to return – with the gift of my life and my experiences – sixty mortal years had passed. All that I knew, all who I loved and would continue to love for the rest of my days were gone. My mother, my sisters and brother were dead, my beloved, gone. All had passed from the world.

And I was a young man still.

I returned to Nuada. He knew what would happen and had not seen fit to warn me. I railed against him, and he – ever fickle – relented.

In exchange for what I had lost, he gave me a gift: I could travel the byways of Tír na nÓg. I could even fashion for myself a facsimile of the old man's hermitage on this side of the gateway. Time in my grove matches the mortal realm, yet it is protected by the mythology of the Fae – time would stop for me unless I stepped on mortal soil, and even then, I would only age in keeping with my time among man. It saved me from Oisín's fate of aging three hundred years upon his return to the world of man.

"Speaking of which, we must move."

Maureen stifled a gasp as she withdrew from Dubh's story. Niamh was standing in the shadows of the entryway, her hands on her hips, looking for all the world like Sr. Theresa when she was waiting for Maureen to stop dawdling. Next to her, Sean was blinking, bleary-eyed, as if he had just woken, and Dubh was staring hard at his hands, open in his lap.

He had just been getting to the good part. "But – but he's not done – you're not done, are you?"

"I—"

Niamh stepped forward. "He can finish the tale on the way to the grove. The scouts have returned. Nuada has called for all but a small group of guardsmen and Seers to retreat to Findias. We think he plans to attack the cave. The mists may not work here, but force is always an option. Numbers won't matter if he allows the Seers to wield their full power."

"You know it could be a diversion – a trap." Dubh's voice was gruff.

"Yes, but I don't fancy our chances calling his bluff. If we can deliver you three to the grove, my people can melt away."

"I'm not leaving them there alone—"

"Then I will send for you once they are tucked up in their beds at the abbey. Regardless, we need to get them out of the cave, now. Where we go they cannot follow, not yet."

He looked at her. "You've opened the way to Tech Duinn." It was not a question.

"And he will not follow. He fears the power there."

"As well he should." Dubh turned to them. "Come, let us make haste."

Sean and Maureen looked between the Fae woman and her Druid. Their words meant little to them but the urgency in their voices was unmistakable.

"It is not your fault," Niamh said as she turned to them, her voice soft. "But you were the excuse. There are things yet you need to know, and Dubh will tell you the rest of his tale as we journey west."

Dubh sighed and rubbed at his face. He looked down at them, his blue eyes wary, as though he did not know what kind of reception they would give him, now that they knew.

Sean and Maureen stared back at him. Hand-in-hand, they waited for him to lead the way.

Living and learning the ways of the Tuatha Dé Danann was poor consolation to what I lost, but I was not ready to lay down my life in grief. Although I had forsworn the gift of future-sight, there was much else I could learn – and I set myself to that task. I set aside my name and became the title Nuada had given me: Dubh Súile.

I could not do the things the Fae could – I was no god of legend – but I could feel the mists and hear the magic as it whispers through them. The knowledge is there, in the whispers, if you listen. You call a gateway the same way you entreat the mist. You focus on what you wish it to do. You two would envision your home – make the memories shine brightly in your minds and your hearts – and the mist would build the bridge between the worlds.

I was also taught to transform – create beautiful pictures in my mind and bring them to life in the world. It was a magic my people only remembered as a distant and fanciful dream.

My greatest teacher was Nuada's Queen, Áine. She was a powerful master of tales, which she wove into tapestry so stunning it could capture the imagination of all who looked upon it. Her weavings told thrilling stories, sung songs of heroes and the lives of those yet living. Sometimes, when the mood would strike, she would weave the tale of those who had yet to come.

Her daughter weaves in a similar fashion, and though Niamh was young when I knew them both, she learned her craft well.

After a time, my studies took me outside the Faerie realm. I had learned enough of the gateways to safely step out of Tír na nÓg, although as a human, I could only build bridges to the world as it was *after* Nuada granted me my freedom. The years I had lost fighting his war were gone forever, but there was still much to see.

My journey began in the middle seventh century, and after what amounted to a year of study here, I could visit the just-completed Winchester Cathedral in the world of man. Áine often tried to tell me that it was possible for me to see into the future of men, beyond my time in Faerie, but I never told her it hurt too much to try. One needed kin in the world to see, and I believed I had none left.

I spent several years with mortal masters, studying the arts of war, music, scholarship and art. Even as I remained separate from them, I learned the ways of man all over again. I could never truly belong, but I did know how to make myself more like them, to shift my visage by drawing on my training as a Druid and the magic of the Tuatha Dé Danann.

At times, I shared Nuada's contempt for the path man had taken. The Druid was gone. Rome had resurrected itself as a holy city, and too many times man vilified and destroyed the wise and innocent. My heart ached for what could never be – ached to see those like me – and I returned to Tír na nÓg often.

I was thirty-five, by my reckoning, when I last stepped foot in Tír na nÓg. In my absence, Áine had passed from the realm. All the Tuatha mourned her, but none so much as her daughter. Niamh retreated to the cave with all who would follow her.

She entreated me to join her, but I would not. Many times, she came to me, but I had sworn to protect Tír na nÓg. It seemed to me her fears would destroy it – tear it and the peace Nuada had worked for asunder. The splendour of Mag Mell had died by then – the magic here was already fading, but I hid from it.

Then the day came when Nuada cast me out of Faerie.

One moment I was striding across Mag Mell, and the next I was in the middle of a busy London street, staring down the nose of what you call a black cab. The steam engine had not yet been invented the last time I stepped foot on mortal soil, and that cab was nearly the end of me. As it was, a young pilot named Patrick O'Malley saved me, and through him, I discovered I was destined to play out yet another war – the Second World War. The gateways were closed to me, and I knew then: Nuada had sent me – banished me – to my death.

I refused to die.

This new world of man was as thrilling as it was terrifying. The war had gone on too long by the time I played my part in it, but the people of the Isles were as stalwart and courageous as ever – contentious too, but that is in their nature, aye?

Where once I mourned the passing of the old ways, now I saw they were not truly gone – just abiding within the hearts of men under new names. It is the one thing Nuada never quite understood, or accepted. As for me, if ever I doubt it, I simply look to the skies.

Donning the guise of a Scottish corporal, I managed to stick close to Pat and his best friend – and navigator – Jamie McAndrew. There was an ease to their companionship, which made disguising myself amid the technological wizardry of the twentieth century a bit easier.

Personally, I think I amused them. I blundered around this new world just like a babe let out of swaddling; old gods and magic could not prepare me for the joy and terror of seeing a plane take off from the ground to soar through the sky.

Pat and Jamie were in their third tour of duty, with just one mission over Germany to go before going home on leave. Meanwhile, I was going behind enemy lines to do some work for 8 Group's intelligence services. We had one last night at the pub before our group was to separate.

Pat spent his time between stories and pints writing a letter to his wife and infant daughter. He gave it to me for safekeeping, and his words touched me deeply. Even with this terrible war taking its toll, his visions for his daughter left me breathless with their hope. Jamie teased Pat about it, but I knew his thoughts were on his own family as well.

I should have known something was amiss when Niamh reached out to me – stopped time right in the middle of our revels in the pub. She had been searching for me, she said, and confirmed Nuada had me exiled. Despite the curses she once flung at me, she offered me safe-passage back to Tír na nÓg. I asked only that she keep the gateway open for a single day – a year for me – and she agreed. I needed to see Pat and Jamie happy and in the arms of their families before I fled to the relative haven of her rebellion.

The next day, they were dead.

If Nuada had planned to crush me, it nearly worked. That these brave men were dead and I was still alive was a mockery. I still had Pat's letter, but I held it close to my heart. I refused to be the messenger of their passing.

Instead, I threw myself at the enemy Pat and Jamie had died fighting. It was the only promise I could fulfil. Whether my actions helped the war or only helped to staunch my grief, I do not know. I do know that at the end of the year, Niamh had to hound me – had to force me to return to Tír na nÓg. Yet, there was no peace for me there, either. I could no more face Niamh than I could your mothers. She rescued me from the war and my exile, but no one could rescue me from the prison I had created in my heart.

I retreated to my grove – barred the door from all who could come seeking knowledge – and slept. Years passed. One war ended, and others began. Babies grew into daring youths with fire in their eyes and magic in their blood.

Maureen pierced the veil. She saw me, and I – well, I saw you both. Your eyes were their eyes, and I knew I could deliver Pat's letter yet. I could ensure those who James McAndrew and Patrick O'Malley left behind knew of their fierce love for them. I would share that which I could no longer share with those I once loved, and love still.

Twelve

"**D**on't let him fool you, my dears. For all his angst, Dubh Súile still led you on a merry chase."

Sean gasped as the king's words brought him out of Dubh's world too quickly. He and Maureen walked arm-in-arm, flanked by Dubh and Niamh. It was just the four of them; Niamh had ordered her forces to hide deep within the cave, deep in the place they could not enter. War was coming, but now was not the time to meet Nuada on the battlefield.

At the sound of the voice, dripping its false concern, all of them stopped and formed a circle. Maureen shifted to guard Sean's back and searched a landscape that was quickly gathering daylight. Nearly a full day had passed.

"Why did he tarry when he could have met with you – explained all this and kept you safe? Have you ever bothered to ask him what it was he was doing while you risked your lives with pirates and revolutionaries?"

Sean stiffened. Maureen had asked that question, many times. Dubh had never given her an answer that satisfied. He looked at her. Her head was high – facing their unseen enemy with a courage that had always given him strength.

She caught his eye and pulled him closer to her

side.

"What could he do, Nuada?" she called. She made her voice strong, despite the jittery anxiety that clung to her limbs, as though she had been roused too quickly from sleep. "How could he explain when he was too busy trying to keep us safe from you?"

She understood now, this was what Dubh wanted them to know. He had tried – had wanted – to be so much more to them. It was not just his despair at their fathers' deaths, either. There was more to it, she knew, and six months of trying to stay alive and hidden was not enough time to forge the bond that would ease the warrior's soul.

Dubh stared down at Maureen, noting as she lifted her chin and glared defiantly into the encroaching mists. There were so many things he would change if he could. Yet, earning the right to be championed by Maureen O'Malley was not one of them.

"This isn't their fight, Nuada." The Druid's voice was barely above a whisper. He looked down at the ground, his stare inward. "This is about me – about the power I could wield here if I so choose." He lifted his head and spoke to the emptiness.

"I do not choose."

Maureen shivered and Sean tightened his grip on her arm.

"I would know peace. I would know the love of my family once more before allowing death to claim me. But know this, Nuada Silver Arm: I will protect the lives of these Changelings with my own."

Hideous laughter filled their ears.

"So brave, so selfless – I had such high hopes for you once, Dubh Súile."

Nuada's sigh wrapped itself around them. The

mists parted. The king stood before them, alone.

"You are too powerful now, as are they. I cannot allow you back into the world, but I cannot have you here – not after their neat trick in Findias."

"You presume it is within your power to do anything about it." Dubh unsheathed his sword. Arcs of light crackled in the mist and danced along the edge of the blade.

The wind was rising and the warrior's hair whipped at his face. Dubh's power was deeper than what Maureen had wielded; he was a Changeling at full power, and it was as beautiful as it was wild.

"I presume nothing. You and yours will fall."

The king moved, he flashed and glittered – he was almost too fast to see, but the taunt was meant for Dubh alone. The Druid lunged after Nuada, keeping himself between Maureen and Sean, and the king.

"Dubh – no!" Niamh's warning came too late and the warrior crumpled to the ground.

"Coward," he panted.

The king made a disgusted sound in the back of his throat. "You think I would allow you to run me through with your blade – your cold iron? Foolish." His gaze shifted to Niamh and his eyes blazed, silver and cruel. "Move aside, daughter. It is time to end this."

"No."

She took Dubh's place in front of Sean and Maureen. The mists thinned and shimmered around her. She put a hand on the warrior, crouched on the ground, and they watched as he slowed his breathing. He braced himself against the earth and waited.

Nuada cocked his head at them. "You would force me to call the demons from your souls?"

No one answered.

"So be it."

With a flick of his wrist, the mists rushed at them, filling their senses. Only Niamh seemed immune. Sean and Maureen clung to one another, closing their eyes against the boiling vapour filled with clawed hands and gnashing teeth.

Maureen felt Nuada slip through her mind, entering dark corridors of her heart and ripping open old fears only recently healed.

"This ends," she whispered. She clenched her teeth, her hands – her entire body – in an effort to throw up a mental shield that would block the king from her mind.

The darkness eased. Her breath escaped her lungs in a rush. She opened her eyes and sought out Niamh. The woman had planted herself behind Dubh, testing her will against her father. The gut-churning fear once alive in the mist was gone, but the howling and gnashing remained. Was Niamh holding Nuada at bay with trickery of her own?

Of course. It dawned on her. Niamh was a spell-weaver. What better protection could she provide from the king's menace than an image woven from their fears?

"Sean. Sean, open your eyes." Maureen shook him and the startling blue of his gaze flashed at her. "Do you remember what you felt at the keep?"

He stared at her, too overwhelmed to do anything else. "I can't – I won't do that again. We can't use this against them. This isn't our war."

She shook her head. He could feel her impatience and ceased his babbling.

He knew what Maureen was asking. She was asking him to open his heart and mind to the magic of Tír na nÓg. But to do that, he had to ignore

Nuada's terrors and focus instead on the realm's simple, stark beauty.

He had glimpsed it, once, when Niamh had entered his mind to speak to him. But since their fever-dreams in Nuada's stronghold, since their magic had washed it clean, he had been unable to recapture the clarity.

"No, no a wall of mist wouldn't help," Maureen was muttering. "Niamh and Dubh are holding him. They are the ones flashing our fears at Nuada – can't you feel it? They let him in just enough to fool him into thinking the fears real – but they aren't. We don't have to fuel the storm, we just need to help them – wait, no!"

"What is it, Maureen? What?" He grabbed her as her arms fell slack at her sides. Her green eyes were panning wildly in her head as she searched the mists.

"We can do it – listen!"

He held her close, clinging to her as an anchor, and life preserver both.

By the gods, boy – this is what he plumbs from your soul? Dubh will have a time training you. You are strong, at least.

He thought he felt Maureen's giggle bubble in his own throat.

Do you feel it Maureen?

Her whispered answer was like a sigh across his skin.

Good. Dubh and I can hold him. We can keep the projection of your terrors in place but we need you to call the gateway.

How? Sean asked. Maureen smiled at him. He had done it.

You call the threads – just as Dubh told you. You have done it before, whether you knew what you did or not. You called the gateway to you that night in 1958. All that followed was the machinations of our king, but you can do it. You must call the gateway. And do it quickly. Once he realizes . . .

Niamh's voice hesitated and Sean waited, holding his breath, for the rest of her words to slide through his mind.

I am sorry. Dubh's plan to send you back to the very night you left will not work. You walked here, and ate. You breathed our air and nothing will ever be the same for you again.

"Niamh!" The king's cry rent the air with rage. "End this. You and yours will fall to me – whether it is now or after much death in battle is up to you. Give them to me, now."

Maureen focused on Sean's face above her. "We have to go."

"What about Dubh – we can't leave him here—"

"Go!"

The single, raw word was torn from the warrior's throat. He spared them a look and they saw all the fire and desperation that once glared at them through smoke and flame aboard the *Excelsior*. His blue eyes were as bright as that night, and now they shone with pride.

"Go," he whispered again. His voice echoed in their ears, and in their hearts.

Live for me.

Maureen slipped her hands into Sean's, and held his eyes in hers.

The white mists of time swallowed them. Niamh's barrier broke and Nuada screamed into the breaking day.

Thirteen

Maureen felt herself dissolve and reform. She clung to the only memory she could find as her awareness sought out the reality that would bring her and Sean home. It was the barest pinprick of light amid the blinding dark, but it was all she had. In the memory, Sean was grinning at her from across the schoolyard, laughing with the lads but watching her as she entertained her mates. It had happened months ago – years ago, it seemed – but it was all she had. She held his smile to her heart and felt her mind coalesce around it.

The nave's marble tile was cool under her cheek. She pressed at it with her hands, tested it to make sure it was real.

Sean was the first to break the silence. "Did we make it?"

"It's solid," she offered as she sat up. Her body ached.

Sean scrambled to his knees. "Do you really think we're home?"

Maureen took his offered hand and they stood together. She opened her mouth to answer but the words died on her lips as the darkened altar began to glow.

Sean's grip on her arm tightened and they backed slowly away, as if the mist spilling to the floor was going to form hands and snatch at them.

Instead of hands, a figure stepped into the boiling mass. It was Dubh – or rather, a vision of Dubh as he stood in Mag Mell.

Drenched in light, he looked like an avenging angel. Lightning etched a halo behind him, and a deep rumble of thunder made the very stones tremble.

When his eyes finally fell on them, his smile rivalled the radiance behind him before his face fell into harsh lines of warning.

"Run."

Even as he issued the command, the warrior's head snapped up. His deep blue gaze pierced the space beyond them and he lifted his sword high.

He was in trouble.

They had to do something.

"We have to go back," Maureen said as Sean began to pull her away. "We can't leave him there."

For a breathless moment, Sean just looked at her.

"Do it."

She tried, but before she could even begin to open her mind to the mists, an inhuman shriek shattered her ears.

The warrior collapsed.

The mists churned violently as he fell, and then were gone.

Maureen stared dumbly at the spot where Dubh had been. It couldn't be true – he couldn't—

Run.

It was a mere shadow of Dubh's voice, but it could not be denied.

They ran.

The lightning and thunder did not disappear with the visions and the mist. It kept coming. It grew louder and louder until the stone church rattled with the violence outside. Rain lashed at the windows, soaking them the moment they burst through the wooden doors.

Their feet reached soil and they kept going. Invisible hands seemed to push them into the woods just as lightning struck. It skittered off the slate roof and the air hummed and cackled in their ears.

Safe in the tree line, they looked back.

Despite the violence outside, the church was lit from within. From what had been dark, spilled a glorious light. It flickered as though through water and gleamed with faint iridescence. It grew brighter until it matched the lightening with its brilliance.

They covered their eyes and cowered before it.

With a deep, reverberating crack, the building blew apart. Boulders flew. Pews splintered. Glass shattered and melted in the heat.

It took only seconds to destroy the venerable building, and the silence that followed was absolute.

Sean and Maureen picked themselves up from the undergrowth. There was nothing left of the church – even the circle of young oaks that once strained towards the sky had been crushed beneath its remains. Already cauterized, the gaping hole where the church had been did not even smoulder.

Maureen clutched at Sean's hand. There was movement on the other side of the destruction. It was a man.

They lurched from the safety of the trees. Dubh. He had survived—!

The man hobbled towards them, leaning on his cane. The storm subsided as quickly as it came, but a few flashes of lightning – far away now – highlighted his face. It was sagging and withered with age.

"I knew you'd come, eventually," he called as he watched them slow, and then stop at the edge of the wreckage. The voice was wheezy, but familiar.

"I knew one day I'd see you two again. When they said you were gone, I knew. I remembered. Oh aye, I'd seen you in church a few times – I started going, regular, like – but it wasn't until you went missing that I knew for sure."

"And what was it you knew?" Maureen asked, her voice clogged with tears.

"That you'd come back. Sean sent me a telegram, after all. I—"

"Gerry."

Sean breathed the name and goose bumps rippled across Maureen's arms.

They skirted the edge of the wound, unable to walk on the church's corpse, until they gained Gerry Ballard's side.

"Aye, the very same. You saved my life, you know – I realized that after we heard Aunt Jenny died at Easter week. I would have been there with her, but you made sure I went home." He shook his head and his voice trembled.

"I never—I never approached you when you were young – wouldn't be right for an auld bachelor, aye? But I did try to tell them old dears that you hadn't run away, that something had happened. I don't know if they believed me – but at least they didn't throw me in the madhouse for it."

He made a weak attempt at a laugh.

"But how did you – why are you here?" Maureen asked. It was not important – nothing seemed important now that Dubh was . . . no, she couldn't think about that. It was better to focus on Gerry.

"I was out for me daily constitutional when the storm moved in and something told me to come up here. Call it premonition or an auld man's daft fancies. I—well, you've been gone a while – nearing two years now, aye?"

He waited for them to acknowledge this but Maureen and Sean just stared at him. Two years? That was impossible.

Gerry shrugged. "If I bring you down to the sisters, they'll either think I helped you, or they'll remember what I said. Either way, you're going to need someone there to stand with you – especially now with the church . . ." He let his words trail off as his gaze wandered over the ruin.

Sean put a trembling hand on the old man's shoulder. "Thank you, Gerry."

Maureen could hear the tears in his voice. Gerry looked between them. Concern and sympathy pooled in his eyes.

"There were all sorts of rumours," he said. "But no one really believed them. They'll start again, but—" He paused and peered at them.

"There's something in your eyes. No one will believe them rumours – and if they do, they'll have Gerry Ballard to deal with, aye?"

Sean's hand found hers and squeezed.

Gerry cleared his throat. "I'd, ah, let the two of you catch your breath before we go down to the sisters, but it seems the old dears heard the show themselves." He nodded towards the abbey, hidden by a wall of trees.

Maureen paused. She could hear them. Their faint calls of alarm sounded from the path – the same path she and Sean had used on a moonlit night two years ago.

Two years.

The words finally managed to break through the dull ache in her head, which had started to throb in time with her heart.

She looked at Sean, but the heartbreak on his face was too much. The passage of time was too much – Gerry, the church, the nuns running up the hill – all of it was too much.

Sean attempted to pull her close but she broke from him. She had to do something – anything. This could not be how it ended.

Heedless of Gerry and Sean, staring at her, she took a deep breath and forced her awareness out into the space between the worlds, only to be met with a blank, seamless wall. She tried harder, tried to scour the darkness for the threads that would build the gateway to Tír na nÓg.

Sean must have felt it and grabbed at her, but she ignored him. Where was it? Where was the mist that so-often snatched at their feet? Where was the tremor of light and sound?

"No. He can't be gone. He couldn't have *left* us here!"

There was nothing. The gateway was sealed, locked away – and she did not have key. The power, once so heady, so readily available in her hands, was gone.

The *other* surged within her, burning through her veins, but she could do nothing with it. She turned to Sean. He was staring at her, looking helpless and lost in the face of her rage. Even so, he glimmered. Magic lingered over him like a second skin but it was just a thing. The power was gone. Dead.

Just like Dubh.

The troupe of nuns, led by Sr. Theresa, crested

the hill. Their voices faltered and died as they stared at the threesome gathered amidst the ruins of the church.

Sr. Theresa was the first to break ranks. Without a word, she lifted her skirts and ran to Sean and Maureen. Tears left tracks on her wrinkled cheeks.

Maureen tore herself from Sean and stumbled back from the nun's reach. No – no, she could not leave the hill.

"Sean, we can't go with them. What if Niamh opens the gateway, like she did for Dubh?"

Sean shook his head wordlessly.

"But, they need us –"

"Maureen."

He put his hand out to her, sorrow and concern at war on his face.

"No, Sean. We have to save—"

"Maureen, stop – you have to stop. He'll *see* us."

Sean's measured words, quiet but firm, slammed into her.

Nuada.

The king was still out there. Suddenly she knew, with a clarity that cut through her anguish: Dubh had died to hide them from Nuada. Somehow, his death had sealed the gateway.

She stared at her friend and did not fight when Sr. Theresa gathered her in her arms.

Dubh's death would not be in vain.

The nun held her close and began to rock her back and forth, whispering calming nonsense in her ear. Slowly, the rage and panic clutching at her gut melted away until there was nothing left but an empty sort of sorrow and a buzzing ache in her head.

At the edge of their little group, Gerry coughed

gently and Sr. Theresa looked up to see Mother Bernadette approach. She released Maureen and put a hand on Sean's shoulder as she passed, as if releasing Maureen to his care.

Gently, Maureen touched Sean's cheek. He mustered a small smile for her before wrapping his arms around her. This time, she did not pull away.

Only a few steps away, Sr. Theresa, Mother Bernadette and Gerry were whispering and gesturing warily at her and Sean. She suspected the joy of homecoming was going to be cut short but she could not muster the energy to worry about it. Instead, she closed her eyes and let the steady beat of Sean's heart sooth her jagged senses.

"We'll find a way back, Maureen," he whispered into her hair. "We'll make him pay – we'll end this, I promise you."

Because, sealed gateway or no, they could not remain hidden forever – one day, Nuada would find them.

"We will." She sniffed and lifted her head from his shoulder to stare at the hilltop, bare and battle-scarred. *"He who sleeps will rise."*

Sean twitched as if she had pinched him. "What are you talking about?"

She froze. The words had slipped out, unbidden, but with them gone, the droning buzz in her head had ceased.

"It's something I heard Niamh say, I think."

"Niamh?" Sean frowned. "When did she—"

"No, no it wasn't Niamh. It was Ionia – it was her song." She searched his face for some inkling he remembered the song sung at Ionia and Aiden O'Malley's wedding feast. Yet, even as she did so, she knew the words had never fallen from the Scotswoman's lips.

"Those who falter and bleed on the plain of man will live again," he whispered half to himself. "No, it was not Ionia who said that."

Maureen's mouth went dry. "No." she croaked. "Not Ionia."

The rest of the phantom prophesy wended its way through her head, but before the words could take a life of their own, Sr. Theresa and Gerry turned to them while Mother Bernadette returned to the small huddle of nuns still on the path.

"Ah Sister, there's no point in bothering them. I'm telling you, there was a storm, and it blew them in just as sure as I'm standing here."

Sr. Theresa gave him an exasperated smile. "And when this storm left, am I to believe it took the church with it?"

Gerry considered this for a moment. "Aye, I think you have the whole of it. There's always a trade with this sort of thing, aye?"

Something unreadable passed over Sr. Theresa's face as she looked between Gerry, Sean and Maureen. "Indeed. Thank you, Mr. Ballard. But as I said before, we'll take it from here."

Gerry's hands twisted his cap into an unrecognizable tangle. "It's just – well, I think maybe I should come with them."

"And do what, exactly?"

"See to it they're safe, like."

Gerry was blushing and Sr. Theresa snorted. "Goodness, Mr. Ballard! We are hardly going to whip them and lock them in the dungeons. They've had a serious shock – they need rest."

"That's not it, Sister. I know you don't wish them harm, but it's just, they saved my life once, and I – well, I want to see to it that—that the storm has truly passed, aye?"

Sr. Theresa seemed to flinch and she turned her gaze to the scarred earth. "Changelings and foundlings – and chasers of faerie gold. Wanderers, the lot of you," she whispered. "The Good Folk always come looking for their own."

Chills skittered up Maureen's arms and Sr. Theresa's grey eyes locked onto hers.

"Indeed. Well, come along Mr. Ballard," the nun said. "It may be that the storm will never truly pass – and you may be needed after all."

The End

By the grace of the gods, he who sleeps will rise.
Those who falter and bleed on the plain of man will
live again. And those who wander will be found.

Changelings: The Coming Storm
Available Fall 2015

Appendix

Cast of Characters

In order of appearance

The teenagers, Maureen O'Malley and Sean McAndrew, are orphans growing up in a Benedictine abbey in 1958.

The dark stranger is a warrior, a monk, and a prince. He goes by many names: Dubhghall, Dubh Súile and Dubhshìth, to name a few, but you may call him Dubh (DOOgal/Doov Sul-e/DOO-she/Doov).

Part One ~ Pirate

Grania Uaile/Grace O'Malley (GRAUN-yuh Wale), while not chieftain of the O'Malleys, she maintains her own strongholds along Clew Bay, and is captain of a fleet of 20 ships.*

Tomás Conroy (tuhmAAs) is a local blacksmith and now-retired member of Grania's fleet.

Liam and Owen O'Neil are brothers allied with Grania and serving on her flagship. Liam is one of Grania's most trusted lieutenants.

Galen O'Flaherty is a young 'ship rat' in the fleet and Grania's kinsman.

Sir Richard Bingham is an English nobleman and Queen Elizabeth's most recent appointee as Governor of Connacht.*

William Pennington is the captain of the mercenary fleet hired by Bingham.

Jamie is a midshipman in Pennington's

mercenary fleet.

Part Two ~ Rebel

Gerry Ballard is a local boy in 1916 Carrickahowley heading to Dublin to race motorbikes.

Mrs. Jenny Mallory is Gerry's aunt and proprietor of the Mallory Boarding House and Mallory Dry Goods Emporium in Dublin.

Patrick Pearse is a schoolteacher and a poet. He is also a member of the Irish Volunteers and Irish Republican Brotherhood (IRB).*

James Connolly is a socialist and nationalist. He co-founded the Irish Citizen Army (ICA), which has recently joined forces with the IRB.*

Seán Connolly is a stage actor from the Abbey Theatre and captain in the ICA.*

Sir Matthew Nathan is the Under-Secretary for Ireland, head of the British Empire's administration in Ireland.*

Colonel H.V. Cowan is the Assistant Adjunct General in Dublin.*

Brigadier-General William Lowe is the commander of the British Forces in Ireland.*

Part Three ~ King

Niamh Golden Hair (Neeve) is the rebel queen of Tír na nÓg, and Dubh Súile's confidante. ±

Nuada Silver Arm (NU ah) is the king of Tír na nÓg. ±

Dian Cécht (deeAAn kay-cht) is the king's healer. ±

Credne (KRA-na) is the silversmith who created the king's silver arm. ±

Macha (mOH-ka) is handmaiden to Queen Áine. ±

Miach (ME-ik) is Dian Cecht's son and a young healer. ±

The Rest

Patrick O'Malley is Maureen's father. He was a pilot in the Royal Air Force (RAF) and died during an air raid in 1942.

Katherine Keefe O'Malley is Maureen's mother. She served in the RAF Women's Auxiliary. She adopted Sean informally when his mother died, and died herself in 1949, from cancer.

James – Jamie – McAndrew is Sean's father. He served as Pat's navigator and died in the same air raid. He was heir to an estate in Strathpeffer, Scotland.

Mary O'Neil McAndrew is Sean's mother. She served with Katherine in the Woman's Auxiliary and succumbed to pneumonia in 1943.

Sister Theresa is Maureen's dorm mother at Carrickahowley Abbey who, while stern, regales them with tales of the Good Folk.

Mother Bernadette is the Mother Superior at Carrickahowley Abbey. She was responsible for arranging for Maureen and Sean's care when Katherine O'Malley died.

Margaret McAndrew is Sean's great-aunt who maintains his inheritance until Sean reaches his majority.

Hon. William O'Malley is Maureen's consumptive grandfather living in Dublin. He has nothing to do with his son's family.

Captain John Bingham is Sir Richard's brother. Grania's youngest son, Tibbot, was reared in his household.*

Sir Hugh O'Donnell is The O'Donnell, King of Tyrconnell (Donegal). He and Grace are allies.*

Sir Christopher Lawrence is the Lord of Howth. Some claim Grania kidnapped him years ago to teach his grandfather the meaning of hospitality.*

Margaret Burke is Grania's daughter by her first husband.*

Richard "Devil's Hook" Burke is Grania's son-in-law.*

Aiden and Ionia O'Malley are Grania's kin, recently married. Ionia hails from Scotland.

Liam Mellows is a governing council member of the Irish Volunteers and IRB in Galway.*

Michael Mallin is second in command of the ICA.*

Sir Roger Casement is a British consul and activist currently in Germany procuring arms for the IRB.*

Countess Markievicz is Constance Georgine Gore-Booth, born to an Anglo-Irish entitled family. She is a socialist, suffragist and member of the ICA.*

Fomorians (F'MoR-e-ans) i.e. the Fomorian Faction is the name used by Nuada's enemies in the Fomorian War. Nuada's brothers, Bres (BRESH) and Balor, led the faction. ±

Áine (AAN-yuh), Nuada's onetime queen and Niamh's mother. ±

Manannán mac Lir (MaNa-Nan mac LEER) is Nuada, Bres and Balor's father and onetime ruler of Faerie.±

Fionn mac Cumhaill/Finn McCool is the leader of the legendary group of warriors, the Fianna. ±

Oisín (Ush-EEN) is the son of Fionn mac Cumhaill, a poet, and a member of the Fianna. He tarried in Tír na nÓg for 300 years. ±

Mairead mac Tadgh (Mar-EAD mac Teague) is the love of Dubhshìth's mortal life and the mother of his child. She was thought to have killed herself when Dubh disappeared in Ireland.

Mártainn mac Aindriú/Martin mac Andrew is Dubhshìth's rival for Mairead's affections. He married her when Dubh was presumed dead in battle, and pledged his warriors to help win the war Dubh had been fighting.

Domnall mac Aindriú/Donal mac Andrew is Dubh's son, who he thought had died with his mother, Mairead. He did not, instead he lived to be an old man whose descendants may or may not include Maureen and Sean.

*Historical figure – these people all exist, however I have put words in their mouths and taken liberties with their actions.

± Mythical figure – all the named Tuatha Dé Danann are figures taken from Irish myth – but as with the historical figures, I have certainly put words in their mouths and taken liberties with their mythologies.

Speaking the language

A note on the text: I used Irish/UK spellings and terminology where applicable. Dialect, for the sake of the reader, has been abandoned except in those rare occasions when it was necessary to define a character.

Regarding the Irish spellings of names, generally I used the simplest, era-appropriate variant while Anglicizing the last names, with one exception. Grace O'Malley – or Grania Uaile as she is called in the story, has a variety of names, including Gráinne Ui Mháille, which is the formal variant, and Granuaile. Granuaile is a term used in folklore, taken from the spelling I use in the book, Grania Uaile. I have always found this last easiest to read, as it most resembles how her name is pronounced in Irish. While Grace O'Malley is the contemporary Anglicization of her name, in her lifetime, her name was often recorded as Grany O'Mayle, or some similar form.

Concerning the Fae, while not specifically of the Seelie and Unseelie Court, the Tuatha Dé Danann (TOO-ha da Dah-n'n) – at once old gods and an ancient Irish race – are here, considered Fae. Tír na nÓg (TEAR na'nog), the Land of the Young, is one of many Irish mythological "otherworlds." Although Tír na nÓg is just one of the realms of Faerie, and the Tuatha Dé Danann just one group of the Fae, I use the terms interchangeably.

Dubh is correct when he says we now know the Cruthin as the Picts, though they likely would not have called themselves such. *Picti* or Pict, meaning painted people, was the name the Greeks and Romans gave them. Cruthin, on the other hand, is an Irish term, which refers to those northern peoples not conquered by the Romans. I could have also called the Picts the men of Fortriu, but as that looked too similar to the Fae city of Findias, I opted for visual simplicity and picked Cruthin.

Dubh's use of a surname was a willfully created fiction for ease of reading. His people would have used patronymics – or even matronymics – that would have changed with each successive generation.

For example, Dubh really should have been called Dubhshìth mac Ciniod, as Ciniod was his father's name, not Dubhshìth mac Alasdair. His son Domnall should have been called Domnall mac Mártainn (or, even better, Domnall mac Dubhshìth) not Domnall mac Aindriú. Additionally, if his family had such great regard for an ancestor named Alasdair, they would have used the "Ó" for grandfather or ancestor.

Finally, Alasdair and Aindriú are Gaelicised versions of non-Celtic/Pictish names, a practice not common in the seventh century. However, the names/surnames have significance to the story – and particularly the next book – so they stay.

Fact vs Fiction

Part One ~ Pirate

Grania Uaile was indeed the Pirate Queen of the Irish seas. She was born in 1530, daughter of Eoghan Dubhdara Ó Máille (Owen 'Black Oak' O'Malley), the chief of the O'Malley clan. In 1546, she was married to Donal O'Flaherty, who was heir to the O'Flaherty titles. They had three children, Margaret, Murrough and Owen. Grania returned to her family's holdings when Donal died, taking with her a significant number of O'Flaherty followers. This was the start of her independent fleet.

In 1566, Grania married her second husband Richard "Iron" Burke. Popular history states they were married under Brehon Law, 'for one year certain,' and at the end of the year, she dismissed Richard, but kept Carrickahowley (Rockfleet) Castle, where this book is set. However, contemporary English records state they remained together – or, at least, allied for a common purpose – until Richard's death in 1583.

There was one child of the union, Tibbot. Captain John Bingham raised Tibbot in his household as a hostage – a practice common at the time, not only to ensure the 'good behaviour' of the hostage's family but also to ensure the Anglicization of the next generation of Gaelic leaders.

Politically, Grania submitted to the English Crown with Burke in 1577.

Despite said submission, she maintained her fleet and seafaring activities, and supported a number of uprisings among the Gaelic chiefs as England's power sought to supplant their own. The prison stay she mentions when speaking with Sean took place in 1577-1579 thanks to the efforts of the Earl of Edmond (Limerick) in an effort to prove *his* loyalty to the Crown.

In 1584, Sir Richard Bingham was appointed Governor of Connacht. He and Grania played a cat-and-mouse game via the various rebellions the broke out in response to Bingham's attempts to enforce English law.

In 1586, Bingham's appointed lieutenant and brother, Captain John Bingham, confiscated Grania's horses and cattle, and murdered her eldest son, Owen. Saved by her son-in-law, Richard "Devil's Hook" Burke, Grania fled to Ulster, where conditions were more favourable for her various enterprises. Bingham was eventually sent to Flanders and Grania returned to Connacht to resume her activities there.

In 1588, Queen Elizabeth pardoned Grania, but as that was the same year Bingham was reinstated as Governor of Connacht, and was still bent on curbing Grania's power, the pardon had little effect. The Queen also interviewed Grania via the Articles of Interrogatory in 1593. The two women finally met in September 1593 at Greenwich Castle, in England.

Although Bingham did attempt to intervene, Queen Elizabeth took pity on an old, seemingly helpless woman. Grania's remaining sons were pardoned and their lands reinstated. Grania was also granted her own personal freedom to act and 'prosecute any offender' against the Queen – which meant she could still ply a trade by the sea, so long as her enemies and the Queen's enemies were the same.

However, as Bingham continued in his position of Governor and curtailer of Grania's activities, he was able to circumnavigate the Queen's orders regarding Grania's ability to eek a living out of the sea.

Despite Bingham, the Nine Year's War that pitted Grania's son Tibbot against her onetime allies in The O'Neil and The O'Donnell, and an impoverished west coast, Grania persevered. She was still an active seawoman well into her sixties, as much out of necessity as desire. Nevertheless, she finally laid her body to rest in 1603.

My Fiction: I am not aware of any oak-circled sidhe mound, shrine or active Benedictine Abbey just outside of Carrickahowley (Rockfleet) Castle. There *is* the Burrishoole Friary, run by Dominican friars, upon which the abbey was based. The Friary, currently a historical monument, was operated well into the eighteenth century, despite the dissolution of religious orders following the English Reformation. It was finally abandoned in 1793.

Furthermore, while Grania did have a fleet of more than 20 ships, I doubt a Spanish caravel was her flagship, nor did she name said flagship "Widow's Weeds." That was just my attempt at humour, considering by 1584, Grania had outlived two husbands. Galleys would have made the bulk of Grania's fleet. Rowers mainly powered these nimble ships, although they were equipped with sails.

Finally, while Bingham and Grania were long-time sparing partners, Bingham did not hire a mercenary fleet to lure Grania to Dublin in 1584, or any other time, that we know of. His ability to curtail her activities was primarily administrative, while his agents were the ones to deal the more physical blows to Grania's way of life.

Anne Chambers, and her book *Granuaile* (1979, Wolfhound Press, Dublin) does a much better – and more comprehensive – job at describing the life and times of Grania Uaile, and it was an invaluable resource in the writing of this book.

Part Two ~ Rebel

On Easter Monday, April 24, 1916, Irish Nationalists, in a bid for independence from the British Empire, laid siege to Dublin. The 1916 Rising – or Easter Rising – was organized by the Military Council of the Irish Republican Brotherhood as well as James Connolly's Irish Citizen Army and members of the Irish Volunteers.

Initially, the rebellion was scheduled to begin via a set of parades and 'manoeuvres' on Sunday, April 23, 1916 – Easter Sunday. However, a series of complications and setbacks – mainly the scuttling of the weapons from Germany and Sir Roger Casement's arrest – led Eoin MacNeill to call off the Rising. He met significant resistance from the IRB military council, which countermanded his order. The Rising began at 11 AM on the 24th.

More than 1,300 men and women turned out for the Rising in Dublin alone, and staged simultaneous takeover attempts on strategic locations throughout the city, including the Four

Courts, the South Dublin Union, the Mendicity Institution, Jacob's biscuit factory, Boland's bakery and St. Stephen's Green. The failed attack on Dublin Castle ended with rebels, led by Seán Connolly, occupying City Hall instead.

Just before noon, James Connolly, flanked by Joseph Plunkett and Patrick Pearse, led 150 men in parade formation before the broke ranks and secured the General Post Office (GPO) as their headquarters. From its steps, Patrick Pearse read the Proclamation of the Irish Republic.

The siege lasted for six days. The British brought in more than 4,000 men and heavy artillery to combat the rebels but it was not until the unconditional surrender was issued on Saturday, April 29 that the fighting ended.

As it was wartime, Major General Maxwell maintained martial law over the city in an attempt to quell any further unrest. Under his orders, the rebels were tried, in secret military courts, for treason.

Ninety insurrectionists, including one woman, the Countess Markievicz, were condemned to death. Of those ninety, only fifteen were executed, including all the signatories of the Proclamation.

Of those met in the story, Patrick Pearse was executed on May 3. On May 4, Joseph Plunkett, dying from tuberculosis and married only seven hours before, was executed, along with Willie Pearse, Patrick's young brother. Michael Mallin was executed on May 8, while on May 12, James Connolly was executed tied to a chair because the wound in his leg had become gangrenous.

Sir Roger Casement, who had spent the Rising in the Tower of London following his failure to land the German guns, was hung for treason on August

3, 1916.

Countess Markievicz's sentence was commuted, and she remained in prison until 1917. She would later become first woman elected to the British House of Commons, although she did not take her seat. She was also the first woman to hold a cabinet position of the Irish Republic.

Of course, another high-ranking nationalist, who did not make it into the story, Éamon de Valera, avoided execution because of his US citizenship. He would later become Prime Minister and then President of the Republic of Ireland.

My Fiction: While there *were* guns under Trinity's Art's Department, they were not claimed by the rebels, nor was Dublin Castle successfully taken.

In addition, the timing of the Dublin Castle siege was different from what I have depicted. There were simultaneous takeovers – or takeover attempts – that coincided with the reading of the Proclamation. For dramatic effect, however, I gave Maureen the opportunity to hear Pearse's words and then stick her nose in history.

Aside from meddling with history, the fiction in this particular part of the book was more in what, and whom, I did not include. There were many historical personages Maureen and Sean could have met, and I had to choose among them, lest I overwhelm the story with a textbook rendition of the Rising.

That said, many of the anecdotes related by Maureen, Sean and Dubh, including Casement and the *Libau/Aud,* Eoin MacNeill's attempts to stop the Rising, and the murder of Francis Sheehy-Skeffington, actually happened, although not always in the manner depicted in the story.

Finally, the 1916 Rising did not happen in isolation, nor did the struggle for independence end there. For my purposes, *A History of Ireland* by Peter and Fiona Somerset Fry (1988, Routledge, Dublin), *Rebels* by Peter de Rosa (2000, Poolbeg Press, Dublin) were incredibly useful in the writing of this book and are excellent starting points to understanding not just the 1916 Rising, but the landscape in which it took place.

Part Three ~ King

So many mythologies, so little time! Tír na nÓg is one of the many 'otherworlds' described in Irish mythology. It is the place to which the Tuatha Dé Danann retreated when the Celts took over Ireland.

As detailed in the *Book of Invasions* (seventh century), first there were the Nemedians, from whom the Fir Bolg and Tuatha De Danann are descended. They fought for control of the land with the Fomorians, a semi-divine race. After a Nemedian diaspora and return, the Fomorians would share the island with the Fir Bolg. Finally, from the four island cities in the north returned the Tuatha Dé Danann – the People of the Goddess Danu.

Following a series of wars against both the Fir Bolg and Fomorians, the Tuatha Dé Danann ruled Ireland until the Sons of Mil – the Milesians – came. The Tuatha ceded the land to the Milesians and retreated to the sidhe mounds, and through them, Tír na nÓg.

Nuada Silver Arm was king of the Tuatha Dé Danann when they came to Ireland, and he lost his arm during the war with the Fir Blog. As the

Tuatha Dé Danann tradition stipulates a king must by physically perfect, Nuada was no longer eligible for kingship and Bres, a half-Fomorian/half-Tuatha prince replaced him

During Bres's reign, the Fomorians imposed an oppressive tribute on the Tuatha Dé Danann. The people became disgruntled and when Nuada's lost arm was replaced with a working silver one by the silversmith Credne and the healer Dian Cécht, he took back his throne. Miach, Dian Cécht's son, would eventually replace the silver arm with one of flesh-and-bone.

Bres then joined forces with the Fomorian, Balor, he of the Evil Eye. Together, they waged war on the Tuatha De Danann and subjugated them completely.

At this point, Lugh – at times an Irish god of storms, trickery and war – joined Nuada's court. Sean accurately recounted the method by which he gained entrance to Nuada's stronghold: while the Tuatha had a wright, a silversmith, a champion, a swordsman, a harpist, a hero, a poet and historian, a sorcerer, and a craftsman, they did not have one who was all those things at once.

Nuada appointed Lugh the Chief Ollam – or official bard – of Ireland and abdicated the throne in his favor. Lugh led the Tuatha into battle against the Fomorians, where Balor killed Nuada. Lugh avenged the former king's death by killing Balor, and eventually claimed victory over the Fomorians.

The Tuatha brought with them four treasures from the northern island cities: From Falias, they brought the Stone of Fal, which would cry out when a true king sat on the throne at Tara. From Gorias, they brought the Spear of Lug which was similar to the Spear was the Sword of Nuada, brought from Findias. No one could sustain battle against it. Likewise, no one could escape the Sword of Nuada once it was drawn from its sheath. It also glowed, bright as a torch. Finally, from Murias, they brought the Cauldron of Dagda, which could feed even the largest of companies.

As for the other Fae mentioned in the book, Manannán mac Lir is a sea god in Irish mythology, and it is his cloak that is responsible for the mists, which separate the mortal world from that of the Fae. Manannán is the guardian of the Irish otherworlds and a lawgiver.

Depending on the myth, Áine is either Manannán's wife or his daughter. She is an Irish goddess of summer and wealth. She is associated with Limerick, and in some myths, she is the queen of the fairies. As an embodiment of sovereignty, she can both grant and remove a man's power to rule.

Also associated with Manannán mac Lir is Niamh, who is his daughter. She is also one of the queens of Tír na nÓg, while Macha is one of the three goddesses of war, or the Morrígan.

My Fiction: All of it. I left out the Nemedians and Fir Bolg, and Nuada was physically unblemished. His silver arm became a silver gauntlet and I doubt he would have been a revered High King of Ireland if he had been as unpleasant as the nemesis I created.

Niamh, a queen in her own right, was not Nuada's daughter, nor was she associated with him specifically. Neither was Áine, but her embodiment of queenliness and nobility was too tempting to not put her into the story. Because she 'has passed' at the time of the story, and not able to speak for herself, Niamh and Dubh use her as a symbol – one they alternately wield for their own purposes and cling to for comfort.

As for the rest of the myths, I had fun weaving small nuggets into the story. Dubh's sword is Nuada's sword from Findias. Lugh became a title instead of a god, and Manannán's misty cloak, which separated man from Fae, became the magical mists of the story. Manannán himself became a dynastic figure for the Fae ruling class. Finally, Dubh's story itself could be a hazy retelling of Oisín's tale, and yet, I know Oisín has his own part to play in the series.

Changelings was not meant to be a direct recounting of the myths, but more a 'what if' story, and an homage of sorts to the tales I first read in a delightful book, *A Treasury of Irish Folklore,* originally edited by Padriac Colum in 1954 (1992, Random House Company, New York). My memory, and the stories, were further fleshed out by online resources available through CELT, the Corpus of Electronic Texts, Ireland's Humanities Computing project.

Acknowledgements

So many people go into writing and publishing a book, and I cannot express well enough how grateful I am for the following wonderful people:

Pat Hitt, when you asked, "can I edit your book?" I finally realized this – this publishing thing – was something I could do. Not only that, but you helped me see the story from another perspective, add drama where drama was needed, and expand it into something I am proud to release into the world. You gave my words the polish they needed, and you have no idea how grateful to you I am for that. And for the smiley-faces that popped up occasionally on the parts you really liked. Those made my day.

Thomas, you are amazing, kiddo. I could not have done this without you – your patience and your support while I willfully spent more time hunched over my computer than, you know, making dinner.

Mom and Dad, you have done nothing but love and encourage me my entire life, even to the point of letting me be the family's weird little throwback Irish kid who decided to move three thousand miles away and live a dream. Thank you for believing in me.

Christine, who else but you would willingly let her best friend and matron of honor obsess over publishing a book at the same time you were getting married? Thank you for being my best friend for the last 20 years. And for pushing me when I did not want to be pushed. And for just being you.

Brad, Helena and Marie, thank you for being my biggest cheerleaders. Thank you for understanding when I could not talk to you for more than five seconds and thank you for just being you. Dean and Tonia, thank you for your perspective and insight. Andra, Charles, Ionia, Jack, John, Pamela, SK and Sue, thank you for being you. Thank you for your creativity and inspiration, which allowed me to take a break from my brain.

Judy, thank you for just being you and listening to me ramble at 2 pm every day. Jim S., thank you for the Diet Coke, and reminding me to live vicariously through my characters. To the Customer Service ladies at Kalmbach, thank you for one of the best work experiences I have ever had. I love you all. Gail, thank you for the last minute save on my cover. I swear, I see everything backwards and upside-down.

Keith O., thank you for giving me Dubh. He is a glorious, epic, marvelous pain in the head, and he made the book – and the series – what it is. Cheers.

Finally, to the readers who have made it this far: Thank you.

Design notes

The title and chapter-heading font is Aquiline Two, which was created by Manfred Klein. It was free for private and charity use, and to use it for the commercial printing of this book, I was happy to donate to Doctors Without Borders. The interior font is Century Schoolbook, a serif typeface designed by Morris Fuller Benton in 1919 for Ginn & Co, a textbook publisher. It is an easy-to-read typeface based on Century Roman, and is still used in textbooks today.

About the Author

Descended of pirates and revolutionaries, Katie Sullivan is a lover and student of all things Irish. Born in the States, she is a dual US/Irish citizen,

Author Photograph by Patrick Hitt © 2014

and studied history and politics at University College, Dublin – although, at the time, she seriously considered switching to law, if only so she could attend lectures at the castle on campus. She lives in the American Midwest with her son, two cats and a pesky character in her head named D (but you can call him Dubh). She can be found writing with said character at her blog, The D/A Dialogues.

Made in the USA
Las Vegas, NV
27 December 2021